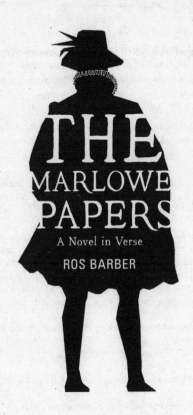

THE MARLOWE PAPERS

A Novel in Verse

ROS BARBER

SCEPTRE

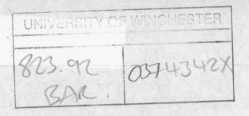
First published in Great Britain in 2012 by Sceptre
An imprint of Hodder & Stoughton
An Hachette UK company

First published in paperback in 2013

1

A CIP catalogue record for this title is available from the British Library

ISBN 978 1 444 73024 1

Printed and bound in Great Britain by Clays Ltd, St Ives plc

Hodder & Stoughton policy is to use papers that are natural,
renewable and recyclable products and made from wood
grown in sustainable forests. The logging and manufacturing
processes are expected to conform to the environmental
regulations of the country of origin.

Hodder & Stoughton Ltd
338 Euston Road
London NW1 3BH

www.sceptrebooks.com

When a man's verses cannot be understood,
nor a man's good wit seconded with the forward child understanding,
it strikes a man more dead than a great reckoning in a little room.
Truly, I would the gods had made thee poetical.

As You Like It, III. 3

The way to really develop as a writer is to make yourself
a political outcast, so that you have to live in secret.
This is how Marlowe developed into Shakespeare.

Ted Hughes, *Letters* (2007)

Poetry is nearer to vital truth than history.

Plato

CONTENTS

To the Wise or Unwise Reader

What can a dead man say that you will hear?
Suppose you swear him underneath the earth,
stabbed to the brain with some almighty curse,
would you recognise his voice if it appeared?

The tapping on the coffin lid is heard
as death watch beetle. He becomes a name;
a cipher whose identity is plain
to anyone who understands a word.

So what divine device should he employ
to settle with the world beyond his grave,
unmask the life that learnt its human folly
from death's warm distance; how else can he save

himself from oblivion, but with poetry?
Stop. Pay attention. Hear a dead man speak.

Dramatis Personae

Writers and Actors

Christopher Marlowe	poet, playwright, intelligencer
Tom Watson	poet, playwright, intelligencer
Thomas Walsingham	gentleman, literary patron
Robert Greene	writer of prose romances, playwright
Edward (Ned) Alleyn	lead actor, acting company manager/sharer
Thomas Nashe	prose satirist
Thomas Kyd	playwright

Government

Sir Francis Walsingham	Secretary of State, head of intelligence
Lord Burghley	William Cecil, Lord Treasurer
Sir Robert Sidney	Governor of Flushing in the Low Countries

Nobility

Northumberland	Henry Percy, 9th Earl of Northumberland
Southampton	Henry Wriothesley, 3rd Earl of Southampton
Essex	Robert Devereux, 2nd Earl of Essex, soldier
Sir John Harington	1st Baron Harington, first cousin to the Sidneys
Lucy, Countess of Bedford	his married teenage daughter
Arbella Stuart	first cousin to James VI of Scotland
Bess of Hardwick	Countess of Shrewsbury, Arbella's grandmother

Intelligence

Robin Poley	intelligencer
Thomas Thorpe	publisher, intelligencer
Richard Baines	intelligencer
Gilbert Gifford	intelligencer
Anthony Bacon	head of the Earl of Essex's intelligence network

Sundry

John Allen	Ned Alleyn's brother, innkeeper
William Bradley	publican's son
Hugh Swift	lawyer, Watson's brother-in-law
John Poole	Catholic counterfeiter
Sir Walter Raleigh	courtier, adventurer
Eleanor Bull	Deptford gentlewoman with Court connections
Venetia	a maiden of Venice
Jaques Petit	Anthony Bacon's servant
William Peter	gentleman

THE MARLOWE PAPERS

Death's a Great Disguiser

Church-dead. And not a headstone in my name.
No brassy plaque, no monument, no tomb,
no whittled initials on a makeshift cross,
no pile of stones upon a mountain top.
The plague is the excuse; the age's curse
that swells to life as spring gives way to summer,
to sun, unconscious kisser of a warmth
that wakens canker as it wakens bloom.

Now fear infects the wind, and every breath
that neighbour breathes on neighbour in the street
brings death so close you smell it on the stairs.
Rats multiply, as God would have them do.
And fear infects like mould; like fungus, spreads –
folk catch it from the chopped-off ears and thumbs,
the burning heretics and eyeless heads
that slow-revolve the poles on London Bridge.

The child of casual violence grows inured,
an audience too used to real blood;
they've watched a preacher butchered, still awake,
and handed his beating heart like it was love.
And now the sanctioned butchery of State
breeds sadists who delight to man the rack,
reduce men from divine belief and brain
to begging, and the rubble of their spines.

From all this, I am dead. Reduced to ink
that magicks up my spirit from the page:
a voice who knows what mortals cannot think of;
a ghost, whose words ring deeper from the grave.

Corpse-dead. A gory stab-hole for an eye;
and that's what they must think. No, must believe,
those thug-head pursers bent on gagging speech,
if I'm to slip their noose and stay alive.
Now I'm as dead as any to the world,
the foulest rain of blackened corpses on
the body that is entered in my name:
the plague pit where Kit Marlowe now belongs.
For who could afford for that infected earth
to be dug up to check identities?
And so, I leave my former name behind.
Gone on the Deptford tide, the whole world blind.

Friend, I'm no one. If I write to you,
in fading light that distances the threat,
it's as a breeze that strokes the Channel's waves,
the spray that blesses some small vessel's deck.

DECIPHERERS

I'll write in code. Though my name melts away,
I'll write in urine, onion juice and milk,
in words that can be summoned by a flame,
in ink as light and tough as spider silk.
I'll send a ream of tamed rebellious thought
to seed a revolution in its sleep;
each letter glass-invisible to light,
each sheet as blank as signposts are to sheep.

The spy's conventions, slipping edge to edge
among the shadows, under dirty night,
mislead the search. To fool intelligence,
we hide our greatest treasures in plain sight.
This poetry you have before your eyes:
the greatest code that man has yet devised.

Captain Silence

We dock in darkness. The skipper's boy dispatched
to find our lodgings. Not a town for ghosts,
and with no wish to be remembered here
I'm wrapped in scholar's garb, the bright man's drab.
A quarter-moon is rationing its light
to smuggle us ashore without a fuss;
the fishermen are far away from port,
their wives inside and unaware of us.

You know I've come this way before; not here,
but in this manner, come as contraband
under the loose concealing cloak of night,
disguised as something of no interest,
as simple traveller. A man of books:
which words will make him interesting as dust
to folk who cannot read and do not care
they sign their papers only with a cross.
My name means more, and yet I shrug it off
like reptile skin, adopt some alias
that huffs forgettable, to snuff the flame
that now would be the death of me. Anon,
now Christopher is too much cross to bear.

The skipper calls me only with a cough.
Lugs, with his lanky son, my trunk of books.
No prop. For books will be my nourishment
in the sightless days without you. And if I
feel strange, or wordless, they will anchor thought,
ensure my brain is drowned in histories
that help me to remember who I am.

The skipper leads as shadows bolt from us
and streets fall back. And in his torch's flame
a flicker of the tongue that can't be bought,
which pirates sliced to secrecy. The rest,
that part he'd curl to make his consonants,
is long since fish-food on the Spanish main.
The boy speaks for him when we reach the door.
We're hurried in, '*Entrez*,' as though a storm
is savaging the calm still tail of May
and has the oak trees shaken by their roots.

The woman might be forty-five, or twelve.
A calculated innocence, a face
so open blank, it seems revealing as
it hides itself. This woman's learnt to blanch
as bones will bleach when left to drink the sun,
as death will creep a pallor into skin
at just its mention. Clothed in widow's weeds,
soft fingers straighten for gold. '*Un angelot*.'
Two months of food for sticking out her neck
for an Englishman. The payment's hidden where
she's still half warm. 'So you will sleep above,'
she states as if she questions us, 'the room
that slopes for Captain Silence and his boy.'
They heft my trunk upstairs between them, just.

'The less we say, the better,' she begins.
'You want some ale? You're thirsty? Or there's sack
if you need something stronger.' Then she pales,
as if she is reflecting me. Some look
betrays my loss to her, and in a blink
her loneliness has fastened on to mine.
'You learnt the tongue from Huguenots?' She nods

and answers her own question. 'That is right.
And you. You are a religious man? But, no,
forget I ask you anything.' In truth,
I am a scholar of divinity
and study the divine with open eyes.
Beyond all question, I would give her truth;
and yet, I cannot save her if I speak.

'My husband was an Englishman, like you.
Or not like you. He had no love of books.
Ballads he liked. He used to sing this one—'
Her brain defends itself by giving way.
'I don't remember it.' But here, her eyes
brim with the silence, break their trembling banks
as though she heard his funeral song. Then he,
her husband, a growl, is whispering in her ear
the rudest ballad he knows, clutching her waist
to spin her for a kiss. And then he's gone,
and we are momentarily with ghosts.
'Forgive me,' she says. 'The silence is poisonous.'

Upstairs, I'm with her still. She's through the wall,
the spectre of a woman I might touch
on any other night but this. I don't
undress so much as loosen up a notch,
for comfort now would later be exposed,
a gift to spot and clear as light to slay;
and bad enough, I'm running for my life
without my skin a beacon for the moon,
a human sheath that swallows blades. I sit
laced in my boots, my stomach tight, my ears
so strongly tuned they model sight from sound.

Next door, the widow braves into her gown
and lies awake. She listens to the house
and reads the whispers that pronounce her safe
though I would have her sacrificed for love.
I know her stares are pulling at the wall
I'm on the other side of, and her bed
feels colder for the want of me. And yet,
as time goes on, she's bidding me *adieu*.

A woman's skin might send a man to sleep,
but I must twitch and listen to the night
say *Nothing's here*. The moon is out of sight
and something gnaws now, in the walls. I write,
the extra tallow that I paid her for
illuminating every sorry word.

How we are trapped in silence; how this night
has brought a silent shipwreck to her shore,
how silence unites us as it chokes us off,
how thick the silence hangs around the door
that dogs might almost sniff it, and the causes:
cutlass, lies or longing. Gathered here,
awake, or sleeping aware, are three full-grown
examples of the muted. And the boy
fathered by silence, slight and safely bred
to keep his trap shut. How the silence grows,
how it wraps around the house like sealing snow
though we are in the final day of spring.

Silence surrounds the men of deepest faith
and, listened to, may call a man to prayer.

I pray that no one follows us tonight;
that in England, rural keepers of the peace
are kept bewitched by corpse and candlelight;
I pray those men are instantly believed
who, having played my dark and murderous friends,
have stayed to stay the executioner's hand;
I pray my soul's absolved in all the lies
that tumble slick as herring from their tongues.
I pray, my friend, you're warm and safe at home,
that doors remain unkicked and truths untold
and we have silence when the daylight comes.

NON-CORRESPONDENT

I have to write to someone. Not the page,
this featureless companion of the road,
this marker of my friendlessness, but flesh
my lips have kissed, a face my mind can shape.
And I choose you, my smart and cautious friend,
my almost love. With you, I'll share all thought,
open my heart's slammed door, so you may roam
among its chambers, sore with what you know,
when I am gone. Some unimagined date,
when I have found a grave I cannot flee,
this trunk will limp its way to the address
pasted inside the lid, and every word
I almost wrote to you will spill from me.

And you will know me, then. And know my wrongs.
That you may not reply: forgive me, Tom.

THE SHAPE OF SILENCE

I dream of Kent. I'm still at school, at King's,
in Canterbury, where my starveling brain
unloaded intrigue from a feast of tongues
that massacre and war made refugees.
Canterbury, where I gorged myself
on knowledge, sharpened up my fledgling wit,
feeding on scholarship an inner flame:
some hot conviction that the world was mine.
Canterbury, from whose huddled roofs
bursts the substantial faith of a cathedral
whose spire aspires to heaven, but whose stones
have been a butcher's block where holy men
were finished off for their beliefs. Vespers.

A whisper: *You're wanted*. Shrinking low, I duck
official eyes and follow the message boy.
He guides me to a room whose door shuts fast.
And clear as sherry there is Robert Greene,
stroking his beard until it points to Hell.
He's master now; the Duke of Chaos reigns.
Envy has whipped the light that shows it bare,
and jealousy has fashioned wisdom's chains.

'Pretending to be dead?' A crow, he caws.
'You'll find death is uncomfortable at best.
You shouldn't mock us with your parlour trick.'
He points me to the iron branks. 'It's yours.
Unless you'll try a smoother punishment.'
I say I will. My legs are rendered stone
and cannot port me out of there. I'm led,
like calf to slaughterhouse, to inner rooms

where boys are gagged with bandages, and on
until we reach the library. 'See this?'
He opens up a box whose gilded clasp
features initials not my own. 'Your tongue
goes here,' he says, and strokes the tongue-shaped mould
designed for it. The velvet's bright as blood.
He turns to the shadows, shouting, 'Cut it off!'
and in the glint of threatened knives, I wake,
a grey light creeping through a widow's drapes.
Only my breathing saturates the dawn.

THE TRUNK

A hand on my shoulder startles me. 'Excuse.
It's best you leave before the dawn. This place.
Its people love the smell of something fishy.
They get up early too.' She's loosely dressed.
I'm at the desk, as though I never slept.
The blown-out candle's stink is barely cold
and she is nursing a flame to light its wick.
'I don't need trouble. Whoever you are. It's time.
You must depart.' She shakes my arm. 'Go! *Vite*!'
She's woken the captain and his boy. In vests
they're readying to shift my trunk downstairs.

Her parlour seems colder now, the fire out.
The candlelight insists it's night outside,
only her rush suggesting otherwise.
'Yesterday's bread. Some cheese.' She packs my bag
as if we are related. 'Best I can do.
Go up the road six miles. My cousin's house
is at the crossroads. He's the farrier.
He'll find a horse for you. Tell him Monique
will cook him a pie if he brings meat across.
Exactly those words, you understand?'

                                        I'm stuck.
Her brittleness unnerves me, like the shock
of a morning wash. She shivers anxiously
as if the changed wind slipping beneath the door
hints at the distant stench of consequence.
Her eyes evasive, fearing mine might lock
hers to some dangerous bond of loyalty.

'The trunk?' I ask. The boy is sitting on it.
The captain yawns. And there I glimpse again
the stub that recommends him to the State.
'I'll send it on,' she says, 'as you instruct.'

Two footsteps on, I'll be reduced to robes,
to paper, quill and ink, a change of clothes.
'The trunk,' I tell her, 'anyone can look.
'It's just some books, some poems. If someone
– authorities – should need to open it,
they will find nothing. It is literature.
Send it to Mr Le Doux. At the sign of the bear
in Middelburg. There'll be an *angelot*
if the inventory's present still.' She nods.
'May God be with you.'

                    Now I'm alone outside,
feeling a pinch no dawn will warm away.
The captain and boy will shuffle off and slip
mooring ahead of mackerel coming in.
I set off inland, towards the brightening sky,
conscious of night behind. All England's dark
that threatens to engulf me is a beast
crouched at my back. And then I remember you.

FORGE

The farrier is shoeing with a force
you'd only use on hoofs. He hammers in
a quarter-dose of good luck for the road,
then puts the fetlock down. 'You wanting me?'
His mouth is battened straight, as if the lips
are still turned in to hold a row of nails.
My mind sets cold; it's hard enough to trust,
and Monique's 'cousin' might mean anything;
they hardly seem related. He's a 'friend',
but not a friend of mine. He runs his eyes
across my scholar's cloak, my library skin.

'I've a message from Monique,' I say. 'She asked
if you would take some meat across for her,
and she'll bake you a pie.'
                                        'That's what she said?
Monique is full of promises. Last time
I did her a favour, she reneged her word.'
He snorts, and turns to wash his spade-like hands
in a nearby bucket. 'So you need a horse.
I hope you're good for payment. Monique's pies
are legendary. Like the phoenix, son.
They don't exist.' His apron is his towel.

Thinking me green, he guides me to the barn
and tries to palm me off with something slow.
'A sturdy beast. You have some miles ahead?'
'A few,' I say. 'But I don't have a whip.'
'Just so.' He laughs. 'For sturdy beasts and mules
have much in common. Some reluctance, no?'

My French needs greasing, but is adequate
to make him laugh. 'Perhaps you're after speed?
In case you're set upon,' he says, and shrugs.
'It happens. The road attracts its travellers
and some are desperate.' His eyes on me.
'Some signs of life would do,' I say. 'This mare?'
'Ten sovereigns.'
                    'That's too much!'
                                        'That's what she costs.'
His arms across his chest, a barrier.
'The price is made of many parts. She's fast
as the man who sells her's quiet. You understand.'
I understand that Monique's words have cost
the doubled price of silence. So it goes;
life will be cheaper once I've disappeared.
I bargain for her tack to be thrown in.
The smell of leather as I saddle up
returns me briefly to my father's shop:
the chatter of my sisters up the stairs
and hammered sunlight leant across the door.

'You know the road to take? Towards Douai?
You have a scholar's pallor,' he explains.
'The English scholars tend to go that way.
But you were never here,' he adds. 'Of course.'

She has no name. I call her Esperance,
blessing myself with hope.
                            Just after noon
we leave the Douai road and plod a stream
that cuts us easterly through woods; a route
less clock-predictable, should I be tracked.

Dear Nowhere-to-go, press on.
                                                        For at my back,
beyond La Manche, one destiny is crouched
still ready to spring: the cell, the lash, the rack,
the gibbet and noose. The vicious slice from throat
to belly; my intestines gentled out
by a dutiful executioner, my prick
hacked off and crammed into my mouth. Good miles
that keep me in my skin, my breath, my mind.
But every mile another mile from you.

CONJURORS

Watching my father at the last, I learnt
that love is a necessity of craft.
Who writes must love their pen and every mark
it makes upon the paper, and the words
that set their neighbours burning, and the line
that sounds against the skull when read again.

Elbows against a schoolboy's desk, I learnt
the dead can be conjured from their words through ink,
that ancient writers rise and sing through time
as if immortal, the poet's voice preserved
like the ambered insect some see as a scratch
but I'd imagine flying, brought to life.

And so to precious paper I commit
the only story I can never tell.

Tom Watson

'He's come to Cambridge. Thomas Watson.'

                                            'Swear!'

'I swear. Staying with some old friend of his.
He's come to see your *Dido*.'

                                 Christmas week.

Nineteen years old, and my first play is born
on a student stage fusty with Latin jokes.
Act One starts in an hour, the snow is thick
across the quad, and crunches underfoot
as Knowles and I make for the buttery.
'You can't be sure.'

                     'The rumour's sound. He'll come.

He'll love it, Kit.'

                   'He'll recognise those lines
where Dido dies. I robbed the pith from him.'
'Be calm. He'll take it as a compliment.'

Our names marked down, I take some soup and bread
but cannot eat. Across the darkened lawns,
the hall is tricked out as a theatre.
Boys are in face-paint; two in Roman gowns
are testing their breasts won't slip. It's too late now
to change a word of it. They've memorised
their entrances and exits, have the lines
under their breath. The night is with the gods.

The final speech. As Dido's sister bolts
headlong into imaginary flames
a silence settles. Then the hall erupts.

A thief's anxiety, worming its nest of holes
in the poet's stomach, softens at the salve
of warm appreciation from a throng
of drunken students.
                              One man stands apart.
As others press to greet me, he leans in
to his friend, his eye on me and whispering
something that makes his neighbour splutter; not
at me, but at the sea of gowns he parts
entirely by the focus of his gaze.

Anticipation makes me blurt his name
in time with him as we are introduced.
He laughs. 'Another Watson? A common name,
I grant you, but Tom too? It's ludicrous.
I've met a dozen Toms this last half-day,
but not another Watson. Peace, my friend.
You're Christopher Marley, and I'm very glad
to meet you. Quite an ambitious play for one
so young. You'll come to town and sup with us?
Gobbo's paying.' He motions to his friend.

Some tankards later, his voice conducts a crowd
jesting at one particular Oxford don
who, 'finding a student tying his laces together,
would correct the miscreant's bows, and demonstrate
the best knot for the job, before he'd rise,
and be felled to the floorboards like a tree!'
The table laughs. His eyes are bright with it.

More beer is hailed as one of his friends chips in:
'And Richard Harvey is another ass.

He wrote a book some years ago, predicting
the destruction of the world in eighty-eight.
The calamity will be fire and water mixed.
And what might that describe?'

'His bowels perhaps,'
Watson suggests, 'when none of it comes true.'
The table erupts, and as the beer arrives,
Tom Watson leans in closer to my ear.
'Dim-witted Dick is rector to my friend.
His brother, Gabriel, is tutor here.
You know him?'

'I have had the dubious pleasure.'
He smiles. 'You'd circle the globe to see two men
more cursed and blessed with brains. Intelligence
is only for the gifted. Don't you think?'
This question pierces me. His eyes, like hearths
to come in from the cold to. Do I think?
I haven't said much since the second beer,
which tugs at me now to head out for the jakes.
'I'm not sure what you mean.'

His friends are lost
in jokes about the Harveys; all the air
around the two of us drawn in, enclosed,
as if his voice has conjured us a room.
His face is serious. 'A lively wit
can only be ridden if it's broken in.
You've heard that phrase? One privy councillor
I know is very fond of it.'

'Lord Burghley?'
'Sir Francis Walsingham. He has some work
for men with languages. If you like travel.

Delivering letters to the embassies.
Paris, and so on. Should I mention you?'

I hope I didn't seem too puppy-keen;
my only other option was the Church.
A life outside the walls of academe,
adventuring in the service of the Queen,
a chance to move among the powerful
and commandeer material for my pen
was more like life than all my lives till then.
The gods forgive me if I wolfed the bait.

'Discretion, though. Should you speak to anyone
about the possibility, it's gone.'

Odd to recruit me there, a public place.
And yet, surrounded by the drunk and loud,
and cloaked in a fog of less important talk,
he carved us privacy. A gale of noise
proves safer to talk in than the queue to piss,
or a quiet street. Words travel far on air,
and leap on the back of silence, riding miles
beyond our sight. But lean in, sup a beer,
exchange a tale. And then rejoin the jokes.
Allude to nothing further: be, and wait.

Thus Watson's first free lesson in the art
of espionage on *Dido*'s opening night:
the safest jewels are hidden in plain sight.

TAMBURLAINE THE GREAT

This banished man is writing you a poem,
the only code I know that tells the truth,
though truth was both my glory, and my ruin,
the laurel, and the handcuff, of my youth.

London seduced me. Beckoned me her way
and spread herself beneath me, for a play.

'They've never seen the like before.' Applause,
a clapping swell like starlings after grain
and Edward Alleyn's striding off the stage,
dressed as the thunderous Tamburlaine. 'Some beer!'
He claps me on the back. 'Look what you've made.
It seems they love a monster. As do I.'

Six years ago is now a life away.
Yet I close my eyes and put my feet up there
as solid as a tavern tabletop,
comfortable as a chair that I rock back
to balancing point, and just sustain in air
because I am young, full of success and praise,
and not yet too much ale.
                          'My love! Some more!'
Dear Ned upbraids the tapster's wife for beer,
orders a double supper, beef and bread,
then closes his eyes as if he hears the crowd
and shakes his head.
                          'Oh, that was something, Kit.
I had them in my pocket from the first.

Your words, I tell you. If I had your words
three hours a night, I'd set the world on fire.'

I say, 'You gave him life, they're clapping you.
My words, but someone had to speak them, Ned.
An author cannot speak his words himself,
the world would lynch him. And his mother, too,
were she to hear.'
                              'The world will hear of this!'

'As far as the world might go. Perhaps not Kent.'
He laughs. 'As far as Beckenham at least!
Come, man, your mother would love the show tonight,
if she had dreams for her son of better things.
A simple shepherd can become a king –
you show us how. And with a crown of words
make kings of both of us. This hollow town
will ring to the name of Tamburlaine for years!'

The man who sidles up behind his back
is red and pointy-bearded, greenly cloaked:
'May it not be so. London's tortured ears
are sick of it already. Is it news?
Congratulations.' Proffers up his hand
as if it were a prodding stick. 'Your name?'

Ned stands to introduce us: mizzen tall.
'Christopher Marley,' Ned says, 'scholar poet –
Robert Greene, author of ladies' romances.'

Greene slides his palm away. 'And scholar too
at both the universities. I write
because I need to eat. There's quite a crowd

of educated masters wielding pens
in London now. You've come to join the throng?'

'He's come to be head of it!' says Ned, quite drunk
on the crowd's applause, and sitting down as hard
as a man will sit on his conscience. 'Come now, Robert.
Did you not see the play? A masterpiece.'

Greene's sigh could strip his beard. 'Not see, exactly,
but rather heard in roars along the street
when I was on my way here. And the chat,'
he motions round the tavern, 'tells the plot.
Tell me, young Master Marlowe, scholar poet.
Is violence poetic? Should you write
so beautifully about atrocities?
I hear your hero has a monstrous rage
and murders his own children. What of love?
Do modern poets not have time for love?
Is it extinct?'

        How wrong a man can judge.
And he heard my second syllable as 'low'.
I let it pass. 'Love is a mystery,'
I say, as a wench's hips sway past my eyes.
'Each person craves it, yet it doesn't sell.
Or so I'm told. We cannot dine on love.
Perhaps too few believe in it.'
                'It's true,'
Ned elbows in, 'the modern public like
their entertainments savage. Buckets of blood,
and heartlessness. Or how could we compete
with public executions? Hanging's free.'

Greene stays with me. 'A Cambridge boy, I'm right?
We might have shared a tutor. William Gage?
I was at Benet first.' He rubs his chin,
as though his beard's a bet he's bringing in
against the fluff of my young moustache. 'You were
a sizar? Not a pensioner?' He trawls,
fishing for scraps that he might hang on me.
What is my father's trade? For he smells trade.
He guesses it straight away, as if my name
has come to him before.
                              'A cobbler's son?'

'But then Our Lord's son was a carpenter.
The trades are honest. Everyone needs shoes.'
My father's words, my mouth. 'Whose son are you?'

'A petty miser. Hard as gold is soft
and can be clipped. He has disowned me, though.
I'm disinherited. A writer's lot,
as you will learn, is not all sweet applause,
and there's no wealth in it. There's ladies, though'
– exchanging winks with one – 'if you're not bent
or too high-minded.'
                              'Robert, will you join us?'
Ned doesn't catch the slurs, his beery speech
too full of them to find a fault elsewhere.
I motion at the chair. Greene hesitates.
'You don't prefer to celebrate alone?
I wouldn't want to steal your evening.'
                                              'I'd
be happy to hear how you live by the pen.
There must be quite an art to it,' I say.
Greene eyes me carefully. 'I don't give tips

to the competition. Nose out. But I'll stay.
So long as there's wine and Ned is paying for it.
The good stuff. French. None of that sherry stuff.'
He pulls a chair in. Ned is scandalised.
'Seems one too many free dinners has spoiled your palate!'
'Too many? Who can have too many?' Greene
twiddles his beard to dislodge evidence.

An hour he drank with us before a whore
was his excuse to leave us. All that hour
he talked about his books and of the plays
he promised to Ned. Occasionally he smiled,
but only sidewise, flinching every time
a groundling came to give Alleyn a slap
for his performance. 'How to follow that?
Great Tamburlaine has clearly conquered all.'
He eyed me shrewdly. 'After such a play,
the next must surely disappoint us, no?'

'More of the same!' cries Ned, still full in sail.
'Tell us what happens next. How does he die?
Who overthrows him?'

              None but God himself,
as I have learnt, but didn't answer then.
I let the bluffers fill the empty space.
Ned offered up a plot. I had my own:
to guard my tongue, but give rein to my pen.

The Low Countries

A room above an inn. The foreign words
on floors beneath me, drifting up like smoke
from kitchen servants, say I'm the stranger here.
The fields are almost marsh. Two days of rain
and still the skies are pouring. Clothing, soaked,
sweating before the open fire. My skin
is wrinkled as the elderly, my feet
as white and sodden as the Dover cliffs
stood out in water. All my papers soaked,
the ink cried out of them: a blot, a streak,
then blank again. Last night, I dreamt of rape.

From the space under my cot, from all the quiet
beneath my sleeping body, came the shift
of someone who had waited for my breath
to slow and mark that I was vulnerable.
A shadow consolidated into flesh,
some man who needed, more than meat or drink,
my soul's destruction. Not a face, no voice,
but the cold desire for what he couldn't have
I recognised. Intrusion was his name.
And the cry of fear he stuffed back in my throat
with fists of bedclothes echoed in the room:

a room with no one in it. Yet, afraid,
I kept my eyes on the door until the first
dull light began to detail me, alone.
I drifted back to sleep just after dawn,
exhausted by my vigilance and fear,

and found myself at the nightmare's end, distressed
and running room to room in some great palace,
with no one recognising me as friend,
and, bursting finally into a hall,
my nightshirt torn, my privacy exposed,
I found myself half dressed before a court
of witnesses. The room was thick with them,
the walled-up souls who manage history.
'Hold her down fast,' they said. 'Cut out her tongue.'

The rain falls still. It's two hours after noon.
The silent shame that followed from my dream
is reeking from the dampness of the clothes
I took a walk in, trying to be clean,
though all the dirt is on the inside now.
And bursting to be told, to be let out,
but, with the stain of it, who can I tell
who wouldn't blame me for inflaming it?

I take my driest paper, mix the ink,
and open where the daughter stumbles in
with bleeding stumps for hands, a bloody chin,
and blood ballooning as she tries to speak;
each word a victim of her absent tongue
translated to an empty sphere of air;
anguished to tell some caring heart who wreaked
this violent silence over their guilty deed.
But speechlessness has rendered her a worm:
no hands to write, no tongue to speak until
she spies the book that spells another's tale –
the silenced woman turned to nightingale
who sings, and in her singing, is avenged.

London. How fondly, thinking of her now,
I conjure up her smells: her market stalls,
the horse manure, the river's fishy taint.
Can hear her in my ears like old advice:
the racket of the carts, the coster-wife
who'd shout out, 'Flowers are lovely,' to the rich
as I wandered back from breakfast to my desk.
I'd make the world in words, I'd show it things
you'd only see in mirrored glass, and then
scratch off the silver, let the truth go through.
The loveliness of youth. The innocence.

Government duty helped me pay the rent.
From time to time, called up as messenger:
the small thrill when my strict instructions were
to give the message personally to men
as close to princes as pond lilies are
to the water's edge. Each courtier, each swain,
was study for my second Tamburlaine.

Watson was newly married: he and Ann
took up a lease above a draper's shop
in Norton Folgate. I lodged in the roof.

'So, Kit, how goes it?' Watson, entering
the room I wrote in through those early months;
the smell of starch and boiled onions.
                                        'Tom,
can I greet you first?'

          I feel that warm embrace
as if his arms are round me now, and not
this blanket. Missing him wells up, like blood
from a fresh wound, as I let my memory bathe
in that early evening as we pulled apart.

'How's the writing going?'
                    'How was France?'
                                    He laughed,
'You first! You know I'm paid for my discretion.
No gossip for you before the third beer. So.
The shepherd king, sir? How's your second part?'

'Obscene. I had to pump the horror up;
dear Ned insisted.'
                    'Have you eaten yet?
Can I tempt you to the tavern? All the light's
gone out of the day. What say you? Save your wax
and dine with me. The Queen is paying for it.'

'I'm halfway through a scene.'
                        'And stuck?'
                                    He read
my mind most clearly when he was relaxed.
'Come back to it tomorrow when you're fresh.
Your brain can solve it overnight, if greased
and given sustenance. Come on.'

                        He was
persuasive, warm. The most insistent arm
ever to link with mine and march me down
three flights of stairs and out into the night
to marvel at mud and stars. He was the shape

I moulded myself to, because he made
such wondrous things as him seem possible.

We strode into the tavern, earned a wink
from Kate the barmaid as she wiggled by,
two trays of food well-balanced. 'Christopher,
you may slip in there; I'm a married man.'
To neighbours, 'Well met, Harry! How's the boil?
My wife can brew an unction. Hunt her down!'
We took the private corner he preferred.

'How do you fare for money?'
                                          'Not so well.'
'Still hiring the horse, though.'
                                          'I must have the horse.
Tom, without the horse, I'm five foot five
and half the world looks down on me.'
                                          'I know.
Create the show and men believe it's true.
Dress rich, ride rich, *be* rich. When will it work
do you think?'
                    'Don't doubt me, Tom. I'm come this far
with nothing but belief. A cobbler's son
who now is qualified a gentleman.'

The corners of his mouth twitched like a fly
in a spider's web that movement fast reveals.

'Don't toy with me, Tom.'
                                          'Oh, we are serious.
I'm glad you have the horse, still. As for money,
the horse might get you more of it.'
                                          'How's that?'

He leant in closer, made our wall-less room.
'A Spanish invasion fleet is being prepared.'
My pulse leapt like a stag. 'Twelve dozen ships
bearing three thousand guns. There will be peace
negotiations. But. We believe they'll fail.'

'The execution of the Queen of Scots –'

'– has angered the Catholics greatly, yes, my friend.'

He dropped his voice two registers, as Kate
yawed to the side to fill our cups with ale.

'A horse eats up the distances,' he smiled
until she passed, 'between the enemy
and us. We need a network on the ground.'
Watson took two short sips beneath the froth
and smacked his lips.
                              'Pack and be ready to go.
You'll not be called until the chain's in place
through which to pass your information. But
be ready to serve your country.'

                              'Tamburlaine!'
The room filled with his roar as Edward Alleyn
created a stage around him. 'Is it done?
I thought I'd find you here. Where is my play?
Have you got time for drinking?'
                              'It's my first!'

'He's lying, this is number three,' Tom said,
and shook his hand.
                    'You poets. Always thirsty.

Can a humble actor join you?'
                              'Certainly!
Where is this man, sir? Let us be introduced.'
Ned bellowed with laughter. 'You are very rude!'
'In the meanwhile,' Watson said, 'please be our guest.
Though our purse is empty, if you might chip in.'

Tom had been writing plays for Ned for months,
though secretly, without his name to them.
'If it's not Latin, it's not scholarly;
I cannot own the thing,' he told me once.

Ned's quick riposte, 'Both spent my money, then?'
was subtle as a knife in an oyster shell.

'I may have information,' Watson said.
'Some advance notice. What will be on the minds
of summer's audience. You could plan ahead.'

Alleyn was interested. 'Go on, then, speak.'
'Better not speak,' said Tom. 'I'll write it down.
Read it and cast it on the fire. And should
anyone ask how you're so prescient,
say you consulted an astrologer.'

Ned tapped his nose. 'Come on, then.' Watson tore
the corner off a playbill on the wall,
borrowed the quill the tapster kept for sums
and scratched some words for Ned.
                                    His brows rose up
like a crowd for an ovation.
                              'This is news.'
'Valuable news?'

      'I'll double the summer gates
with the right plays in place.' Handing a purse
over to Tom unconsciously, his eyes
still taking the words in.
                        'On the fire,' Tom said,
and Ned obeyed. It curled up, black as nightmares.

'We will defeat them,' Watson said, quite firm.
'We will defeat them, Ned. You mark my word.'

At Middelburg, the printer's twitchy eye,
its odd, incessant winking, puts me off.
My accent deteriorates. 'Monsieur Le Doux.
You have a trunk for me?'
                              The facial tic
suggests he has it hidden. 'Not at all.'
'It didn't come?' His wink says nothing more.
'If I give you this angel?' 'There you are.'
He snaps the money up. 'It's stored out back.'
I follow him through. An apprentice at the press
brings down black letter on to pristine sheet.
I check the contents. 'Everything is there,'
he says politely. 'Books are valuable
but far too heavy to stand in for gold.
I have some English titles you might like.
Things you can't get a licence for. You know?'
The one time winking might have seemed to fit,
his face is motionless as masonry.
'Religious tracts of various persuasions.
Wider debate than the English Queen allows.'
'You publish poetry?'
                        'If it will sell.
None at the moment. You have written verse.'
He knows. It's not a question. 'I have seen
your manuscripts.' He shrugs apology.
'When I was checking things against your list.
There might be a market for the saucy ones.'
'We may do business later,' I reply,
tucking a ream of paper beneath my arm.
'For now, I'm at these lodgings. Send the trunk

as soon as you can manage.' He folds the slip
into his pocket, winks me to the street.

I write all night. The lady of the house,
who provided extra candles for a mark,
is snoring on her purse. The moon is low;
a cat is prowling shadows on the stairs
and when I stop, my losses crowding in,
I think of your lips, one kiss. As though I live.
But I am the ruined queen of ancient Rome
who killed herself, and left her words to sing.

At noon, the trunk arrives between two boys
who frown at my shilling. The tall one kicks the short
to dig out a piece of parchment, firmly sealed:
'Arrived this morning, sir.' Another coin
and both skulk off. It is addressed 'Le Doux';
the seal's unknown to me; the hand inside
is unfamiliar. But beside the words
is sketched the outline of a marigold.
'Meet me at one. The Flanders Mare. T.T.'

'Oh, that was something. This'll run for weeks.'
Over my shoulder, 'Robert, sir, you're late!
Where were you at this young man's play?' Ned barks.
Greene almost flinches. 'Though there's nothing I
would rather do than laud another's art,
I was unwell.' There is a hint of truth
around his lips; the lightest tint of green
reflected from his cloak, or in his blood
from the rumoured diet of fish and Rhenish wine.
Tonight, exaggerating for effect,
Greene is his name, his nature and attire.

'On rewarding myself with a pint or two of wine
for finishing that script I promised you,
I find my head inoperative, too full
to take this young man's pounding poetry.
But, Marlowe, you're well, I trust. Another triumph?'

'Marley,' I say.
                'That doesn't have the ring
an author needs, my boy. Whereas Mar-lowe
seems altogether fitting, since the sound
paints you with either syllable. Mar, low.
The play went well?'
                Ned chips in, 'Like a trollop!'
The insult doesn't land with him at all.

'That's just as well for me. These fashions change,
sometimes before a man can capture them.'
He pushes a manuscript in front of Ned.
'*Alphonsus, King of Aragon*. The part
is made for you, Alleyn. Bold bombastic verse

in quite the style you're used to. Guaranteed
to pack the house as full as *Tamburlaine*.
Ten pounds is not too much to ask.'
                                'Ten pounds?
I paid half that for *Tamburlaine Part Two*!'
'But this is twice as good again, at least.
(Excuse me, no offence intended.) And
the Spanish title makes it topical.
You'll more than make your money back again.'

'Can I distract you?' Watson, at my side.
'A friend from Paris would like to meet the man
who has a shepherd turn kings into beasts.
Sir Francis' cousin, Thomas Walsingham.'

Thus, you have joined me in the tale I tell:
your gentle face beside him, framed in curls.
'Perhaps you'd call me Tom. Another Tom.'
You grasp my hand. 'I've read your poetry.
You're Watson's heir. In English. And your play –
it's very brave.' Your eyes are so intense
I'm speechless for a moment.

                        'How so, brave?'

'To scold religions, have an atheist
depose both Christian and Muslim kings.'

Is it natural for a memory to scorch,
word upon blistered word, that first exchange?
Do you recall as clearly my new gaze
falling upon you? Yours was torching me.

'It isn't bravery, but metaphor.
Impassioned right slays cold hypocrisy.
Those who swear oaths on sacred books and break
their promises should surely feel God's wrath.'
'In the form of a shepherd?'
                                        'Why not in a shepherd?
A shepherd's a man like any king. But rarer:
he keeps his word.'
                              'You don't see danger in it?'

Instinctively, I draw back from the cliff
of my own confirmed opinions, wondering if
you fish for your cousin also.
                                        'May I speak
not as intelligencer, but as poet?'
'Can you separate yourself so?'
                                        'Certainly.'
As though you'd entered, verbal sword half drawn,
and we were locked now, hilt to hilt.
                                        'Then do.'

'Truth's dangerous to liars. But in art
it's softened by beauty. If we put both sides,
as dialectic training teaches.'
                                        'Where
were you educated?'
                              'Cambridge.'
                                        'Tom, I swear,
he works for you already. Interviewed
by Sir Francis himself.' The jest from Watson there
only voicing my own discomfort. You stay fast
on the subject as a ship's own barnacle.

'One of the sceptic colleges, no doubt.
Not Christ's. Say, Corpus Christi?'
                                        'You are sharp.'
And serious. 'My father kept blades like you
for skinning rabbits.'
                        Trying to prick a laugh,
to distract you from your purpose. To no avail.

'They train good heretics,' you say as plain
as if I'd just assented.

                        'I would say
they train young men to question and debate
both sides of all positions.'
                                'And is there
a bar on what may be counter-argued?'
                                            'No.'
'The existence of God?'
                            'Ah, come now.' Watson leaps
ahead of my answer. 'Let us get to know
each other first. Thank goodness it's a play.
As quite opposed to something serious.'
He clasps your shoulders. 'Come now, gentle friend!
A play is only playful. There's no threat
if we are entertaining make-believe.'
Your eyes assess the set of my mouth and jaw
precisely as a housewife squeezes fruit;
remain there lest I slip away. 'I don't
believe he's made it up.'
                            'What are you saying?'
'The atheism. *Are* you an atheist?'

Watson laughs loudly, 'Faith, he isn't, Tom!
He's toying with you.'
                                'No, I'm not,' I say.
'Not an atheist?'
                        'Not toying with you.'
                                        'Oh,'
you say, and I watch your face fall like a bird
hit by a slingshot. So surprised by 'Oh'
that the fight quite leaves me.
                                'Nothing more than "oh"?'

There is a folding sadness in your face.
'If you don't know God's not an argument,
I cannot help,' you say.
                        'You want to help?'
'A talented writer like yourself? I do.'
The strangest sense, then, of your tenderness
washed over me. I'd read you very wrong.
'I'm open to help,' I say, 'all kinds.'
                                        And Tom
slips in, 'He hasn't any money, Kit.
He's a second son. His brother has the manor.
Handsome place, too. At Scadbury, in Kent.
But Tom's as penniless as the rest of us.'

We spent some borrowed pennies anyway
on further beers. You softened visibly.
and as we parted, grasped my hand and said,
'You know God's name is Jove?'
                                'Of course.'
                                        You dipped

my finger in the frothy head that lay

at the bottom of my exhausted cup and spelt
across the tabletop: 'I-O-V-E'.
'As it is written,' you said, quietly.

I close that memory, and sleep alone.

Just two days later, I was called away
to the continent. The Spanish invasion fleet
was building off the Netherlands. Inland
the Duke of Parma's army gathered strength.
I crossed the Channel as a pious man
and quoted verse at those who challenged me,
defrauding death by blasphemous degree.
Yet in the honest service of a faith
and that faith's defender; loyal to my Queen
by counterfeiting service to a God
I couldn't quite believe in. If that God
despised my actions, he left me unharmed
to estimate men and horse, artillery.

Flushing, the English garrison where I
reported news that they might use at home
was base to every spy and volunteer.
The inns were choked with soldiers on alert
exchanging rumours over watered beer;
with tables squeezed, it wasn't possible
to eat alone, unless one was diseased.
But I was halfway through a history play,
preferred to eat alone than make small talk,
and the inn, at least, had candles. I was glad
scribbling in public frightens people off.
It kept me out of trouble.
                              'Can I sit?'
The gentleman who joined me had a voice
as singular as Fortune.
                              'Be my guest.'
I hoped he couldn't read things upside down.
'Do you mind my asking what you're working on?'

'Do you mind my saying yes?'

He didn't blink.

'It can't be secret if you're writing here.'

'It isn't secret, but it's personal.'

'Looks like a play.'

'Excuse me, have we met?'

'Henry,' he said, his hand entreating mine.

I took it. 'Christopher Marley.' Back to the page.

'Marley the poet?'

'So they say.'

'What luck!

I finished reading, only recently,

your fine translation of Ovid's Elegies.'

'That manuscript has travelled well.' I wondered

how the stranger came by it.

'Indeed. Like fire

through August hayricks. You have quite a skill.

I write a little myself. Not fresh as you.

I'm more of a reader.'

'Very interesting.'

I admit my patience wore a little thin.

'I'm sorry. I'm interrupting. Pay no heed.'

He sat and tapped his fingers on the edge

of the beery table. Like he dabbed the keys

of some invisible virginal to scales.

'Curious how, on the very edge of war,

our thoughts are drawn to the wars of history.

I couldn't help noticing it's a battle scene.

Apologies.' He'd been quiet a good two minutes.

Time to give up. 'You're fond of history?'

'I'm fond of learning. Fond of the arts, and science,
debate. Though I avoid theology.
As wise men should. But knowledge interests me.'

Clearly he was no soldier. Though in clothes
as practical as mine, there was an air
of velvet and silk about him, suddenly.
I wondered I hadn't noticed it before.

'When all this is over, if they don't invade,
perhaps you'd like to use my library.
Come stay with me. I have two thousand books;
you might find one or two of use.' He grinned.
'Do you know Thomas Watson?'
                                                    'He's a friend.'
'A mutual friend. Delightful. Well, I'll go
and leave you to your play. We'll meet again.'

I asked the tapster to supply his name.
'That's Henry Percy, Earl of Northumberland.'

NORTHUMBERLAND'S SUBJECT

At summer's end, I crossed the Channel, thin
and ready to rest, and made his Petworth home
my own for several weeks. His own pet poet:
he asked me to read my verse aloud to him,
and had my portrait painted. We discussed
Copernicus, that whispered heresy
all clever men must orbit. But religion,
which killed his father with a pistol shot,
we never mentioned. Had I lingered there,
and caught the habit –

                          Oh, this thorn, regret.
I catch my eye upon it every time.

FIRST RENDEZVOUS

A half-hour early, I search out a seat:
a shadowed place, a good view of the door.
As midday nears, the Flanders Mare fills up
with Flemish conversation; working folk
taking repast. At noon, a slender man,
tall as a cobbler's story, enters the inn,
a drooping marigold in his lapel.
I've never met the man, he can't know me,
and yet he logs my face and, ducking the beams,
traverses to my corner. 'Thomas Thorpe,'
he says; a proffered hand. I let it hang
limp in the air, an unadopted flag.
In both ways, he's unshaken. 'Marigold!'
The hand I spurned leaps to the sad gold flower
and dumps it on the table. 'Am I right?
It was murder to get it. Sorry. Figure of speech.'
His eyebrows flash an inkling of the fate
I'm rumoured to have suffered. 'You'd be surprised
how detestably obtuse the local soil:
it's not the soil for marigolds, I'm told.'
I don't know whether to take this literally
or as a metaphor, since 'marigold'
has long been the service code for Catholic.
I haven't said a word to help him out,
provoking the eager man to ask me straight,
'Monsieur Le Doux, have I made a mistake?'

'What makes you think that I'm Monsieur Le Doux?'

He pauses thoughtfully, and tucks the flower
back where its drooping head offsets his air

of confidence. 'Three men here are alone.
One is as old as Christmas. One possesses
a wooden leg. The other one is you.
Your caution's admirable; but you've the air
of someone set upon and robbed, my dear.
Thus I concluded you have lost something
that's as yet unrestored. Your name perhaps.
I have on my person, however, something of yours.
A publication fresh picked from St Paul's.'
He places the volume gently in my hands.
'An author of some promise, I understand.'

It's *Venus and Adonis*. The long poem
I wrote the previous winter when the plague
had closed down all the theatres. The works
I wrote while living never bore my name.
Anonymous, to save me from the fools
who thought that I was Faustus, Tamburlaine.
And still not mine. What's new belongs to him:
my fabricated self, my pseudonym.

> He insisted that I meet him personally
> in an empty room at Richard Field's shop,
> above the bang and clatter of the press
> on the floor below. The deal already sealed,
> the price agreed. 'But I must know his face.'
>
> He had a hard, unmoving quality:
> rough country hewn, that quietly withstands
> the shoulders of bulls. I've never met a man
> so much like a dry-stone wall.
>   I watched his eyes

travel my clothes and calculate their cost –
cambric sixpence a yard, slashed satin sleeves –
I'm totalled, underlined.
                              'So you are he?
The writer?' I nod. 'We all should learn to write
and live so sumptuously.'
                              And I could say
I've other work, or I have noble friends,
but choose this line: 'I'm kept well by my Muse.'
A tightness in me, constricting like a wire
across my Adam's apple.
                              'But not safe.'
He closes his ledger, states my truth as bare
as Lenten tables. 'So. We have a deal.'

How sharp to see his name beneath my words.
Print makes it real. Erased. I'm written out.

'It's causing quite a stir,' Thorpe offers, pouring
himself a beer from the jug he whistled up.
'Lusty young men are learning lines by heart.
It's selling. The second printing's due next week.
I have an interest in the trade,' he says,
as he notices a question in my face.

'And there's no inkling?'
                              'Not a doubt, my dear.
He's fresh discovered. Conjured out of air.'
He throws his hands up like a small bouquet
which falls again, and crumples in his lap.
'The public love a new thing.'

                    'So they do.'
And there! A spike in my blood, an inward punch
against myself, and all that nourished me.
So long as the public swallow up this lie,
believe me written out, then I am saved.
And yet I'm starved. But *good* he's believed not me.
Yet dreadful, my work condemned to bastardy,
conceived as if my Muse had slept with him.
Now see, my beautiful daughter on the street,
admired by white-limbed, languid youths, and she
crediting him, while I am buried warm.

'And has he kept his head down?'
                              'That he has.
He's happily in the country where the folk
don't read a lot of poetry.' Thorpe smiles
like a reopening wound. This agent's young;
younger than me, I'd guess – yet old as wine
kept in its dust.
                  'You'll want to spend some time
alone with this,' he says. 'But we must meet
again. I have a letter. No, not here—'
He must have read my mind, which jumped like a fish
in hope of a mayfly. 'Not here. Somewhere private.
Where do you lodge?' I give him my address.
And so he weaves his height back through the chairs
and leaves me with my poem, half his beer.

As I walk out, a pair of Englishmen
fall into step beside me.
                          'Pardon us.
We were wondering, sir, what you were reading there.
It seemed to provoke such interest. Is it new?'

They are both in continental clothes, disguised
in local jackets. The second man chips in:
'My friend and I are lovers of literature
of all persuasions.'

     'And so inquisitive,'
I remark politely. 'But I have no objection.'
I hand it over like a piece of bread
I don't mind sharing.

     England's spies are quiet,
thumbing the pages, finding only poem.
No code, no masked sedition, only poem.
One shrugs, gives up. The sharper of the two
returns to the title page. 'What phrase is this?
Can you translate?' He jabs the epigram
which, naturally, is Latin.
       'It's a quote.
"Let base conceited wits admire vile things.
Fair Phoebus lead me to the Muses' springs."
From Ovid,' I add gently. 'The Roman poet.'

'I've not much taste for ancient history,'
the sharp man says. 'And though I like a verse
or two, a poem this long is tedious.
Perhaps another time.' The pamphlet's pressed
into my chest, and they give me *Good days*
and doff their hats. I'm free to walk away.

THE FIRST HEIR OF MY INVENTION

I cannot bear to check it for mistakes.
Can hardly bear to look at it at all,
and tuck it in the trunk. So it is mine.
So young men parrot it. And there is praise
inherent in the printer printing more.
But the accident of needing some disguise
to write beneath means all the praise belongs
to my invention, Shakespeare. Who is me,
and yet divorced from all my infamy.
The poem designed to rescue me from shame
now wreaths its laurels round another's name.

I smuggle a quart of liquor to my room
and drink the afternoon into a blur:
filling the hell-hole of the thoughtless mouth
that occasioned this disaster to occur;
drumming the dumb skull of this idiot
who pushed the gods of fame to such degree
that no one, now, can know that he's alive.
And no one abroad has been as fooled as he –
or me – for I forget now who I am,
drowned both in liquor and unyielding grief
for all that's shipwrecked with identity.

THE JEW OF MALTA

At the launch of my fourth play, I'm holding court.
London is drunker with me every month,
and tables pulled together, flagons poured –
and how my mouth is like those beery jugs,
pouring a liquor that could ruin us all,
clear and intoxicating all at once.

'Religion is made by men, not made by gods.
Its purpose is to keep the world in awe
while we are robbed to gild the candlesticks.'

Tom Watson, sucking the meal out of his teeth,
allows his mouth to crawl towards a smile.
'Not all religion, Kit. Those candlesticks
are Papist props. So be a Puritan.
Eschew the pomp.'
                        'But that's his favourite bit!'
This gibe from Nashe, then recently arrived
in London: a gag-toothed youth I rather liked
for his insolence.
                        'The scarecrow isn't wrong,'
I say, not quite declaring he is right.
'At least the Catholic Church puts on a show:
paintings and music, incense. What *we* get
for our pennies on the plate is threats of Hell,
and pious hypocrisy, with rituals
dead-dull enough to send a spark to sleep
if the pews weren't hard as sitting on your bones.
Nothing to look at, sermons sour as lime
and fines for not attending.'
                        Watson smiles,

intent on baiting me. 'So be a Jew!'
He fills my tankard to the top, then his.

'Tom, could I change my blood, I'd rather die
than offer my quill to have the end snipped off
– of all ungodly things man ever dreamed –
and join a people scorned even beyond
players and poets. No, for all their skill
at making money.'
                          'Be a Muslim then.'
His smile says, 'Give up, friend, you'll never win.'
He pitches it against my seriousness
hoping I'll yield and turn to lighter things.

Might I have saved myself by heeding him?
Not without gutting me of all my passion;
the past can't be rewritten. And time's shown,
for all Tom's lightness, he too found his prison.
My bars were forged inside my drunken mouth.

'My point is, all religion is the same.
I can't see why a man may not just be –
defined by no allegiance. Hold his spirit
outside religion.'
                          Quietly, you were there.
Folding your jacket, speaking with that calm
that lifts your opinion over louder mouths,
entreating, 'Kit – be careful what you say,'
your eyes intense.

                          'Can I not speak my mind?
Is England ancient Rome? Are we all slaves?'

How patient you were with me. A doting parent
whose love prevents all discipline.

                                  Your voice:
'In principle we're free, but bear in mind
the times. You could pick a safer subject. *Be*
a safer subject.'
                  Like a father.
                            'Kit!'
Tom Watson interjects. 'The Bible says,
Be still and know that I am God. What say
we let it rest at that?' There's nothing stirred
until Watson gets his oar in. I respond,
'The Bible is a storybook for babes.
And the New Testament is filthily written.
It's hard to credit that the word of God
would have no poetry.'
                        'But it speaks of love,'
says Ned, objecting. 'Loving one's fellow man.
You surely can't find fault with that.'
                            Nashe snorts,
attempting to contain within his nose
a laugh that Edward Alleyn would not enjoy.
Not to blame friends for my misfortunes, but
he cues me in to further mischief.
                          'True.
Christ loved St John extremely, don't you think?
Actors have ingles, Jesus had his John.
I can't help but approve, yet worship him?
How has this man, professing love, puffed up
a cult that suckles bishops? Feeds them larks
on golden platters in their palaces?'

'Abuse of power,' you remind, 'is not
specifically religious. It's a trait
that occurs throughout humanity. But love'
(oh, you were always speaking love to me),
'the concept of God as love, is *that* not worth
the flaws in either Testament? Is love
not central to religion?'

               There, Nashe twitches
with such involuntary violence that his beer
flies into his lap and soaks him. Christ, your laugh
is blessed relief, but when the ragged roar
of hilarity dies down you ask again,
'Do not the Gospels testify of love?
Are we not urged to love?'
                      'But has it worked?'
You know I hate to lose. I do not lose.
'As one and a half millennia attest,
religion kills more people than the plague.
Love neighbours, yes. But not if their beliefs
rest in some other holy book.'

                  These words
provoke a burst of laughter. Ned is cut.
'But, Kit,' he says, 'you do believe in God?'

'I believe in truth and beauty. The divine.
But literal miracles? Water into wine?'
('If only!' shouts Nashe, shaking his empty cup.)
'The raising of the dead? A virgin birth?'

'So Christ was a bastard and his mother dishonest?'
Watson desires to see how far I'll go.

'He was a carpenter. A mortal man.
What are we meant to worship? Didn't the Jews,
among whom he was raised, know who he was
and whence he came? And they had him crucified.'

Ned's brother, John, is listening from his post
behind the bar. 'Now, now, that's dirty talk.'
His moustache and hairy lower lip are paired
to make a second mouth, which I enjoy
watching as he negotiates the burr
of the faint West Country accent Ned has lost.
'My customers are all God-fearing men.
Or ought to be, for all the ale they swallow.'
He crosses and sits among us, next to Ned.
'*Brother! You've brought in reprobates again!*'
(A hammy whisper.) 'And Master Marlowe too.
Always a pleasure to learn what's in those books
and have the company of gentlemen.'

Nashe grimaces. 'We're happy to oblige.
Now back to the fun. So who is next?'

                                'Moses,'
Ned offers. 'Now *he* was a holy man. A prophet,
most surely.'
                I snap the offer from his mouth
as a hawk takes bacon.
                        'Ned, he led the Jews
to wander the wilderness for forty years,
a journey that should take no more than one.
Appalling poor direction? Or a jape
so all those privy to his subtleties
would perish before they found the Promised Land?

Raised Egyptian, he wouldn't find it hard
to fool some unsophisticated Jews.
The man was a conjuror.'
                                        'A conjuror?'
'Most certainly, for when—'
                                        'Who has my chair?'
A kingly roar comes from a stubbled man
whose friends tug at his elbows, rein him back.
'My chair!' he says. 'Has my initials on.
See? William Bradley. Give me back my chair!'

It's the chair I'm sitting in that bears his mark,
carved on the armrest like a schoolboy's desk,
and I rise, as light as thought, until a hand
presses my shoulder. 'No, Master Marlowe, you
should stay right there. The chair belongs to me.'

The chair man stumbles back a step. 'How so?'

John Allen: 'Because you owe me fourteen pounds.
Deny it all you like, I have your chit.'
The men lock eyes as if those eyes were horns;
John, as innkeeper, snorting from his turf
at next door's bull. He growls,
                                        'Now pay your debt.
Or you will lose more than your furniture.'

'You broke into my house.'
                                        'You broke your word.'
John Allen's accent thickens under stress.
'And I will break your neck without a thought
if you make any trouble.'
                                        'That a threat?

I'll have the law on you.'
                          'We have the law
with us,' says Watson, fingering Hugh Swift,
his brother-in-law, a Middle Temple man.
'Now pay your debt to John or bugger off.'

Bradley is pissed, but with this taunt he stiffens,
shakes off his helpers, and engages me
directly. 'That chair's mine. If you know what
is good for you, you'll stand and pass it here.'

I feel my throat go dry, and every face
around the tavern tense for my reply.
I take a sip of beer and settle back.
It hasn't passed my notice that his hand
is on his dagger's hilt. 'Dear man, I would,
if I thought you needed it. But you can stand
up by yourself, despite – how many pints?
This chair's so comfortable, I fear you'd slump
and lose all benefit of being tall.
Once sat, a man must rely upon his wit
for his defence. Take no risks. If you stand
you can rely upon your knife. Although –'
I nod to his twitching fingers, dancing round
the hilt '– I wouldn't. There are more of us.'

His anger narrows. 'So superior,
with your clever words, your friends with velvet capes.'
It was you he was referring to, our lord
without the manor. 'All is levelled though
by your being flesh. No wit is quick enough
to escape my knife. Who are you anyway?'

'He wrote *The Jew of Malta.*'

                              'Good for you!'
the bastard leers across the tabletop.
'At least you'd sense to boil the big-nosed crook.'
The farce's subtleties were lost on him.
'The Jews and money lenders should be hanged'
(grinning at John Allen), 'and all the tapsters
who wait on buggerers.'

                    Now Watson stands,
now Edward Alleyn, now every one of us,
comes to the battlements with daggers drawn.

'You pus-filled cullion.' Watson's voice is steel.
'You privy stool I wouldn't shit upon.
If you're a gentleman, procure a sword
and find me any weekday at my house.
If not, admit that you're a parasite
who borrows from friends and doesn't keep his word.
Let's settle it like men, and not like scum
who murder with their eating implements.'

Bradley is reeling back and grinning wide.
Pleasure has dropped his voice to baritone.
'If you're a man, then I'm a Persian whore.
We'll settle it as you say, though. Call it a duel.
Then, when I kill you, I'll have my defence.'
He and his cronies shamble to the door
half checking us, half fearless. As he leaves,

'You challenged me. My brothers are witnesses.'

Everyone sits, and no one says a word.
Four heartbeats pass before I break the air.
'Tom, that was madness.'
                              'Well, he made me mad.'
'The man's a brawler.'
                              'He'll not get a sword.'
'Who says he won't come at you anyway?'
'He'll be sober tomorrow.'
                              Our eyes meet, sharing doubt.
'I liked your speech, though,' Nashe says, 'very neat.
Your mental side-step stole the wind from him.
You juggled him smartly.' So the table warms
and I am toasted: 'To Kit! To the play!
To *The Jew of Malta*!' And Nashe contributes:
'To pus-filled cullions, may they rue the day!'
'To pus-filled cullions,' we agree, and roar.
I notice Greene come in, turn round, and leave.

LURCH

'I must abandon London, Kit,' you said,
catching me as I left the inn that night.
'My brother's fallen ill.'
                              Perhaps the drink
had magnified my feelings, but your news
felt like a blow. And that surprised me so
that I staggered back.
                              'Woah, Kit!'
                                          You pulled me up
from the path of a carthorse and its fatal load.
'All well?' you asked.
                              'No, Tom! All isn't well.
Why are you going?' You helped to brush me down
unaware your touch was setting light in me
a thousand fuses. And confusion too,
tipped up, the drink not helping. 'For my brother,'
you said. 'And Scadbury needs managing.'
'Is he very ill?' I asked. 'Will you inherit?'
The drink, the drink. You smiled all your forgiving.
'I do not know the upshot, Kit, only
that I am called away.'
                              'Don't go, dear friend!'
My sudden passion shocking even me
as I went to kiss you.
                              'Kit,' you reeled, 'be sober!'
The boy holding our light looked sharp away.
'I need you here,' I said.
                              'You don't need me.
You have Tom and the others,' you replied.

These days you know how much I needed you,
my voice of caution, and my gentler side.
How differently this story might have spun
had you remained with me. But your advice
faded in time as clothes do with the sun.
For I remember, parting, how you gripped
my hand in both of yours with urgency.
'Work less for my cousin. All the lies required
are dangerous for honest men like you.'

'When money comes more readily, I'll stop.'

You went to Kent. And what was I to do?

THAT MEN SHOULD PUT AN ENEMY IN THEIR MOUTHS

Liquor kicks doorframes while the Lowlands sleep.
It shoulders blame for my catastrophe,
swallows my life and pisses it in the sink,
blurs what I hurt to look at, pillows sense.
Drink fogs a future which is only dark
and endless tramping into foreign towns
until tomorrow narrows to a point
on the nose's tip. Then soaks and hardens thoughts,
weighting them into bruising hammer blows

which wake me, not as senseless as I wish
I was. Each leaden limb thuds with the poison:
self-administered. As I lift my cheek
from its crumpled resting place, and shift my head,
the world shifts with it, wobbles, settles down.

'And Christ is risen.' Thomas Thorpe is sitting
four feet away, his hands placed on his knees
like handkerchiefs. 'You're lucky I'm a friend.
I could have had eggs and bacon off your back,
you'd not have noticed.'

                              'How did you get in?'
I squint my eyes at the daylight's acid burn.
'Old-fashioned charm,' he says, smoothing his hair.
'A drop of rose-oil too. The ladies like it.'

My brain is coming back from somewhere cold,
finding its way by following the steps
it stamped out yesterday. 'You have the letter?'

'The letter, yes. All in good time, my dear.
There's something else more pressing. A request.
We need a play.'
                    'The theatres are closed.
Unless you're saying they're open?'
                                        'No such luck.
The plague's still rampant. Gathering for sport
is quite forbidden. All the same a play
has been requested. You'll be paid for it.
A comedy.'
            'A comedy!'
                        'Indeed.'
He keeps his mouth straight, though it longs to smile.
'The Queen, apparently, likes something light
at Christmas time.'

                    I launch towards my desk,
pick up the papers I was writing there
and wave them like a fist. 'I have a play.
A tragedy of violence and revenge.
Titus Andronicus. The crowd will love it.
Henslowe will make a mint. Though he'll complain
about the cost of bull's blood, and the slopping
and mopping for each performance. Here. It's done.
Or close to done. I've had my fill of it.'
A wave of nausea forces me to sit,
my heart capsized.

                    'And then the comedy?'

'What? Are you mad? Pray, find me comedy
in the nonsense that my life's become. Go home.'
I press my aching head between my fists
as if I could squeeze him out of it. 'Go home.

Go back to – where you came from.' Thinking Hell
might be the place. 'But give me the letter first.'

'Touchy,' he says, and offers it from afar
like meat on a stick that's pushed towards a bear.
The seal, and the hand, Southampton's, and not yours.
I break it open. Not a word of you.

'There's nothing else?'
                                          'There's gold if you'll write the play.
I assume you're running low by now.'
                                          He's right,
and knows he is, but quiet in victory,
stares out the window at a distant cloud
feeding his hat brim through his hands, to mime
that velvet wheel of Fate, necessity.

'I'll try,' I say, my hand out for a purse,
aware of my own petulance. 'Perhaps
the joke will come to me in Italy.'

'Commedia dell'Arte! I saw it once
in Padua. What larks!' He stops the flow
immediately, though a boy had bubbled up
beneath the beard. 'You've travelled much?' he asks,
dropping the gold into my open palm.
'A little,' I say, with unmasked bitterness.
'In service of the Queen. What I've not seen
I'm sure to make up for in the coming months.'

'Do you know Padua?' 'Just by report.'
'A scholar ought to go there at least once.
You're travelling as a scholar, I believe.
You might want to visit the university.'

'If I have time,' I say, aware of time
stretched out before me in an endless rope
that I must climb towards the heartless gods,
its end fraying behind me. And the drop.

I tuck the purse inside my shirt. 'I'll try,'
I say to his eyebrows, arching up like cats
at an enemy. 'No promises.'

                              He picks
up the *Chronicles*, that volume from the trunk
that groans with England's misery, and flicks
to a page that wants to open. Reads for a blink,
then puts it down as gently as a babe.

'There's humour in every tragedy,' he says.

'Not this,' I answer, stabbing the title page
of the bloody play that hacks out my revenge.

'The troubled mind is a creative one.
But have you watched the crowd's reaction when
the blood starts gushing? Faces turned away.
Barbaric as humankind might seem to be,
most cannot look. The point you mean to pierce
is deflected. No one sees. But make us laugh
and we're toys for you to play with.

                              Just a thought,'
he says when a silence follows.

                              Though that thought
is tugging a mental sleeve, points at the door

of my own imprisonment. Which is unlocked.
Liquor, however, clouds the hall beyond.

I turn to Thorpe. 'What was amusing once
seems less amusing now I am obliged
to forgo my native tongue. Go by a name
I cannot tune my ear to when it's called.
Good conversation, which would feed my heart,
is fields and seas away, and barred from me.
Banished from friends and loved ones, putting miles
between us daily. That's my life. Perhaps
you'd like to suggest the humour in it.'

                                  'Well . . .'
He thinks for a moment, scratching at his chin
to make a cloud of fairies. 'You're alive.
Whereas Marlowe, so they say, is horribly dead.
Stabbed through the eye. Some drunken tavern brawl.'
I startle. 'Sorry, what?'
                         'That's what I heard.'

'He was a gentleman! A Cambridge scholar.
He never would have died in such a manner.'
He knows. I know. Third person is a sham.

Thorpe shrugs. 'Does it matter now? Kit Marlowe's dead.
And no one looks for a dead man. So. Be glad.
Get out in the air and breathe it. Friends of yours
have taken risks that you might do so.' And
with that, he turns, gathers the play, and leaves.

THE UNIVERSITY MEN

No one dared breathe *succession*, but the stage
was clearing for the coming deathbed scene
of the Virgin Queen. Vibrating in the wings,
the noble houses and the royal courts,
a dozen hopefuls. She would not discuss
such certainties as might endanger them.

For power's an intoxicating brew,
and plots begin to cook in seething heads
that ache to overthrow the old regime
with cold assassination. So we were placed:
the university men. The tutor spies.
The secretary agents of the State.

For a change of head may bring a change of faith,
and the careful man will shift from foot to foot
and listen to the words that will determine
who will be judges, who will be hanged and burnt.
The university men, known for their wit,
would use intelligence, and gather it.

The God of Shepherds, Poley named himself.
In charge of the poets: as if poets can
be ruled by anything except their dreams.
But still, we drank with him, and called him Pan,
alive with the danger he might put us in
to serve our country, and to serve the Queen.

Watson went to Cornwallis, while my charge
was the King of Scotland's cousin, Arbella Stuart.
We were to guide our pupils down the road

of strict obedience and loyalty.
We were to note who called, who crept to church.
The loyal man at work. Yet still, I played,

dandled that toy, religion. Spun ideas
to jet above Ned's buskins on the stage.
For it was God – at least, it seemed like God,
who kept me up at night, and scribbling
those thoughts humanity might understand.
Only, I wrote – and signed them – in my hand.

THE PACT OF FAUSTUS

'So should I sign in blood?' My joking words
fell silently on the official's face.
I put my name to paper anyway.
And so I set the wheel of my disgrace
trundling towards me on some distant road.

Knowledge. It sounds as gentle as a bell
at three a.m. from the neighbouring parish clock.
It sounds as safe as wood does to a tree.
It guides me dreamily, from book to book.
But certain volumes, authorised in Hell,

are dangerous to know. Some knowledge lifts
and some intoxicates. Jesters and clowns,
pretending they know nothing, are the wise.
Some knowledge airs the mind; some knowledge drowns –
and yet, I couldn't drink enough of it.

I had such faith in me, such certainty
the licensed bloodhounds couldn't do me harm;
dull thinkers not equipped to sniff me out,
who missed the jokes, too slow to see me palm
the words from hand to hand, or hand to mouth.

But the universe has lessons, tailored tight
to fit the sin, and I was set to fall.
Proud of the name I signed away that day,
as former cobbler's son who had it all
but shared with Lucifer the sin of pride.

Bright Lucifer, once so beloved of God
but tumbled out of heaven, and his wits;
the universe correcting for its gifts.
True knowledge of humanity confirms
that this is Hell. Nor are we out of it.

THE TUTOR

'You have been recommended. And your name
is Morley, I understand.'
                              'It is.'
                                        She's still
as a spider who has felt a fly alight.
The Countess of Shrewsbury knows the Queen as Bess,
a name they share. A cold, entitled look:
three husbands haven't lasted her. The fourth
is not at home in London.
                          'Hear me then.
My granddaughter deserves the best of minds
to guide her education. Rhetoric'
– she enunciates carefully, lest I mishear –
'will not be taught to her. No woman should
be trained for disagreement. Literature
will do. The classical sort. Not Ovid, mind.
She's just thirteen.' She scours me with her eyes.

'Come closer, Master Morley.' Lifts a sleeve.
'Now. Velvet? Surely a scholarly gentleman
cannot afford it.'
                   'I have generous friends.'
'Do you indeed? Tom Walsingham, no doubt.'
She casts for the reaction on my face;
I give her nothing. Still, a narrowed gaze.
'Oh, I know all about it. Why you're here.
The eyes and ears of the Queen range far and wide
across our troubled country. There are those
who fancy Arbella on a *Catholic* throne –
please don't insult me with your feigned surprise –
and she must be protected. You'll report

to Walsingham or Burghley. So be it.
Then the government shall pay you. I'll provide
paper and books, and ten hot meals a week.
A room when we're not in London.'

                                  Like a thief
cutting the purse strings – certainly as quick –
but with deservedness.
                        'Your ladyship,
What if I can't afford those terms?'
                                 Her brow
rises as gently as the sea. 'Then I
will find someone more flexible,' she says.
'Someone who understands the value of
tutoring she who might one day be queen.'
'My lady, we can't discuss succession.'
                                 'No.
But be aware succession will occur.
Dear Bess is not immortal.' Flashing teeth
as black as widow's weeds. 'If not Arbell,
then her cousin the King of Scots. This royal charge
is valuable. Be aware that I could ask
for any prospective tutor to pay *me*
and have a hundred applicants.'
                              It's true.
And bowing to greet her rug, I sniff the bait
of royal stories. Close to history's forge
as a cobbler's son could ever dream to be,
think not of danger, or grey poverty
gnashing its teeth. Just opportunity.

Small Beer

'Not pay you?' Nashe is shrill, incensed. 'Not pay?
The richest English woman beside the Queen?'
'But how did she become so?' Watson nods,
filling a pipe. 'Think on. The woman's shrewd.'
'Not pay you, though,' Nashe murmurs.
                                    'I'll survive,'
I reassure him. 'You should see the meals.
Quality fare, a ransom on their own.
The books and paper are invaluable,
and time to write in. And the rest of it –
the beer and ink and horse food, I can cover.
Intelligence will serve if the playhouse shuts.'

The tapster's girl, collecting empty jugs
at this point trips, almost into my lap
before I help her onwards. Watson blinks
at the accident. 'You mean your wits, of course.'
'Of course. These were expensive wits to train.'

SOLILOQUY

Listen. The hoot owl sweeping from the woods
marks, like a breath expelled, the starlit air.
The moon scores loneliness across the fields,
slow as the rolling ocean, and a breeze
slides to my cheek and whispers, *He's not here.*

The road might carry love upon its back
like a dusty serpent winding from the hills;
you might be sleeping one night's dream away;
and yet your absence crawls inside my bones
and makes its home there, like a broken vow.

Two things remain: the thudding of my heart,
that drumming clown whose audience dispersed
to leave only litter, tickets . . . and the sound
that thought makes when it's battered on a wall
that won't admit it. Oh, love, let me in.

I grieve myself. This shadow I've become
that berates itself for being out of doors,
the rusty nail on which my name is hung
now on the edge of falling; I'd be yours
were I not crushed and bootless. Who is this?

I grieve that boy who practised walking tall
around the quiet squares of academe;
who, like his father, aimed to fashion souls,
envisaging the awl as poetry.

I grieve that young man, choking on the jests
that he and friends had conjured from their dreams;

of how it will be when all the world is theirs
and they will fall to bed in satin sleeves . . .
oh, clod, oh, stupid man, where was your head?

This age abhors the truth. It beats it down
like a smart unruly servant, like a dog
whose eye reflects his master, club in hand
and poised to destroy him. Meanwhile, churches cram
with poisoned congregations, social ticks
who nod to each other, followers of faith
who don't believe the words, but sing the song.

Oh, irreligious world, so scant of good
that good, when it comes, cannot be recognised –
a tolerated foreigner, who's blamed
the moment we're engulfed by our own sin.

Oh, sacrilegious world, to kill a man
for the form his prayer takes, when we need all prayers
to pull us from this darkness into light.
But snuff us out, who cares?

                              Oh, shameless world.
I'll hold a mirror to your ugliness
until you see you contribute each squint,
each pustulence, to the grotesquerie.

Oh, former loved but never-loving world.
We poets have a duty to believe
in goodness, beauty and the human heart.
Forgive me, then. How deeply I must grieve
that I'm struck down for having better faith.

A rabbit screams its murder. Bullies read
the bloodied claw of nature as a cue
to justify themselves as predators.

The landscape sits as passive as a priest
receiving our confessions, and the globe
revolves beneath the heavens: night, then day,
then night again. A lifetime falls away
as water poured on sand until we ask,

What is a human being? Are we clay?
Excrescences of light? Bright animals
adopting gross stupidity? Or gods
pelted in human skin, come down to play,
create, destroy, find joy in misery?
The moon squats on the mountains like a pearl.
It only has to rise, and will be free.

The Hog Lane Affray

Hog Lane, just after two, three years ago.
After a meal of mutton and cold beer
with Thomas Nashe, I'm strolling back to work
on *Doctor Faustus* when the Devil himself
calls out behind me: 'There's the beardless man
who slandered me!' It's Bradley and a friend,
George Orrell, full of ale and parsnip stew
and outrage. 'I believe I complimented you
on your uprightness,' I said.
                                        'Untrammelled shit.
Give me your sword,' he says to Orrell, 'quick.
I'll slice his head off. Then we'll see whose brains
are bigger.' Clumsily, he wrests the sword
from his large friend's scabbard. Orrell shoves him off,
annoyed to be handled. Yet eager to assist,
he hands his yeoman friend a soldier's blade.
The rapier at my waist weighs half as much,
but neither of us has experience.

'That's not a duelling weapon.'
                                        'I don't care.
A fighting weapon's all I'm looking for.'

'Don't start this thing.'

                                        'You started it yourself.
The night you wouldn't get out of my chair.
I'm here to finish it.'

                        He hawks and spits
a fat green slug of phlegm on to the dirt.

Nashe whispers, 'I'll get Watson,' and flits off
through the gathering crowd, who, with their stink and breath,
are drawn by the hope of blood and spectacle
to make our arena. I watch my flame-haired friend
like an urgent signal flashing up the street,
dodging the foul discharge of a chamber pot
before he's swallowed up in passageways.

'I've got no fight with you, my friend,' I say.

'I'm not your friend.' He slides a greasy hand
across his mouth, as if he's tasted me.
'Draw if you call yourself a man.'
                                        'I do.
But a gentleman.' I slide the rapier tip
into the air with a flourish, though my heart
is knocking to be let out. 'And I would rather
settle with words. But if you're disposed to fight
I'll prove that wit's superior to sword
by dodging you.'

                    He narrows blazing eyes.
'I'll have your wits on a skewer. Come here, boy.'
He beckons with his free hand. 'Let's have some blood.'

'Show him what for!' A shout comes from the back.
It's Eric, the local butcher's lad. 'Now, Eric' –
my sword tip drops to the ground – 'should you not be
about an errand, running joints of pork?'
A grin splits through his pimples, cracking sore.
'I wouldn't miss a murder for the world.'

'Murder? There'll be no murder here.'
                                        'That's what
you think,' says Bradley, charging like a bull
that has broken tether. Instantly, the cuff
of our weapons clashing, and his heavier blade
has snapped mine seven inches in.
                                   'Oh dear,'
says Orrell. 'Now look what you've done. You've snapped
the boy's toy sword.' A laugh bristles the crowd.
I'm hard against the brute, our wrists are locked
until I push, release and slip aside
like a sudden opened door, so that his force
throws him on my behalf.
                          'You little shit,'
he growls, brushing the dust off as he stands.
My breath, from the exertion of his weight,
is rasping a little, and my rapier
is blunt as a whore's remark. Bradley, now sore,
is more determined. Slow, perhaps, but slow
in the manner of a seasoned torturer
delighting in his work, delaying pain
until the expectation's made it worse.
He calls for a swig of ale, as if to savour
his victory before dispatching me.
It appears from the audience. 'I'll have you now,'
he says, with a cellared voice, 'you worthless tick.'

'Go on, Bill, finish him off!' a woman squeals.
I turn round, shocked to notice 'Mrs Peat?'
'I meant him, dear,' she reverses. 'Finish *him* off.'
And no hard feelings, offers me her gums.
Bradley's delight reveals two broken teeth
inflicted in another brawl; he comes

like Judgment Day towards me. As he swings
the unwieldy blade, I snatch from a crooked man
his walking stick, rush 'Sorry,' as he falls
and his crutch, braced in my hands, prevents an act
of unfair decapitation, then is dropped
as I duck beneath those ape arms. Bradley turns
but trips on the crippled man whose stick I stole.
'You whore's son with your la-di-dah brocade.'
Several assistants help them to their feet,
the old man winded, Bradley in a stew
now boiling over. 'Fight, you poncy turd!'

'I believe you're a little drunk. There are children here.'

It's Watson, breathing sharply at my side,
with Nashe not far behind. He claps his arm
around my shoulder, saying, 'Honestly.
Gentlemen duel at dawn. It's almost three.
You're keeping good people from their work. I'd guess
that your opponent's not a gentleman.'

'So you've come now?' says Bradley. 'Very good.
I'll have a bout with you, then finish off
your wheezy friend.'

                    There goes his fish-stock rage,
bubbling over his lip as if a fire
were stoked beneath him. Watson keeps his calm,
and his hand on the hilt of an unfamiliar weapon.
'That's not your sword.' 'No, it's Cornwallis's.
I borrowed it just in case,' he whispers back.

Having emptied his verbal armoury,
the brute has another swig of someone's ale,
a pat on the back. A breeze whips up the air
like a hand up a lady's petticoat. A thrill.

My mind cooks up the shiver; brings it here
with a flavour of its aftertaste, the bite
of unalterable history. But then, what felt
like theatre was real: not choreographed,
the lines to come unwritten and unknown.

'Kit, hold my jacket,' says Watson, stripping quick
to his undershirt. 'It cost me two months' pay.'
And he's in the fray, and fencing.

                                    I've seen cocks
go for each other's eyes more cautiously;
Watson, perhaps pumped up from running there,
is bright, ferocious; Bradley swinging wild
like a blinded man who doesn't know which way
the blows will come. The gathered crowd step back
to accommodate raw spleen. A boy left stood
in the way of danger, awed by spectacle,
is collared to greater safety.
                              'Ha! Take that!'
crows Watson, scratching blood from Bradley's chest.
'I've taken worse,' his gruff opponent says,
and turns as ugly as a thunderstorm,
thwacking his heavy sword again, again,
across the spaces Watson occupied
split seconds earlier. Tom leaps back and back
to make some space for the depth of Bradley's rage
as the bull man presses forward. The heavy sword,

now lightened by fury, flashes there, then there,
slices at arm and thigh.
                              I watch the blood
that feeds that friendly heart spread like a plague
across the cambric of Tom Watson's shirt.
Bradley is grinning. Now the crowd grows quiet,
and the steel on steel that follows cuts a hush
as still as the full-stop of a funeral hymn.
As tremors in my legs, those staggered steps
of Watson, backwards – backed now to a ditch
where his breath comes shallow, sharp as that bare inch
between him and his end – a sudden end,
rearing up black from the afternoon's bad joke.
And who would leap into that deep unknown
we're told leads to the gods, but comes up void –
is always walked alone – without a stab
at another's heart?

                              I hear the blade go in
with a crack of bone, a squeak along the rib;
Watson's eyes widen, close. The heavy groan
is Bradley's. He slides – as easily as snow
laid thick on a sloping roof, but thawed beneath –
clean from the blade, and crumples to the ground.

No one moves, though the wind tugs at their cuffs,
their hats, their hems. And then a wail begins
on a note like a rising flood in someone's gullet:
a dusty woman pushing through the throng,
knocking aside the goggling passer-by,
the death-dumb neighbour. 'Bill,' she's sobbing, 'Bill,'
and it's Bill that's drowning. Blood bursts from his mouth
in eager blossoms as his love winds through

to cradle him in her lap, 'Oh, Bill, oh, Bill,
oh, William' – so intently locked with him
that she's blind to us, his murderers, until
she finds on her blood-soaked dress a heavy corpse;
and no one in that flesh.
                              'What have you done?'
Her hate disintegrates to disbelief,
then melts to loss as she returns to Bill,
what used to be her Bill, what kissed her neck
to wake her up, and twirled her in a dress
when he promised her a future, always good
for the rent no matter what. And now, no Bill.
And she's sobbing no, and no, and no, and no,
her hair stuck to her tears, her hopeless cheek
stamped with her lover's blood. The bud of her lips
murmuring prayers.
                              'I'll get the constable,'
says Nashe. 'Don't worry. The both of you stay put.'
He's sprinting down the street. I steer Tom's arm
to sit him gently down, remove what's left
of his shirt and tear it into strips. There's not
one protest, joke. With frightened care, I wrap
his wounds until the cloth stops soaking red,
then drape his jacket gently on his shoulders
as though he were a general. He shudders,
grips round his knees, and dimly stares away.
Someone offers a flask: 'Good liquor, sir.'
I put it in his hand. He swigs it, gulps
and winces, gives it back, still gazing straight.
I don't partake myself; return it to
the glove of a quiet man I recognise,
a friend of Richard Field.
                              Tom's skin is cold,

so I put my arm around him, stop his coat
from flapping on his chest. I want to say
'Are you all right?' but the question is absurd.

What good are words? There's a woman sobbing on
her slain provider, comforter and mate –
and her sobs are your creation. How should words
presume themselves as bandages or slings
when the world limps onward, and you've darkened it?
And words be damned, for if we're 'gentle men'
then what hope does the world have? Words are lost.
They've plucked their eyes out rather than see this,
have jumped from clifftops.

                                    Finally, Tom thaws.
Stone quiet, he murmurs, 'What will I tell Ann?'

'Tell her the truth,' I say, after a pause.
'I killed someone? She'll like that.' There's no smile.
'I thought I was a better man,' he says,
'but there's no such thing. Just look.' He nods his head
at the sobbing woman, mingling tears with blood,
Orrell and Bradley's brother lifting what
used to contain her love, and staggering,
off-balanced by its weight. 'Ten minutes ago
I was a writer. Now I'm a murderer.'

Envoi

And he was not the same. If prison broke
some part of him, it was a secret piece
below the cough he carried eighteen months
beyond the blessedness of his release.

Within his former swagger now, a limp
was hinted at: some slight imbalance stayed.

Behind each joke the deadly serious
would tug a gulp, provoke the listener's stare.

And he was out of time; his laugh would ring
two beats beyond the point where some of us
would find things funny.

                   Yet the strangest jest
Tom ever played on us was losing faith
that the world would let him off on self-defence
another time. And so he wrote his end.
Three years would pass before we buried him.

LIMBO

Thrown into Limbo, Newgate's deepest cell,
to await our pardons, and to join those souls
who spend their hours watching rodents fight
for a crumb of something rotten.

       'Fuck, the smell,'
says Watson, as we're harried down the hall.
Gaol costs, and those who can't afford to pay
to shit in a pot have smeared it on the walls.
Here, we'll await the pardon of the Crown.
The stink of resignation follows us down.

The third night in, the gaoler lets me out
for a visitor who's paid him handsomely.
And there, in a private room with a solid door,
is Robin Poley.

      'So. You're faring well?'

'The God of Shepherds come to find his strays?'

He likes the metaphor. 'A little beer?'
He passes a jug across. He has a face,
as Watson said, uncoupled from his thoughts.
A windless lake that mirrors the serene
even when lightning cracks the sky above.
I wanted more than drink.

      'Some paper and ink?
A decent quill? A pen-knife?'

         'Not in here.'
'But you can get me out?' I say. Again,
that lake of a face shows only silver calm
over its fatal depths.

      'Come sit,' he says,

proof that the man can smile and slip the noose
over your head before you feel a thing.

'I cannot bear to be here,' I begin.
'The shit, the fleas—'
                              He stops me. 'Who are you?'
'I'm sorry?'
              'The Queen's own servant, are you not?
No livery, grant you; you're of a higher grade.
A trusted agent, and a royal tutor.'

I gaze at his throat. 'No doubt that's over now.'

'Not so, my friend. Your Poley had a word.
Her guardians were most distressed to know
about your mother's sudden death.'
                                    'Her death?'
'Indeed. You must remember that she's dead
next time you need excuses.'
                              'But she's not—'
His smile is broad. Untrustworthy as fog.
'I've no idea. Shall I send someone to check?'
I take a seat. I let him pour me beer.

'An event is like a coin,' Rob Poley says,
palming an angel deftly out of sight
and back again. 'It has two faces. You
might see them both, or choose to muse upon
the one side only. Most folk here see tails:
the arse-end of the problem . . . like the stench.
But on the reverse: our queen, all majesty,
and the cool suggestion one might use one's head.
There are advantages to prison life.'

'The exceptional banqueting?'

He meets my eye.
'The food gets better for a little cash.'
'Which I can't earn in here.'

'And yet, you can.'
The angel is gone; then reappears again
as if by its own free will. 'A shortish stay
at Her Majesty's pleasure brings its own rewards.
And you might learn something.'

'To earn that coin?'
I wish I could say I had no need of it.
I tried to affect disdain. It didn't fit,
my poet's poverty too overgrown
to wear indifference lightly.

'It is yours.'
It's flipped to the air and, like a falcon's beak,
my hand has snapped it cold. 'Look closely now.
And judge the weight of it. Test that it gives
like a woman's flesh between your teeth.'

I test.
'Seems good enough,' I say, and slip the coin
beneath my belt. I scrutinise his face
for the fading pleasure of a punctured ball
but Poley is unmoved. 'It might prove hard
to break so large a sum; you'd rather change?'

'I'll keep the gold.'

He hefts a heavy pouch
of lesser coins. 'I'll give you twice the value
in pence and ha'pennies.'

                    I weigh the offer.
'All right,' I say. 'Let's see them.'
                              He makes stacks
and I inspect them, tally them, and then
surrender my angel.
                    Poley's smile's unchanged,
and yet I sense a satisfaction there
as though he's swallowed something.
                                        'Yes indeed,'
he says. 'The highest quality I've seen.
You're smart, yet they got by you. You've been gulled.
How much more easily fooled the common man:
the grocer, the soldier and the publican.'

It dawns on me. I've swapped my gold for dirt.

'But coins this small are never counterfeit!'
'Sadly untrue,' he says. 'Still you can spend
that shit in here. The light is very low.'

I pick out a penny, turn it, looking close
as I've ever looked upon the Queen's gnarled head.

'Perhaps there's something off,' I say.
                              He nods.
'And yet you'd hardly notice, you'll agree.
It's expert stuff. And there are chests of these
buying rebellion on the continent.
You know of Sir William Stanley?'
                              I adopt
that look I practised in the glass when young:
unwashed contempt. 'The man who quelled the Irish,

but gave Deventer to the Spanish. Yes.
England's most famous turncoat. What of him?'

Poley is like a draught beneath the door
that slides around one's ankles barely felt,
then whispers up the spine.
                              'He has command
of a regiment of soldiers near Zutphen.
He keeps his troops in beef with coins like these,
having spent all legal funds. This is much more
than a treasonable insult to the Queen
and Lord Treasurer Burghley. It feeds mutiny.
It pays those who are only building strength
to slit the throats of fellow Englishmen.
We cut those strings, the threat will melt away.'

'What can I do in here?'
                          Rob Poley's face
is an unturned hour-glass. 'Why, you make friends.'

His foot, snapped like a belt against the floor,
flattens a cockroach. Now tapped from his sole.

'There is one Poole, a prisoner you might know
thrown here on a misdemeanour. He made these.'
He touches one as if it's a weevily biscuit.
'At least, we think he did. We have no proof.
We found him shaven-headed, like a priest,
loaded with coins and not far from the coast.
Sir William Stanley's sister is his wife.
That's all I'll tell you. You'll tell me the rest.'

'And when I do?'

'If you get in with Poole
there will be more employment in the world
outside these walls.' He rises from his chair
and calls for the guard. 'Poole's brother-in-law is cousin
to Ferdinando Stanley, future Earl
of Derby. He keeps a troupe, Lord Strange's Men,
who masquerade as players, though they act
abominably, in my view.'

There's the latch
undoing our meeting. 'You, I hear, write plays.'

'When I've the time.'

'I'll leave you with this thought.
A servant of Lord Strange would have the time.'

John Poole, a big man, like a side of beef
hung till the blood drains out of it, just chews.

'Limbo. The biggest joke is in the name:
we're in a place the State denies exists.'

He doesn't fence a smile. 'If you're amused
in eighteen months, explain the humour then.'

'You've been here eighteen months?'
                                    'And seven days.
I don't need friends.'

                    That told me. But a week
of watching me cross myself before I eat
and he has softened up.
                        'You keep the faith?'

'This? It's a mime to scare the flies away.'
His grimace is a gift of blackened teeth.
'That's good. I'll try that one.'
                                He eyes the bread
that I've paid extra for. Watson's asleep;
shedding the time.
                    'They say he killed a man,
your friend.' Poole nods at him. 'He don't look tough.'

'How looks deceive. Were we to go by looks
I'd say you were a shaven-headed priest
whose locks grew out.' He cackles. 'So you heard.
Arrested for a haircut.' Runs his hand

across the lank lengths of his grown-out sides,
the crop on a once-bald pate.

                                        'You're not a priest?'

He laughs. 'No Latin. I *dressed* as a priest.
For a private joke on my sister's wedding day.
A crime of clothing, though no law exists
until they make one up.' Those teeth again,
like headstones, lean and list above his gums
as though the land has slipped. He slides his back
down the wall and sits beside me. 'Sir. You seem
like a gentleman,' he says, 'whose charity
I'd not want to abuse. But I am short
of the grease that moves the gaolers. Would you have
a groat or two for a brother?'

                                Now, my purse
is fat with coppers which the very hand
that asks for them has minted. What to do?

I think of Ned; how he can wear a thought
or state of being, shrug on innocence
and make it fit. I put the broth aside,
with its balanced bread, and hand him several bits
which he slides, no questions, underneath his belt.

Fear has my stomach clenched, I don't pick up
my bowl again. 'Are you not having that?'
he asks. 'I'm full.' He grabs it like a thief
would grasp a chicken by its neck, and eats.

And after wiping his mouth, he's glad to talk.
'You know Lord Strange?' he asks, thus saving me
two days of round-the-houses. 'He's the cousin
of my brother-in-law. My father dines with him.
I have connections, see. Your kindness here
will add to your account when you get out.
You're getting out, I take it.'

                               'Yes, due course.
Both of us filed a plea of self-defence.
You?'
               'When the wind slides round. Which I think it will.'
'You do?'
                   'Connections.' Taps his nose.

                                   Some men
fear they might fade away unless they talk,
and will at the smallest chance unleash their thoughts
to anyone who'll listen. And John Poole –
whose best advice is keep things to yourself –
is one of those. I'm blessed.
                         'My brother-in-law.
Sir William Stanley. You'll have heard of him.'

'Christ!' I shush him. 'Not in here. The guards—'
'They're deaf as posts, I tell you.' My attempt
at quieting him provokes a greater urge
to spill himself. 'He keeps a company
of disgruntled soldiers, growing by the day.
He speaks of religious freedom on these shores.
A Catholic Head of State.'
                         'But this is—' Here,
I stop myself to barely mouth the words.

'*But this is treason!*'
                    'She is getting old.'
His whisper would reach back to the cheapest seats.
His cupped hand doesn't shield, but magnifies.
'I don't say kill her; though I know some do.
Simply, when death vacates the English throne
some Catholic will replace her. And the gaols
will be for Protestants.' His fingers spread
to offer our grim surroundings to the foes
that occupy his head. He fiercely smiles.
Watson drifts over. 'Kit. You coming back?'
'Up!' is the word that sends us to our cells.

It was a fearsome and unbalanced smile
that I adjusted to in several weeks
over the conversations as he poured
his life into my hands. Until one night,
returned from ablutions, with his hands still wet,
he had me by the throat, pinned to the wall,
lavender sickly over the smell of shit.

'You tricked me,' he says.
                    'I'm sorry?'
                                        'Don't pretend
you don't know anything. Your money's bent.'
Believe your innocence. (Thanks, Ned.) My eyes
must speak for my closed-down windpipe, and they do:
he drops me like a wool-sack. Rubbing my throat,
'You mean it's worthless?'
                    'Yes.'
                                        'How do you know?'
'Because it's mine. I made it.' If the guard

ten yards away has heard, he doesn't care.
'I hadn't seen it closely, in the light,'
he spits, as if I'd called him stupid. No,
neither had I. Light was in short supply.
He comes at me, 'Which suits you, weasel man!'
Getting me by the collar leaves my throat
a corridor of air to answer him.
'Where did you get it?'
                              'From my cousin, sir.'
'Where did he get it?'
                              'I don't know,' I say,
squeezed like a pimple in his pinching hands.
'He gave it to me' (coughing) 'so that I
would not die here for want of sustenance.
I didn't question where it came from. Why
would I suspect him?'
                              'Why would I trust you?'
Poole growls. 'Has your cousin ever been abroad?'
and he twists my collar. 'Often,' I reply,
though the word's half lost for choking. 'Often, sir.
He is a soldier. Half his life's abroad.
Recently Flushing. And he plays at cards,
perhaps he won it.'
                              Like a house at night
where a fiercely burning candle's pulled away
from a window, and seen flickering elsewhere,
at the back of other rooms, or up the stairs,
Poole's thinking pulls away from murdering me.
He lets me slide on to the earth, sits down.

'I couldn't know it wasn't real,' I say.
I dig some coins from the purse beneath my belt.
'It still looks real to me. Extraordinary.

Do you jest with me? You made this?'
                            'Yes.' He nods.

And on some grains of truth, I build a plinth
to set us on again. Within an hour
he's marvelling at coincidence and Fate:
and how two brothers, for we almost were,
might use some slivers of cathedral plate
that he had minted for a higher cause
to buy some privy time, and newer beef.
And I am complimenting him on work
so finely wrought that very few would know
except perhaps himself.
                            'It is an art.'
He glows.
              'Astonishing. How do you make
the points so fine?'
                      He grins.
                                'There is a method.'
He mimes an action, but does not enlarge.
'Obtaining silver is the harder part.
The higher coins are better worth my skill.'

'I have a friend,' I say, 'a noble friend
whose greatest interest is in alchemy.
He has a well-equipped laboratory.'

'A wizard?' Poole is wary.
                            'No, an earl.
Northumberland.'
                    Thus are our goods exchanged:
his counterfeiting knowledge swapped for hope
that basest metals might transmute to gold.

The information that I gleaned from him
will only lead me further up the chain.
His parting gift the day I am released:
a letter of introduction to Lord Strange.

A TWIN

'The trouble a writer has,' says Thomas Thorpe,
breaking the local flatbread, 'it seems to me,
is his writing calls to be attended to,
yet he fears too close attention.' Knocking snow
off his boot, he snares me with a look that hints
more information may be read therein,
then fondly eyes the fire. Some travellers
have gathered there to thaw themselves and drink,
soaking the welcome heat. It is the eve
of St Stephen's night, and I feel more relieved
to see Thorpe's face than I'd care to admit.

'Something of interest to you. I've a tale
of a man who was mistaken for another.
London is talking now of William Shakespeare.
A man who shares that name had come to town
attempting to broker the sale of Stratford grain.
The keeper of the inn where he is staying
puts out the rumour that the famous author
William Shakespeare is a guest of his.'

'Oh, God.'
            'Just listen. So the word goes out
and a young man comes one evening to the inn
and asks this merchant, Shakespeare, if he'll sign
a copy of the book he wrote last year.
A certain erotic poem you might recall.'
'But the man can barely write.'
                              'Don't second guess
the tale before it's told. You'll spoil my fun.'

He takes the carafe between us by its neck,
as though he holds a goose, and tops our cups
with warm spiced wine. 'So.' Takes a sip of his,
devoid of urgency. 'This Shakespeare says,
"I'm afraid you have the wrong man."'

                                          'Honestly?'
'He waves the youth away.'
                              'But—'
                                      'Let me finish.
The young man asks the tapster, is it true,
that the man in the snug seat, polishing off some tripe
is the author William Shakespeare. "That he is,"
says the tapster, "and as modest as could be.
You'll never hear him boast it, but it's true."
"But he says he isn't." "Ah," the tapster says,
folding his arms and chewing tobacco leaf,
"and there's your clue. Imagine you're mistaken
for an author of genius, would you not be tempted
to soak up the praise and let the error pass?"
The youth agreed he would. "There's half your proof.
And might the actual author, shunning the gaze
of an over-zealous public, shy away
from acknowledging his progeny?" He might,
the youth agreed. "You peg him closely now,"
the tapster says. "Look at his balding brow.
The heat of the ideas inside that skull
have burnt away his hairline." It was true,
his hair was fast receding. "See his hand,
poised on the table ready for a quill,
the thumb and finger open." The student stares,
then notices something awkward. "Where's the ink?"
"I'm sorry?" says the tapster. "Where's the ink?

The pad of his middle finger should be black
from pressing on a pen." The tapster stares
to the middle distance, like he's watching wheat
as it's harvested and stacked. "Ah, yes, the ink.
The absence of ink. You've found the final proof.
The man is such an expert at the craft,
so practised in the art of wielding pen,
he never blots a word." The youth's convinced
and the tavern picks up custom from his friends
as he spreads the word. Our gentle merchant packs,
ready to head back to the countryside
where he can do his business unperturbed.'

'And there the story ends?'
                        'Ah. Were it so.'
Thorpe motions my attention to the cup
I drained while he was talking. 'Please.' I nod.

'He took his business straight to Richard Field.
He is a private man, he says. This fame
that you have courted, settles ill with him
as a curdled syllabub.'

                    'But he was paid!'
My throat is sticky. I rinse the lump of fear
back to my stomach with a swig of beer.
'He took the money.'
                  Thorpe taps on his lip
with a slender index finger. 'If you wish
to use his name again, he wants a share.'

'In what?'

'In the players' company. Stay, stay –'
he stops me rising to my feet in rage
'– your Privy Council friends have seen to it.'

He lets the information sit with me.
The fire munches on damp conifer,
popping and whining when it hits the sap.

'Well, I don't like it.'
                        'No. But it is safer.
A false name is a wall made out of paper.
A finger can be pushed through it. But flesh
will not give way so easily.'
                              'As long
as he is paid.'
                'Indeed, but then your plays
will see to that. And as a shareholder
in the players' company, he seems more like
the thing he's meant to be. A purveyor of plays.
You might see this as help from God on high.'

'Divine assistance. Really.' And I drain
to the bottom of the cup. Waft back the smoke
that, failing to find the chimney, stings my eyes.

Thorpe rubs his hands together. 'Well, it's cold,
but never so cold as six feet underground.
Don't you agree?'
                  He likes to use my death
as a cheery tool to demonstrate my blessings.

'Can we get away with this?'
                            'Who knows? Who knows?

It's strange how the truth is seeded. Take a lie
and give it plausibility: *voilà*!
You have a truth.'
                    He mimes a magic trick.

'I prefer true truths.'
                    'Spoken as a poet.
Be glad that truth's like that. Though half the time
it works against a man, the other half
it puts the Devil off his scent.' He fills
my glass half full. 'I have another letter.
I'll slip it under your door when things are quiet.
You have a play? You have the comedy?'

'Oh, yes,' I say. 'I have the comedy.
And you have put in mind another one.
Two gentlemen, identical in name,
and how each is mistaken for the other.
I have them fucking one another's wives.
The room for comedy is infinite.'

He surveys me like a plot of land for sale.
'Be careful how you spend your humour, though.
Store in the light. You may be needing it.'

'How needing it?'
                    He stretches his legs towards
the longed-for grate before he answers me.

'Nashe is in prison.'
                    'What for?'
                              'For the book

he wrote in repentance, mourning at the death
of dear Kit Marlowe.' He gives me the look
that tells me he knows everything. 'He laid
some juicy insults on our much-loved town
and all who dwell in her. So he was gaoled.
It isn't safe to write so openly.
As he should know, having had such a friend.'

I see the puckish one light up a pipe
only a year ago, when we were free.

'Poor Nashe.'
                'Indeed, poor Nashe.' The silence falls
over our conversation like a hood
to protect the guilty. I have run away,
though all my friends might go to Hell for me.
'How is he?'
                'I hear he's railing even now
that the city's corrupt.'

                        The news was heartening.
We all might come through this. 'And how is Ned?'

Thorpe's wall goes up. 'I'm sorry. It seems we've drunk
a little too much. I blame the Christmas cheer.
It isn't good to name a person's friends.'
He fakes a yawn. 'I'm done. We'll meet again.
More soberly the next time.'
                        And he's gone.

NECESSITY

Necessity, the mother of all art
and half the population, brought me square
to a shared room on the knee of Bedlam gate.
My rent was gladly absent, but my sleep
was patterned by the cries of the insane.
If madness sucks in madness, then perhaps
that room made sense.

                I shared with Thomas Kyd,
the both of us employed to furnish plays
for the good Lord Strange's Men. A bed thrown in
and a desk at either corner. Thomas Kyd
was a white-skinned creature who avoided sun
and drooled in his sleep. He had a lodger's cough,
winced when I cursed; he'd beg me to be quiet
lest I bring the Devil on us. So I teased.
He was a toy, an instrument for me,
a winter amusement, and I played his tremor
as perfect as a lutist plucks a string;
it fed my humour through those long dark months
without Tom Watson's wit.

                We wrote in stints.
He had the daylight, squinting at his scenes;
I chose the dark, the quietude, the sense
of the world asleep wrapped round like a cocoon
where I plotted to shake them rudely, candlelight
making a pool so all I could see was play.

We sat there under blankets. Kyd was blocked.
He ground out word by word, a line an hour,
stumped by *The Spanish Tragedy*'s success,

his sighs enough to cure meat, but his words
uncooked or overdone.

              'Hamlet, revenge?
What kind of cry is that? A fishwife's cry.'
Kyd draws in his neck and covers up the script
I'm reading over his shoulder. 'It's a draft.'
'Should the man broadcast his plots for all to hear?
He's mad indeed.'
                   'It is a draft, I said.'

'Apologies.' I sit down on the bed
and tug my boots off. 'Surely what we need
when we've put good plays behind us, is hard truths.
Better you hear it now than when it dies
and they laugh the tragedian off the stage.
Can you feel how he might feel?'

                     'The tragedian?'

'Your Prince of Denmark. He that needs revenge.'
Kyd screws his forehead up, as if he'd strain
to wring the feeling out.
                 'Not in your head,'
I say, 'but in your heart. You feel it *here*?'
Thumping my chest. But Thomas Kyd looks blank,
and then, as if he's stumbled on a road
that shaves his knees of skin, his eyes grow dark
and wary. 'It's not yours. It's my idea.
You think you'd write it better. Well, you're wrong.'

I clasp my hands behind my head. 'I think
no such thing,' I say. (Though his complaint

plants the suggestion.) 'I still have the Devil.
He's meat enough to try my teeth upon.'
Still scratching at religion, light or dark,
contained or uncontrolled. Kyd shivers sharply.
'I wish to God you'd finish that.'
                                        'I will.'
I lie back leisurely, my elbows spread.
'When his time runs out. And you must finish yours.
I mean to be helpful, truly. Perhaps the Fates
put us together for that very purpose?
A second opinion can be valuable.'

Kyd bites his lip. He picks off scabs of wax
that cling to the table. Rubs an eyebrow tired.
Picks his nose. Then gathers some scenes and dumps
them on my chest. 'All right. What's wrong with it?
In *your* opinion.'

                    I read with his eyes on me.
Awareness of his breeding restless thoughts
intrudes on my concentration. At one point
he jumps from the chair, like someone badly stung
by an unseen wasp, and orders on his shelf
some books and papers. Then he's up again
to stand at the window, flinching at the sound
of each read page. The last sinks to my lap
and he turns to me, tight as drum skin. 'So, go on.'

'It could be good. It is a courageous yarn.'
I must admit, I was half writing it
in my own words even then. Pressed back the thought.
'But in order to fill the stage with guts and gore,

you've sucked the blood from every character
that ought to hold our interest. Chiefly, him.
The lost great Dane.'

                    Kyd makes a slow retreat
back to his chair. 'I don't know what you mean.
Revenge is the interest, isn't it?'
                                        'Revenge
could work like a canker on the man beneath.
Dissolve his metal, even as it shines
through his despair. I can't find his despair.'
I hand the papers back.
                              As if they weigh
much heavier than they are, his outstretched arm
weakens as it receives them. Kyd's response
is wheedling, pleading for his words to be
interpreted more kindly. We indulge
in a kind of mental arm-wrestling until
his irritation bores me. I must work.

'Hamlet is all of us, put in his place.
You need his hesitation, or the deaths
are done with by the end of the first act.
But where's his anguish? His humanity?
Is he a thoughtless murderer? Your Dane
is a writer's puppet. Wooden. Yanked on strings.'

He sinks to the floor. I've holed him, like a ship.

'Go out,' I say, 'get supper. Try to tup
some juicy barmaid. Put yourself in the way
of some other humans. Life's experience
may feed you when imagination fails.'

Much worse I was to do to him. Much worse,
by the accident of sharing a room. My taint –
the very taint he feared – smeared on his name,
and knowledge of me would be drawn out, in pain.
I never meant to be another's curse.

After he left, and took his seething with him,
I sat at the window seat and watched the shade
of a winter afternoon becoming night.
Across the street, De Vere's house, Fisher's Folly
– newly acquired by the Cornwallises –
was lighting up within. Ann Watson's hands,
over the red-brick, castellated wall,
unpegged the laundry in the kitchen yard:
mistress's nightshirts, napkins, tablecloths,
her charges' clothes.

                    Ann couldn't keep their house:
a prisoner can't earn, and former rent
prevented her husband's gaolers making more
of his punishment. Her brother, a musician,
employed to teach the eldest daughter songs,
had wrangled her some duties, and a room.

Now, as the sky shuts down, I strike a match
and light a candle, breathing out the name
of dear Tom Watson as a form of prayer.
But I'm alone. And I must write from there.

THE SCHOOL OF NIGHT

Still, the past draws me like a jug of beer
back to the moments when my star was high.
The greater the heights, the more extreme the fall.
And in those glorious nights, the splintered how
of waking up breached and broken on my now.

'You stir them up,' Sir Walter Raleigh says,
beating his pipe until the ash submits.
His West Country burr like John Allen, but soft
as the lace of a courtier's delicate handkerchief.
'It's more than entertainment on the stage.
You show us ourselves. Uncomfortable to see.'

My own discomfort is the feathered brooch
he has perched in his hair. He mustn't see
I'm fighting to keep my eyes fast on his face.

'I write what comes to me.'
                              He motions I
should sit down in a heavy, cushioned chair
less throne-like than his own. Behind his head
the river's sultry darkness softly winks
with a barge's lamp.
                     'This was the lantern tower,'
he waves at book-shelved walls, 'when this dear palace
belonged to the Bishop of Durham. Now I've made
a study of it.' Enjoying his own pun.
Self-educated, he displays his books
as peacocks do their fans. 'Knowledge entails

the shedding of new light on old conundrums.'
Perhaps he believes his riches make him wise,
or that his knighthood, and the Queen's good favour
entitle a sailor to school a Cambridge scholar.
'This room's a metaphor.'
                              A laboured one,
I think, but say, 'A perfect place to write.'
'Yes, isn't it?' He pours us both a drink
– 'The sailor's delicacy. You don't mind?' –
and offers me tobacco. 'Do you smoke?'
'I haven't tried it.' 'Well, you should, my boy.
The native Indian tribesmen of Virginia
will claim it brings you closer to your soul.
Relaxes one. Here. Borrow my spare pipe.'
It's carved with naked women. Raleigh laughs
as I study it. 'I'm told they run around
like the nymphs and dryads of antiquity.'

'The New World is an old one, then?'
                                        'Perhaps.
I have a mathematician in my pay
who calculated they have been around
for sixteen thousand years. Ten thousand more
than the Church gives all Creation. Some would call
him heretic. But how d'you account for that?'

He lights my pipe, and his. I watch him close,
and suck, as he does. Bitter on my tongue
and puffing my words to clouds. 'I'd trust a scholar
before I'd trust a bishop with the truth,'
I say.
         'Too harsh!' He laughs. 'What can you mean?'

'We're prone to take the Bible literally,
forgetting it was written for the flocks
of a simpler age.'
                        'You're not an atheist?'
he asks, half casually.

                        'The word of God
must be interpreted,' I say, 'by man.
And man is full of ignorance and sin.
The Bible tells us so.'
                        Raleigh guffaws
and throws his head back, so his pointed beard
pokes like a mason's trowel into the air.
'You priceless man. It's true, then, what I've heard?'
'What have you heard?'
                        '*I count religion but
a childish toy*. That line is yours?'
                                        'It is
a character's.'
                        'You hold it true yourself?'

To buy a pause, I suck and blow out smoke.
'You should inhale,' he says, concerned. 'Like this.
To feel it in your lungs. Not much at first.
You'll find it powerful.'

                        So I inhale . . .
and cannot speak for coughing. Raleigh smiles,
and passes a lacy napkin.
                        'Apologies.
Perhaps a little less than that. More drink?'

To mend my throat, I gulp rather than sip,
then wipe my mouth and say, 'My view is this.
Religion is irrelevant. What counts
is faith in God, and love of humankind.
A Catholic's as human as a Jew,
a Muslim, Moor or Puritan; though he,
the Puritan, will aim to enjoy it less.
But only the pure intentions of the heart
connect us to our source. Not ritual,
not superstitious oath, not form of prayer,
nor literal translation.'
                              Raleigh nods
his sage approval. 'Truly. To preconceive
is to imprison thought, which should be free.
We will discover nothing if we bind
ourselves to accepted wisdoms. Questioning
is necessary for discovery.
The best minds in the country think like yours.'

I find I'm liking him a little more.
Though he is fishing, I'm a fisher too.
I suck at my pipe more cautiously; this time
a sudden airiness, a head as light
as a gust of autumn wind.

                              'Oh, yes,' he says.
'I wanted to show you this. This lyric's yours?'
He brings out from a drawer the song I wrote
for lute, 'Come Live With Me and Be My Love',
expertly copied in a stranger's hand.
'It is.'
          'Delightful! I have made reply

from the love-shy maiden. Would you like to see?'
Without a pause for my assent, he thrusts
the answer in my hands. 'See how the form
has followed you precisely.' He is pleased,
and breathes like a panther, softly, in a tree,
digesting. In my flesh, tobacco buzzes
like a woman stroking all of me. His praise
could almost bed me if he shaved the beard.
I read, but cannot take it in.
                                        'So to
the reason why I sent for you,' he says.
'We have a meeting, once a month, held here.
We would be very grateful if you'd speak
on a subject of your choosing.'
                                        'Who'll attend?'
'Lord Strange. Northumberland. George Carey too.'
These names as powerful as laudanum
dropped in my glass. He has my 'Yes' right here.
'George Chapman, Matthew Roydon, fellow poets.
Thomas Harriot. Others I shall not name.
But men of some education, with a bent
towards the improvement of humanity.
Many of these you know.'
                                        'Matt Roydon, yes.
And the Earl of Northumberland made me his guest
this summer last. I used his library.'

'And of course Lord Strange has furnished you a room
to write for his players.'
                                        'You are well informed.'

Sir Walter rises. 'London's alive with gossip.
If people are bones then gossip is the flesh.

The power goes to he who controls the flow.'
He turns the globe that sits upon his desk
until I'm faced with the Americas:
his prize, his conquest, feeder of his pipe.

'As a lung for gossip, this house does not exhale.
Thus we speak freely here,' he lifts his eyes
to catch mine on a hook of seriousness,
'but nothing of these meetings must be breathed.
Not who attends, or what is said. Agreed?
Swear on your word.'
                              'Upon my life I swear!'
I speak with a rush of passion. Raleigh smiles.
'The word of a gentleman is good enough.'

And in that word, the wide world opened up.
As Sir Walter Raleigh completed the winding in,
I felt so close to Court that I could taste
the powdery kiss of my good Sovereign's hand.

'The Queen delights' (he sucks) 'in clever men';
he blows a loop that wobbles in the air.
'Our full potential as creative beings
requires that we adventure to our souls.
Though we explore the globe, map out the stars,
the greatest mystery remains in here—'
He thumps his chest. 'Which is where poetry goes.
Tobacco too. Why don't you stay tonight?
The servants can lay a chamber. Stay, let's talk
over some venison. I'll tell the Queen
I've fed the master of Mephistopheles.'

THE BANISHMENT OF KENT

Gallows festoon the road with rotting men,
left as a warning to the vagabond;
their eyes pecked out, the flesh dried into strips,
their bodies gently twisting in the wind.

I am struck dumb. Expelled into the air
like the nation's cough, because there is no cure
for the liberty of thought it won't endure,
for certain uncertainties it cannot bear.

The truth is silent and the lie believed;
all through man's history, this gaping gulf.
The lamb is slaughtered to preserve the wolf.
The son of God is drying on a tree.

TOBACCO AND BOOZE

It's small beers and a trencher at the Lamb.
Three fools: Tom Watson, Thomas Nashe, and me,
Watson a little thin since his release.
'Two Toms and a Kit,' Greene called us once, half cut.
A very feline crew. But quite without
a cat-like wariness, gold blinking eyes
that take the world in, opting not to speak.

A celebratory day, a guzzling day.
A day to be remembered at one's death,
exceptional. For it was on that day,
full of lamb cobbler and my latest play,
friend of Sir Walter, satisfied to be
the tutor of the maybe future queen,
that I tipped my chair back, lighting up my pipe
to savour its sweetness balancing sour hops,
and seeing a man's face crumple, loud declared,
'All those who love not tobacco and booze are fools.'

'Tobacco and boys?' Nashe laughed. He was half deaf,
the close ear dull. 'Dear post, tobacco and booze!
But boys go just as well with sweet Virginia
pressed into a pipe.'
                    Misheard, offstage,
the quote that would define me for an age.

COPY OF MY LETTER TO POLEY

To Pan, the God of Shepherds, Fontainebleau.

Mercury sends his greetings. Please excuse,
if this should meet unfriendly eyes, the stop
of rhyme to force them skywards. I have news
of a Spanish metaphor. This, I will swap

for whatever letters you can bring this ghost
that might not find him safely otherwise.
Risk no one, yet deliver the enclosed
to the man whose servant stabbed a poet's eye,

that perjured eye whose sharp continued sight
sees nothing, lately, but the worst of men
and longs to feel the beam of friendship's light
break from the clouds and fall on him again.

A man condemned to silence may still hear.
Speak to me softly. Lest the ghouls appear.

How Do I Start This?
Let Me Try Again

The night is very silent. Though the days
are marked by the dull percussion of the miles
away from you, the night brings me up close
to its empty collar and breathes your absence there.
A blow in the chest. A heaviness of air
that I must carry with me, to my bed,
rather than mistress, lover, drunken friend.
Forgive me. At times, I almost sense your face
in front of mine, and bring it to my lips,
only to see myself the foolish man
in the window's mirror. Love. You know my heart:
so quietly murdered, yet it beats as loud
as a funeral drum that sounds the death of kings
when I feign sleep and, when I dare your name,
leaps lively as a trout caught on its fate –
so quiet for some, but far beyond dead things.

Where are you now? And do you sit, like me,
endlessly conjuring your lost friend's face?
Or do you sup and laugh with newer friends,
more cautious friends, who would not court disgrace?

I spill out words, more words. Where do they go?
I see them landed in a distant pond
and sunk to the bottom, covered up with silt,
then seen no more.
                    It seems I have no breath
if I'm kept from all reaction: if a puff
on my palm does not bounce back to stroke my face

then I am truly dead. And so I wait
to hear that I am missed.

                         This damnable silence
that I agreed to, bargaining for my life.
To do what? I forget. Then I remember.
To write. To write. To write. To write. To write.

BURYING THE MOOR

An April night. A distant bell tolled ten.
The cobbles glittered recent rain; the elms
fringing the church shook drips from newborn leaves.
Chilled moonlight traced a figure at the gate
that turned out to be you.
                              'Tom. Kit. You came.'

Watson's whisper was louder than my boots.
'How could we not? A secret funeral?'
He was a little drunker than we'd planned.

'Go in,' you said. 'The coffin's on its way.'

Throughout, Tom Watson ran a commentary
into my ear like a gnat's unsettling whirr.
'He seems upset with us.'
                           'With us?'
                                      'With me.'
Sir Francis Walsingham, or what remained,
came past in a simple coffin made of pine.
'The man was like a father to him, Tom.
And his brother's only six months in the ground.
Has drink made you stupid?'
                               'Maybe. Maybe so.'

The bishop cleared his throat.
                               'So few are here!'
Tom whispered. 'All that effort for the Queen
only to die a pauper's death. How rich.
Or not.'

The candles flung their shadows high
into the vaulted roof.
                                'Lucky there's room
in the tomb of his son-in-law,' Tom hissed, 'or he'd
be dumped in a common hole with the rest of us.'

Widowed, now fatherless, his daughter Frances
stood in the pew beside you, holding tears
and her three-year-old until the youngster squirmed;
a servant arrived to take the babe away.
Watson remarked, 'As well she looks good in black.'

The bishop called you up. You read some words,
the emotion in your throat like broken glass
for the man who filled your father's shoes.

                                        'Is that
the Earl of Essex?' The once deft whisperer,
his volume faulty, caused two mourners' heads
to turn and glare at us. 'By God, it is!
A sterling comfort for an orphaned girl.'

She wept a river on that noble chest.
A stand-in for her father, so I thought;
but nine months later, she would bear his child.
A night so marked with endings and beginnings.

'So who will pay intelligencers now,
seeing the debt it drove Sir Francis to?'
Tom Watson muttered.
                                When I heard your news,
my thoughts too had been half upon your pain

and half on my pocket. But I was all with you
as you closed your reading, crumpled like a rag
that has polished until it should be thrown away.
I wanted to hold you.

                     Watson said, 'I must
be sick,' and stumbled outside as we rose
to sing one economic psalm.

                              Which left
just me alone to greet you afterwards,
as we stepped from candlelight into the dark.
We clasped like brothers, though your cheek on mine
felt like the moment Phaeton took the reins
of his father's horses.

                     'Can you stay awhile?'
You shook your head. 'Too many creditors.'
'I miss your company.'

                              'And I miss yours.'
A silence between us like a pact of kings
exchanging truces.

                     'You could come to Kent.'
The orchards of my boyhood; sallow fields
and not a theatre. Only mumming plays.
'I cannot leave London. All my work is here.
At least till Arbella returns to Derbyshire.'

And silence again, a wall we couldn't breach
which needed no words, but some intense collapse
into the truth of what we had become.
Too hard to be the first.

                     And then came Tom,
grinning skeletal, so recovered from
his beer-fuelled sickness that he startled me.

'That's better,' he said. 'Sometimes one needs a purge.
A vomit and leak. And as I tucked me in,
who should pass by but our Lord Treasurer,
leaving the church, but not without a plan.
He stopped, and most conveniently conversed
about our working for him. Come this way.'
He tugged at my sleeve. 'Shall we meet you anon?'
Addressing you. 'The Golden Bear's still lively.'

'I'm staying tonight with Frances.' And your eyes
engaged with mine. 'So we should say goodbye.'
Embracing Tom an unknown final time,
a punch on his arm to seal it off.
                                        Then me.
'Goodbye, good friend,' you said. The weight on 'friend'.
'Goodbye.' Another clasp. Another taste
of fiery horses hammering through my veins.

'Be well!' Tom said to you, and tugged me out
into the churchyard, cluttered with its stones,
towards the road where two grey horses stamped
and steamed. And waiting by his carriage steps,
'Lord Burghley,' Tom whispered, nodding at the man
in robes and chains. 'He wants to speak to you.'

'Morley? Or Marlowe?'
                                        'Either will do, my lord.'
He rearranged his gown, fussing his thumbs
around the chain of office. 'Very good.
I hear you write poems in English. Latin's fine'
(addressing Watson), 'but the young prefer
poetry in their native tongue. I have
in my charge the young Southampton. Quite a fine –

no, quite is ungenerous, inaccurate –
an exceptionally fine young man, with all the arts
a responsible guardian should train him to:
a taste for poetry, debate, good wine,
but not, alas, for women. That is to say . . .'

I noticed how bright the stars, how velvet black
the sky this conversation fell beneath.

'. . . not so much that he looks the other way
but dreams of sport and of a soldier's life
and says a wife would hamper him, where I
would have him settled down. He is sixteen,
and listens far more to poetry than me.
I wondered whether, for a generous sum,
you might persuade him of . . . the benefits . . .
that is to say, desirability,
of marriage.'

        Watson's smirk, behind his hand,
he had to cough out, and excused himself,
leaving us momentarily.
           'My lord,
if you're imagining I could write a poem
which would turn his thoughts to women, I'm afraid
my friends have made too much of me. Though women
boast charm, some men are naturally averse.
I could no more turn a fox into a frog
than persuade your ward to marriage.'

              'No, no, no,'
the Treasurer demurred. 'He's not *averse*.'

Watson dipped in, then out. His suppressed mirth
was proving hard to wrestle with. 'My lord—'

'He's simply not inclined. Indifferent.'
Lord Burghley was very used to being right.
A splat of late-stopped rain, held on a leaf,
was shaken upon him, yet he wiped it off
without distraction. 'Certainly not *averse*.
No verse would touch *averse*. And yet a verse –'
(nodding the pun to congratulate himself)
'– or several – might turn *him* in his course,
if executed with sufficient . . . grace.'
Watson rejoined us, his rebellious mouth
repaired on his sleeve.
                        Lord Burghley skimmed him over
but remained intent. 'For a substantial purse?'
'Very well,' I said. 'But I must meet him first.'

SOUTHAMPTON

The first of his words to me were angry ones.
'Why should I marry who that man decrees?'
He was a boy, four months from seventeen.
The sky was in his eyes, intensely blue.

His second sentence was in praise of love.
'Love is what brings us close to the divine.
To wed for less is shabby compromise.'
The simplest shiver rippled through the trees.

He softened to me then. 'I liked your play.'
He patted me beside him on the wall.
'So tell me, you're a poet, am I wrong?
Should I forget my heart?' There was a song
sung from an open window, light as lace
upon the moment. 'Never that,' I said.

'My mother loved,' he said, 'another man.
It killed my father. Truly. Broke his heart.
Women are fickle. Love makes lovers damned,
a marriage bed a deathbed.' Yet his face
had all his mother's tenderness; his rage
was all his father's. He, the argument
for marriage, procreation, and disgrace.

'What is a woman for? The servants cook
and clean, friends entertain, and whores are cheap.
Why do I need a wife? For what plain good?'
The lavender was thick with scent, and bees
hung round the beds like baleful courtiers.

Above, his eyes, a sky's idea of blue.
The thought occurred: 'To make another you.'

In his perfection, here was Love's excuse
for all her misdemeanours, every heart
that split to feel her bastard offspring's dart.
And here was Love herself, conducting songs
from neighbours' windows, rustling up the trees
to shed the spring's confetti for his hair
and bring this moment, begging, to its knees.

Love is oblivious. All the love was mine.
And all the wisdom of a dozen plays
of wit and genius will not assist
the motley fool whom sudden love enslaves.
Except this was not love, but pure desire
for perfect beauty, for a taste of it.

For he was both man and maiden, boy and girl,
the consummate alchemy of human form.
Unworldly, godly, in his countenance,
a blazing sun round whom a room must turn,

yet utterly insensible to his power.
Three years have gone, and still that blessed sight
– the jewel of Southampton, sitting on that wall –
accompanies me to my oblivion.

ARBELLA

Arbella was wild as a clipped goose smelling fox.
She lurched from wall to wall. 'Why not go out?
There's education in the wind and rain.
We could get wet and you could teach me why
it bounces off the sparrows.'
                                    'Read this book,'
I offered, patiently, the only poultice
that's ever worked for me.
                                    'Pah! Read a book!
Another dusty book? Another wedge
of dead man's brain? No, thank you. What is it?'
'It's poetry.'
                    A snort. 'What good is that?
What good are words? Words are not real life.'

'But they create in here,' I tapped my head,
'whatever's locked out there.'
                                    Another snort.
She stamped her boot, and spun towards the view.
'But not the Earl of Essex,' she replied.
'You can't create him, can you?'
                                    She was hooked
two years before, at court, when she was twelve.
Imagined they might marry, though I knew
by then your cousin Frances had his child
tucked in her belly.
                    'You might be the Queen
one day,' I said. 'How to prepare for that
except to read and imagine how it feels?'

Knowing she'd marry whom the Queen decreed.
Be pawned to the Duke of Parma's son, Farnese,
to end the war. Be dangled like a threat
to keep her cousin James obedient.
And me, determined to get close to both.
How powerful I felt myself to be.

'Very well,' she said. 'Prepare me.' Still outside.

I turned the pages silently and found
the lines where the sultan's riches glow like fire,
the pulsing light of each delicious gem
its own confection, savoured on my tongue.
And drawn across, as though the jewels were real,
Arbella knelt in front of me, her hands
open as though she thought this spell of words
would conjure and drop into her lap those stones.

I closed it, and we listened to the weather
beating itself against the window pane.
'Now love,' she said. 'Now tell me how love feels.'

ALPINE LETTER

Love? If you'd asked me yesterday, I'd say
love is a saw that amputates the heart.
I'd call it my disease, I'd call it plague.
But yesterday, I hadn't heard from you.

So call it the weight of light that holds one soul
connected to another. Or a tear
that falls in all gratitude, becoming sea.
Call it the only word that comforts me.

The sight of your writing has me on the floor,
the curve of each letter looped about my heart.
And in this ink, the tenor of your voice.
And in this ink, the movement of your hand.

The Alps, now, cut their teeth upon the sky,
and pressing on to set these granite jaws
between us, not a mile will do me harm.
Your letter, in my coat, will keep me warm.

WATSON'S VERSE-COMMENT ON MY FLUSHING ASSIGNMENT

(translated from the Latin)

'A horse has summer flies; a sheepdog fleas.
A swift will harbour lice, a brook its rocks.
Bright days breed duller endings, and a girl
of perfect beauty's not immune from pox.
An apple has its worm, a rose its thorn,
the noblest seat of earls, its ghost in chains.
Good books will suffer misprints, will they not?
The gods have sin. And you have Richard Baines.'

POISONING THE WELL

One of Tom's favourite tales was Richard Baines.
The priest of spies; the spy who was ordained
while under cover with the Jesuits,
his ear out for their plotting as his mouth
swallowed the wafered lie: 'The body of Christ.'

How you and he, that Paris summer (there
to receive each message at the embassy:
who went to England, under which false names)
watched as he crumbled like a papal biscuit.
The Old Religion drove the man insane.

His identity submerged beneath a fib
that even he believed: so who was he?
A hundred per cent pretend; and Richard Baines,
who sucked in incense and incensed himself.
Who counted tedium on his rosary.

And once he was ordained, bad faith took hold:
rotted his humour, and disturbed his sleep –
the laughable sinful mismatch of his roles
as Father Baines and agent of their foes,
betrayer of the faithful, took him deep.

The stink of fish on Fridays up his nose,
he salivated at the thought of meat.

He took to sneaking pork pies to his cell:
'God cannot be concerned with what I eat!'
Began to gibe at prayers and snort his truth
beneath his breath, not knowing that he spoke.

Love was his downfall, though. There was a youth
– for who can bear so much deceit alone? –
he shared a bed with. Stroked his novice head,
while plotting ways that he could take him home.

The boy was a thorough Catholic: convinced
that the seminary served a holy cause.
Baines moulded him like warm wax, dropping hints
that darker secrets lay behind locked doors.
'And will you plot against your natural queen?'
The boy's uncertainty filled up the pause.

This, how Tom told it, dramatising scenes
over the tavern table, playing Baines
as he existed afterwards, post Rheims:
shocked into greyness, with a limping sway
not yet inflicted on the loving priest
who stroked the boy's anxieties away.

The lie would send him witless: he must leave.
But not without the boy. And not without
shutting the college down; no, no reprieve
for the priests whose mumblings broke his sanity.

Think: Tom's cruel mimicry of Richard Baines
watching the morning gruel, the evening soup,
with sudden insight – every bowl the same!
How easy to wipe them out, this nest of rats,
with poison in the food. He would be loved,
he told himself, by government and queen.
And now to persuade his lover.

                        Could he blame
the boy for running to the powers that be?
Baines had been breaking slowly ever since
he donned that itchy robe, humility,
and now had shed the cloak of decent man,
exposing the loveless murderer beneath.

Enter the later version, Richard Baines,
crippled by vengeance that he cannot take
and joints that creak and groan each time it rains,
betrayed by the youth who still comes to his dreams.

How easy it is to get a laugh from freaks.
'Incense and blather!' Tom's adopted twitch
that Baines himself developed after weeks
of the strappado – hung like butcher's meat
with weights on his feet, and dislocated arms,
in a new mode of confessional for priests –

forgetting it was a man they'd broken there.
Forgetting that we weren't immune from sin.
Forgetting how whispers travel on the air
and get back to the subject.

                        If I wrote
a play whose central character was him,
I never dreamt his hands around my throat
or thought that he might recognise himself.

He didn't matter. He was just a tale,
material I foisted on the shelf
of a London stage or two. He was the Jew,
the counterfeit believer, counting gold

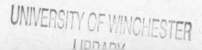

above all human life, tainting the stew,
out-plotted to a most theatrical end,
and played for laughs. And that it tickled you
was all I used to think about, dear friend.

Danger Is in Words

Thom Nashe's lip relaxes to curb his teeth.
'You're not concerned he's seen it?'
                                        It is cold.
We're standing in the doorway of a shop
festooned with carcasses; and half a pig,
eviscerated, sawn from snout to tail,
spins gently round to eye me.
                              'Richard Baines
at a public entertainment? Heaven forfend.
Watson says Baines was made more serious
than sentence of execution. Anyway,
I go as Morley. Marlowe wrote the play.'

FLUSHING

When the winds decreed, I sailed to Vlissingen:
Flushing to English ears; and English ears
were everywhere: in street, in crooked inn,
on frozen river, at the chestnut stall,
stamping in garrisons and coaxing whores
from frosty doorways. I reported there,
leaving my passport with the governor,
then through snow, up a creaky flight of stairs
to the cold room I would share with Richard Baines.

He wasn't there. I poked amongst his things.
Some jottings in a crabby, slanted hand
and half in cipher. Flints and candle stubs.
Some undergarments draped over a chair
like unwrapped bandages. A locked-up trunk.
A Douai Bible with a broken spine
and scribbled in. And when the stairs complained,
I closed and set it down.

                              Baines, coming in,
froze in the door. Eyes flicked around his things,
then back to my face, and narrowed.
                                        'Who are you?'
'Morley,' I said.
                    And something on his face
like pan-burnt porridge, betrayed an aftertaste,
as if he knew that name. But only now
do I understand that look.

                              'Why are you here?'
he asked, not watching me, but limping in

to gather his papers up like promise notes
snatched from a fire.
      'I believe we have a friend
in common. Richard Cholmeley?'
         'Drury's "mate"?'
He spat the word like bones. 'What kind of friend
will put a friend in prison? You should leave.'
My information fatally out of date,
or set up to label me. Quick thinking due.
'I'm glad to hear you've stronger loyalties,'
I doubled back. 'These are unsettled times.'

He knelt now to undo the trunk, his hair
all in a circle, monkish round his pate
and prematurely grey from torture's jolt.
He fed the papers in, replaced the lock
and turned the corded key around his neck.

'Why are you here?' he said again, like ice
at the heart of sleet.

      'In truth, I have a message
of some delicacy. And understood you might
know a way to send it onwards.'

        'Oh? To whom?'
'To Sir William Stanley.'
       'Ha!' Baines gave contempt
both vent and volume. 'You are very young
if you imagine I would commit myself
to knowing the Queen of England's enemy.'

On this point, some years later, I'd agree.

'I'm nearly twenty-eight.'
                              'You are a babe.'
He grimaced, approaching close until his breath
assaulted me. 'Do you know who I am?'

'You're Richard Baines.'
                          'I'm Richard Baines,' he echoed,
glaring the broken vessels of his eyes,
'who spent three years at Rheims to serve the Queen
and took a punishment you'd not survive.'
His lip curled back, trembling as if his teeth,
filed by their rottenness to tiny points,
had terrified it into revealing them.
'I don't take kindly to the implication
I'm the Duke of Parma's whore,' he said, and spit
fell softly, unintentionally, like rain
upon my cheek.
                'Sir, I apologise,'
I said sincerely. 'I meant no such thing.
Only, I understood you knew of ways
to pass a message. If I was mistaken,
forgive me.'
              'I don't forgive,' he breathed. 'That job
I leave to God.'
                  But stepped away at last,
if only to appraise the whole of me:
if I were a joint, how long I'd take to cook.

'If that is so, then I'll be on my way' –
re-shouldering my knapsack with relief
at the prospect of escaping his foul air,

fair swap for failure. 'Please, forget I called.
So many rumours fly about my charge
I would not wish to stir them.'

                    'What? Your charge?'
He pecked the words, half starving. 'Who is that?'
I confess, I used Arbella like a worm
to jerk before that grasping mind. 'Her name
has caused great trouble to the bearers of it.
If you don't know, I'm glad not to expose her.
I come on another matter.'
                    Though her marriage
to the Duke of Parma's son was brokered there
in Flushing – in that month.
                    And when he knew,
boiled down the stock of his deductive broth
to the royal bones, he said, 'Forgive my haste.
It was un-Christian of me to suspect
your motives. These are awkward times. And yet' –
drawing his hesitation on the air
like an unsheathed sword across my exit door –
'I might know ways to help you. You have money?'

FISHERS

Which of us had the net, I couldn't tell.
Both of us fishers, sounding out the depths
of the other's beliefs. I'd not declared a side
and nor had he. He offered to make enquiries
on condition – to keep the closest eye on me –
that I shared his room and rent.
                            No, not his bed,
though I felt those pink grey eyes upon my back,
like cold on my buttocks and my shoulder-blades
undressing at night, conscious he never snuffed
the candle till I was covered.
                            No, not his bed,
dear absent friend, whose ear these words address
in the silent theatre of my empty head
some two years since they brought the curtain down,
and the cheering crowds dispersed to pick their teeth
and the plague played kill-kick-jenny on the streets.

A sea away, two countries' width away,
a war away, a mountain range away,
each sentence that I form, I form for you.
You are the love I tell my story to –
who knew so much of it, and yet the truth
eluded both of us. Yet, I've begun
to understand.

                    All histories are fictions,
so if I skip the worst, forgive my fault.
Though you would not condemn me: like the sun,
my imagined perfect audience of one,
your light seeps through this darkened, shuttered room

somewhere in northern Italy. But grieve,
and remain with me, as I return to Baines,
confess my part as I reap the bleak remains
of the game I played with him.

                        No, not in bed.
For even then my body's touch was yours.

A RESURRECTION

The game was simple. It was not to lose.
The game was complicated. It was this:

If he was Catholic, I was Catholic too.
If loyal Protestant, I mirrored him.

Neither of us committed to a thing.
I let slip nothing that was not my view.

And yet I bathed in contradiction, sharp
to each shade of his behaviour. Faith, we were
chameleons trying to conceal ourselves
in the ever-changing colours of the other,
so standing out against the barren hues
of that bitter coastal town. And like a scene
unravelling before me on a stage,
my mind's eye conjures up the day it changed.

Baines is as bony as a beaten hound.
And me? Cocksure, bright-eyed, ridiculous.
Our pie has just arrived.
                         And spying us,
across the tavern, munching gristled beef,
is a dead man.
                 Gilbert Gifford.
                             '4,' I breathe,
and his jaw falls open as he reads my lips,
then fiercely resumes its chewing, eyesight dropped
to read the grain of the table.
                             'For? For what?'
Baines is intrigued to read the shock on me.

Six years before. My first assignment. 4
was the spy we most admired. As slick as wax,
and warming the kirtle of the Queen of Scots
as he passed her coded letters. Ordained at Rheims
the year I left Cambridge. Later caught in bed
with a whore. Jailed by his Catholic friends. And dead.

'For pity's sake,' I say, 'that meat is tough.
Look at him chewing. Do you know that man?'
(*My God*! What was he doing in a port
so full of spies, when Poley had fixed his death
in a Paris prison not three months before?)
But Baines is in the dark. 'I've seen his face
these last few days but don't possess his name.
I'll ask.'
     'No—'
           As he leaps up, deathly keen
to inflict a meeting, I forget myself.
'He may be offended,' I explain, 'by me.
That I was staring.'
           'Tush. Don't be a mouse.'
Baines stride-hops over like a half-chewed goose
and stops at the other's table. Though I strain
to catch their conversation, it is lost
in the songs of a dozen soldiers at the bar
comparing wives to liquor. Gifford laughs;
they both glance over.
           Then the dead man nods,
abandons his bowl of stew, picks up his beer,
and follows Baines towards me.
           Baines is pleased.
What odds, two former bogus Catholic priests –

one rumoured to be dead, one broken-kneed –
have come this way to sift me?

                         'Since his beef
was inhumanely tough, I said he might
share some of our rabbit pie.' Baines stands aside
for the weathered man who once looked like a child
to introduce himself. 4 has a skill
more powerful than Ned's. The lie is steel.

'It's Gilbert. Gifford Gilbert.' He gives his hand
as though I'd never taken from its clutch
the notes to Walsingham that laid the trail
one Queen of Scotland followed to the block.
An oddly bloodless hand, and glacial look.
'Gilbert,' I echo, as if the name reversed
has turned him inside out. 'I'm Morley, sir.
Called Christopher.' So begins another game.

'What brings you to Flushing?'
                         Not a hint of sly,
deception's signature not in his voice,
no hint of recognition in his eye.
'I come as a messenger.'
                    'Ah, Mercury.
My favourite of all the Roman gods.'
Had I imagined that some Paris brick
had knocked all memory clean from his skull,
his use of my codename clarified the rules.
'Are you staying long?'
                 'Not long.'
                         Just long enough
to ascertain Dick's contact. And to play

another round of Who's In Catholic Pay?
'And on what business do *you* pass this way?'
I ask the handsome corpse.
                                  'Oh, for my trade.'
'What is your trade?'
                          'A goldsmith,' Gifford lies,
audaciously demanding my belief.
'I give shape to the precious. What of you?'

'For my sins, I'm a scholar,' I reply.
'I give shape to the precious also, but the gold
flees to the hands of others.'
                                  'And your trade?'
he asks of Baines.
                          'I trade in human souls,'
Baines mutters without blinking. 'I'm employed
to find good men wherever they may be.'

'Is that a trade?'
                          'Recruitment? Possibly
it's more of a vocation.'
                                  Baines has sliced
a section of pie and hands it to our guest
on my empty trencher.
                                  'Who do you work for?'
Gifford's pretence at innocence demands
he asks such forward questions. Baines, exposed
by a twitch on his cheek, replies, 'Whoever pays.'

We laugh at the sour joke, and make a toast
to the paymasters, whoever they may be,
that feed this poet, crippled spy, and ghost.

A COUNTERFEIT PROFESSION

So we became a threesome, thick with spells
we might cast on each other. Gifford made
some sad excuse of homelessness: some bill
for a phantom signet ring due any day –
was grateful to lodge his body in that room
where we might frisk each other's souls, unheard.

A week went by, during which time we stuck
so closely to each other's sides, we stank;
needing the privy all at once, like girls,
so as not to miss a whisper. What we lacked
we held in common: the coppers to pay our chits
and the knowledge that might furnish us with gold.

Grief! The pretence we made, of being friends,
began to wear in like a favourite cloak,
and I relaxed into that dangerous state
as though too deaf to understand the joke
that every one of us was counterfeit,
and more in need of truth than we'd admit.

THE FATAL LABYRINTH
OF MISBELIEF

Money was almost all we spoke about.
Baines wanted more.

                 Unsummoned comes his voice,
edged like an axe. 'A crown is just enough
to pass your message. A reply costs two.'
And again the past comes vividly alive:
that room, my younger self, and Richard Baines
limping this way and that to warm his bones.

I weigh him up. 'I'll pay you when it comes.
I'm clipped at the minute.'
                 'I will need it first.'
He shakes his head at the floorboards. Cold, so cold,
and I back against the warmth of a chimney breast
fed by the heat from someone's fire below.
Baines fidgets at the window. 'Here he comes.
Back from the docks, I see. Not looking well.
He's ill-clad for a goldsmith, don't you think?'

'His cuffs are a little worn.'
                 'Yes. And his shoes,
two seasons old at least.'
                 'Your point is what?'
'Our friend may not be all he seems to be.
Or more. You know this town is full of spies.'
His eyes on me.
                 'If you suspect him so,
then why invite him to come in with us?'
I ask. He limps to the bed to relieve his bones

from the stress of standing. 'What you do not know,
young scholar, could be stretched between the stars
and hang the world's washing. There's great benefit
in keeping close those folk you do not trust.
Though half a wheel keeps stiller than a whole,
only the wheel that turns is immune to rust.
Gilbert!' he greets him. 'What a nice surprise.'
(Leaving me to decode his homilies.)
'I thought you would be gone two hours at least.
You have your money?'
                              'No.' The boyish face
that, legend has it, charmed a dozen nuns
into breaking their vows to Christ, is sour with age.
He throws his jacket off. 'The boat has sailed.'

Had coinage passed between us quite as freely
as talk of it, we would all three be rich.

Over some broth: 'Stanley's in want of funds.'
Baines offers common knowledge like a gift
I should be grateful for. 'That is well known,'
I answer.
              Did the slight lead me astray?
Why would I add, 'And more in want of funds
since the man who pressed his coins was put away.'

'What man?'
                'John Poole,' I say. 'I met him once.
In Newgate.' This news ignites our Richard Baines
as a spark strikes out of flint. Here is the key,
I think to myself, engaging with the lock
of Baines and turning him. 'And did he speak?'

The veins of his eyes are like faint trails of blood
across some week-old snow. I make him wait.
Gifford is leaning inwards, though he feigns
to pick dirt from his nails.
                                    'So? Did he speak?'
'Yes, a most prodigious speaker.'
                                    'That is he,'
Baines nods and sits back, coldly satisfied.
'If words were food, he'd vomit himself skeletal.
You spent long with him, did you? Dear John Poole.
How was he?'
                    A sudden rush of chilly air.
'Alive,' I say. 'Grateful to be alive.
Look smart. The drink is coming.'

                                    We put coins
in the wench's hand; Baines takes no pleasure in it;
remarks, 'How quickly money runs away.'

'Yet how many ways to make it,' Gifford muses,
sipping a drowsy beer. 'If we but knew.'
'You are a goldsmith,' Baines says, 'surely you
could press a coin or two.' Gifford's awake
immediately to the danger. 'Do you ask
could I commit a treason? No, I couldn't.'

But Baines's smile is serpentine. 'Not tried?
Even for fun? To see if you've the skill
to make a coin that's passable.'
                                    'I've not,'
Gifford says firmly, his conviction melded
with the fact he's never handled molten metal.

An opportunity to whip away
my former contact's cover; bond with Baines
in his unmasking. And in doing so,
remove his complication. Sorry, 4.

'Why, Gilbert,' I say, 'what treason could there be
in testing a goldsmith's talents?'

                         Baines concurs.
'Should anyone find out – and how would they?
we'd vouch for you. That it was just a game,
and not in earnest. Why, we'd not strike coins
in any quantity. And not in gold.'

'But pressing coins? That is a specialist skill.
My talents lie in crafting jewellery.'
Yet mutinous pearls of sweat had broken out
across his temples. Me: 'It isn't hard
from what I understand. John Poole described
the process in some detail.'

                         Richard Baines
picks up the thread. 'I'd truly like to see
how easy – or hard – it is to press a coin
that is persuasive. If Marlowe would tell us more.'

'Morley,' I say.
                'Of course. What did I say?'
'Another name.'

              Gifford objecting then,
'I have no metals. Until my bill is paid.'

'We *do* have metals. Why, this pewter spoon
would make five shillings.'

'Poor ones.'
                              'All the same.'

How did I miss that Baines knew both my names?

We needed wax, and clay, and crucible.
Inn candles were purloined for wax; the clay
brought from the shoreline by an eager Baines.

'I don't believe I have a crucible,'
said Gifford, and moments afterwards,
                                    'What's this?'
Baines lifted the unused prop from Gifford's things.
'Is this not a crucible?'
                    Defeated, 'Yes.'

The fire in the room was lit and fed.
Enthusiastic, Baines laid out the tools
while Gifford stood and contemplated flames.

'Now, what shall we copy? Who has got a coin?'

We'd nothing between us higher than a shilling,
and Dutch at that.

                    'You don't have something English?'
Baines asked. His eyes most pointedly on me.

I part supposed – misreading his intent –
he meant whatever coinage we produced
might go to Stanley's English regiment.

And sewn inside the lining of my coat:
a dozen English coins. But something said,
Just shake your head. They're for emergencies.

'No matter,' said Baines, 'press on.'

                         The mould was made.
My mouth gave out instructions, word for word
almost as Poole had given them, my mind
well used to memorising sentences.
Gifford was rattling in his skin. His hand
shook like a beggar's cup. More ale, more ale
to still it. I drank too. Baines stayed as dry
as a heath in summer, cracking tiny smiles
whenever I looked to him.

                    'Please, can you help?'
Gifford addressed me. Steadier of hand,
I poured the liquid metal into moulds.
We waited and drank some more.

                    And, 'There. It's done!'
One coin is uttered; an imperfect fake,
and yet the birth of it, miraculous.

'Bravo!' I say. Gifford hides his surprise
in a slow, professional nod. He's passed the test.

'The method seems sound,' says Baines. 'Though I've seen Poole's
and they were sharper.'
                    'With a little practice,'
says Gifford, 'I would do better.'

             'Would you, now?'
Baines rubs his chin. He contemplates the shilling
by the hungry fire.
             'Except I would not coin,'
Gifford says, hastily. 'Not as a rule.'
'Because?' says Baines.
             'It is a capital crime!'
He starts to pack away the crucible,
the evidence.
          'Well, let us celebrate
your show of skill in any case.' Baines pulls
from his trunk a bottle of liquor.
             'From the monks
at a certain bolthole in the heart of France.'

Two logs on the fire. By the time they have collapsed
into their embers, breathing dragon bones,
Gifford is snoring heavily in a chair.
The liquor's warming. Baines is tight and quiet,
turning the shilling over in his palm.

'More of this would be useful.'
             I agree.

'And do you figure this act is treasonous?'

I couch my answer in philosophy.
'All men are equal under God,' I say.
'Beneath God's gaze, I've as much right to coin
as the Queen of England.'
             Something slips apart
in the fire; provokes a brief, unruly flame.

'Sir William Stanley, whom you wish to meet,
would like to have this knowledge you possess.
Poole's knowledge. And he'd pay the goldsmith, too,
past his objections. I could take you there.'

I said I would be happy to be taken.
His hand slid to my knee.
                              I took a breath
and told him it was time I went to bed.

The liquor knocked me out, but how long for
I couldn't tell. What woke me was the cold
of Baines's bony body in my bed,
rubbing against me. I pretended sleep
and lay as unresponsive as the Fates
as he wheezed and grunted. Praying silent prayers
that all my duties for the Queen would not
include forced penetration. By the dawn
he'd satisfied himself, or given up.
And more than once I've wondered, had I let
the bugger in, if I would be here now.

Baines, in the morning, like a change of sheets,
betrayed no inkling of the night before.
As if his memory were wiped by drink,
he gave out nothing, even in his eyes.

'Stanley is outside Flushing. You will need
your passports.'
                      'Mine is on me,' Gifford said.
'You're sure he will pay me just to see this coin?'

Baines was packing clothes for travelling.
'For your trouble, yes. And confirming how it's done.'
'My passport's with Governor Sidney,' I replied.
Baines tied his bag up smartly. 'Yes, of course.
You came in by the port. To the governor's, then.
We'll call in on the way.'

                          And so we slipped
through snowy streets to Robert Sidney's house.
I put Baines's speedy limping down to cold,
to the icy leaks of less-than-perfect boots,
so blind was I to the fate he planned for me.

BETRAYED

'You must arrest this man!' Baines flings at me
a shaky arm. 'Go on! Arrest this man!'
'No! On what charge?' I startle as the guards
take both my arms behind my back. 'What charge?'
'This man's a traitor. Counterfeiting coin
of the realm. Sufficient crime, I think you'll find,
to hang you,' he says, switching his words to me.

Gifford begins to leave. 'And this man too!'
Baines says decisively, through crumbling teeth.
'He is a goldsmith, and he struck this coin.'
As guards take Gifford's arms, Baines struts across
and slaps upon the desk our one Dutch shilling.
I glance at Gifford, but his eyes are fixed.
The embassy clerk in charge considers it.

'A sorry thing,' he says, soothing his beard.
'It wouldn't pass. It's pewter.'
                                    'It's a test.
With practised skill they meant to strike in silver,'
Baines is insistent. 'And the Queen's own coin.
They're traitors, both.'
                                    'This man is lying,' I say.
'We struck this coin, agreed, but for a wager.
To see the goldsmith's cunning. Let me see
Sir Robert Sidney on my own. I can
explain.'

            But we would not be seen alone.
Sir Robert was very busy. A two-hour wait,

messengers running in and out like bees
depositing nectar; visitors summoned forth
and clacking their leaving heels across the tiles:
all more important than three feuding frauds.
Even though two of us might meet our death,
the crime was 'petty' treason. Common. Small.

Gifford was steeped in silence, staring down
at a spot that looked like blood just by his feet.
I rehearsed what I would tell him, any words
that would keep me from the gibbet. Richard Baines
was impatient, jiggling his legs like rattling sticks,
and yet each time he caught my eye he grinned,
like a cook who holds a lobster by its claw.
Finally we were summoned.

                                    'Very well.'
Sir Robert surveyed us with the saddest eyes
I've ever seen in government. He seemed
as under water as a drowning man
whose white face sinks away from you.
                                         'I have . . .'
the effort was painful '. . . understood the claim
and counter-claim. Now speak one at a time.
First, Master Baines.'

                        Baines rises to his feet.
'I'd prefer you sitting,' Sidney says.
                                    Baines sits
reluctantly. His voice scratches the air
like a thing that claws the door to be let in.
'These two men struck that coin upon your desk.'

The sorry thing that looks more like a stain.
'This man' – his bony finger points at me –
'is an enemy of Her Majesty, who means
to go to Rome.'
                    'I do not!'
                                'Sir, sit down,'
warns Sidney, for indeed I'm on my feet.
'*You* mean to go to Rome!' I finger Baines.
'Sir, *he* is the Romish agent.'
                                'Sir! Sit down!'
The governor's anger silences the room.
I melt to sitting.
                    Sidney takes a breath
of perfect patience. 'Master Gilbert next.'

Gifford says only, 'They both pressed me to it.
They wanted to know my skill.' Eyes earthwards still.

Behind the governor's head, the worthy spines
of perhaps three hundred books are calling me
to confess myself a poet. 'Like your brother,'
I imagine myself saying, 'in whose tomb
I saw Sir Francis buried.' But my tongue
is stuck in my cover.

                    'A scholar by profession?'
He reads the notes taken on my arrest.
'Marley,' he says. (I gave the family name;
poised as it is between the poet's and spy's.)
'You pressed the goldsmith to demonstrate his skill?'

'We both did. For a wager.'

                    Sidney clacks
the roof of his mouth. 'A very risky bet
to take with a man who's clearly not your friend.'

'I did not think—' I stop and realise
the truth of that. Sidney seems sadder still.
'You're aware that coining is a capital crime?'
I nod.
            'Why should this agent want you dead?'
Baines's objection he stops with stony eyes.

I splutter, 'Sir, my purpose . . .'
                            Falter there.
For the noose is sooner put around the neck
of government traitors. 'Sir, I cannot speak
openly of my purpose. But wish to say
I'm very well known to the Earl of Northumberland.
And also my lord Strange.'
                            I watch his face
register the significance of these names:
two earls of Catholic family whose claims
to the English throne are watched by those like me.

'Excuse me, sir,' Baines says, 'but who he knows
is not of relevance. The man should hang
for counterfeiting coinage of the realm.'

Sidney considers once again the coin,
a thing inconsequential in itself,
handed across a bar, or flicked into
a beggar's hat. But here, potential doom,
the tiny price a man's life hangs upon.
He raises his eyes, surveys all three of us.

'Of this realm,' Sidney says, 'but not his own.
The case is not so clear.'
                              'Sir, it is clear!'
Baines senses he has tugged a little hard,
and the hook not quite inside the lip; and here's
a chance I might swim free. 'Excuse me, sir,
but to counterfeit's a crime in any land.
Simply imprison him, let a judge decide.'

Sir Robert Sidney rises like a spark
sent up the chimney. 'I will not be told
my course of action by – what are you, sir? –
a snivelling groveller whose loyalties
are not detectable.' Those words are like
the lifting of a boot that pressed my chest.
I thank him with my eyes, and anger him,
it seems, a little more. 'It is not clear,
and I will not unravel it from here.
Lord Burghley will decide what shall be done.'

He ties the papers. 'Masters Marley and Gifford,
you remain under arrest. As prisoners
you'll sail tonight for England. Master Baines,
you will go with them.'
                         'Am I prisoner?'
Baines asks, most aggravated. 'Sir, I have
important business here.'
                         Sir Robert asks,
'And what is more important than the law?
Than justice being done?' Baines cannot say.
He's fleshed in secrets. 'You will go with them.'

The river's frozen, sullen as it's wide.
The town sits on the river like a toad
swallowing flies. We are its meal today,
and half digested, we're pushed out to home.

Returned to the
Lord Treasurer

Before we reached London, Baines had slipped away.
Along the Strand, the air was a mist of rain,
which flecked and relieved our faces with its cold.

Burghley was livid.

    'Now, what have I left?
Two unmasked agents and a scheme undone
which took four years to put in place.'
        'My lord—'
'Don't *my lord* me.' He vibrates like a bee
that can't decide to sting us. 'You are dead,'
he says to Gifford. 'I cannot have you hanged
without unravelling a dozen lies
that serve to protect Her Majesty. Though God
knows I am in the mood to have you hanged
for your destructive interference.'
      'Sir—'
His attempt to speak is severed by a hand.
'Expressly, Gifford, you had been retired
and put out to pasture. It was not your place
to be in Flushing, let alone intrude
on matters of delicacy.'
      'I saw a chance
to be of some service.'
     'Only to yourself!'

Burghley dismisses him to wait outside.

'And you.' He turns to me. 'Can you explain
what violent arrogance possessed your brain
to demonstrate how counterfeiting's done?'

'I thought – I felt – if he was Catholic,
and keeping Stanley's gate, then it would prove
that I was close to Poole, might be of use.'

'You set the hook by which he wound you in.'
He turns to the desk and thumps it. Rubs his fist
and returns to stalking, up and down like thread
from my mother's darning needle. 'Can't be fixed,'
he says, as though he too perceives the hole
I just imagined. 'You are too well known.
But not as an agent. No.' He meets himself
on coming back. It seems they have agreed.

'You were on Her Majesty's business. An arrest
on petty treason necessitates your death –'
He pauses for breath. Perhaps to make me sweat.
' – which plain incompetence does not deserve.
Yet your release . . .' Again he ventures short
and this time, won't complete. 'You're on your own.
I recommend a daily dose of prayer
that no news of your liberated state
gets out to Baines.'

                              'Then I am free to go?'
'For now, you're free. Return to tutoring.'

Crossing the marble entrance hall, I hear
a gentle voice behind me: 'Marlowe, sir.'

The Earl of Southampton, hair down to his waist,
and dressed as if Tuesday morning might be host
to some fine occasion.
                    'I enjoyed your poems.
Remiss of me to let so many months
pass without saying so. Forgive me, please.'

I nod. 'I understand they didn't work.'
'Not as my lord intended,' he replies,
with a momentary flash of summer's warmth.
'But something of love is kindled by your lines.'

A servant appears, as if a fairy's curse
has summoned him from smoke to break the spell.
'My lord Southampton, you're required within.'

Gifford was just outside. We left as one,
all hope of further service work undone.

Light-fingered rain had thickened in the hour
and now fell hard enough to clear the streets.
Though the door closed at our backs, we hovered there
to shelter in the doorway. 'Disappear,'
said Gifford. 'Baines won't keep this to himself.'

COLLABORATION

The consolation prize I called my friends
was out of sorts when I returned that night
to the lanes of Shoreditch, freshened by the rain,
rinsed of the stench of urine. I could kiss
their crooked timber houses and the dogs
half bald with mange, prepared to brave the wet
to nose the butcher's leavings. Much the same
as when I left to tangle with Richard Baines,
excepting those friends of mine. Some argument
had splintered them into separate inns.

                                   First Ned,
nursing a pint of stout between his paws
in the Cock and Bull. 'The man's impossible,'
he booms like an ancient king. 'What? Robert Greene.
I only added six lines to his scene
and he took offence. Called me a pea-brained clod,
a country parsnip, if you please. My God.'
'And you stayed calm?'
                        'I may have said some things.'

Nashe in the Horse and Groom, his mischief sealed
behind a troubled stare. 'It's not my fault!'
he says straight off. 'Though Ned is blaming me
for laughing, the pompous oaf. Greene lost his temper.
Now Ned won't even pay him what he's owed.'
'And what of the play?'
                        'The play? The play's a mess.'

My play. That Ned persuaded me to leave
half finished when I went abroad. Had said,

'Good hands will finish it! You'll have your share.
The lion's share, indeed. Go on, be gone!'
My play was at the core of what went wrong.

Greene had moved in with a strumpet named Em Ball,
who cradled his head between a squelch of breasts,
eyeing me sharply. 'Don't be upsetting him.
He isn't well.' Greene peered up through the pain
of a whole day's wine. 'You can sod your blasted play
unless you've come with money from the Crow.'
'Ned isn't happy.'
        'Good.'
                'About the play –
you have some scenes?'
                'I fed them to the fire,'
he growled. 'Delightful words, but we had need
of kindling.'
        'Greene, for God's sake!'
                'What of God?
What's God to do with this, you atheist?
I know what you've been up to, gone abroad
to pretend at being Catholic, setting traps
for Jesuits. How taxing it must be
to believe in nothing.'
                'Robert, that's not true –
and protecting Her Majesty is honest work.'

'If lying through your teeth is honest work
no wonder I'm facing death through poverty.
You're no more honest than your friend the Crow,
for both of you live by acting. And beneath
are puffed-up nothings, like the fungus balls
we find in the woods, and stamp to clouds of spores.'

'Greene—'
          'You address me decently. Try "sir".'

'What have I done?'
                    'Whose brothers have you sunk
with your information? Who now rots in gaol
as the result of your "intelligence"? While I,
with twice the education and the skill,
am hired as a scribbler to complete your play?
And then insulted. And, what's worse, not paid.
What have you *not* done? You have left a trail
of devastation in your wake, while you
reap every glory. God will bring you down.
I have that faith.'
                    'In God?'
                              'He spoke to me.'
He fills himself with air like a balloon.
Em grabs his arm as if to steady him.
'From the bottom of a cup?'
                            'Oh, you may mock.
There is no God for you, of course, but Fame.
Get out. And do not speak to me again.'

His mind diseased, I left him with his whore
and went in search of my own sanity:
an evening with Tom Watson, to offload
the horror that was Flushing, knowing he
would find the joke in it. And we'd share Baines,
and the resurrection of dead spies, with glee.
He'd shore me up.

                    But no lights in his rooms.
And no Tom in the local hostelry.
And no wife to explain where he might be.

The night was turning filthy, with the rain
harried in all directions by a gale.
In case his tutor's duty kept him late
I knocked at Fisher's Folly, spoke his name,
and the door was shut on me.

      So I trudged back
to Nashe. 'Have you seen Watson anywhere?'
'Oh, Kit. My word, I'm sorry. I was so –
preoccupied. I forgot you didn't know –
it happened weeks ago.'

      'What happened?'

          'Kit,
he's in the Fleet.'

     It's true that I had then
a vision of his body, bloated dark
with the sewer water, floating to the Thames.
Rather that than think our friend in chains.

'Explain,' I said, winded enough to sit
and help myself to cider.

       'He – oh, Kit,
it isn't good.'

    'Explain.'

       'The girl, the girl—'
And so he blurted it. Tom's brother-in-law
falling for Cornwallis's young daughter,
and how Tom – as a jest – suggested that
he lend ten angels to the miser's girl,
and have his brother Hugh draw up a deed
to say she'll repay it on her wedding day,
but worded in such tortured legal speak
that he, the brother-in-law, must be the groom.

——— 172 ———

'And all is blamed on Tom? He's in the Fleet?'

'He's in the Fleet, accused of every crime
the family could muster. Chiefly this,
for instigating blackmail.'

                              'Have you tried
to bail him out?'

                  'They wouldn't set a price.
His employer's livid. And in any case
I'm hardly equipped to lend a surety.'

The wind was at my back and in my face,
the links boys scattered by the howling rain,
and only a lighted window here or there
allowed me to thread that mile across the city.
In time, the sullen shadow of the Fleet
reared up its walls and smell.
                              Though it was late,
I offered what I had in silver coin
to a hook-nosed gaoler.
                        'Watson. Tom. It's me.'
I shook him, and his soul fell into place
behind his eyes: still him, but somehow changed.
'I'm done for, Kit.'
                    'Don't say that.'
                                      'Smell the place.'
The torchlight lit him wildly, but the draught
that ripped through the building couldn't budge the stench.
'That's death,' he said. 'Three corpses leave a day.'
'Not yours,' I said. 'You're coming out alive.'
He smiled as if I was insane. 'Let's pray.'

And closed his eyes. I waited for the joke
to end. Instead, his eyes steadfastly closed,
his lips were murmuring. And then, 'Amen.'
'Are you all right?' I asked.
                              He looked at me
as though I spoke in Flemish, and the pause
was for his own translation. 'Am I? No,'
his words as brittle as an ancient book.
'Tom, you'll escape the charges.'
                              'You don't know,'
he said. 'Cornwallis doesn't go to church.
You understand? He has me for a spy.'
'I'll get you out.'
                    'With what? A locksmith's pick?'
'I'll think of something.'
                         'Yes. The genius,'
he said, unusually sour. 'Well, think it quick.'

'Where's Ann?' I asked. He threw his head back hard
against the stone. 'With relatives. My wife
must resort to charity. It was a joke!'
'What was?'
           'What do you think? The bastard note.
I never thought they'd write the idiot thing.'
He smacked his head against the wall again.

Two hours I stayed, entrenched in his despair,
and each week after, dragged myself to him,
with pies, and paper that he had no heart
to fill with words. The spark in him was out,
and his estate too damp and treacherous
for it to be relit. What was my friend
departed months before the final pinch.

And though I strove to paint his freedom there,
a future for him, he only saw his end
creeping towards him, inch by stinking inch.

My own fate crept towards me too. How frail
is the bubble reputation. On a pin.

What starts with only rumour, just the fluff
of some poor servant's ignorance and fear
becomes corporeal, trails a snaky tail,
until the tale's found devilish enough,
and scurries to the dark, as lode to pole.

An anonymous agent writes of how we meet
to spread the unholy creed, and from my lines,
twists joke to accusation: how we teach
scholars 'to spell God backward'. We who thrilled
at Raleigh's phrase 'adventure to our souls'
begin to understand we may be damned.

'Faustus!' A stranger hails me in the street.
'Send my regards to Hell!'
                              I grab his throat
and thrust him against the baker's door.
                                        'Who said
that I am Faustus?' The sweetest smell of loaves
warms in the air between us.
                              'Why, it's known,'
he stammers. 'Is generally known.'
                                    I see his hand
making a surreptitious cross, and growl
into his face, 'What's known? What's this that's *known*?'
'That the author of *Faustus* is an atheist.
That you are he.'
                  'Who said this?'
                                    'Robert Greene.'

HOLYWELL STREET

'Greene! Open up!' I hammer on the door
of his digs in Holywell Street. A passer-by
skirts me like I'm a pothole. 'Mistress Ball!
I need to speak to Robert.'
                              It is May.
Enfeebled sunshine warming up the roofs
and the foul load of the gutters. 'Open up!'

Movement. An upstairs window creaks its joints
and the woman's face appears. ''E isn't well,'
she says in a voice as sharp as splintered wood,
'and not receiving visitors.' She's gone.

I could have left. Perhaps, had I turned my heel
and left them well alone, his spiteful pen
would not have felt it had to set in ink
the vitriol he'd drafted with his tongue
and freely spewed in taverns and hostelries.
But I was righteous. Full of consequence.

I hammer again. 'Greene! Open up this door!'
It flies from my fist. 'Whaddya want 'im for?'
Miss Ball was Greene's protector, those last days,
her shrew-like features screwed up like a page
whose scenes he had rejected. 'He is ill,
I said, and if you do not know the word,
then please acquaint yourself and catch the plague.'
Her diction was deliberately strained.

'He has the plague?'
                      'Whaddya take me for?
Would I be 'ere without an 'andkerchief?

No. No, you fool. Although a plague of "friends"'
– her tone has marked the word for quarantine –
'seems to descend here daily. What's yer beef?'

'I want to speak to Greene,' I say, and take
advantage of the open door to bolt
like lightning up the stairs. She follows. 'Hey!
Don't push me! Don't go up there! Bloody men.'

Greene is indeed in bed, but fully dressed,
as though he's just retreated there.
                                    'Ah, Marlowe.
I thought I recognised your dulcet tones
drifting up from the street. And such a rhythm
you played on my door, as if it were a drum
and I should break out singing. But, alas,
I am unwell. They say the very air
can spread contagion. You may note the smell.'
There was, indeed, a stench.
                                    'One cannot catch
the slow death wrought by liquor, Greene,' I say,
stalking across the room to pull the sheets
away from his booted body. Emma swears,
arriving in the doorway out of breath,
and hands him the olive cloak draped on a chair.
'And you have been well enough to venture out
and smear my name amongst the taverners.'

'So? I must eat. My Em's a dreadful cook.'
She scowls at him; he smiles and grasps her hand
to pull himself up to sitting. Clears his throat.
'A dying man should have his fill of fare
while time allows. If I should stagger out
for breakfast, an evening meal—'

                'You miss my point,'
I say. 'Eat what you will. And where you will.
But keep your mouthparts busy mangling food
and not unravelling slanders. Several men
in this last week alone, have savaged me
for views I do not hold, and claimed that you –'
(I jab my finger in his chest. He coughs.)
'– were their source of information.'
                       'Oh? What views?'
All innocence he is, all empty-eyed,
though his lips are curled like paper by a fire.
'A man's religious opinions –' I begin
'– that is, beliefs – should not be simplified.
Not in these times.'
                'What times? I'm out of touch,'
he sneers. 'Dear Em, will you fetch me a mug of wine?'

'The Queen herself once promised, we are told,
not to make windows into her subjects' souls.
But if others, spreading lies—'
                    'What have I said?
No more than you've said yourself a dozen times.
"Christ was a bastard and his mother dishonest."
The atheist highlights, if you please.'
                     'For God's –
for pity's sake, you cannot spread this stuff!'

Nashe said I should have run him through, right there;
but to witness one man die was enough for me.
And I am not a natural fighting man.
I prefer the bright and bloodless cut of words.

'What fiendish foul excuse for a human being
would put my life and liberty at risk

for his private entertainment? The powers that be
have cooked up fear until it bubbles thick
in the brains of the ignorant, and you would stir
it further, give them names? And give them mine,
as if this mind is fodder for the ropes
at a public hanging? Damn you, Greene, you may
have bitterness against me, but this life
of graft by pen and ink, and several friends,
we have in common. Say what you like of me,
but do not say I am an atheist.'

Emma returns with wine. He curls a hand
around the mug, and pats her on the bum.

'Say it? I'll write it. Publish it indeed,
under my name. *Greene's Devils*. That would sell.
Greene's Former Friends, the atheist and the clown,
who feed their best lines to an upstart crow.'

'But you will ruin me. For mercy's sake,
if you call me an atheist in print—'

'You'll soon be back in gaol, where you belong.'
He takes a gulp of wine. 'And I'll be dead.
Chettle will publish it when I am gone.'
A smile spreads on his face as though a stain
has crept across a tablecloth. He coughs
and pats his mistress's hand. The spill of glee
has spread to her lips, which curl up like a cat.

'Well, damn you both!' I pace across the room
and, in a surge of fury, draw my sword.
'What maggot in a cloak, what pickled turd,

would find this shit amusing? And what sow,'
I skewer her with a glance; she looks away
'would suckle this poison? In the name of God –
for now you swear allegiance, like a cur
licking the foot that kicks him – damn you, Greene!'

He eyes me like a sore. 'How very choice.
In the name of God you damn me. Does that work,
I wonder, when your blood's so thick with sin?
I will not fight. So murder a dying man,
be witnessed by my Em. I am unarmed.'
He coughs again. She pats him, eyes all spite
in my direction.
                    'Sin? You hypocrite.'
I sheathe the sword with difficulty. 'Sin?
You're the high priest of sin. You've said as much
yourself. Full house. Let's lay them out to see:
pride, envy, greed and lust.'
                              This last word licked
against Miss Ball, who steels each dwarfish inch
of herself towards me. 'Get out of my house!
I'll call the constables. *Flo! Get the law!*'
she shouts at her neighbour's wall. '*A man in 'ere
is causin' trouble!* 'Andsome. Now ye're cooked,'
she says, self-satisfied. 'Go on, clear orf,
before ye're clapped in irons.'
                                'Don't do it, Greene.'

'I'll do whatever I please.' The mug set down.
'Perhaps if you had come on bended knee,'
he smoothes his beard into a sharper point,
'and not on a horse that you can ill afford,
full of yourself and your self-righteous wrongs,

full of your friendships with the sirs and earls,
trussed up in velvet like a bloody lord.
You're all pretence. An upstart cobbler's son
who dresses up as pounds what is worth pence.'

'You filthy weasel!' I am at his throat
with my eating knife before his breath is out,
and Mistress Ball at the window, *'Murder! Help!'*

'You piece of shit.'
                                    He's not the least alarmed,
knowing I've not the heart for it. 'How quaint.'
His Adam's apple bobs against the blade.
'You've reverted to your class. I've heard distress
will do that to a man.'
                                    'This way! This way!'
the shrew shrieks at the window. ''Ere they come.'
She grins at me. 'Ye're really for it now.'

It could have been worse. I was bound to keep the peace
and warned to stay away from Holywell Street.
But had I hoped to stem the bleed like this,
I was mistaken. 'Marlowe the atheist' –
the rumours thickened, reproduced and spread
from house to inn, from corner shop to bed,
from maid to fishwife, serving man to priest.

A Groatsworth of Wit

Death came that summer, dressed up in a heat
as unforgiving as the smelter's fire,
stalking the alleyways and London streets
as hot and unrelenting as desire
will track a woman down and smear her sheets.

So many deaths, they couldn't count them all:
the cry, *Bring out your dead*, soon emptied complete
houses. It heaped whole families with its call
and tipped them into everlasting sleep.
Summer burnt on relentless. At St Paul's

the thinning buyers milled more thickly where
the stationer stacked Greene upon his stalls.
A freshly dead contagion in the air
as accusation gossiped round the walls
the plague of rumour. I would not be spared.

And the fear that gripped me as it spread its wrong
ensured I would be perfectly ensnared
by throwing me into a dark despond.
For the flavour and appearance of despair
looks much like guilty truth when stamped upon.

Such heat. September came without relief,
the summer furiously clinging on,
killing exhausted mule, pernicious weed
and sucking the river dry. Thom Nashe was gone
to spy on the Church; our friend was in the Fleet

sucking the humid air, while like a fly
my brain buzzed madly round the corpse of Greene
pressing to find a window to the sky
but only knocking into stink. A priest
confused me with Doctor Faustus as if I

had damned the world to gulp his curses down.
So merged the playwright and the Queen's own spy,
by the power of language flushed from underground;
my fictional creations now not mine,
but *me*. And in their mythic flesh I drowned.

DISMISSED

Fear sends the mad man running off a cliff.
I asked Arbella Stuart for forty pounds;
an annual sum, to save me from the list
of poverty-murdered poets. I could hear
Fate drumming at the window. But the doubt
surrounding my religion reached the ears
of the countess. Like a flea, I was dismissed.

The Cobbler's Son

The backward movement of returning home
thickened my blood as I approached the walls
of Canterbury. Passing through its gates
like a child squeezing back into the womb
of a mother he has out-suckled.

                          There, the fence
I used to daub with chalk when I was small,
was clipped around the ear for. There, the school
whose books propelled me into fantasies.

Autumn was shedding summer in the churchyards
and the leaves blew giddy down familiar streets
as though afraid of something.

                          At his awl
just as I'd left him some three years ago,
my father bends and straightens like a willow,
predictably nattering a customer
into a better pair of shoes. At first
his eye mistakes me for a gentleman
he needs to cozen, misled by my clothes.

'Young sir, how are you booted?' Then, 'Good grief!
It's Christopher!' Out back, '*It's Christopher!*'
My mother comes with sodden hands, 'My son!'
and wets my shoulders with them. 'Why, you've come
so unexpectedly! What brings you here?'
Between the two of them, a glance, a nod:
I wondered then how fast, from man to man,
the word might travel.

With her in the yard:
'You have leave from your tutoring?' she asks,
wringing a tunic dry. As if she knows.
'I'm finished with that,' I answer, tapping grit
out of my shoe. 'I am on government work.
I need to rest here for a week or so—'
The truth stuck in my throat.
                              'You'd let me know
if you were in trouble?'
                              'Ma, you know you'd know.'
She eyes me like a button that won't fit
through the hole she's made.
                              'I know you less these days.'

I was foolish to go drinking; but what else
is a man to do to stop becoming boy
when he's moved back with his parents? Darkly lost
in wondering how to rescue me, 'My God!'
feels like an assault; a cheery parrot's cry
from a man I fail to recognise. 'Topher!'
He spits through his teeth the name they used at school.
'Come on, it's me, Corkine! The tailor's son.
Indeed, a tailor now. With a son of my own.
How's cobbling?'

              I confess, it grated me,
his sense that we were equals. I had lost
a job instructing England's maybe queen,
been slandered by a drunken, envious pimp,
but still was raised to gentleman by degree.

'Excuse me, sir, I do not cobble now.'

His cheeriness was irrefutable.

'They call you the cobbler still. You cobble up
some trifles for the public stage, I hear.'

'I am a scholar. And a gentleman.'

'You jest!' He laughs, and jabs a bony digit
into my ribs. 'Our Toph's a gentleman.
If you're an esquire, where's your rapier?'

It was in London, stored amongst my things,
and just as well, the mood that I was in.

'Are you suggesting, sir, that I am lying?'

His eye tics nervously, as if the smile
is breaking off in pieces. 'Not me, Toph.
Just asking where your sword was, that was all.'

He sits beside me, pulling up a stool.
'So do you have a family? A wife?'

For twenty minutes, I put up with it,
answering trivial questions through my teeth
in one or two words only, but Corkine –
either convinced his cheer will gladden me,
or unaware of how I seethe and boil –
remains there like a birthmark.

                                    'Well, Corkine,
it's been a pleasure,' (said so sourly

my mother could pickle herrings in the tone)
'but it's time for me to go.'
                              He stands up too.
'I'll walk down with you to your father's house.
My own is just beyond.'
                              'I'd rather walk
alone,' I say. Yet ten steps down the road
I find him at my side. 'It isn't safe,'
he says, 'to walk alone at night. Not here.'

The wind spoke malcontentedly through signs,
creaking the baker's loaf, the glover's glove.
It wasn't safe for him to walk with me
against my wishes. Though I bit my tongue,
and though I'm not a natural fighting man,
my ruined life was overcoming me.
I was so close to punching him, I swear
my fist was itching.

                              'Look, I need to think.
I have some troubles and must be alone.
Please let me be.' So firmly to his face
he couldn't mistake my meaning. Still, he said,
'I hope we might be friends. Now that you're back.'

You understand that I must say all this
in mitigation for what happened next.
The facts alone – if you had seen the facts,
laid out, as they were, in court – tell only that
I assaulted the man. But I did so much more.

'I am not back. And we will not be friends.
I don't make friends with tailors, any more
than I would marry the shit upon my shoe.'

I watched his face turn crimson in the light
of the tavern window.

                        'Furthermore—' But I
had said enough. And felt it, even through
that bellyful of ale. I turned to go

and Corkine shouted out, 'You stupid sprat!
You upstart sprat of a man! You know you're nothing!
You're nothing at all.'

                        And did I batter him?
You bet I did. Did I hold my dagger close
against his throat as I had done to Greene?
Did I growl in his face, and cut his buttons off,
saying they'd be his fingers if he crossed
my path again? With certainty, I did.

My father bailed me from the local cells
and talked me home. The shame in my mother's eyes—

I knew then that I couldn't stay there long.
To go back to the ground-nest of your birth
when you have fledged, have learnt to use your wings,
flown across oceans, sung with friends at dawn,
is to shrink and rot as surely as a worm
will hole an apple. London, though, was death
tricked out in temptress clothes.

And then you spoke.
Your voice came clearly: '*You could come to Kent.*'
Yes, there was more to Kent than Canterbury.
I rode, next afternoon, to Scadbury.

RE:SPITE

The birds sang my arrival through the woods,
along the path, and through the entrance gates.
Had I believed that all would turn to good
the moment you embraced me, I would wait
only two weeks to learn that pain was still
coming for me, and as relentlessly
as a bloodhound closing in upon its kill.
Tom Watson turned to death to set him free.

A Fellow of Infinite Jest

Had I forgotten Tom? No. Nor can I
erase from my mind the pained, unruly grin
that took possession of his face the night
I told him I was leaving town.
                              'You too?
Of course. Yes, bugger off. I'll keep the rats,
my loyal companions. I shall press my face
against the bars and gurn at passers-by
for entertainment. Though if this keeps on
there'll be no passers-by. All London town
will be a prison, which we prisoners
will govern by witchcraft while we slowly rot.'
'Tom—'
        'Don't apologise. You have your troubles.
I don't wish to be one of them.' Like lard
slides off a cooked goose breast, he changes tack.
'This heat is insufferable. When will it end?'

I left him there, it's true. No coin of mine,
no words that I might write, would set him free.
And yet, if I could go back to that night,
I'd boot the guards and wrestle for the key,
rather than standing in that dripping yard,
wondering which unholy mound was he.

SCADBURY

We wintered quietly. We fed the fires.
You let me write for hours, and touched my sleeve
when meat was served. December's ice furred thick
across the moat; fish torpid in the depths
of the fishponds' cloudy cataracts. I wrote
as deep as I could inside the ancient tales,
as if afraid, should I come up for air,
I'd find a bank of prosecutors there.

When geese cranked spring's return across the sky,
you rode to town and back, to bend your ear
to the Privy Council's whisperings, while I
sank deeper still, but all my blood aware
that half those men still pressed to have it spilt
as a fine example of the rebel's heart:
He who abandons God cannot be saved.
Those men could not imagine how I prayed.

A Slave Whose Gall Coins Slanders Like a Mint

You'd spent two days in London. You had news.
Your wolfhound greeted you with a slow wag;
you stroked him distractedly, and gave your cloak
to Frizer.
             'Bring some wine,' you said. His brow
showed silent concern. How strange to write him now
bearing only the weight of your cloak along the hall,
knowing how he would bear a greater burden,
and all for love and loyalty to you.

Anxious, I followed you into the room
where so many conversations, games of cards
and quoted poetry had sealed us tight
in friendship: every night held in those walls
as though the wood, still tree, were living witness,
rather than seasoned panelling.
                                 'Frizer.'

                                      'Sir?'
'Dismiss the servants. We're not to be disturbed.
And you may go to bed.'
                        It wasn't late,
and he raised a single eyebrow, but complied.
The crackling fire, which he'd lately fed,
filled up the silence as we listened then
to the quieting of the house.

                        'There is a note,'
you said, with blunt despair. You turned your glass

around in your fingers, staring at the wine
as though you wished to drown there. 'Kit, it's bad.
Lord Burghley gave me sight of it. It says—'
You shook your head to free you of the thought.
'Kit, they've enough to hang you.'

                                        So it fell,
the sword of Damocles. I barely flinched.
'What does it say?'

                    'Your words. It's all your words.'

You left a gap, allowing me to summon
which words it might have been: and strangely, then,
I could only remember triumphs. Faustus, mad,
as he fails to save his soul. Or Tamburlaine,
whose bereavement serenades the loved, lost wife
in emerald, ruby words. Leander's song
for the woman he will throw his life upon.

'It's every quip you ever made on drink.
Your arguments against the Trinity:
Mary a whore, the Holy Ghost a bawd,
and Jesus a bastard.'
                    'Jesus.'
                                'All set down
in a comprehensive list of blasphemies.'

How much I would prefer I had been damned
by the words I crafted carefully in ink.
Instead my pen was cancelled by my mouth,
and scholarship drowned in an hour or two of drink.

If I had drifted into my own pain
on the damp, unstable wreckage that was Kit
you barely noticed, locked in paraphrase:
'That the Bible's filthily written. Every gibe
you aimed at religion, recalled perfectly.
That Christ deserved to die more than Barabbas
though Barabbas was a thief and murderer.'

The reference woke me up. With that, I knew.

'Barabbas – Baines. He wrote this.'
                               'Signed his name
with a flourish. Says he can bring witnesses
to affirm his accusations. Ends the note
to plead that every Christian should ensure
your mouth be stopped.'

                    'I'm done for.'

                            Silence sank
into the room as a stone sinks in a pond;
the shadows thrown up by a welcome fire
dancing like hordes of demons on the wall.

'What if you disappeared?' you said.
                              'To where?'

'To Scotland, where your friend went. To the King,
Arbella's cousin.'

               'How could he take me in?
A wanted atheist? No, I'd be sent
home with an escort.'

                    'You could go abroad.
We have the contacts.'
                              'What, and have to hide
for ever after, fearing for my life,
or end my days in some unsavoury hole,
stuck on the end of an assassin's knife?
I'd rather die right here.'

                         I watched your face,
as tender as though I'd kicked it. In a breath,
I'm on my feet, and stalking up and down.
'Damn it! What do I do?'

                         'You die right here,'
you said as quietly as fear allowed.
Still walking nowhere, everywhere at once,
I barely heard you. 'What?'
                              'You die right here.
Not here, not in this house, but somewhere safe.
Under another name, you slip these shores
with passport to travel. While Kit Marlowe meets
a proper death, observed by witnesses,
with documents to prove it.'
                              'How?'
                                   'Sit down!'
you said, more forcefully. 'I have to think.'

THE PLOT

The plot you devise for me is scrupulous.
In every detail – entrances, exits, marks,
contingencies and props – no blank is left.
No improvisation. Nothing left to chance.

If I'm arrested, Burghley will have me bailed.
He wouldn't want me in a torturer's chair,
blubbering awkward secrets, crying his name.
We will have days to set the plan in train.

>My perfectly accidental death. A fight,
>a scuffling over something trivial.
>The reckoning – I saw you enjoy the pun.
>Most folk would say that I had gotten mine.

To be controlled it will occur inside.
At the safe-house. Widow Bull's, close to the Thames:
easy to sail from, and inside the Verge,
jurisdiction of the Queen's own coroner,

ensuring that this too-convenient death
is stamped by the royal seal: no doubt allowed.
The Queen will sign it off, conditional
on an obedient silence spent in exile.

>Exile. In all the haste to save my neck,
>I hadn't sounded out that word at all.
>It sings its empty promise in my ear
>like the coffin of a wife that I must join.

But now your job is: make me disappear.
A minimal cast whose loyalties are sound.
Chief witness: Robin Poley, king of lies.
Abroad, but he can be sent for. Offering

his life in your service, as he had once sworn,
Ingram Frizer will play my murderer,
armed with his stone-faced plausibility,
and a plea of self-defence, to dodge the rope.

    Was there no other way it could be done?
    My reputation snagged upon that nail:
    a man who'd stab his patron's loyal retainer
    over a tavern bill, and from behind.

You brighten it up. You polish it like brass.
The second witness, Nicholas Skeres, a friend
to each of us in the past, dog-loyal, and skilled,
like Frizer and Poley, in the spotless lie.

You bat away my doubt like summer flies,
distracting my mind with Italy: the art,
the poetry, the theatre, the wine.
'And months of sunshine, Kit. Escape the rain.'

    Yet rain is the stuff of home, a constancy
    that drums its comfort on familiar roofs,
    washes the face awake, peels back the blooms
    and lifts the smell of growth out from the grass.

My friend, you wrought a most ingenious plot.
As wedding to marriage, its complexity
masked future troubles. But no more than a scene
when I must go on acting to the end.

WHITGIFT

The privy councillors are cleanly split.
The half that want their spy alive lock jaws
with the half who'd have me roasted on a spit.
Archbishop Whitgift has the faggots lit.

Fear and the plague are one. What horrifies
is the thought of death come calling: close, now, close
as a neighbour's son, the tailor, an old friend,
as each is smacked to bed, and rendered numb.
Carted to grey stone walls, dropped in the earth,
imprisoned in the lea of Christendom.
And fear is the contagion passed along.

Blame anyone, blame anyone but us.
Blame foreigners for eating bread and ale,
for speaking words we cannot understand.
Blame women for the looseness of their tongues,
for doing work we wouldn't do ourselves.
Blame slaughter for the smell but relish meat;
blame sin on God, but heed the worship bell.

At Lambeth Palace, cool upon the Thames,
heads come together. *Walter Raleigh spoke*
against the Dutchmen, yet we passed the Bill
to welcome them; we need more Protestants.
Now the people riot. And who stirs them up?
Plotters and Catholics. Upstarts, atheists.
They work a plan. Two birds. A single stone.

The page is sent to get a literate man
who's paid to keep his secrets. 'Make a verse
condemning foreigners. Make *them* the plague.
Then have it written neat enough to read
and post it on the wall outside their church.
And you should allude to Marlowe. Marlowe's words.
Let Marlowe take the blame, should any come.'

KYD'S TRAGEDY

The London streets are thick with discontent,
and someone must be blamed; and someone sought,
and someone's cheek be forced against a wall
and someone's parchments whipped up into snow.

They arrest my former room-mate. It's not hard
to get a nod to all they need confirmed:
they only have to crank his fingers out
and press a coffin's weight on to his chest.

Out spills my name. Are these my papers? Yes.
They are not his. They are not mine. A scribe
copied some lines against the Trinity
from some old book. But I'm weighed against his spine.

My confidence, he took for arrogance.
I teased him. Now his muscles tear like lace,
his fingers too divorced from knuckle joints
to hold the pen he'd sign confessions with.

A year or so from now, Tom Kyd is dead,
his ribs a cage around his silenced heart,
unable to sever by penitence or pen
his name from mine, or that word atheism;

from the fact he set inquisitors on me.
But for now, he scribbles – starving, from a cell –
of his innocence, and of my crimes as well,
as he tries to hold his index finger in.

SMOKE AND FIRE

Some twenty miles away, I knock a pipe
ash-free. But where the habit once relaxed,
it now rides agitation, stroking hackles
which rise on its passing; aggravates a throat
where emotion clusters with expectancy,
like schoolboys for the whip. Another smoke.
My fingers shake to press the new stuff in.

'Kit,' you said, 'they won't come looking here.'
But gave me a room with sight across the moat
to the arch bad news must broach. Now dusk descends,
and a mist lies on the water like a bride
waiting to be disturbed. Only the sigh
of trees, a moorhen's cackle, and the bark
of a distant fox send quivers through her peace.

My days I fill with telling another's tale,
playing the loved and lover all at once:
lighting the lamp and swimming the Hellespont.
Evenings, we eat, and gulp wine by a fire
that crackles with hope, and prompts our talk of soon,
how this will pass. But this hour, in my room,
my faith deserts as swiftly as the light.

They'll come for me. They'll come as sure as sleep
comes to the man who's been awake too long.
With warrant and dog, they'll come as sure as sound
comes to the drum that's beaten. Even now,
the name of Marlowe leaps from lip to lip:
not wonder of the age, but atheist.
You're gentle on my shoulder. 'Kit. Come down.'

By Any Other Name

Greene's Marlowe has stuck. Now half of me says 'low',
the sound of which is like a cobbler's knee.
And something of the flavour of the ditch
resides there also, if you listen for it.

Marlowe, the name that even friends adopt
because it means me now. But dangerous,
a shifting name that has me kiss the clay
and barely props my soul against the wind.

Marlowe the name that slips into the ear
of blind authority and sleeping dog,
the name that rustles up the fishwife's sleeve
and rattles dice across a tabletop.

Fractured into a dozen parts; yet one.
For surely he sold his soul to understand
the nature of evil. Faustus. Tamburlaine.
My name slipped by degrees out of my hands.

They call me what they will. A devil, too,
and Machevil, as if my words have power
to topple kings and princes. Or the Queen.
It's Marlowe on the warrant sent for me.

DRAKES

'What will you need?' you asked, your quill hand poised.

'I'll need my books. Paper and ink. Some clothes.'

'A decent horse. Money to get you through
until you meet your contact overseas.'

You scribed it all with such efficiency.
I couldn't bear to watch you shape that list
when all that was essential would be left
behind, in the very room I breathed in.

                                        'You,'
I offered. At first, you didn't understand.
'I'm sorry?'
              'You. Come with me.'
                                  'Kit, I can't.'

You set the pen down gently, and stepped over
your sleeping hound to meet me at the warmth
of a dying fire, where I'd been standing, propped
for the last half-hour. You took my hands in yours
and a feeling shivered through me. 'If I go
the minute you are dead, what will they think?'

'That it was faked.'

                  'Or that I murdered you,'
you said, the words distasteful in your mouth
as a swig of milk that's turned. The thought of it.

Your eyes dropped, and my hand rose to your cheek
as to a statue, banished from my touch,
whose beauty compels that most forbidden act –
to know you through my skin. My love. To feel.

You didn't flinch. Indeed, you placed your hand
in the curls of my hair, and quietly met my gaze.
And as we kissed, the wide world looked away,
not understanding anything at all
about two friends who've never spoken love
but find themselves born helpless in its arms
embracing the silence that my death demands:
pretended death so resolutely played
that heaven might admit me, but not you.

And what possessed me then, surprising you,
was the ageless hunger of a starving soul
who needs to eat and be eaten, to be one
with the feast that fills him, so he might be whole.

Later, aware of morning's creeping chill,
you led me like a puppy to your bed.

We lay until eight: one sleeping like a lord,
the other, awake, preparing to be dead.
And when the stirrings of a country house
had you in breeches, I remained quite still.

'Where will we get a corpse?' I asked again.
'If the man's already dead, and I presume
you don't mean to murder someone, how will he
seem fresh to the jury?'

            You pulled on your shirt
across the urgent signature my nails
had made on your back. 'He will be freshly dead,'
you answered, once again so matter-of-fact
the night might not have happened.

                              'Dead from what?'
'From the same disease that would have you dispatched.
Religious intolerance. There are enough
rogue preachers who await Her Majesty's noose
for us to borrow one unfortunate.'

So practical. I hated that in you
that morning. Though my life depended on it.

'So he will be hanged?'
                        'Ideally. And not stiff
before he is delivered.'
                        All the 'he'
was making me nauseous. To discuss a man
as though he were a sack of grain.
                              'This corpse,'
I said, 'how will it pass for me?'
                              You paused
at the window: some commotion on the pond
took your attention.

                    'Drakes will sometimes drown
the ducks they mate,' you said. 'By accident.'

My friend, each thought we have is meaningful.
The lightest observation weighs like lead
on a friend as vulnerable as I was then.

You turned your gaze to me. 'How will it pass?
The men will swear it's you, and be believed,
as friends of yours. The bulk of England knows
nothing of what you look like.'

                              'But the servants,
and Widow Bull? If they see me arrive?'

'Oh, death's a great disguiser, Kit,' you said.
'And we will add to it. A gory wound
will make the sternest-stomached soul recoil,
look anywhere but at the corpse's face.'

'What do you have in mind?' I asked, afraid
of your calm, phlegmatic answer.

                              'It's the eyes
where we feel vulnerable,' you said, your gaze
proving your point. 'A stabbing in the eye.'

My Being

How could I give up writing? You might ask
a man to give up breathing, or a hawk
to drop a strip of fillet in your hand
and starve itself. I am compulsion's fiend.
And thought is as an irritating itch
that can't be reached except in pen and ink.
I covet paper. Nothing inside is still
till I empty out my mind and order it.

How could I give up writing? You might ask
a fish to give up swimming, or a horse
to ditch his kick and neigh, his stamp and snort.
Or ask a man brought up inside the trades
and elevated into velvet halls
to soft-relinquish everything he's earned;
swap cloak for leather apron; kneel as if
he is a common man, and not to mind
his life turned back to nothing.
                                    Rather ask
a god to be your servant than request
I gag myself without complaint, when words
are all I have to stay this side of Hell.

My Afterlives

Two names were needed for my afterlives.
A name to travel under, and a name
to write beneath: believable, yet blessed
with meaning, in the way that names can be
when not devised by parents. For the first
I settled on Le Doux: the gentle man.
A name so sweet, so radically at odds
with how my enemies would have me viewed
that I'm disguised completely by its sound,
the merest tap of a tongue inside a vowel.

The pen-name, though, kept me awake for hours.
What power might I invoke to hide behind
when every word I write, stamped with my voice,
might summon, like a sneeze in hide-and-seek,
my swift discovery?
                        Do you believe
in the power of dreams? I drifted, with my mind
hooked on the question, and when I awoke,
the name of 'Shakespeare' spoke itself. A gift –
or thus I was persuaded by the dawn –
from the goddess Athena, warrior of the wise,
whose shield, protected with the Gorgon's head,
would freeze all those who tried to look behind.
How perfectly it works, that verbal spell.

The Christian name delivered like a foal
slipped all at once on to the stable's straw.
I knew a boy at school called William Good.
Will I Am Good, we laughed; for he was caned

most often. And the Will I Am came through
as a floated prayer; the breath of my desire.

'Will I Am Shakespeare, then,' I mouthed to the face
in the polished mirror as I shaved away
the roguish beard I'd grown to give me age.

'William Shakespeare.' Memorable yet bland
as a pat of butter shaken without salt.
If the name seemed half familiar, I took it then
as a sign of its rightness, not the distant knell
of a long-lost conversation overheard.

What destiny hunkers in coincidence?
What paths are knitted for us by the gods
who pull such strings together? Thus was summoned
like Hecate's curse on any future road,
the printer's friend who'd worn that name since birth,
discreet as married sex. It was agreed:
a grand idea. A cloak, an extra layer.

The name is mine, I tell myself, it's bought
as a doublet's bought. Yet worn by two, not one,
it chafes where he narrows, rubs where I'm not free,
itches, fits neither of us perfectly.

Yet I am Will. I am. I say these words
over and over, like a hopeless spell.
Will I am Will. I'm Will. And Will is me.

A Passport to Return

Two classic narratives of thwarted love.
A pair of poems, like a pair of gloves,

conceived together. One, discreetly lodged
with Field in my new name. The other dropped
with 'Marlowe' on its cuff, on Kentish soil,
to circulate in manuscript, unspoilt;
the hero strangely living. Leander swims,
not to be published; for his finish begins

when my death's undone.
                              In each, the other sings,

their source identical. Brought side by side
the lie can be exposed: this author died?
Then how did the matching poem come to be?
And notice the motif: the telling scene
embroidered on the sleeve of Hero's dress
from the other poem, authored by 'W.S.'.

So brought together, these two will confess.
The perfect bookends of this man's distress.

DEPTFORD STRAND

On Deptford Strand, the famous *Golden Hind*
whose fine prow Drake encircled round the globe
sits broken to its bilges: souvenir'd
into a ship of bones. On breezy air,
the blackhead gulls are circling for a spoil.
The river laps at mud and, on this turn
that loops a noose around the Isle of Dogs,
slides swiftly round the bend. A hint of salt
and fishiness betrays how close the sea
is to this widening gullet. And to me.

We meet at ten on the path up to the door.
Frizer's eyebrows greet me, and he nods
at Nicholas Skeres. Frizer is strangely calm
for a man prepared to stage some murderous rage,
only Nick Skeres betraying signs of nerves
Frizer will shortly douse with beer. A twitch
as Eleanor Bull invites us: 'Gentlemen.
The room's upstairs,' she says. 'Young Martha here
will show you up. Dinner is pork and beans.
I'll serve you there myself around midday.'

Frizer enquires, 'Is Master Poley here?'
'He's been delayed. He'll join you presently.'
How does she know? 'He arrived here yesterday.
Come from The Hague, or somewhere. He went out
first thing this morning, "tying up loose ends",
he said I was to tell you. Never fret,
Master Poley is most reliable.' She pats
me on the arm as if I were her son.
'I expect you'll want some drinks.'
                                    'Small beer,' I say.

The window rattles with a puckish breeze
as I stand there looking down upon the lawn
lined by whispering bushes, and the path
that I expect him on.
                              'A friendly wind,'
says Frizer unexpectedly. 'So long
as it keeps up its direction.'
                              He returns
to playing patience, Skeres pouring a glass
of warm ale down his gullet. Here we are.

This is the house from which I'll disappear
and swap my comforts for a dead man's clothes,
give up all public substance, with my name
sloughed off like the reptile's skin he has outgrown.
Kit Marlowe dies here. And with that thought, a pang
for a younger self who dreamt of being hailed
a wonder of the age, but now is holed,
like a galleon in warfare, and will sink
to the mud of history beneath a lie:
the coward conquest of a wretch's knife.

Poley arrives at last. I hear his smooth
placating patter in the hall downstairs;
the laugh of Mrs Bull, charmed to her corset.
'Good fellows,' he greets us, making sure the door
is firmly shut behind him. 'Excellent news.
We have our substitute. John Penry's dead.'

And I must break this narrative to pause
and say a prayer for Penry, whose young wife
had begged for clemency. Who was condemned
for tracts he hadn't written; for belief
that his eloquence might turn the hearts of men

to a different church. And almost, we were twins
exchanged at death, not birth; for it was speech,
and love of liberty that brought us both
to a silencing. And had he not, in truth,
been executed hurriedly that May,
I might have joined him in a common grave.
Our only difference, this twin and I,
was the influential aspect of our friends.

'Backgammon,' Poley says. 'You'll have a game?
With money on the side perhaps?' He throws
his cloak over a chair. 'Come, come, man, sit.
We have three hours to kill before the corpse
can be delivered. A penny down to start
us gently?'

        So we play away the hours
as though the time has no significance:
I lose two shillings in distractedness.
Food comes at noon as promised, though I have
no kind of appetite.

        Poley seems charged
with a strange kind of enjoyment. Full of meat,
he stretches – 'Time for a little fresh air, perhaps?' –
as though he must put on the play for us,
though we are actors too. 'A gentle turn
around the garden?'

        The breeze is playful still.
We walk in quiet conference; ahead,
Poley and I, the other two as close
as midday shadows.

'The north side of the house
is windowless,' says Poley. 'By the gate
that backs on to the lane, there are some shrubs
that grow there thickly. Enter them as though
you must relieve yourself. You'll find a trunk
containing Penry, separate from his clothes.
Leave yours behind, use his and flee from here
to a barque named *Pity's Sake*, which waits for you
on the eastern pier.'

                    'That's it?'
                              Rob Poley smiles
that noose of a smile he saves for lethal words.
'This is goodbye. The three of us will dress
the body in your gear. I'll keep the Bull
and her Martha occupied with pleasantries
while Frizer and Skeres lump-shoulder in their friend,
the loll-headed drunkard who must sleep it off.
That's you.' He brims with the beauty of his art,
the joy of his own deception. 'Go. Be gone,'
he says, 'before we wheel around again.'

Penry is in his underclothes, and pale
as the winding sheet he lacks; a crumpled ghost
of indignity. One eye is not quite closed,
gleams jealously as I adopt the clothes
his wife had stitched, that he had buttoned up
to go to the gallows, opened at the neck
for the hemp to tighten on his throat; which wound
would be concealed beneath the awkward ruff
that you ensured I wore. Oh, guilty thief,
who slides on so efficiently his shirt,
without its preacher's collar, and the gift
of being alive, in front of Death itself,

and slips on to the lane as casually
as one engaged in some delivery
of goods, and not himself.

                    The eastern pier
is poking its sullen finger through the flow
that now sweeps swiftly seawards. There, the boat
Poley had named jerks hard against its ropes
as though concerned to leave, knocked by a breeze
still keen for France. On the vessel sits a boy
picking his teeth distractedly, who swings
his legs round when he sees me, calls a word
to the boat's invisible skipper. From below,
as unexpected as a perfect bloom
emerging from a plant that seemed diseased,
you show yourself. An innocent mirage
but, for a breath, I let myself believe
you're coming with me, though your face says no.

'Your papers. And a letter you must give
to the Flemish contact. Certain points in France
where you'll link with the network. And the name
of a guide who'll safely take you through the Alps.'
You tuck them inside my jacket, and your hand
so warm, so personal, I want to grab
your wrist and keep it there, close to my heart.
Instead, I watch you like a wounded child,
saying goodbye to me. 'And I will write
when it's safe to do so. Not for several months.
I'm bound to be watched. But, Kit, please write to me.'

And I am wordless, powerless to speak
the sentences that stampede to be said
and trample upon each other. In my head

I tell you my every feeling in a form
that changes the ending; thankful, warm with love,
we sail together.
                        In truth, I stand there, dumb,
watching us both as if we're on the stage
forgetting our lines; have stumbled on a scene
that I stayed awake, not writing.
                                    'Kit, be safe,'
you say, your hand extended to my face
and almost touching.
                        'Master Walsingham.'
The young boy, come like a shadow to your side.
'Father thinks we should go.'
                                    The hand withdraws.
'I leave you then. The trunk has all the books
you asked for. Paper, ink.'
                                'My manuscript?'
Perhaps the waves' unsteadiness beneath
the thin shell of the boat reminded me
of those lovers separated by the strip
of the Hellespont.
                        'I have a copy of it,
and you have yours,' you answer, 'to complete
when I, and other friends of yours, secure
an end to your exile.'
                        'Tom.' I grasp your hand.
'I shan't forget your help.' We grip goodbye,
brief as the pat the farmer gives his cow
before it's sent to slaughter.
                                'Take my cloak.'

Though you read my shiver wrongly, I was glad
to wrap myself up in the scent of you
when the salt tang of the sea unleashed its spray.

And half across Europe, something of you stayed
in the practical fibres of that everyday
reminder of you. The smell of Kent lay thick
like turf inside its hem. Sometimes I swore
as I slept beneath it, you were lying with me.
And then I'd wake, from the stare of John Penry.

I FORGET THE NAME
OF THE VILLAGE

There is a village, shadowed by the Alps
where early evening paints the snow as blue.
I still play French in northern Italy,
nodding '*bonsoir*' when I'm bid '*buona sera*'
and traipse the lane towards my rented room,
letting the creak of snow beneath my boots
return me to the quad on *Dido* night.

'Poley.'
        He must have seen me long before
I noticed him. Already looking bored,
he's taken in my clothes, my health, my mood,
and need not ask me.
                'So. You're still alive.'

'Another year. And yes. No thanks to you.'

He squints for a sun that set an hour ago.
'How did you conjure that? Without my help,
you would have swung last year.'

                        'Without your help
I wouldn't have been projecting for the State
and stuck my neck out.'
            Poley's like the snow
on the field beside us, untroubled by boot or hoof.
'If I suggested work when you were broke,
you didn't have to take it. I was clear
about the risks involved. Who serves the Queen

must travel with the currents, like the tide
is pulled by the moon – you poets have compared
her to the moon, I think. You may wash up
on a foreign shore and find yourself alone.
Unfortunate, but true. Yet see the light.
You could be dead.'

                    'I *am* dead.'

                                    Poley's face
shows unimpressed in the December gloom.

'And yet, you'll shortly take me to an inn
for something mulled, while I recount to you
the tale of your revenge. And think on this:
no poet is ever valued till they're dead.
I've brought you greater fame than you could buy
idling your hours in meadows. If that fame
is notoriety, so much the better.
Rather be infamous than buried bland.
Your favourite Ovid was exiled, was he not?
And doesn't exile burn into the heart
a greater fire to speak, and all the wisdom
that comes with a wide perspective?' He was right,
though I left his question hanging. 'Look, it's cold.
Let us continue somewhere off the road.'

The tavern's quiet, and we have the fire
all to ourselves. Rob Poley contemplates
a log he adds to embers, as it tempts
the fire into life again. I know there's news,
but I am not as eager as I was
to hear it from him, and refuse to ask:

for he would have me dangling on his words
like a dog who fetched a stick but won't let go.

'Not long to Christmas,' he observes, at length.
'So I have a present for you. Baines is dead.'

THE GOBLET

'There is a loyalty' – Poley cups his hands
around warm earthenware – 'that's rarely touched
upon, between intelligencers. But
it binds us.' He glances up to catch my eye
as sharp as any hook into a fish.
'Some of your friends felt I should look for Baines.'

He's quiet above the crackle of the fire,
which spits and pops the winter damp from logs
to punctuate his tale.
                              'But he is dead?'

Poley nods slowly. 'Yes. Perhaps you'd like
to hear a fuller version?'
                              'Carry on,'
I say, though I'm afraid of feeling glad;
of bathing too deeply in my enemy's blood.

'At first, he'd gone to ground. As will the fox
when hounds pursue it. But a year had passed,
and you were safely dead. Your reputation
as something of an enemy of the State –
excuse me –' he said, reacting to my scowl
'– enabled him to think heroically
of his part in it. So summer brought him out
as it brings out rashes and the cheaper whores
who ply their trade on Turnmill Street. Of course
he was startled when I approached him, but my meat
and ale is convincing friendship.'
                              With a smile
he instantly admits me to his heart –

a sample of his wares – then drops me cold.
Poley delights in savouring his tales,
but this, served to a storyteller's ears,
has extra gravy.

              'So we fell to talking
and I tempted him to a tavern where I know
the host and hostess passing well.' He grins,
and I see in the corner of that curl
his hand glide gently up a virgin's thigh.

'From the friendship I was offering, he assumed
we'd murdered you, and no bad thing, he said.
His conscience seemed troubled all the same. No, truly,
I noticed that he couldn't stop your name
peppering every sentence.'
                    I bless the fire:
its cheery destructive crackles fill the gap
that he has left for me. I don't react,
holding myself a heart's breath from the glee
I sense he feels at taking my revenge
for me.
        'Go on,' I say.
                He shakes it off,
that bothersome sense that I am not with him,
like a nuisance fly.
              'At length, I offered him
the hint of some private work. Said we should talk
in another place, less public, and we moved
out of the tavern to the stable block,
taking our cups. Mine was a special thing,
a silver goblet that the hostess lets
her favourite drinkers use. "You hold my cup,"

I say as I hear footsteps, "while I write
the contact's name. It's foreign." Like a child
he takes the goblet and, instinctively,
he hides it as the taverner comes in
(this, prearranged). The hostess challenges him,
the cup is discovered, and I wash my hands
of the whole affair.'

                 'He couldn't hang for that!
Just moving it within their property?'

'The stable block belongs to someone else.
They only rent it.'

               Poley is clearly proud
of his plan's simplicity. 'And since they were,
both of them, in their house, that's robbery.
No benefit of clergy. He was hanged.'

He sits back like a predator whose game
digests inside his stomach. What a trick!
What practised magic with a legal sting
he brought to bear upon my enemy!

And yet I cannot thank him, for his sin
has doubled injustice in a world of wrongs.
And Baines cannot recant now he has swung,
cannot be pressed for truth, cannot undo
the document. A cinder from the fire,
spat out, smokes patiently beside my boot.

'Poley,' I say, but then can add no more.

In a Minute There Are Many Days

Between our letters, this adopted death
becomes more real. My heart slows to a crawl,
chilled by your absence, waiting for the fall
of written words to warm it up like breath.
I'm cut like a lily water cannot save.
The endless nights are stitched into a shroud
that takes my shape, and has my weeping bound.
The weeks until I hear gape like the grave.

But when your letter opens in my hands
my heart starts up, a wild bird to a clap,
and air fills lungs as though some arid land
were suddenly ocean, charted off the map.
Two pages of your hand can bring such bliss;
and yet, without your love, I don't exist.

THE HOPE

I dare not breathe it, yet it lives in me
as sometimes the single reason why my heart
must go on beating. Let me name the hope,
and do not take it, never tug the threads
that I've secured it with; I am afloat
by only the meanest margin, buoyed by this:
that I might be restored to life, and name.
That I might walk the London streets again
as Christopher Marlowe, not an atheist,
but wronged by suborned informers, jealous wits,
and ignorant plebeians. And not dead:
but no, the Lazarus of modern times,
raised by the new incumbent Head of State.
If only that is James. And so I wait
for the Phoenix not to rise; the crab-haired queen
to crumble in her bed, relax the grasp
tight-knuckled fingers have upon my fate,
and gasp her last.

            Do not dislodge the hope
that holds in place a thousand racking sobs
for all I've lost: the stink of London town,
the cry of hawkers in my native tongue,
an English tavern's simple fare, warm beer,
an afternoon at the Curtain or the Swan
amongst good friends; though half those good friends gone
already, and the rest of them as dead
to me as I've become to all the world,
because I may not touch one's face again
or hear another's laugh.

And still, I hope,
and the hope sits like a lump beneath this poem,
and under every play, it hatches dreams:
that every word might be restored to me.
That my name be cleared, and sounded round the court,
that good King James release me from the bonds
of unjust exile. Oh, let it be James
that hefts the crown, and not some specious wretch
who wins the throne by murder.

For my hope,
it is the smallest thing, a captured bird
that beats against the bars with beak and wing
and often breaks itself, exhausted, frail.
The Queen must die, that I might tell the tale.

My hope is threaded to that soft word, *home*,
though home is a foreign country to me now,
a fabled kingdom where I cannot tread
because I am a ghost, and must be dead.
But do not kill the hope that I might breathe
some mist on the glass my mother shows my mouth,
or stand once more to savour every smell
that permeates the hall of my father's house:
new leather, shoe wax, iron, elbow grease.

Where I am staying now, the smell of fish
assaults me awake each dawn. The merchants' clothes
grow less peculiar daily. Random bells
become my certainties. Though there is heat
in every square and pavement, every voice
raised in a bet or bargain, still I keep
watch for more English weather. Sudden rain.

Friend, send me word. If I could slip ashore
and live in secret on some quiet estate
far from the eyes of London, let me learn.
The Queen has the best of doctors, and my hope
is struggling to breathe. Help me return.

SICKENING

Doctors, I said. The night I wrote those words
I fell into a fever. As if the pen
reminded my body of an ancient trick
to provoke the care of others, I fell sick.

The Latin from which 'delirium' derives
kept me awake all night: *out of the furrow*,
vexed as a hare that's tortured mad with spring,
or mad, just mad, with nothing, nobody,

short in the breath and long in sweat, a jerk
out of the straight-ploughed earth, out of my mind
for the cooling touch, for the whisper at my bed,
for the *Try some soup*, for the *How did you sleep, my love?*

For how do you sleep with Death camped by the door,
and the night as long and cold as a drawn sword?

They have not come for me. They have not come.

Oh, bile.

        I throw up till there's nothing left,
sick to my stomach of regret. Each curse
I damn on others, damning only me,
condemned to the long death of obscurity
when all I had created's inside out
and me expelled – a fact I can't digest.

Oh, hold me, mop my brow, my love. But, no,
some seven hundred days have passed alone
and nourishment is more than tavern soup,
or chicken wrangled off the bone.

                                        The man
who should bring cash and letters hasn't come.
I am forgotten, stuffed in Europe's boot,
and starved, my hopeless stomach shrinks to stone,
admitting nothing, no one. What is thrown
into this rented bowl is only bile,
and the wine that washed it down.
                                        Anatomize
this fever: boiling rage not shouted out,
expressed in the quiet overheating cage
of a soul whose spirit languishes repressed
by a time too ignorant to hear, or see
what every human being is in heart:
intelligent, divinely conscious, free.

Yet frail, still. For the shivering that plagues
this clammy skin is mortal fear, for me.

God's wounds, how easy it would be to die.
To collapse against this bartered door unheard
and not a creature come for days. No sound
except for the sainted and persistent flies
that with their buzz persuade me I'm alive.

And should I be found, slumped cold, oh, not a word
of blessing on the stranger's grave. And years
gone by, what would you say? I disappeared.

Beyond your powers to save. Dead anyway.
Oh, Lord. I need to get me out of here.

Some three days in, my brain boiled up like stock,
I drag myself, wrapped up in sheets, downstairs
to scare the landlord's daughter. '*Spettro!*' she gasps,
knocked by the sight of me into a chair,
then up, remembers herself, and helps me sit:
brings wine, and bread, and flaps about the door,
wishing her parents home. 'Don't you dare die.
What's wrong with you?' she asks, in savage French.

And I forget pretence; my native tongue,
too burdened with disease to hide itself,
spits out, 'What kind of illness does one get
from swallowing the world's neglect? How do
the symptoms manifest?'
                                    She swears, '*Inglese!*'
Wondrously – how the fevered mind expands! –
then crosses herself. Flits out into the square,
a songbird suddenly freed.
                                    I grip the bread,
smear it with butter, salt, gulp down the wine
and fall into dreams of deportation, cast
adrift in my queasy stomach.

                                    She returns
to find me asleep on elbows, bathed in sun
from the open casement, hair at the temples wet
as though I've been baptised. Her mother wide
behind her,
                'You are English, Louis Le Doux?'

'I am a child of all the world,' I say,
expansively, half drunk, and half undone
by days of throwing up. 'Check, if you will,
my Italian blood.' I cough, my handkerchief
catching the finest spray. 'See? Marcus Lexus,
a Roman soldier, garrisoned in Kent,
lifted his leg across a Kentish maid,
herself of Viking stock. Norwegian eyes.'
I blink my heritage. 'Though the blue in mine
is buried beneath French conquest – a Gallic shade
fruited from Norman chestnut. And who knows
what branch of Turkish empire, Asian slave
or native African is written there
in a litany of humpings?' I thrust the rag
towards them, though they shrink from inspecting it.
'Ladies, I'm from the world, and so are you.'

I've no idea how much they understood.
The presence of English was assault enough.

'You have to leave this house.'
                                                   'Then I will die,'
I say, with far less drama than I might.
'But I will go. It is your house.' I push
myself up on the table, and at once
collapse to the floor like laundry.
                                                   'Apologies.
Perhaps you'll help me to the door.' They run
to lift me by the armpits (pity them)
and do my bidding; I am light as bones,
and the hefty mother hefts me off my feet
on the left-hand side. The daughter breathes on me
a lunch of peaches. 'Woah! I am not dressed,'
I remember, coiling the sheet about my loins.

'We'll bring your clothes down presently,' the whale
of a woman replies. 'Let's get you outside first.'
'But my things. My trunk.' I stop them at the door.
'Can you send my trunk to—'
                              Here, the comedy
collapses. Christ, I can't imagine where
my trunk might safely be received. What friend
would take it in, and me, except at home?
Some leafy, rutted lane in England's shires:
the vision, clear as through a polished glass,
comes bridled with a shiver as I feel
the wind in the hedgerows, hear the clattering cart
that hauls my books and bones the final miles.

Then heat returns, and I am in the square,
undressed and homeless, manhandled by girls.

'*Scusi*,' I say, embarrassed by the tears
that squeeze their way past every last defence
and fall, now, freely.
                        Melt the landlord's daughter.
She leads me like a lamb back to the cool
of the kitchen, sits me down, and takes my head
on to her bosom, which I wet with grief.
Her mother tuts Italian. 'He can't stay here.'

'We cannot simply throw him on the street.
Have some compassion.'

                        'Who is he, anyway?
Pretending to be French. Dishonesty
is not a pleasant house guest.'
                                'Mother, please.
He understands Italian.' She takes my cheeks

between her palms and looks into my eyes
as kindly as a sister. 'Tell me, sir,
why the great sorrow? And why disguise yourself?'

She presses her handkerchief into my hands
and sits beside me as I dry my face.

'I've never told my story,' I explain,
'except to ink and paper.'
                                    'Then you must,'
she urges me. 'An untold story sits
like rust in the heart. It makes the blood go sour.
Press on.'
              So, hesitantly, I begin.

'At home – and I still call it home, although
I'm almost two years exiled – I wrote plays.'

'Exiled,' she breathes. 'So, so. There is the grief.
Go on.'

              'I wrote a comedy. A farce.
Most popular. The protagonist so extreme
in his two-faced treachery, you'd have to laugh
or despair at humanity.'
                                    'This is a tale
that promises to stretch to suppertime,'
the mother sighs. 'All poets are the same.
Enamoured with the beauty of their words,
they spin three yards when half an inch will do.
Skip quickly to your banishment. What crime
have you committed?'

                    'Why, the crime of truth,'
I say. 'For every fiction has a core
of honesty. The seed of the idea
plants in the mind from life. This "character" –
though I changed his name, location, race and creed –
was a man my friend had worked with. And his tales,
those tavern entertainments, spun the plot
that then became my play. I didn't dream
the dangers of my profession. I was glad
only to see the theatre glutted out,
the play a staunch success.'

                        'What of this man?'
the daughter asks. I wish I knew her name;
protecting myself from that was purposeless,
and I am half in love with her already,
for caring enough to ask me who I am.
'He recognised himself?'
                        'He must have done.
Although, I told myself, this was a fiction
and, therefore, how could he find fault with it?
Stupid.' I stop. Once more, I'm almost floored
by the weight and depth of my own ignorance.

'What happened?' she asks, as gentle as a breeze
lifting a tattered poster from the wall
for an event long past, and half forgotten. 'Then?'

I skip the coining, and the failed betrayal.
Speak only of 'invented' blasphemies.

The mother has turned her back, and has a hare
stripped of its skin and on the chopping block.

'A fishy tale,' she says. 'If they were lies
then you could surely say so.' And the knife
chops off a haunch.
                    I flinch. 'In England now,
religion is the tetchiest of notes
that one might pipe on. Since our Virgin Queen
passed the point of bearing issue . . . laws have changed.
Even to be accused of heresy
is taken by the courts to signal guilt.'

'My mother's right,' the daughter says, as soft
as a pillow I could expire on. 'Surely lies
could be turned out and booted down the street.
Be honest, please. Was there some truth in it?'

Her eyes search into mine so tenderly
I cannot think of lying.
                         'As a student
they trained me to debate theology;
a habit I enjoyed. Sometimes with friends
I openly expressed opinions which
I'd not want written down.' She turns her face,
ashamed for me. 'But who when they are young
is prudent every moment? Which of us
can claim great wisdom when we're primed with wine
and the company of those we love and trust?
If I have sinned – and I confess I have –
it is against myself. I'm in the hands
of God completely and, by his design,
I never sinned enough that I should die.
Or I'd be buried now.'
                       She takes both hands
and reads me quickly, scans me like a script
to find her part.

                    'And where would you be now
if not consigned to exile?'
                                        'Why, in love.'

The shock to both of us has cleft the air
into a silence, following the thud
of her mother's cleaver, finished dismembering.
Was it my need for rest that brought that word
out of my lungs? Or just the strange relief
of finding kindness in a world of stones?

'You barely know my name,' she says.
                                        'It's true.'
'Venetia,' she says.
                    'And mine is Christopher.'

'Clear off, she's spoken for.' The mother's lunge
towards us with a cloth to wipe the table
shocks us both to our feet, and I, unbalanced,
weak in the legs, am floored a second time,
and coughing my surprise into a rag.

Venetia crouches to help me up. 'It's true
I'm spoken for. And you are far too ill
to imagine yourself in love with me. Your fever,
and fear of death, can be the only cause.
But I will help you – Mamma, stop clucking, please –
I'll help you find some passage back to home.'

She's leading me to my bed. I say, 'But home –
they think me dead at home. All but a few.'
'Then one of those few can nurse you back to health,
before you're truly dead,' she says.

                    'But what
if I'm recognised?'
                    She stops us before the mirror
at the foot of the stairs. Says, 'Do you see yourself?
Do you recognise that man?'
                              A sallow face
whose skull shows through his skin. A ragged beard.
'No,' I admit.
                    'Then no one will know you.
And if they do, and you're imprisoned for
the crimes you fled, what difference will it make
to die that way, or here, so far from home?'
I glance at her breasts. 'I'll have nowhere so soft
to rest my cheek at home.'
                              She laughs and shakes
her head at me. 'You are delirious.
Lie down, Christopher, Monsieur Louis Le Doux,
whatever your name is. You are not in love.'

I lie down meekly. 'Why are you so . . . kind?'

Her eyes, then, spring with tears. 'I had a brother.
Had others been kind, I'd have a brother still.'
Then, brushing the thought to air, 'No more of that.
I'll find a merchant willing to take you home.'

How powerful that one word has become.
I might as well die there as anywhere.

STRAITS

What part of her she gave – they had no gold –
I'd rather not imagine. In a week
my nights were sweated on a merchant ship
above a hold of Orient silks and spices
bound for an English dock.
                                    Across the sheer
blue of the Mediterranean, the threat
of Barbary pirates threaded through my prayers.
And in Gibraltar's strait those prayers contained
the damnable Spanish, who might scupper us.
Yet we sailed through as smoothly as a promise.

Montanus

Only the sea becomes my enemy.
As we plough northwards through a deeper swell,
it builds the waters mountainous and cold
as the Alps I had avoided. I awake
to a storm whistling the masts into a creak
that would awaken monsters from the deep.
And we are rolled and yawed, and tossed and dumped
as a dandled plaything on a Titan's knee.

I light a candle, prepare my ink and pen
and record that simile before it flees,
follow with how it feels inside my skin,
then the ominous eerie whistling of the wind,
the slewing about of all that's not lashed down
(retrieving the ink that slides across the boards),
and how a part of me's already drowned
in the fatal fear of knowing I cannot swim.
Then the door bursts open. If the seaman's face
were a single word, it wouldn't be polite.

'The cap— What are you doing?'
                                          I can't explain.
To most folk, this would be no time to write.
'The captain wants you.' His glance suspiciously
on what I'm writing, which he cannot read.

'We must turn into port,' the captain says,
shouting above the racket of the wind.
'The storm is too much.'
                            'What country?'
                                          'Maybe France.

Or maybe Spain. The pilot's lost our course.'
He nods at the man twitching above a map.
'You have your documents?'
                                    'He has a pen,'
says the seaman who fetched me. 'Likes to write with it,'
and smiles with Venetian coldness.
                                    Like a king,
the captain dismisses him and stares ahead
into the howling dark as though it might
unpeel, revealing stars. 'So earn your keep,'
he says. 'Make a note for the vessel, something that
will pass in either country. And for yourself.
And, oh . . .' he stops me as I return below
'. . . the English are hated everywhere,' he says.
'Be anything but English.'

                                    Friend, we survived
our docking and mending, and the curious eyes
of Spanish officials on my forgery.

Now ploughing the sea again, I have prepared
a passport, in perfect secretary hand,
and dated almost exactly one year ago
in the name Pietro Montanus, faithful servant
to the honourable Anthony Bacon. By this name,
which ties us to our common love, Montaigne,
Bacon will know who it must be that sails
into the Thames to seek his sanctuary.

BISHOPSGATE STREET

It's May again. Two years have cycled round
as I return, unrecognisable,
to a neighbourhood that used to meet my boots
with a cheery ring. I scrape and hobble now,
pared to the bone by sickness. Here, the street
slides deep into the skirts of Bishopsgate:
the former mistress who disposed of me
and now mistakes me for a foreigner.

She smells the same. I catch her foetid breath
as a Gascon servant ushers me indoors
beneath a blanket.

             Through the afternoon
she gossips through the window like a wife
or former lover, oblivious to my pain,
quite blind to the man who's aching to chime in –
and almost says my name a time or two,
Mar-something – but she's moved to lovers new
while I am dying quietly within.

So close to Hog Lane that I hear the pigs
driven to slaughter. And the laughing whores
that kick about these evenings are the same –
I swear, at least for certain *one*'s the same –
that I have hired to celebrate success,
have sat on my lap and tickled, pouring beer
into my mouth, and flooding hers with it
in a drunken, lustful kiss. She glances up
but doesn't know this shadow of myself.

Half of me dreams up schemes where I will kneel
upon this bed and roar across the roofs,
'Hey, England! Look, it's me! Your fool is back!'

As if I had a voice. As if a ghost
could solidify to flesh and hope to live,
when he scares both wives and horses. I'd be struck
back to the graveyard of my deep pretence.

I sleep the first few days. Good Anthony
(a kinder man I could not hope to serve)
appreciates that love can mend disease.
He stations a boy to see I'm fed and clean,
visits me frequently. 'What do you need?'

And still – despite the letters not received,
the last two months of silence on your part,
the change in me, embittered by disease,
a silent voice is mouthing, 'Walsingham.'

How close you are. Now, not an inch of sea
roughens the air between us. You might ride
just half a day and touch the lips of me:
except these lips are blistered, and my pride
can't bear that you would see me broken down,
the tattered sail of that good barque we planned
holed and gone under with the barest sound.
I want your love to know a better man.
So I sleep. Imagine the air I'm breathing in
came straight from your lungs, disguised as summer wind.

I lie, within a lie, in Bishopsgate,
the name entirely false, the heart still true.
I long to hear 'Kit' or 'Christopher' again.
And when I think of love, I think of you.

MADAME LE DOUX

'Come. I've a treat for you.' My gentle host
responds to my better health with a surprise.

He leads me to a draughty room. A dress
is draped on the bed as though just recently
vacated by a princess. 'It's your size,'
he says. I try to read his face. Contained
within those eyes, the quiet expansive hint
of naughtiness.
                    'My size, but not my colour,'
I say, addressing my fingers to the cloth.
'I'd rather blue.' I'm playing out the joke,
whatever the purpose. 'No,' he says, 'this green—'
I interrupt: 'The colour's surely "sludge".'
With a teacher's patience, he repeats, 'This green –
an oceanic green – it sets your skin
off beautifully.' And holds it to my chest,
tilting his head as if the angled light
has made me feminine. And then he laughs.
'Perhaps the moustache might go.'
                                    'What? My moustache?
You will not have it, sir!' I fence him off
with my forearm. 'Swive, it takes three months to grow.'
'A soft, half-hearted thing.' He smiles. 'Believe
me, Kit, it will be worth the sacrifice.'

My name dropped like a stitch. We hold the air
and listen for servants. Not a creaking board.
And in that stop, I breathe the nectar in –
to be myself, and to be 'Kit' to him –
I almost dare not say what that is worth.

He starts again, contrite, 'Monsieur Le Doux,
if you might play your *wife*, then we have seats
in the balcony to see the latest play
by a certain William Shakespeare.'

                                   Me, see me?
In one disguise to watch my other's work,
pretending I don't know it? Can I fake
indifference to a script I'll know as well
as my tongue knows every crevice of my mouth?
Might I pretend those phrases new to me
whose words have kept me up at night? And not
demand some public credit for what spouts
out of the actors' mouths? 'I cannot do it.'
I sit down, heavy.

                     'Fie!' He gives a laugh.
'It's Ferdinando's Men. Now working for
the good Lord Chamberlain. You cannot miss it!'
He sits beside me softly. *'Richard the Third.'*

What spirits ride the draught I dare not name,
but ghostly fingers stroke me to a thought
that stirs a shiver. 'I heard they poisoned him.'

Bacon looks puzzled. 'Though my history
may not be deep, and I've not seen your play,
I recall that he was stabbed.'
                       The curtain breathes.

'No, Ferdinando Stanley. My lord Strange.'

Anthony nods. 'The Earl of Derby's death
was most mysterious. If Catholics

were the cause of it, I have not found the proof.
I have been looking, trust me.' And my hand
is taken in his, and held, and gently placed
back where he found it, just before it's missed.

'Do come,' he says. 'Come for your old friends' sakes.'
'Which friends?'
     'The quick, the dead, and all those souls
who've wished you well, who've kept your secret safe,
and hoped that you might one day see on stage
the final quarter of your history play.'

'Does anybody know?'
     'No. Not a soul.'
'And is it safe? Can I pass for a maid?'

He laughs more loudly than the room can take.
'A maid? Certainly not! Though it heartens me'
– he crosses the room to open a chest of drawers –
'that your vanity's survived such tragedy.
No, but your shaven face is soft enough
to make a widow of the plainer sort.'

'The sort no one will look at?'
     'That's the plan.
Best not to draw attention to the man
in woman's clothes, by making him beautiful.'
'It's risky, still.'
     'I regard your biggest risk
as wearing my mother's hair.' He throws the wig
into my lap. 'I stole it years ago
for some revels at Gray's Inn. You'll find the itch
is somewhat testing. Like the woman herself.'

'And if I look male?'

              'I will not let you out.'

But 'out' is what tugs me, strongly as a hook
this fish has swallowed and life is winding in:
the street with its hum of voices, and a stink
as homely as my armpits – even now
I'm savouring the ride to Gracechurch Street,
past a dozen taverns I know well enough
to stumble from, and maybe with a glimpse
of someone I might know.

              But then, the show.
And all the bloody deaths that it entails.
And all the ghosts that curse and swear revenge.
And me without a sword to fight for them.

'I wish that you had booked a comedy.'
'Could you have laughed?'

              'I'd rather laugh than cry.'

He comes to join me, looking at the street,
which, this midsummer evening, light as noon,
is filling up with revellers and song,
the shriek of swifts and martins, stitching roofs
in gentle loops.

            'Yet welcome what tears come.
They'll only enhance your womanly disguise.
Now don't be long. See? There's the coach outside.'

As he turns to go, I halt him. 'Wait! Will he –
the man from Stratford who is playing me –
will he be there?'

           My host laughs. 'Have no fear.

He comes to London only twice a year.
More often, and he'd be fending off requests
to rewrite scenes. You will not see him there.'

Curious, glad and sorry, I stepped in
to the sludge-green dress, arranged the wig with care.
Persuaded by my metamorphosis,
I left that house obsessed with who I'd see,
and not concerned enough with who'd see me.

THE THEATRE

Perfumed and powdered, I am led inside
on Anthony's arm. The smell of roasted nuts,
of beer and sawdust, brings me close to tears.

My place. My home. Yet no response to me.
No hush, no cheer, no recognition sound;
no lump in the throat to correspond with mine.

As though a hound I'd raised up from a pup
forgets his old master, trotting past my scent
to sniff the hands of new adopted friends

I choke unnoticed on the loss. There's cheer
around me, and I in a bubble of different air,
mull how the past included me. Our seats

are cushioned and shaded in the balcony.
Anthony pats my hand, and grins. 'Not long.'
Then, surprised to see me suffering, 'What's wrong?'

I wave his concern away. There are no words
in the moment ever. Only emotion's saw
hewing and hacking at the grain of me,

which won't for hours make verses worth their keep;
no words that I won't have to labour for
in the quiet distillation of no sleep.

Those who don't write – or, like dear Anthony,
knock off a poem when the Muse allows –
imagine we who live and breathe the pen

are eloquent and better-equipped than them
in the face of feeling, to describe that pain.
How could they know it's we who are struck dumb,

and ill-equipped to process what we feel,
are urged by that loss to find our horror's name?
For this we scratch while others safely dream.

Not to be known is such a slicing pain
I find myself half wishing for a cry
out of the crowd, a finger quivering:

'It's Marlowe!' and the sudden press and throng
and even swift arrest, even the rack,
the hangman and the slit from throat to prick

seems longed-for resolution, comforting
against this bitter nothingness, this blank.
In my nostalgia, I forget to fear.

Dick Burbage sidles on: the crowd falls quiet.
Some offstage music ruffles him; his eye
ranges with joyful hatred, drilling deep

into the groundlings. Now he grins and limps
to the centre of the stage. Here come my words.
Later, later, I shush my heart. I want

to be alive to this experience,
however sharp. And taste the blade go in,
the better to know the fruits of human sin.

INTERVAL

All through the gasps and jeers, the groundlings' boos,
I entertained this suicidal prompt:
Throw off the costume, let what happens come.

But then, and then . . . I pulled upon the thread.
Investigations, friends called to account:
your certain execution at the end.
I may not care to live, but love my friend.

And love, as if summoned in another form,
to seal my commitment to the raft of life,
weaves like a spring breeze through the drinking crowds.
Anthony whispers suddenly, 'Don't speak!'

And there, making straight towards us, is my past –
the Earl of Rutland, whom I barely know,
and the Earl of Southampton. If his beauty shone
in that garden once, then it is blinding now.
And the three years since we parted in the lobby
of my employer's and his guardian's house
seem shallow, thirsty years, and he a draught
both delicious and refreshing. Though at first
he doesn't see, sees only Anthony.

They greet each other. Being feminine
I'm less important and uninteresting.
I'm able to take him in, this sweet mirage
who'd pass for a girl more easily than me
for all his adopted swagger. Then he sees.
Stops dead.
              'Excuse me,' he starts.

'My lord, may I
present Madame Le Doux?'
'Why, *enchanté*.'

Something has passed between us. Is that eye
so suddenly fixed on mine because it sees
what others can't? Did I communicate
so accidentally, in the way I stared?
He kisses my hand, at no point looks away,
and I'm almost shaking. '*Comment allez-vous?*'
Though he's turned twenty-one, he bears the cheek
of a schoolboy with an earl's authority.
'I'm afraid,' says Anthony, 'her voice has gone.
A terrible summer cold. You know how travel
can weaken the system.'
'Yes, indeed I do.'
He smiles. I swear he knows.
'She is the wife
of a friend of mine,' Bacon adds. He's feeding rope
to a man long overboard.
Southampton's face
is a fairground of delight. 'May I enquire
how long she's staying with you?' I am lost.
He knows, he knows!
But Anthony holds firm.
'A month or so, I think. There's no fixed plan.'

'I'll call on you soon,' Southampton says, elated
at discovering me.
'We may be leaving town,'
says Anthony, nervously.
Southampton shifts
as a summer sky will thicken up with cloud;

takes my host's hand. 'Sir, I seem frivolous.
I apologise I can't mask my delight
at meeting a lady so *exceptional*.'
His eyes address me. 'But I am dedicated.'
To Anthony, 'Truly, dedicated to
the same good cause as you. The life of a friend
is no mere bauble. If dedication serves
as a token of trust, then you must let me call.'
To the Earl of Rutland, 'Come, we'll take our seats.'

He leaves me speechless, Anthony in sweat.
With *dedication*, he picked out the word
that signifies precisely what he knows.

For in order not to draw the hounds upon
those hands that helped me slip out from the noose,
and needing to launch my pseudonym in print
with works protected by a noble name,
with his permission, granted through his kin,
I dedicated both those poems to him.

A Change of Address

'We have to get you out of town.' My host,
turning his back as I step from the dress.

'I believe he can be trusted.'
                            Bacon sighs.
'Gossip follows him everywhere. As dogs
will follow the heels of every butcher's boy,
his beauty drags jealous tongues in tow. Besides,'
he turns for a moment, catching my bare skin,
then studies the wall again, 'I have to move.
I'm sunk with debt. The agents I maintain
abroad for the Earl of Essex from my purse
have proved too costly lately. And the rent
is two months overdue. I'm taking rooms
in Essex House, at my lord's invitation.
I can't bring you.'
                    I button up my shirt
and feel him watch me. 'I should leave you, then.
Go back on the road and take my chance.'
                                        'No, no,
I have a plan,' he says, grasping my hands.
'Come, let's go down for supper. I'll explain.'

He's generous with wine. 'So is this plan
that I pass out, you stuff me in a sack
and throw me in the Thames?'
                            He shakes his head,
amused. 'A Kittish joke. Not every kit
that seems unwanted ends up bound and drowned.
But the play restored your humour. I am pleased.'

He tears some bread with difficulty. He
has the gout again.
                    'That cough of history
is not the last,' I say. 'I'm put in mind
of another Richard.'
                    'You knew many Dicks,'
says Anthony, gamely.
                        'No, the royal sort.
Tell me your plan.'
                    He has to finish chewing.
Holds up a finger, swallows, sips some wine
and spills the arrangement: through a maternal aunt,
his relative is Sir John Harington,
a cousin of the Sidneys. Friend to poets.
He has a son in need of tutoring.

'In Rutland?'
                'At Exton. Burley on the Hill.
A fine house. Far enough away from here
to save you from pryers. But close enough for friends
to visit at Christmas, when I hear he lodges
over a hundred guests.'
                        'When should I go?'
'Tomorrow,' he says. 'My instinct tells me so.
I always heed my gut, when it persists
in griping pain. The last three hours were Hell.
To you, my friend.'
                    Our glasses rise and kiss.

How *Richard II* Followed *Richard III*

My brain's at work. What further history
chews on the flavours I have licked from life
like the tale of Bolingbroke? First, sent away
on the lies of false accusers, by his king –
that second Richard, limp as the third was lame –
and banished into exile, suffering
the loss of his native tongue, and his good name –
anguish as known to me as my own hand.

Then he returns, still loyal, yet conquering
the rank injustice that set him aside.
And just as my *Faustus* captured my own doom,
perhaps this script could write me back alive.

No, dream, but do not plot, dear Posthumous.
The way back into life is hard and strange
and doubtless more complex than I write some lines
and let God make them true for me. But this –
the thought of where I'll start, the opening scene,
inspires me. Imagine this, my dream.

BURLEY ON THE HILL

If I must be imprisoned, let it be
in a house like this one. If I must be kept
from all that once informed me I was free,
then give me marble floors, a sweeping drive,
three dozen colonnades. A stable block
more sumptuous than my father's cobbling shop.

Give me its broad façade, its generous arms
embracing those invited to approach;
its lofty chambers where the words of kings
can echo back from ceilings, magnified;
this hilltop seat, its broad commanding view
laying the country out like a tablecloth:

perspective, now, on all that I have lost
and all that I might conquer, given room.

CORRESPONDENT

A fine place to retire, if I were old.
A good position, if I favoured sleep
and didn't mind oblivion. A house
to settle in, as dust upon a stair.

Safe as a nut, for who can even find
the county on a map? Rutland's a fleck
in the eye of God, and I am holed in it,
hugged in the murder of inconsequence,
and teaching numbers to a three-year-old.

My host, discretion's knight, is deathly kind.
With paper freely given, I retreat
into the grand adventures of my head:
the plots and coups that forward history,
where I would be, with sword instead of pen,
in a finch's blink. Your letters urge me, *Wait*.

For Elizabeth to die? I could be dead
myself before the pampered girl expires.
My loyalty to her strung up this noose
that tightens slowly, day on gag-bound day;
the suffocating knowledge every play
my heart creates, lifts high another's name.

You ask if I, now well restored to health,
would not be more content in Italy,
with drier reds, and weather as a friend,
and not so tempted by the closeness of
the familiar haunts and homes of those I love.

I answer: this master keeps an open house.
All visitors welcome. There is here a man
who used to count your friendship as a jewel,
and how the sight of your face would bring relief
from endless lake and hill and cloud and sheep.

I sing and pretend and play the perfect guest.
I chant the alphabet for a rich man's son.
I finish the play that no one knows is mine.
Your letter arrives, saying you will not come.

Some dark wind huffed and made her manifest.

The first week of October. Coming in
from a stroll by Rutland water, I am met
by notes as strangely tuned in to my heart
as a mother's lullaby: faint in the hall,
but strong, insistent, as they beckon me
towards the drawing room where at the keys
of the virginals, a woman sits and plays
such melancholy music that my eyes
begin to fill. If she has noticed me
she doesn't break her step: indeed, she starts
to sing just as I wander through the door,
as though I am the ear she's waited for.
The song, in French, seems penned, alone, for me.

Sweet bird in exile – so the first line goes –
why do you sing so distantly of love?
Do you not know the cage has an open door?

I paraphrase; perhaps if I had seen
the words on the sheet I might find I was wrapped
in some sorcerer's illusion and the song
was a list of gizzards, scales, and contumely.
How could I tell? For watch me, I'm entranced.

She comes to the end and halts. 'Monsieur Le Doux?'
'How do you know my name? I don't know yours.'
'Excuse me. I was sent by Jaques Petit.'
Anthony's Gascon servant. 'With a message?'

'With just myself. I do apologise.'
She rises. 'Chevalier Harington is out?'
'Until tonight. The servants let you in?'
'With a letter from Jaques, who suggests I could be nurse
to Chevalier Harington's infant girl.'

                              Her eyes
have the promise of storms; a power that augurs change.
'Where should I wait? I don't know where to go.'

I sell my afternoon into her care.
She spills her story out as if her trust
were won just by my asking for her name.
'I go by Ide du Vault,' she says. 'Why laugh?
What's funny?'
               'Sorry, the name comes to the ears
as Hide the Fault, in English.' Hide the Fault.
Much more of a giveaway than Louis the Sweet.

She looks ashamed. Her eyes drop to her lap.
'That is the name I'm given for my sins
by a wicked man. A joke at my expense.
I see. And now I can't escape the joke,
for all my papers bear it.'
                    'It is false?'
She looks at me accusingly, my twin.
'No falser, I know, than yours.'
                      'What do you know?'
'Just that you're not a Frenchman,' she replies.
'Your accent's true: but the lascivious gaze
a Parisian would deliver has betrayed
you, by its absence, for an Englishman.'

So dangerously smart; so unafraid.
Yet vulnerable, for in the next rich braid
of the beautiful tale she's weaving, she reveals,
'I'm hiding from my husband.'

                             'You are married?'
'Unfortunately, yes. Though in that name
I shan't be known, I'm Madame Vallereine.'

So open, so bare, a field prepared by plough
for whatever seeds Fate plants; the ruffled wind
is lost on her. Her tongue reels out her woes
and reels me in upon them. How Monsieur
had betrayed her publicly, then set a slur
against her name to furnish his excuse –
'And all the eyes of Paris were upon me.'
Hers fall into her lap again. 'And he,
believing his own story when he drank
began to beat me also for the shame
I brought on to his head. Such wicked men—'
She broke her thoughts. 'I shouldn't speak of him.
He is a curse that gives me nightmares still.
For there are men who prey on women's minds.
I only hope you are not one of them.'

I try to look softer. 'I was raised with sisters
and a mother I respected.'

                       Though her head
shakes at this point in open disbelief
it's not my information, but her own
losses she's moved by, like a weather vane
bothered from both directions.

     'Do go on,'
I press her, gently, noticing a tear –
a tear as fiercely wiped as though it comes
from the scoundrel husband.

       'So one night I fled
to a nunnery in the hills. I did not say,
of course, I could not tell them I had wed
two years before. It's true I told them lies –
but also true, I gave my heart to Christ.
Still, when he found me—' Here she blanches white

and I will stop. For though a woman's tongue
will often shake off secrets, that report
does not become the listener's currency.
What matters is the love that had begun
to surge through my veins, like running down a hill
with the wind behind me, sure her body was
calling me with its longing; love so strong
that it washed me from my reason. I was won
the moment she lied to me and hooked the truth
of my own pretence. She was both warming sun
and rain on the shoots of hope, perched on that stool
with all the beauty of a ruined nun.

THE GAME

My mistress plucks my strings, and I am played
as expertly as any lute. She first
encourages, then shoos my love away,
reluctant to intensify my thirst.

She promises nothing. Sweet as nothings are
an urgent need for something keeps me up
long past the hours where lovers sigh at stars,
wishing my love were pure, and not corrupt.

Wrapped in her arms, with all my hope unwrapped;
between her legs, and breathing in her must,
she chides I mustn't. I am free, yet trapped,
a moth who beats his own wings into dust.

As she completes me, so I fall apart.
Love then, my Muse. For she has all the art.

PETIT

December chills the sheets. Much warmer they
become when doubly occupied. She stops
resisting me, my garrulous, lovely Ide,
to obtain my furnace in her bed. The month
brings more than sharpening frost and softening thighs.

A party descends, two weeks before the feast
is due to start, some forty men and maids
on horse, on foot, in carriage. It's the Earl
and Countess of Bedford, daughter of Sir John.

With Jaques Petit. He is a stick-limbed man,
plucked from his mother's dugs too soon, a face
like a smear of butter on a stale bread roll.
Yet Anthony sends him; and with him, a list
of friends who will descend here presently:
a Christmas to crown all Christmases!

                       A glow
must shine from me as I extricate myself
and this knowledge from the room; first Jaques Petit
attempts to trip me on the stairs with 'What
did my master say of me?' I freeze. The sheer
effrontery is baffling. 'If he
had wanted you to know, assure yourself,
he would have scribed in French,' I say. His flinch
is measurable. His spine contorting like
a sausage shrinking over flame. 'But you
will recommend me to Sir John, perhaps?
To stay for Christmas?' And a smeary smile
is plastered on with effort.

　　　　　　　　　'When he asks
to see me,' I say. 'He's with his daughter now.'
I'm turning on my heel when he remarks,
'Be careful with the woman.'
　　　　　　　　　　　　　　　'Woman, sir?'
'Miss Ide du Vault. Her tongue is very free.
I do not think it wise—'
　　　　　　　　　　　　　'Excuse me, sir,'
I interrupt, 'but you exceed your place.
Did Anthony speak of Miss du Vault?'
　　　　　　　　　　　　　　　　　'No, sir.'
'Then neither shall we. Good day, Monsieur Petit.'

The manner of the Frenchman bothers me,
but I brush it from my mind, as one might brush
a cobweb from a velvet sleeve. My friends,
Southampton among them, coming here! Again
the joy so strong it draws into my path
its opposite – the darkness of my love,
who is pouting more than usual because
of Jaques Petit's arrival. He it was
who gave her the punning name, apparently.

'He's full of evil, as an egg-bound hen
is full of egg,' she says.
　　　　　　　　　　　　'Sorry, my love?'

'That stupid man you left not seconds ago
fawning and crawling. Petty Jack. The spy
from Anthony Bacon's house.'

　　　　　　　　　　　'Shush! He's no spy.
Anthony's sound. We're friends. The man is just
obsequious. Loves Anthony too much

and the rest of us too little, for the threat
or competition that we pose. My love—'

'Love is for later on. The letter he brought.
It lit you like a candle, and you ran
away from us all to read it, like a cat
who caught a bird. Since I share all with you –
most intimately – what will you share with me?'

'My body,' I say, stroking her shoulder.
                                        'No,
you cannot sell me what's already mine.
I have your body. I would know your mind.
The letter. What moved you?'

                        'It is just some news.'
She waits.
        'Of friends,' I say.
                        She's waiting still,
her tongue ticking against her palate.
                                'Friends
who are coming to visit.'
                'So!' she says, and smiles.
'I will know more, but not in corridors.
The rest you will tell me when we are alone.'

With her tongue on my thigh, unholy in its course,
intent on torturing out of me the name
that most delighted me. 'So he's an earl?'
A fire is blazing in the grate. A touch
of her lips, like coals.
                I groan, 'So you're a nun?'

She laughs like broken glass. 'A woman has
so many faces. I have worn the veil.'

'You didn't learn this at the convent.'
                                        'No.'
She leans back on her elbow, drags her hair
across my belly like a paintbrush. 'No,
the skill is natural. It comes from liking.'
'You have experience.'
                    Her eyes grow dark
as if turned inwards. 'What have I to sell
except the thing men most desire, myself?
My flesh is only ever a hired mount.
My heart, I'm saving.'
                    'Saving for me?'
                                    'Perhaps.
If it pleases me. And then I will move on.
Perhaps I'll move on now,' she teases, 'go
to the other wing and find myself a man
who does not keep such secrets.'
                                'Ide—'
                                    'Not Ide!
Call me my name, Lucille. And tell me yours.'

'I can't. It's dangerous.'
                        She makes a noise
like swallowing poison; turns her head away
when I see her eyes have filled with sudden tears.
She shrugs off the hand I reach to her, 'No good,'
she says. 'No good, we do not use the names
that we were born with. Lovers should be true
to themselves, they should be honest.'
                                    'Ide—'
                                        'Lucille!'

She's half across the room now, every inch
as naked and angry as a trodden snake.
More blaze in eye than grate. 'My name's Lucille.
And what is yours?'
                           She looks so beautiful,
my sulky temptress, that the ache for her
might almost conquer reason.
                                    'Here. Lucille.
Come back to bed.'
                           Her skin, so biscuit brown,
shivers a little.
                    'Not without your name.
I do not sleep with strangers any more.'

The fire spits some gobs upon the hearth
of wood it has rejected, all in flame.

'There is a tale attached to it,' I say.
'And you must hear the whole tale in my arms
if you're to have my name. For they are one,
the name, the story, and they must be held
between two lovers, closer than the child
that might come from that union. Lie down.
I promise you, you will be satisfied.'

So in her bed, with all the house asleep,
kissing her neck to warm her up to me,
I make her promise on a future child
(which I may plant in her, should luck decree)
to keep to herself the story I'll reveal
or know her tongue itself will be the axe
that severs her lover's head, and turns these lips
cold and unyielding as the winter ground.

The thrill of being entrusted with my life
quickens her sighs, and she responds as wild
as I have known love, tugging me inside
and reaching instantly that mounded peak
few women ever climb: two stops of breath,
then blushes flooding to her chest and cheek
like soldiers running on to battlefields
when war is over. Softened,
                            'Tell me more,'
she says, half satisfied. 'What is your crime?
What do you hide? Who are you, man of mine?'

WILL HALL

Come. Am I stupid? Maybe for as long
as it took to watch her climax on the thought
she could be the death of me. A woman's tongue
is looser than a man's, and half as loyal.
Desire, which might have told her everything,
grew sober to feel her hot, unruly mouth
feed fiercely on my danger. So I switched
the name in an instant. And the name I gave
bore ounces of truth for being worn before
in government service; so nudged past her doubt,
though she did repeat it twice: 'Will Hall? Will Hall.'
And chewed on it, momentarily. 'How strange.
I had an inkling of another name.'

'What name?'
                'Oh, you would laugh at me.'
                                        'Not so.'
'I thought perhaps I was kissing Kit Marlowe.'

'Why him?' I say too quickly. Then, 'Who's he?'
'You silly, the man who wrote the play,' she says,
'about the Paris massacre. There is –
you must know, there is rumour that he lives?'

My heart is beating like a captured bird.
'He died in a house in Deptford. In a fight.'

'He was a wanted man. It is too neat.
I like to think he lives,' she says. 'Don't you?'

'Not if you'd leave my arms for his,' I say.
'What made you think I was him, anyway?'

'I don't know. Something. That you hide away
all day in your room, just writing – don't deny!
The ink is here on your fingers, look!' She holds
my hand to my face for evidence. 'And that
you pretended to be French. He wrote in French.
And the name, Le Doux, I thought could be a joke
that one so dark could call himself "The Sweet".
So why are you hiding? What for, the pretence?
Who do you run from? What is your offence?'

I tell her a little of my narrative.
The part that does belong to William Hall,
the government agent who was sent to Prague
to mix with necromancers, alchemists,
and sniff out the Catholic plot that cursed an earl –
my former good Lord Strange – towards a death
of sudden twisting poison. She is quiet.
'But why must you hide?'
                              'So I will not be next.'
'And what do you write all day?'
                              'Religious tracts.
Pamphlets to turn the Catholics from sin.
I publish them beneath a pseudonym.'

'I've seen such things,' she says. 'They are' – she smiles –
'useful to wipe oneself upon I think.
What a pity you're not Kit Marlowe.'
                              'Why?'
                                        'Because.

For him I have a passion. You, perhaps,
have grown a little stale for me.' She turns
her back as though she's keeping shop and must
now tend another customer.
                    'Lucille.'

She doesn't answer. 'When I write those tracts
I make things up, you know.' The fire now
is burning lower, crouching in its grate,
but my bare need is fuelled by her rejection
and I must heed the ache. 'Imagination
can be a place to stoke desire, Lucille.'
She breathes as though asleep.

                                     'We could pretend.
I could be any man you want.'

                                      'Of course,'
she sighs into the pillow.

                             'I could be
pretending to be Will Hall.' Her shoulders shrug.
'I hope so. William is my husband's name.
I have too many Wills already.'

                                    Yes,
and one more than she knows. 'Perhaps you could
imagine me Kit Marlowe.'

                          Now she turns
and smiles with teeth.

                        'So tell me I am right.'
'You're right, Lucille. You found me out.'

                                These words
unlock her like a casket full of jewels,
and I have her glittering eyes, her ruby tongue
suddenly willing. 'You are famous, then?'
she coos, stroking my cheek. 'Oh, infamous.'

'Tell me again how famous!'

                             'You yourself
had heard of me in France.' 'Yes, as a rogue!'
'And the playwright of *The Massacre*.' 'Say more!'

I talk her to her climax seven times.

'What would they do to you?' 'They'd make me dead
as I'm supposed to be.' She chews my arm;
she grinds her pelvis into me; she groans.

And is she done? She sighs. 'But people know.
Your friends know.' 'Some of them.' 'How can you hope
to keep yourself a secret?' 'No one talks.'
I flop beside her, grateful her desire
has come to some conclusion. Not so mine.
'They know the danger to myself, and them.
In any case, the Queen has sealed it tight.
She has me writing plays, just as she likes,
but through her censors. She would not be pleased
to have me exposed and killed. That I still live
is purely through her will.'
                                         'She has a will?'
She giggles. 'She has grown too manly then,
in her man's position. I prefer this will.'
She seeks it out and grips it.

                              Why the mind,
so glorious in all it apprehends
should be encased in flesh, I do not know.
And why its workings shudder, stall and drop
to the call of base desire's a mystery
no priest has ever purposed. Thus enslaved,
I lose all higher sense, all urgent goal
except the spilling of myself, in her.

'Call me his name,' I urge, 'call me his name.
Tell me you want Kit Marlowe.' And she does:

the name huffed out of her with every thrust
resurrects me by degrees. My hungry corpse
fiercely asserts its need for life and love,
like the soldier soon to risk his all in war.

And afterwards, the silence almost throbs
with the bruise of my forbidden name. What chance
that the walls, or sleep, contained it? 'I must go,'
I whisper, though I sense she isn't there,
but in a dream of goose-down infamy,
fresh bedded by the rogue she thinks is me.

I pull on clothes, now greyed out by the dawn
and make for my room. But as I cross the floor
I swear that something scuttles from the door.

Yet I was not uncovered, and the quiet
that hung over breakfast tables, white as cloth
prepared for a christening, was shaken off
in under an hour by more distracting things:

the Countess of Bedford's evident delight
at the Christmas plans, which she swore quite the best
of the fifteen years since she was born. 'See here,'
she squealed to her father, waving in his face
the letter that occasioned her to dance.

'The Earl of Southampton's hiring Pembroke's Men
to come from London with a play. A play!
How wonderful! Let's hope a joyous one,
full of romance and clowning.'

                                   Lutes and drums
were in her head, but I thought, *One of mine.*
He's bringing one of mine.

                            'And Rutland too,
with quite an *entourage*.' She mouthed the French
with gusto that the dogs around her feet
took as a cue to whine as though they sensed
a hare on the lawns outside.
                            'Twelve days of fun!'
She twirled with the thought of 'Lords and ladies here!
So many lovely gentlefolk!'
                        My mind
was stuck on the play, what play, and would the cast

be old familiars, fooled by no disguise?
Until a certain name fell from her tongue.
Undid me, straight.
                    '. . . and Thomas Walsingham!'

STOPPED

Could time run slower? Only if God's hand
were pressed against the sun to keep it still.
If shadows made to inch across the floor
were painted in their places. Come. Please come.
Before the weight of waiting buries me.

The boy's sums take for ever. Afternoons
grow whiskers, even though the days are short.
And nights would stop completely, but for Ide
pestering me to look into her eyes.
'What's wrong with you?' she says. 'Where have you gone?'
I say I'm nowhere but between her thighs.

But I'm lost in you, beyond my boots in you,
and the blessed future day when you arrive.

Dogs

A faithful dog, I raise my head to see
each visitor arrive. It's never you.
The hurt of half imagining your arms
on a coach's door, or seeing at the end
of the drive, on horseback, someone of your frame
melting to unfamiliar on approach
has steeled me thus: I'll have no faith in you.
I'll not believe you're coming till you do.

I immerse myself in scripting thwarted love
while the hubbub grows around me. Christmas Eve,
and a hundred guests expected down below
as I scratch doomed love towards oblivion.
A knock, as soft as a servant's, come to feed
some logs to the fire.
                        'Come,' I say. 'Come in,'
intent on my sentence, finishing the line
before I sense no housemaid at the grate
but a solid, watchful presence.
                              'Hello, Kit.'

And there you are, like a month of blessed rain
on a field of sun-blanched wheat: too much, too late,
and yet embraced at once. I clasp your flesh
like a storm would tear me from your mast, the chair
I've abandoned faking a gunshot as it falls.
I hold you like a once abandoned babe
clings to its mother, though your arms, round me,
seem hesitant, as though you're scared to touch
something so live, so hot, so not the same.

You smell of Kent. You smell of Scadbury.

'I dare not let you go,' I tell your ear,
and feel your breath draw in. 'And yet you must' –
you unclasp my arms as gently as you might
undo the bonds of a prisoner soon to hang –
'or how can I look a dear friend in the face?'

Your own is plagued by nervousness. 'The door—'
'I'll lock the door,' I say. 'Don't move an inch.'
And you obey, as if the world will fall
should you exhale. There is a chill in you
like you brought the outside inside.
                                        'You are cold.
You've only just arrived?' I feed the fire
with all the logs there are. 'That ought to help.
Sit down,' I say, and offer you the chair,
put right on its feet, while I perch on the bed.

'Tom, I'm so glad you came. I thought perhaps—'
Though words are what I worship, mine are lame
straight from the mouth, uncrafted. 'You had said
you wouldn't come.'

                        'That was the safest course.'
Your eyes are troubled. You barely look at me
as though afraid I really am long dead,
a spectral illusion. My own eyes are slaves
to the face I worked so hard to conjure up
that effort erased each feature over time:
they relish and restore to me the slant
of cheek, of neck, of nose, the different hues
within your hair. I wait for your voice, which comes

like a rumble over mountains: 'Kit, I fear
I put us both in danger being here.'

I reach to take your hand. Cold as a bed
no one has slept in, but the pulse in it
connects me to your heart. 'But, Tom, you came.
You cast off fear and came. What made you come?'

Twelve weeks without a letter was the start.
And as you told the tale of how you'd sat,
your heart as heavy as a mason's stone,
at Chislehurst Common, at the crossroads there,
unable to point your horse towards your home,
or spur her to chase a chosen compass point,
my heart rose up to kiss the thought of you
statued by doubt, and every ounce of me
sang that your strange paralysis was love.

The smallest tug of your arm, and you are mine.
You are the puppy suddenly, and I
the master commanding that you kiss my face.

The strangest transformation's wrought by fear:
you are quite melted, subject to my will.
Though all these thirty months you've held like rock
to a separateness, you now consent like snow
consents to its thawing underneath the sun;
consent to let me in, consent we're one.

So let the fire crackle that perfect hour
when we, again, go deeper now than friends,
swim in our Hellespont, and hope to drown.

FRIEND

You dress yourself; each button carefully
replaced in its hole as though it never left.
The evening lights you coldly, now the fire
has dimmed to embers. It is only six,
just gone, and the house below us thrums *halloo*
as the hunting set return.

                        'Thomas, you said—'
It's hard to be naked when you're fully dressed;
I pull my shirt on also. 'When I left,
you said you couldn't follow me because
some might suspect your role in it.'

                            Your boots
are going on now, laces tugged as tight
as a good spy's cover story. 'That's still true.'

I picture the cobbler measuring your calf;
of how you'd talk more easily with him
than you do with me.
                 I say, 'But time has passed . . .'

Your eyes stay with the laces, concentrate:
this notch, that hole, criss-cross. 'Nothing has changed,'
you say. Then glancing up, 'We cannot be
together, Kit. You want a dozen whys?
Because you're dead. Because you're known in Kent.
Because I have a house and estate to run.
Because what we are sometimes drawn to do
is a capital crime. Because I want a wife—'

You read my eyes and save the other seven.
I'm washed up into tears so easily
that I might be your wife, but for one thing.

'Sorry.' You watch the floor as though your words
are spilt on the rug between us. 'Kit, I swore
I wouldn't—'
             You leave me to fill the line.

I don't oblige. I concentrate on dressing
to distract me from the tightness in my chest.
As long as I'm turned away from you, you stare:
I feel it hot as a brand upon my skin,
an undisguised desire to drink me in
that slides to the fixtures when I look your way.

I shiver.
        'Come sit by me. It's warmer here.'
I move as I'm bid. Again, you apologise,
and this time touch my arm. So you're forgiven.

'Nobody doubts I'm dead?'
                  I watch your eyes
rest anywhere but on me, like the bee
that lights from flower to flower. 'Not nobody.
But mostly, yes, your death is very famous.
More famous than your life was.' There, a smile
like the sort I knew of old. A tug at me.
I sneeze; the thought of my death is full of cold.

'But you might safely visit me abroad,
if I'm forced abroad again?'

Your sigh's released
like old tobacco smoke: 'It won't be safe.'

You pick up the poker, stir the dying fire.
'Kit, I can't live pretence. For years my job
was setting up secret schemes, devising lies
for others to populate – and I can bite
as hard on my tongue as any man, but not
if I'm in your company. Who are you now?
Will Hall? Louis Le Doux? What if I slip,
one night, in the grip of wine, and call you Kit
in a public place? It only takes one ear,
one English-speaking, sly, take-profit ear
to root through my history and dig you up –
and snap, you're jigging on a hangman's rope
and your heart cut out still beating. No, I'll not
be a part of it. It's bad enough I'm here
to spend Christmas with you. I should not have come.'

Again, constriction. You, the conjuror
whose words alone can starve me of my breath.
Just one word more, and I might turn to stone.

You prod and poke, and tiny tongues of fire
burst into silent speech, and then subdue.
Somewhere, I find inside of me, your name.
'Tom—'
        'I believed—'
                We stall.
                        'You first,' I say.

But a knock at the door is first. It is a maid
with a supper tray, and wine: 'Monsieur Petit

said I should bring it for your gentleman.
He said the two of you would dine alone.'

As if he had intruded in the flesh,
all thin-stretched smile and stale obsequious French,
a flicker of annoyance finds me words.

'Monsieur Petit has overreached himself –
but as it comes, this suits us very well.
The fire is dying also – will you tend it?'
She bobs, and in her smile, the signature
of a private joke unnerves me. She brings wood
stacked up like consequences. When she leaves
we break the bread in silence.

                      'What I lost—'
I take a gulp of wine to steel my blood.
Afraid of what is written on my face,
you blurt, 'Say nothing more. I understand.'

No appetite at all, I watch you chew
until obliged to say it anyway.
'What keeps me hidden is my love of you.'

You swallow. 'Then love me constantly,' you say,
'if you cannot love yourself.'
                      'What's there to love?'
And I begin the list of all my faults.
And you turn off the faucet with a kiss,
your only weapon.

                'Kit, you must stay hidden.'
There is a quiver in you, in your eyes.

I suddenly understood your presence there
was underwritten not by love, but fear.
You feared that I was breaking. Hence, you came.
And after that, I watched you differently.
As a lover who gifts his mistress beauty's dress,
but then insists she never take it off.

'I'm not the only thing that keeps you sane.
You've said it yourself before, you live to write.'

A sudden laugh downstairs. All out of time
with our private bartering, yet to my ears
the laugh of the universal gods. 'I do.
What else do I have but writing? Where my friends
and drinking used to be, or riding down
to the river for a boat, or afternoons
engaged in the playful fare of theatres,
there's pen and paper and those endless hours
in which to fill it.'
                              'You speak bitterly.'

As if to sweeten me, you fill my cup.
Drink loosens resistance. Still I play along
to numb the pain of understanding you.

'If there were no hope, Tom, I might be restored
to my former life and reputation—' Here,
my mind lets go and free-falls at the thought,
unable to fill that gaping 'if'.

                    'Oh, Kit,'
you say, and though my name means more than gold,
and to hear you speak it still delights my heart,

that Oh, that empty Oh's another hole
that can't arrest my falling.
                              'Do you think
I can't be rescued? I can't be restored?'

Your eyes, which testify the truth of this,
look anywhere but mine. 'We worked so hard
to have this lie believed. It isn't time
to undermine it. They would have you killed.'
'Who, they?'
                    'Archbishop Whitgift and the rest.
Come on, Kit, nothing's changed. You can't go back
to the life we've buried. There is nothing left.'

Your silence closes like a coffin lid.

The fire spits something burning at my feet;
you stamp it out.

                    'So there's no hope for me?'

'All hope is in our current plan,' you say.
'The plan to keep you writing, and alive.'

'But no one knows it's me.'
                              'That is the point!'
Infuriation shoots you to your feet
and you settle, swaying, plant yourself more solid
before you say, 'You have to live with it.'

'What if I can't?' I watch you steadily.
Your eyes are focused on the fire whose light
flares up in them.

'Then you will die for it.
And I will swing beside you.'

                    Dearest friend,
I wondered then if it was me or you
that you feared most for. I'd not have you dead
through any fault of mine. Should death weigh hard,
I'll take my life alone, in privacy.

I felt that night you had abandoned me.
Forgive me, then, if I abandoned you.

Hal

Deserts stay rainless year on chafing year.
Then glutted with months of water in a night
they bloom, their hidden sand-beleaguered seeds
seeming to conjure flowers out of air
in sudden, excessive beauty. My blessings too
fell fast and all at once.

                    Coming downstairs
from supper with you, into the banquet hall
they clear now for a dance, I glimpse his hair
and the glowing face of the girl he's talking to.
You notice I've stopped, and must retrace three steps
to hiss at me, 'Don't stare.' My feet are stuck,
so thank you for the words. They are a jolt.
'Your obsession with that boy's insufferable.'

Your eyes are angry, and your mouth's a wound.
Insufferable is right. I too have wished
his beauty didn't draw me like a sword
I cannot wield, which cuts me constantly.

And yet I'm drawn. As I reach his side, you've gone,
slipping away as thieves do in a crowd,
unwilling to make believe. This is a move
too dangerous for you.

                    'Monsieur Le Doux!'
I'm beckoned close to meet the youth I know
too well, and not at all. 'Young Henry Wriothesley,
the Earl of Southampton. Meet Louis Le Doux.'
Sir John's a little drunk. Southampton turns

and a ripple passes through him. So intent
does his gaze become, the girl is melted free
from his company as wax from flame. 'Le Doux?'
Cracking his voice, a hint of broken boy.
'I believe I met your wife some weeks ago.'
His lips smile playfully. 'At the theatre.'

'At a public playhouse? Surely not!' Sir John
puffs stiffly.
                    Southampton soothes our host: 'Sir John,
the Queen herself brings those same plays to Court
as highly suitable for men and women
of the finest breeding.' And to me, 'Was it
your wife?' The boy must play. All his delight
is focused on how I'll answer him.
                                            Breathe in,
exhale. 'My lord, forgive me, but I fear
you must be mistaken, for I am not married.'

He can't resist. 'Perhaps it was your sister?
Now I think of it, there was a likeness there . . .'

'My mistress, perhaps,' I say.

                            'Too many dogs!'
Sir John barks, shocking us silent till we see
he's waving his arms at servants, and the hounds
marauding beneath the table. 'Get them out!'
and he stamps away.

                    The laugh is a relief,
and the absence of his ears a blessing too.

'Kit, how are you?'
                              'Le Doux!' I say, alarmed.
'My lord, though I would have it otherwise,
we're not alone.' As if to make my point
young Rutland brushes past us with his arm
on the waist of Lucy Harington. The room
is light with Christmas, crammed with gentlemen,
their wives and sisters. Yet between we two
the air is close and intimate.

                              '"My lord"?
Surely the time has come to call me Hal.
I loved your poems. The second was very dark,
but the story clear. You are the nightingale,
singing of your destruction. Have a glass
of wine.'

              He puts his own into my hand,
and takes another from a passing tray.
The spot where his lips have kissed the sheen away,
he turns towards my own. 'You need a drink
to warm you through.'

                              'My lord, it isn't safe,'
I say. 'The tongue behaves like an unschooled child
when doused in wine or ale. I am the proof.'

'The smallest sip,' he says. 'The smallest sip.'

So, yes, I press my lips where his have been
and taste a draught of his intoxicant.

He smiles at me. 'So many things aren't safe,
yet pleasurable. Come to my chamber, then.
But you shan't enter till you call me Hal.'

'And may another know this Hal?'
                              It's Ide,
all bosoms in her dress, or largely out,
and lips as wide as the Thames at Deptford Strand.

'The Earl of Southampton. Ide du Vault,' I say,
and watch her almost spill out of her dress
as she curtsies deeply. 'Please forgive me, sir.
I'm French. And may be "tipsy", that's the word?'

For a moment, he is fazed, as if his wit
were wiped by the candid beauty of her face,
erased by her perfection. 'Miss du Vault,
you are forgiven.' Lifting up her chin
to fall into the disaster of her eyes.

It's clear at once: he's struck. Her look alone
transforms reluctant boy to aching man,
turns Ganymede to Zeus. One glimpse of her
could pull the moon to hang before her face,
abandoning its celestial course to stare
lovingly into her oblivion.

She senses instantly her hook is in,
and takes my arm to sink it deeper. 'My
Monsieur Le Doux has mentioned you before.'

'I don't recall,' I say. She says, 'Of course.
You were asleep.
                    He will talk in his sleep,'
she says to my lovely boy, all matter-of-fact,
as though she hasn't strung me from her keel
as she ploughs her way towards him.

                              'Is that so?'
Southampton eyes me archly. 'Walls are thin
in the tutors' quarters?'
                              'Thinner than the wing
of a butterfly,' she says, so prettily
that I forgive her everything. 'But I
can keep a secret. If I have my Will.'

I swear the woman spoke in capitals.
Her meaning landed there upon his face
in a look of intrigue. 'Then you must come too.'

'Must come? To what?' All wine and innocence.

'To a private party hosted in my rooms
just after midnight.'

                              'What – with only men?
You have mistaken me for someone else,
Monsieur my lord.' But hangs there like a fly.
A dazzling fly, all emerald and lace.
And when, for a moment, she has turned her face,
he grabs my arm: 'And you must come at ten.'

YOUR FOOL

I find you waiting in my room, your face
an accusation.
                        'What? Two years alone
and I should stay a hermit? Never trust
another living soul apart from you?
You think that after all these friendless months,
just one should be enough? You're going away.
You said so.'
                'Kit—'
                        'I have lost everything!
My reputation. Work. The very name
my parents had me blessed with at the font
is flushed like so much turd into the ditch.
Am I to sit here cloistered like a monk?
What's left to nourish me that I should pass
on this sudden feast of friendship?'

                                'Kit, you're drunk.'
The disappointment sinks you to my bed.

'What if I am? What is the bastard point
of sobriety?' You flinch. 'And it's not wine.
I'm drunk on the rush of feeling loved again.
And if it's fleeting, all the more reason why
I should have my fill of it.' What's in your eyes
is sobering, however, and it brings
me to my knees in front of you: the boards
as hard and cold as penitence. 'My fill.
Yet you would be enough for me, I swear,
if you would make a promise . . .'

                         'Kit, the girl.'
'The girl?'
           'The dark-skinned girl. Hung off your arm.'
The supplicant's position I am in
has weakened me, and chafed against your mood.
I stand, brush off my knees.
                         'Who is she, Kit?
I've never seen a woman look so knowing.
What have you shared with her? And who is she?'

I stalk across to the window.
                       'Jesus' balls!
What have I shared? Who is she? Tom, a wife
would ask less prying questions. She has been
my comfort, is all.'

               'You cannot be familiar,'
you say, 'with anyone. What does she know?'

I bite my lip.
              'She knows I am not French.'

Your eyes say *idiot*.
                'What could I do?
She's French! She knows a Frenchman from a nail.'
You punch the bed, send up a cloud of dust –
both your dead skin and mine launched into air –
then stand, your hands in fists, as though you might
punch me for satisfaction.

                    Dearest friend,
        forgive me, that I keep our argument
        fresh in my head as new earth on a grave.
        Had you not left, I would have more to save,
        but can't discard this moment, or its pain.

'There's quicker forms of suicide,' you say.
'And ones that don't put friends' necks in the noose.'

People are leaving. Carriages outside
rattle towards the gatehouse.
                            'Tom—'
                                    'And worse
you've let Southampton in on it.'
                                    'That's not
my fault! I met him at the theatre.'

Your eyes roll to the panelling above
as if you hope for God to intervene
and bring the ceiling down. I'd been so ill,
I want to say, if you had seen me thin
you'd take me to the theatre yourself –
for all the risk – to let some life back in.

'Your obsession with the earl cannot protect
you from his fickleness. You are his pet.
And now his thrilling secret. But be sure
the moment he sniffs disaster, he will shrug
you off like last year's codpiece.'

                            And the rest,
the comparison with you, you leave unsaid.
Your loyalty thickens in my heart, like glue.

'You've lain with him?'
                'Never!'
                                'But you've lain with her.'

I cannot lie to you; you read the Yes
in my dumb response. And like a beleaguered boat,
you half set sail, then lurch back to my dock,
quietly sinking.
                'Tom. This all stops here.
I promise. But be with me.' I pull you close.

At first you are a sack of wheat; your arms
hung loosely at your side. But then your breath
responds to my kisses, and the huge machine
of mutual longing slides us into bed.

THE AUTHORS OF SHAKESPEARE

You cannot know how often I replay
our conversations in my head. Your voice
inhabits the space where friendship used to be,
which rattles less when I rehearse these scenes,
tell them like bedtime stories, tell them fresh
for ears beyond our own, should one day this
sad tome of cipher meet posterity.

I see us clearly: pillowed in our sweat,
recovering our breath and sanity
in the gentle flicker of fire and candlelight;
coverlet kicked to the floor, a trail of clothes
like offerings to the god of sodomy.

What livens our bed-talk is the threat of death;
the scythe of its humour cutting me my lines.

'You said you would not have me here, and yet,
I do perceive you've had me thoroughly.'

Though serious, your smile's no more contained
than a rabbit captured in an open sack,
and yet you say,
                        'I *would* not have you here.
My Kit—' Your hand, a blessing on my cheek,
removed. 'I swear to God, you are not safe.
The public are sheep and fall for any lie,
but private rumours circulate amongst
the curious and literate in town.
A lawyer playwright told me in faith last week
that *William Shakespeare*'s not a real name.'

'He's a real man!'
                    'But not that can be seen.
He comes to London only twice a year.
Picks up a play from Bacon, drops it off,
collects his cash. He is invisible.
To all intents and purposes, not here.
The masses are none the wiser, but the cream
of literate society suspects
the name's a front for someone else.'
                                    'For me?'
'For Bacon. Or the Earl of Oxford.'
                                    'What?'

'Don't be offended, Kit! You had a death
more documented than most royalty.
The lewder gossips spin it off in yarns
you could strangle cats with. Since you're loudly dead,
the suspects are the living.'
                              'Oxford, though.
The man's a nincompoop. He churns out verse
fit only for lighting fires.'
                              'It could be worse.'
'How so?'
            'They could be gossiping it's you.
The clues you keep leaving, Kit, for pity's sake.
As if your style itself weren't badge enough
for your friends to work it out. Your enemies
must be gifted nothing. *Non licit exigius*.
Let them chase shadows. Let them not chase Kit.'

These words float from that bed across the years.
And thus, the Turnip kept my greatest prize
and earned for his silence more than I was paid

for my verbosity. That a man discreet
as a bolted door, by nature taciturn,
should be rewarded handsomely to keep
counsel, is like a housecat crowned a king
for being good at sleep. And yet I knew
he could be trusted not to puff and crow –
and never claim he wrote them: only show
his face, and not his handwriting for then
he'd show he was a stranger to the pen
and risk his death as well as mine. So. So.

'Let them chase shadows. Let them not chase Kit.'

Writing these words I sense the tenderness
your staunch good sense kept from me. Finding my fist
resting against my lips, I kiss that flesh
lightly, as if to say, again, goodbye.

Mr Disorder

'Who are you watching?'

                You, in winter garb,
mounting a chestnut mare, exchanging talk
with our host in a cloud of breath.

                        'It's just the hunt.'

I came down to the east wing's sitting room
for a panorama of your exit scene
through its windows' tall, wide-open eyes. Ignoring
my mistress installed in a chair, and quietly sewing.

Lucille is clipped. 'I have been hunting you.
Three days you've avoided me.'

                        'I have been ill.'
'You don't look ill.'

                I answer 'You're a nurse
as well as a nun?'

                'I'm more things than you know.
Today a seamstress. This dress has a tear
would make a harlot blush.' I turn to see
the green dress she was wearing Christmas Eve;
her smile as she sews the rent across the breast.

'How did that happen?'

                   '*Chéri*! Do you care?'
'Sarcasm doesn't suit you.'

                  'Nor do lies
suit you. Your friend is leaving now?'

                        'He is.'

'He won't stay for theatricals tonight?'

Horses are stamping in the yard; the hounds
sniffing and milling round their hoofs. But you
will head not for the fox, but for the south.

'Pity, I hear the play is very good.
If a little bloody.'

                    Titus Andronicus.
You couldn't bear to see the players come.
Or watch Southampton's surreptitious gaze
in my direction as my words were staged.
You found the play 'too vengeful, anyway'.
'Forgiveness,' you said, 'might bless you. Not revenge.'

You kiss the countess's hand. Some final words.
From the portico, a thin-lipped Jaques Petit
steps forward, slides a letter in your hand.
You tuck it in your breast, oblivious.

'He calls you Mr Disorder.'
                    'Who?'
                              'Petit.'

Despite the window's frost, I watch you leave
through a clearing my hand has made upon the glass:
a static wave you never turn to see.
How perfectly you have forsaken me.

'Do you not care?' she says.
                    Do I not care?

I care beyond all measure, and my heart,
already three-way splintered, sinks with lead.

'I've been called worse,' I say.

                              'He is a rat,'
she says. 'He means to poison everything.'
I turn. She is unpicking stitches made
in anger's error. 'I don't like the man.'

'What do you know about him?'
                              'Only that
he stirs the gossip in the servants' hall.
And often enough, I leave my room to find
him in the corridor, starting away.'

'Perhaps he is protecting you.'
                              She snorts.
'Write to your Anthony. Tell him he must leave.'

You're at the gatehouse, now, and rein the mare
to the right. A six-day ride to Scadbury.

'I think he's here for me.' Said absently,
but her hiss gets my attention. 'I despair!
The man is running rumours, sure as rain.'

Yet Anthony's trust was not won easily.
And though the man was welcome as a flea,
obsequious and greased with copious smarm,
he seemed to serve a purpose. And perhaps
that purpose was to keep this ghost from harm.

She folds the dress across the chair, as if
it is the limpest girl, dragged from a lake,
and comes to my side. Her hand is on my cheek
as tenderly as yours has ever been,
and plants a simple need that I be held
as if you'd never left, and she was you.

I go to kiss her.

            'No,' she says, 'not safe.
No more for you till you shoo that rat away.'

REVENGE TRAGEDY

The real play is offstage. It's her and him:
the Lord of Gorgeous and my fatal nun.
She's squeezed beside him, palms beneath her chin,
pretending to watch, but gleefully as sin
distracting him with whispers. I'm the one
he should be eyeing, yet he's eyeing her,
as if forgetting who the play was for.
The once or twice he glances, I am stern
and he half guilty, like a man disturbed
in the act of stealing ripe fruit from a tree
that tickles his fence. Now hungry, now unsure
whether it's right to lord it over me.

While players strut, while boys bake in a pie,
while throats are cut – she hums the line, 'Say aye.'

So

Example of foolish thought love makes occur:
'I'll win his heart with poems about her.'

In Disgrace with Fortune and Men's Eyes

Three weeks have passed since I last scratched a note
to you in this book of sorrows. I confess
I've written only sonnets to a lord,
sliding them, nightly, underneath his door
adorned with the initials 'W.S.'

As well you are not here. As well that I
shan't send the bulk of this until my death.
As well it's all in cipher, for Petit,
I know, has 'borrowed' papers from my desk.
Nothing of consequence: I do take care,
despite your certainty that I'm a fool;
my drafts are burnt before I leave the room.
But he is always up and down the stairs,
outside my door, or hers; cleaning his shoes,
wiping a smirk, pretending to polish air.

More of him later. First, I want to say
forgive the weakness that your absence spawned;
this dawn tiptoeing for want of him, or her.
Love is the only point of drawing breath,
and I'm marooned without it. The poems seemed –
given Hal's love for those I wrote before –
my only power. But so much for art.
My stormy, merciless mistress has his heart.

She tugs us on a double-baited hook.
She kisses me swiftly, then returns to him.
'Banish Petit,' she says.

                    Tonight, in tears
she came to my room with letters for two friends
in London. I am to deliver them.

For a letter in cipher came from Anthony,
compelling me to leave. Her every fear
about Petit is true. He's threatening
to expose us both for our moral laxity,
his own disgust.
                    Oh, moral laxity,
how you have sweetly leavened my flat dead hours,
deliciously inspired both prick and pen.
Only a juiceless man denied such good
could call it evil.
                    Lucille placed her head
upon my shoulder, sobbing properly
how sorry she was, and she was in my hands,
and could I deliver, please . . . and all my thoughts
I must confess, were on her bosom there,
most warmly pressing. Even as her tears
soaked through my shirt, I went to raise her head
and kiss her mindlessly.
                    I leave at dawn.

ESSEX HOUSE

January ends, but passes winter on
as seamless as this river meets the sea.
The edge of the Thames is creaking. Ceaseless snow
falls from a sky white as a winding sheet,
obliterating what marks street from street.

As light fades, I dismount at Essex House,
swaddled against the cold up to my eyes:
disguise itself disguised as keeping warm.

Anthony's strangely cheerless.
                                              'I am here
myself by the earl's good grace. Which may be stretched
as far as lodging dead men *if* you stay
stuck fast in this room, in case you're recognised.
We'll find you service shortly.'

                                    I'm in pain.
I've warmed my feet too quickly by the fire
and my toes are aching. His good-natured smile
is cooler than I remembered it. The source
is soon apparent.
                          'Tell me, does the air
in Rutland cause conversion?'

                                    I'm unclear.
I run my mind through maths and alchemy
while he gulps liquor.
                              'I believed we shared
– proclivities.'
                    And though his meaning dawns

with that word's hesitance, I feel compelled
– annoyed perhaps that he should limit me –
to tease him with 'Montaigne? Italian verse?'

'Your Edward the Second and his Gaveston!
Your Gany— Ganymede.' A stuttered halt.

I massage my foot to urge the chilblains out.
'I write of killers, yet I am not one.
Nor am I Doctor Faustus, though the world
would have it so. Though Adonis disdained
the arms of Venus, must I do the same
because I write the tale?'

                  No answer comes.
He's picking at his thumbs.

                    'Although it's true
I might enjoy male intimacy too.
But what I value most, experience,
is not found compassed in a single shape.'

He shifts uncomfortably.
                    'I cannot share
your taste for female flesh.'

                    No remedy.
I slide the foot back in its chilly boot.

'And I don't ask you to. But don't ask me
to love no more than half humanity.
Beauty is sexless. It's found everywhere.'

He lowers his gouty frame into a chair
and watches me as though I might combust
and turn to ash in front of him.

                          'It's clear,'
he says, 'that we must find some task for you.
And more engrossing work than tutoring.'

THE EARL OF ESSEX

A bear of an earl. This cousin of the Queen
requires to meet the man he's sending off
to serve him on the continent. He stands
like a monument to pure nobility,
his back to the room. Though younger by a year
than me, his person breathes entitlement.
From his padded shoulders to his slender knees,
he's dressed like a king in waiting, and might seize
the whole air of the room to draw a breath.
His beard is red as embers, and his eyes
– now rested on my face – as shocking soft
as tenderness upon the battlefield.
And in his presence, one might quite forget
what one is for. He clears his throat.

                              'My friend
the Lord Southampton tells me you're discreet.
And Mr Bacon, that you pass as French.
I gather you're a victim of this war
against the Catholics.'
                    'I served the Queen
until I was slandered grievously.'

                         He nods.
'And now you may serve me. I pray, sit down.'

I take the seat that faces him.
                         'My aims,'
he says, 'are much as hers. Protect the realm.
And gather knowledge of our enemies.
But where Her Majesty refuses flat

to favour a successor . . .' In his eyes,
the spark of meaning I am meant to catch.
'Say that you had a preference for the throne . . .'

He leaves the silence open as a hand
that I must shake correctly, brotherly.

'The King of Scotland.'
                                    'Good. Then we concur.
Plans cook abroad, and thicker year by year,
to plant a Catholic. Though Lord Burghley has
averted many plots, he isn't well.
A younger man must take the mantle on.'

The beard seems fiercer, somehow, in the sun
that filters weakly through the window pane.
Some six weeks' snow has settled.

                                    'So. We're done.
Here is a memo, written out in French
by Mr Bacon's servant. You will find
all your instructions. You'll accompany
the Baron Zeirotine to Germany,
and send news from the court. Then on to Prague
and, should conditions suit, to Italy.
I gather you have the language.'

                                    'Sir, my tongue
has peeled that fruit, and others.'

                                    'Has it so?'
One eyebrow rises like a proving loaf.

'I trust you won't resort to poetry
when filing reports.'
                              I'm chastened. 'No, sir, no.'

'My wife's first husband favoured poetry.
You know his work, I'm sure.'
                                        He pares his nails
with some device he's fished out from his desk.

'And I know yours,' he says, letting the weight
of his words sink in my chest. 'I know the names –
true names – of all my agents. That includes
the slandered one you left behind.'
                                          I try
to meet that gaze: that steady, kingly gaze.

'My lord—'
            'No, please. You'd best to hear me out.
Should you prove true and loyal to my cause
I will ensure your restoration comes
as surely as the King of Scots is crowned.'

'I swear—'
            'And you are eager, I can see.
No oaths are necessary. That's the point.'

He hands across a seal: the name Le Doux
and a man whose face is masked.
                                    'This, I will trust.
Work diligently, then. For both of us.'

Small Gods

Small gods they are that shuffle men like cards,
dealing them into courts, minding their hands,
and laying wagers they will stay ahead.
Again, I'm alchemised to Mercury.

Letters delivered. Nobles led to Prague.
Messages tramped across the lines of war.
Armies estimated; counts dispatched.
Rumours reported and alliances forged.

And though I miss the semblance of a home,
and a dark-eyed mistress I might dream upon,
the European air is savoury
as wine to a man just recently set free.

For I shape more than one boy's alphabet.
Licensed to roam, observe and scribble down,
to mingle amongst the gossip of the troops
and privy councils both, to taste the sounds

of history thrashing to be born, to breathe –
my usefulness to England warms me through
Bohemia, and the cold of Germany.
When you know this, may you be proud of me.

For though I've put you away, as soldiers do –
folded and dog-eared, sewn into a coat –
still all is done in reference to you
and love is inclined to catch me at the throat

when it sifts from the crowd a voice that rings like yours.
I fill my head with duty, discipline,
but when I sleep, my heart slides from its post
and slips on the outfit of a future year

when I'll reclaim the plays I send from here
and reimburse the man who's loved me most.

MERRY WIVES

My fear, at first, was that familiar tropes
would shout my name in each delivered line,
hanging their author from a stylish rope.
Could they tell my invention's work from mine?

My fear now is, they do. This sheltering name,
beneath which wisdom grows as sorrow's fruit,
is fathering plays I still hope to reclaim
but sharper, without the arrogance of youth.

And who will know them mine? How can I snag
some threads of myself to show I passed this tree,
and not stuff Kit into the drowning bag?
I write in fits and starts, a comedy,

between the inns and lodgings of the road –
bizarrely peppered with some scraps of me
too ghostly for the ignorant to see,
disguised, as truths had better be, as jokes.

IN THE THEATRE OF
GOD'S JUDGMENTS

A book stall in Frankfurt. How the ear homes in
on the English language, as a lamb's attuned
to its mother's bleat and trots with wagging tail –
in my case, to be startled. For within
two steps I heard my name at Cambridge, 'Merlin.'

There by a pile of English tracts, a man
I didn't recognise – who had not called
across to me, but read out loud a book
he cradled in his hands for a laughing friend.
Adopting a preacher's tone despite the scorn
in his Rhenish accent:
                         'See what a hook the Lord
put in the nostrils of this barking dog!'
Some joke in German. Then, 'May the good Lord
preserve the English from their atheists!'
A scoff, and the book's rebalanced on the pile
before they saunter back into the crowd.

What do I do? What joke is this of Fate's
to drag me over Europe to this spot
for the moment that a stranger turns a page
– a random page, just where the spine decreed –
and reads my name aloud?
                         And 'atheists' –
it surely *is* about me.
                         No. Too mad.
If raw coincidence can cook that up

then I'm a pig in pastry.
                              Sweat breaks out,
like catcalls in a madhouse. Who is here?
Whose eyes are on me, who paid them to bait
me with that tome, that conversation?
                                        Fear
stamps my heart, rapid as the rabbit's foot
that warns the warren. Fake it, saunter past,
or find a dagger's hilt between your ribs.
(I'm told you never know it instantly.
That to be stabbed feels only like a punch
until hot fluid soaking leads you to
notice your life blood leaving, stem the flow.)

At the edge of the marketplace I find a spot
beside a wall, and sink me to the ground.
I breathe as if a fist has winded me,
but slowly return to focus. People mill
and natter. There are children playing chase.
The sun shines meekly. Browsers move from stall
to stall like cattle, grazing. I'm alone.
I am prey to senseless terrors; this I know.

For half an hour I fidget with my thoughts.
What is it called, this book? How can I find
it elsewhere, when I know it only by
its uppermost position on that stack?

But if this slander's published, I must know
what else it says about me. To be sure,
what's snacked upon in Germany will be
meat and potatoes to the London crowd.

I could ask a boy . . .
                              I do not have enough
to buy it, though . . .
                              I could return disguised . . .
Yet by that time, what book will be on top,
and that one buried?
                              Thus I venture back
a little closer, testing how it goes,
and fret discreetly, sifting the market stalls
for suspicious loiterers, for patent spies
who might be focused on that book, and me
(the most suspicious loiterer of all),
until the vendor, free of customers,
descends upon that teetering stack of wares,
beginning to rearrange it, as a trickster
will whisk a marble underneath three cups—
and I'm running like a child,
                              'Nein, nein, nein, halt!'
and wrest the book from where he buried it.

A thick book, though. Author, one Thomas Beard.
I skid my thumb through pages, nothing, where?
Then set it on its spine to fall apart.
And again. And again. The fifth time, it is there –
the page where 'Marlin' leaps into my face,
the phrase 'a poet of scurrility'.
And worse, far worse. All Baines's points transcribed
and summarised as fact. A gory death
painted as if Beard mopped the blood himself.

I close the tome, disgusted. Come, sweet blade,
into my guts. Sharp steel could do no worse
than printer's ink to wound me.

                              Then despair's
consumed in the heat of anger. I will fight.
By God, I will set sail to England now
to claim my name, to shake this lying Beard.

Did I die swearing? No, see how I live!
Swearing most certainly, but full alive.

And how does God perceive me? See this eye,
this unstabbed brain?

                              And am I wretch? A villain?
Do I look filthy? Tell me to my face,
so close and living you can take my pulse;
judge for yourself the odour of my breath,
and what is a fact, and true. And what is death.

WHO STEALS MY PURSE
STEALS TRASH

I drink it out, of course. Drink out that rage
into a pool of vomit by the road.

For some time after, I sit with my head.
How helpless we are to write our histories.

As I made Richard crookback, so these flies
lay maggots in my life's realities
and print bestows them with authority,
cold worm-gnawed fabrications.

                                My side of it –
these papers that build quietly with me –
become the very breath of me because
else *there* I am, and *that* is what I was.

SLANDER

Because I can't fight back, because we've sworn
my disappearance from all mortal men,
new stings arising from the angry swarm
are sunk into the name I left for them.

A corpse can't shake itself, so slander sticks,
encasing the mind as heavily as wood –
as lies, far more delicious on the lips,
obliterate my every trace of good.

Poor truth, already exiled in disguise
is truly now deceased and heaped with earth.
For what slim chance this man could ever rise
to claim a name no longer wreathed with worth?

Yet join me in my silence. Don't defend
that man, and put at risk his dearest friend.

A Kit May Look at a King

Reviled as brawler, traitor, heretic,
as resident in lies as in my skin,
my loyalty remains with England still,
my skill with knowing chaff and wisp from will.

October 1598. The Hague.
Burghley is dead. And I am working for
the French. So say my papers. Since the King
of France signed peace with Spain, my mission is
to ascertain the trueness of his heart
as I shuttle his general's letters back to him.

The road to Paris. More familiar now
than boyhood lanes; though conkers rain here too.
Then through the northern gate, down city streets
where you and Tom Watson, many years ago,
wrestled each other into inns.

                  The Court
swallows me as a snake slips down a mouse
whole, for digestion later. I may walk
around the fountains, through the panelled halls,
or rest in my chamber until I am called.

'And have you heard from Anthony?'
                         The King
and he spent years together in Navarre.
'How is his gout?'
                'He's been in bed two months,'
I say in French.
                'Bad business. Why the good

are struck with such afflictions beggars me.'
His warmth to me seductive, friend to friend.
'You stayed with him in London?'

                               'Three years past.'

'You know Petit?'

                         'I hesitate to say.'

'Why hesitate?' The twitch around his mouth
appears to invite my playing. I have missed
banter more keenly than an English ale
with beef and kidney pie.

                  'Because to *know*
suggests a depth that I have failed to plumb,
Your Majesty.'

                  His smile cracks in his beard,
breaks like a sunrise. 'Yet he's surely not
a shallow man,' he answers graciously.

'Oh, no, indeed.' *En garde*. And then engage.
'Since I have failed the fault must lie with me.
He wears misanthropy like battle-dress.
I'm not equipped to pierce it.'

                         'I perceive
some modesty. You seem amply equipped.
Where were you schooled? I reason, not in France.
Our academies are dull.'

                       'In Wittenburg,
Monsieur Le Roi.' I chose it playfully,
having once immersed myself inside the head
of its most famous heretic.

                          'I see.'

He beckons a servant carrying a bowl;
announces, selects, 'A juicy gift from Spain,'
and breaks a fig between his thumbs. 'Like Faust,
you tired of scholarship and sold your soul
for power and influence.'
                                    'Your Majesty?'

'You might have been a fellow. Write and teach.
But you carry post. A most intriguing choice.
I'll know you better. Come, sit by my hand.
I've several other messengers to see.
Observe them, and recount their traits to me.'

Thus is my afternoon accounted for,
amusing the King as though I were his fool.
How this man's eyes could not leave off his boots,
and how another's collar did the work
his mother left unfinished, strangling him.
Jests for that mangled turn of phrase, those shoes.
Easy unkindnesses.

                        'How did you find
the ambassador from Norway?'
                                        'Full of puff.
He wears his limp as if he made it up.'

'And none of these fellows, note, do as you do.
You're easy with the Crown. It's puzzling.'

'I believe we are both men.'
                                    He takes me in:
a drenching, sideways look. 'I am a king.'

'Respectfully, Your Highness, so might I
have been, had your mother borne me.'

                          I detect
that the servants, locally, have turned to stone,
as though afraid Jehovah's thunderclap
might singe them as it smites me. I might choose
to be afraid myself, except my taste
for subjugation has grown less of late.
He stares at me all seriousness, and when
he fails to find the crack, starts chuckling.
'How very odd you are!' He claps his hands
delightedly, and makes the servants jump.
'The show is almost through. Who have we left?'
He reads the courtier's finger. 'Ah, just one.'

And what a one.

                   My breath stops in my throat.
The great hall is in shadow by that door,
and what steps through it glimmers like an ounce
of wishful thinking. Caramel, chest-length hair.
I thought he was a figment, made of dust.
But no, he is announced, and I am stuck
watching him bow before me, then look up –
and almost react. As startled as a horse
spooked by a gust of nothing, and reined in.
He stares, tries not to stare, then stares again.
Then builds a wall between us in the air.

'I came at your request,' Hal says. 'You asked
to see me, Your Most Christian Highness?'

                                                                    'Yes,'
the King replies. 'I wanted to confirm
you had returned from England quite unchanged.
You left the embassy so suddenly
in August, I was most concerned. And since
your return, there have been rumours. I could not
accept them without seeing you myself.'

A fleeting tiredness shifts across the face
I've loved so pointlessly. And then a steel
glints into it; the glittering eye of pride.

'You've heard that I am married, then.'
                                                    'Indeed.
And are you?' 'Certainly.'
                                        Here, I am cut
down from love's gallows with a hearty thump.

'Then you must dine with me, to celebrate!'
the King says cheerily. 'Return at eight.
And bring your wife with you.'
                                            'She is – detained.
In London.' Hal replies. His halting words
betray an awkwardness the King has dammed
and now is fishing, smilingly.
                                            'Detained?'
Hal nods his lovely head.
                                        'She'll follow you?'
'More likely I'll return to her,' he says.
I sense, where tenderness might be, regret,
an aching to acknowledge me expressed
in the stiff tilt of his neck. He and the King
exchange more formal pleasantries before

he is dismissed. And as he bows, I swear,
a glance at me from underneath his brow,
swift as a spark, and instantly snuffed out,
too brief to be understood. Southampton sweeps
out of the room like summer warmth.

                        '"Detained"!
Wonderfully delicate. She's in the Fleet,
disgraced by a swelling belly. Are you well?
You've gone quite pale.'
                     'Your Majesty, I am –
fatigued.'
               'By all that gorgeousness, no doubt.
How did he strike you?'
                      'As a man who knows . . .'
And here I blank. Should I betray myself?
Or sift myself and lump here as I am,
a lonely, shamed pretender of a man?

The King is sharp. '"Who knows"? Do you not know?'

More knowing than I wish. So I restart,
'Your Majesty, he strikes me as a man
who knows how he's regarded, as he sees
himself reflected in the eyes of men
with hair that tumbles on imagined sheets,
lust for a mouth, and jealousy for skin,
but nothing inside of substance, since their gaze
falls only on the crust of him.'
                    'Bravo!'
the King applauds. 'You've earned yourself a drink.'
More claps bring wine. His smile is quivering.
'He looked at you most oddly, don't you think?'

A ROSE

The King has proved a friend. Not through my art –
all cleverness was dashed upon that glance –
but through his willingness not to unmask
an English agent felled with a single Rose.

A Rose with whom I now seek audience
at the embassy, where you and Watson played
tables till dawn, some sixteen years ago.
Since all you described is laughter, this is new:
the marble floor, the yellow curtains snagged
like sour cheeks into smiles. The chairs, too high,
that lift feet from the floor, make one a child.

He leaves me twitching in the corridor,
hours, it seems, until
                        'Monsieur Le Doux?'

Excusing his secretary. Yet alone,
maintaining the pretence. 'How can I help?'

By recognising me. By being the same
man who passed me his glass two years ago
at Burley, asking me to call him Hal.
I look at him amazed. Wait for the ice
to thaw. He asks again, with feigned concern
for something on his desk, 'How can I help?'

Perhaps some spy is hidden in the room.
I search his face, and ask, 'Are we observed?'

'I took you at your word,' he says, surprised.

'You must no more acknowledge me, you said.'
'In a poem, yes.'
                        'I took you at your word.
"I may not evermore acknowledge thee,
Lest my bewailéd guilt should do thee shame,
Nor thou with public kindness honour me,
Unless thou take that honour from thy name."'
'In public, Hal. May I still call you Hal?'
His hand, like snow inside my leathered palm,
melts out of it.

                        'I do not think it wise,
even in private. Circumstances change.'
'What circumstances?'
                        'I am older now.'
'Your marriage—'
                        'That does not come into it!
Your dangerous position is the point.
I've taken your advice.'
                        'I wrote in pain!'

He urges me to hush. 'If you must shout,
then shout in French. Or with an accent. Sound,
Monsieur Le Doux, stays not within four walls.'
He invites me to sit down, as if my hurt
might be contained by horsehair and brocade.
'You wrote acknowledging your name's destroyed.
In England, to love Marlowe is to swear
allegiance to the Devil.'

                        He says love!
How stupidly my heart sings at the word,
like a girl sings as she launders her own blood.

'What kind of dead man are you? Turning up
all over the place. The plan was disappear.'

'And to all the world I have!' I stand again,
my lungs craving more air. 'Except to you.
Perhaps we are drawn together.'

                         'By the stars?
By sun and moon? Then I am truly doomed,'
he says, and does seem stricken. 'Your disgrace
will not be mine.'

            I whisper, 'My disgrace?'

'It's said you died blaspheming. That the knife
into your brain was punishment from God
for all those statements in the note from Baines.'

'But I didn't die!' I grip his arm to prove
how alive I am. 'And the rest is all made up!'

'The note from Baines was real.'
                            'But it was lies!
At least, exaggerations.'

                  Like a splat
of mud, he shakes me off his arm and stands.
He's very tall. Willowy, yet more broad.
So young, so splendid. I catch sight of me
in the window's dusk: a shorter, balding man
whose clothes are slightly crushed, whose older face
is quivering, and shadowed beneath the eyes.

How cruel an instrument, imagination,
to paint me a future where he welcomed me,
offered protection, loved me for my words.

What fiction had I spun to picture him
a greater friend than you, because you left,
because you could not risk my company –
and how did I sell myself this fantasy
with him a titled earl, and more to lose?

'Forgive me,' I say. 'May life be good to you.'
I make for the door, my throat as lumped and tight
as if Eden's apple chokes me.

                  'Wait,' he says.
His eyes are also brimming. 'I would like
to give you something dear to me.' He pulls
open a drawer, extracting a small book.
'Your friends are working still, to save your name.
Shore up your reputation. This I thought
quite beautiful.'
             He hands the book to me
as a nurse would hand a baby to its mother.

So full was I, of taking last goodbyes,
I didn't read the words upon the cover,
and twilight on the frosty Paris streets
prevented me from knowing what I held
until, in my room, I lit a candle on
this – what can I address it as, but horror?

And dedicated by Ned Blount to you,
who gave my script away for this to happen.
'*HERO AND LEANDER*, BEGUN BY CHRISTOPHER MARLOWE'
and no. No, no.
                 'AND FINISHED BY GEORGE CHAPMAN.'

CHAPMAN'S CURSE

How dull a dead man is. How short on wit.
How absent at the dinner table, too.
How tedious in friendship, how like air
to every sense that used to hold him true.
Dissolved into a fiction of your making,
how unreal I must seem, these days, to you.

The proof sits in my hands. The smallest book;
and yet, between its covers, I am slain.
This poem we agreed I would not finish
until some king brought me to life again,
you have allowed another man to end,
who adds more wordage than the story needs,
alters my structure and destroys the tone,
then dedicates it to your recent bride,
flourishing friendship that I thought my own.

One poet not enough for you, perhaps.
Or this first one so lamed by Fortune's spite
that you craved other architects of verse,
and seeking my echo in the school of night,
found ghost-eyed Chapman, swaying from the pipe,
fresh from communing with the spirit world.
And he might pass, for he can turn a line
you might develop fondness for, or worse.
Although your heart is still attached to mine,
the difference is that he can come to Kent.

And did you, pray, invite him to complete
the interrupted story of our love,
relinquishing all hope of my return?

Or did you, so convinced of your own fraud,
in the absence of letters agents fail to pass,
begin to believe that I was truly dead
and ask the man to channel me?
                                        I rage
through the dutiful plodding of these stolid lines
Chapman has patched where I would write with fire.
But I don't blame him. He believes the dead
are guiding him.

                    But what has guided you?
Has five years in perdition ruined me
and you must plunge me now into the dark?
Or has mere absence puffed your love away
like so much Old Man's Beard? I understand
how unrewarded longing bursts like song
upon the merest kindness, after years
of knocking its head against the lost and gone –

but you have given up my words, and let
another write my ending. Brother, friend,
how should I read it? Even in Judas' kiss,
Christ was never more betrayed than this.

Bare Ruined Choirs

All in a day, the birds were stripped from trees.
The flowers lost their petals, and their scent
dissolved like an echo of forgotten song.
Yet nothing changed: for any other man
who walked this lane would swear there's nothing wrong;
not holding in his heart this heavy stone.

The fault lies not in you, not in my Rose,
but in that youth convinced he couldn't fall:
proud of his swift ascension, scorning Hell,
oblivious to the feathers falling from
the wings he fashioned in his prison cell,
that room above a home-town cobbler's shop.

Words: he commanded them. Called them his slaves.
Yet the rope that Fate would put around his neck
he wove himself with words too freely spent;
youth's certainty, a preening arrogance
born out of turning shepherds into kings.
If I could travel back and shake that boy –

no good would come of it. He had a friend
who warned him ceaselessly, said, 'Hush,' to jokes
whose laughter came from outrage. Chide me, then,
as Fortune does, for my stupidity.
No massacre occurred. There is no husk
of glory to mourn. No ruin here, but me.

Knives

Of course, you are Brutus. Moral, careful man,
persuaded my death is for the higher good.
Chapman perhaps your Cassius, whispering knives.
So many stab me that the blame is lost.
Your blade the last: and my surprise enough
to kill a man not used to shocks. But I,
old hand, am merely robbed of sleep, my brain
wrestling words to make some sense of pain –
burning the stinking tallow, gulping wine,
and scratching another version of this tale.

My cure, the manuscript. The first scene goes
to a rabble-rousing cobbler. You'll recall
a witty friend once free and sharp as him.
Later a poet's murdered by mistake,
confused with a conspirator: his name
condemning him to death. Shall I go on?
I'm already Caesar, whose swift rise was feared,
a conqueror of men, too confident.
Mark Antony, who moulds the crowd with words
to any shape he wishes. Portia too,
the swallower of fire, transparent, true.
Most any part is me, but you play Brutus.
Sleepless counsellor, wisdom's constant friend:
haunted by ghosts, loved to the bitter end.

Concerning the English

Dispatches received by my lord Buzenval,
at Antwerp, this year, 1599.

Essex is sent to Ireland. It is said,
in a fierce debate, the Queen had boxed his ears
and his hand, instinctive, touched the hilt of his sword.
Undrawn. But her silence slicing off his head.

Essex sets off with sixteen thousand men.
A four-mile double line of citizens
cheering him and the troops until the sun
gives way to rain and hail. They scatter then.

The largest army ever to set foot
on Irish soil arrives in Dublin close
to St George's Day. He throws a lavish feast.
The Earl of Southampton's Captain of the Horse.

Can that gentle face bark orders? Do men ride
into battle blinded with their love for him?

The rebels, marched upon, melt into woods
and bogs, know where to ford and how to milk
their native land's advantage. Essex rides
to empty battlefields. His marchers tire.

The army's provisions falter. Rebels strip
horses and food from land beyond the Pale.
The Queen stamps feet to hear Essex bestows
copious knighthoods, dwindling loaves of bread.

She sends the order to attack Tyrone
directly, but his force outweighs the troops,
now dwindled to five thousand. Essex has
some ailment now, perhaps a kidney stone.

Essex decides to parlay with Tyrone
against the Queen's instructions. Rides a horse
up to its belly in the River Glyde
for private conversation. Half an hour.

And so, cessation. All that cost and not
the promised victory. Peace rests on the oath
of a man who can't be trusted, in a tongue
that slips interpretation like an eel.

In mid-September, sources intercept
an order from the Queen: he must stay put.
On no account must the Earl of Essex leave
Ireland without the Queen's express command.

I pick up this news in Zeeland. If all hope
for resurrection rests with Essex, this
rage of the Queen adds mortar to my tomb.
He's falling as fast as I did.
                                        I get drunk
in a back room with two soldiers, wake up bruised
unsure of why or how. My friend, I fear
I'm falling sick again. It's in my bones:
a deep appalling ache. Each morning leaves
more hair on my pillow as my body fails
to restore itself to health. And then worse news.

September 24th. The earl has sailed
for England.

An act as close to treason as
that twitch for his sword. And two weeks on, a whirl
of gossip. My friend, confirm if this is true:
that the Earl of Essex burst upon the Queen
ungowned, unwigged in her chamber, so intent
on explaining himself, he glimpsed the royal dugs.
That since that day he's under house arrest
and Cecil entreats Her Majesty to press
a charge of treason. Friend if this is true—

I broke three days, not knowing what that 'if'
should lead to. Beset with shivering and pain.
Anthony writes: the earl cannot sustain
intelligencers. He is growing debts
as lesser men grow buboes, and the court
whose will he needs to know lies close to home.

My misery, no longer so inert
or held in its place by hope, is moving in;
and others see it in my eyes, I know.
The weather, and bad fortune, weakens me.
It rains five days.

I dreamt of him, the earl,
magnificent, his beard a ruddy spade,
his armour bloody from the battlefield,
about to offer me all that I crave:
my reputation, my identity,
the right to be called Kit Marlowe and be safe.
But as his mouth opened to say my name

what fell out was a fish, another fish,
gag after silver gag of fin and scale
which servants bagged in nets and took away,
and then the earl himself, all shrunken, pale.

No further letter, and no payment comes.
The network of agents I've depended on
now falls apart, and I must make my home
wherever I am useful. And away
from incessant rain; the wide, tormenting grey
of the English Channel.

                    Once or twice this year
I imagined I had seen the Dover cliffs,
and even the dots of samphire pickers there.
But the pickers were gulls, feeding above the sea;
the land a bank of cloud, and not my home.
I long for warmth, and rest; some sanity.
I leave with a mission travelling to Rome.

ORSINO'S CASTLE, BRACCIANO

Spring, and the first flowers of the century
break colour to me gently. There's a rash
of narcissus running southwards to the lake,
visible even as I lie in bed
in this stony room. It pains me to get up
when I have slept so little. I make lists.

A list of things I might have died without.
My linguist's tongue. My rapier and knife.
My trunk of books, the lock upon it. Jokes
Tom Watson told me, which I shared with thieves.
Your cloak. Ten angels from the King of France
concealed in the hem of it. Remembered words
from the Bible, Ovid, Virgil's *Ulysses.*
A letter of introduction to the Duke
Orsino in the name of William Hall.

A list of Bracciano's benefits.
The peace to write. A room to settle in.
A view of the lake, and sunlight on the wall.
A climate kind to grapes, and wine as good
as the host who serves it. Somewhere to read books
and not depend on memory alone.
The sense of permanence that comes from stone.

A list of reasons I am still myself.
I write.

I'm writing more, and better than
I could, contented. For the sting in this
prison of circumstance stirs in my blood

more honest wit than comfort ever could.
And as my mouth was stopped, so must my pen
speak volubly, and clear – and cleverer
than those who would be my decipherers.
Those who would have me killed, led by the nose
to a wall that butts them stupid. Those called friends
led through the forest, note by rhyming note,
to find me in my exile. If they would.

Writing the date alarms me. That sixteen
obliterates Kit Marlowe's century;
the zeros like a slate some hand wiped clean
when I had all my thoughts chalked down on it.
New spring, new century: if these spell hope
to other men, they toll 'all gone' to me.
No plan except await news of the Queen.
Meanwhile my days are sluiced down castle walls
like yesterday's food; passed through and poisonous.

I'm writing a comedy. Oh, you will like it.
A fairytale, adapted as all tales are.
I've added a stupid William, who would woo
and win the love of Audrey-Audience
despite his blunted wit and Cuntry Ways.
There's a threat for him. And melancholy Jaques
in a tribute to my little friend, Petit.
For me, whose folly made him wise, Touchstone,
by whom base metal can be told from gold,
expounds on the truth and fake of poetry.

And yet, the long nights won't let go of me.

GHOST

I met me on the stairs. I had an eye
bloodied and scabbed as our poor story told,
and I, or it – there was no human there –
urged me, 'Revenge! Revenge!'

                                  Startled awake,
I swear the shadows dragged me out of bed
to mix my ink, and tell—
                            What would I tell?
Kyd's fishwife tale, written this time from Hell,
with all the suffering that whips me mad
in castellated prose: in tricks and turns,
and watching the dark, and how the candle burns,
and God preserve us from these men of stone,
their murdering of truth.
                          To be?
                            To not?
Might I set straight this crooked path we paved
with a shadowed laugh, a play within a play?
Where does the playing end? I rip the speech
from *Dido, Queen of Carthage*, like a badge.

He hesitates to act. And yet he acts
with constancy. With words, he sets a trap
to catch the confession of a guilty look.
While faking kills his love, he hides in books.

Yet how to end it all? For, could he kill,
nothing would separate him from his Hell.

THE AUTHOR OF *HAMLET*

He is only a piece of chaff. He is a blot
that trails persistent sickness page to page.
A dying man's drool. A mad dog chasing smells
to the corners of his brain. A puppet king
with not a string to his fingers, miming shows
in the back of his head. A tempest, all his rage,
that might sink fleets or tear the steeples down
dissolving into out-breaths on a stage.

What a clown he is, this prince of perfect souls,
dragging his thoughts to dinner to be chewed
by dogs beneath the table, though he's raw
as a mutton chop, as helpless as a stew
that's served to drunkards to be puked outside
and cursed in the morning. How at sea he is
in his pain and motley; only a fool writes plays
and hopes to be understood. He is unhinged.

Christ, how the nights possess him with their dark,
mocking the stench of his extinguished light
as he stalks through rooms he cannot call his own,
wrestling a thousand wrongs, and fencing Right
till he slides the point through its throat, and feels the blade
unleash *his* blood. If he could choose again
he'd choose oblivion in the world of men
who save their violence for a proper fight.

But no. He builds his muscle like the worm
that crawls through the apple, bittering its taste.
He paints with private torment of the waste
and rank injustice of a sleeping world

carved into gargoyles by ambitious men
who stage this blazing farce upon a pin.
He dresses the hurts of others with his skin
until they heal, his own wounds festering.

He is Ophelia, gathering up her weeds
when love has blown her out. He is the Queen
who takes the poison, tasting in its bile
the bite of love. He is his father's ghost,
tricked of his life and kingdom, who now roams
the silent battlements, and when he speaks,
asks him for vengeance like a thing from Hell.
He knows him not at all. And very well.

Quiet. I hear him knocking in my head.
I've nothing for him. Nothing. Words, just words,
like countless grains of sand that shift and blow
until a world is buried. Oh, this brain,
made mad with faking, and with playing dead,
condemned to ever clevering the tongue
until it cannot say the simplest thing.
There is no fool in *Hamlet.* Only him.

IN PRAISE OF THE RED HERRING

A storm. The mountains light up like the bones
of shattered Titans. Every past disgrace
is blasted by God into a reliquary.
The heavens' sluice gate opens; crackling air
converts to deluge in a single breath –
a wall of water fit to drown all woes.
The ceiling weeps, two inches from my desk.

I snuff the candle, better to watch the land
flash into being, disappear again,
like lives across an aeon.
                                        A night like this,
in my ungrateful country, years ago,
a friend ran through the rain.

                                        'Kit! Thank the Lord,
you're safe.'
                        'And dry. The gods have pissed on you,
however. Tell me, why would I not be safe?'

Southwark, two years before the bastard Note.
'I thought you were dead,' Nashe said. 'I had a dream.'

Described how I was 'pale as baker's dough,
your right eye hollowed out, and in the air,
hovering by your head, a dagger blade,
so real I went to touch it, and awoke—'
He showed me his hand, three fingers cut across.
His voice was trembling.
                                        'You sleep with a weapon
beneath your pillow?'

He swore that he did not.
'Come, friend,' I smiled, 'this is a foolish joke.
Did Watson put you up to it?'
                                    He swore.
'You think I'd cut and drown myself for fun?'

In my back, a muscle spasmed, three times, four;
as though my spirit pinched me to wake me up.
'It's nothing,' I said. 'It's not a prophecy.
It's pointless to fear what we cannot explain.'
I ribbed him on that dream relentlessly,
squashing all claims of 'vision'. Till the month
I left my dagger in the curtained room
where the dough-pale face of Penry would play mine.

So understand, that when you write he's dead,
but no one's seen Thom Nashe's corpse, or grave,
I doubt your news. I doubt it grievously.

For surely, if the reaper stepped his way,
Nashe would get wind of it, and pack, and flee.
Might even now be on his way to me,
crossing the mountains in this flashing storm,
to talk himself around the guards, the gates,
to clatter up stairwells, nattering to maids,
until I greet him, dripping, at my door.

Sojourn

A year ago, my ear perceived as strange,
the sing-song 'a' or 'e' or 'i' or 'o'
most every word must end with. And the sun
whose midday fierceness sends all men to sleep
was alien, its kiss a souvenir
on English skin. How I have changed since then;
an incremental metamorphosis
adapting me to exile.

            This is home.
The language comes to my ear, its sense intact
as I slip my shadow through the marketplace,
a neighbours' quarrel entering my head
in violent detail. And my skin, once pale,
is tanned antique: the native patina.
The street cries spell out food. Only the eyes,
which stare so brightly at me when I shave
out of this darkened face, surprise me still.

I'm not the man who travelled stealthily.
I wear each pseudonym as second skin;
answer to almost any name except
my own. Here, I'm Will Hall, elsewhere, Le Doux.
So comfortable as that sweetened *monsieur*
that I've feigned ignorance to Englishmen
who've then conversed their secrets in my face,
believing that I couldn't comprehend.

And yet, inside, I'm England. I'm the clay
that clogs your boots on Kentish lanes, the cloud
that lowers itself like London's muffling shroud,
to soften the sleep of cutpurses and whores.
The sudden shower that sends the cats inside,
the blatant rose that blooms above its thorns,
the nightingale that sings to spite the dark.
My dreams are hybrids where historic kings
are tricked out of their crowns by Harlequins.

And England, Italy, are much the same –
though one eats anchovies, the other stew;
one basks in heat, the other suffers snow
late in the spring; one likes its women slim
but plumps them up on marriage, while the shrews
of England make for better wives than sheep.

Both countries forged in human contradiction,
in ignorance and perspicacity:
in smug and blind assumption sent to sleep,
in envy, greed and folly forced awake,
in love and loyalty, hauled from the brink –
and neither one is better, neither worse:
two different coats both keep the weather out.

But no. One sits more soundly in my heart,
without the gaps a sudden wind might frisk.
It's England's shores that call me to return,
embrace my fears and shoulder any risk
that I might spend another night with you.

So this most welcome message in my hand,
deciphered into being in the slant
of Italian morning sun ignites my heart.
'Meet me at six, beyond the olive grove.
I am to take you where you wish to be.
Special commission from her H.   T.T.'

T.T. & W.H.

Beyond the olive grove, there is a hill
that twists the stony road around its hip.
A stone-built barn whose roof is not repaired
open-mouth laughs some rain to fall in it,
but the sky's relentless blue, the earth parched dry
as crumbled bones. A tremble in the trees
reminds me to check my dagger's in its sheath.
As I reach the barn, the road's old curves reveal
Thorpe sitting on a wall in meagre shade.

'My dear,' he says. 'You're looking very brown.
I had imagined you encased indoors,
shunning the sun and penning tragedies.'
He's reading a map that's laid out on his knees.
He pats the wall beside him. 'Come. Sit down.'

Cicadas scratch the gap between his words
and my lack of movement. As I seek his eyes
beneath the generous brim that shadows them
my stallion heart kicks at the stable door.
Harder to trust Her Highness, since she slapped
the Earl of Essex under house arrest.
I do not know the game. And though Thorpe seems
an unlikely cold assassin – flaccid hat
and rose-oil scent, his slight unmuscled calves
that surely never walked here, and a flower
drooping in his lapel – that's just the sort
one shouldn't bare one's ribs to.

                              'Suit yourself,'
he says. 'I thought you'd like to see the route

I've planned for us.'
                              'As long as it's not to Hell.'
'Tush tush! Does the Devil wear Venetian hose?'
'I've never met him personally,' I say.
'Unless you're he.'
                              'My darling boy,' he laughs,
though still my junior by some years, 'are we
old friends, or not? What's changed? Did I betray you?
Or speak your name without due care? Or cut
your purse while you were sleeping? Though dead drunk,
you'd not have noticed. I remember well
the state of you, though it seems your memory
of me is somewhat hazy. Sir, give up!
Accept the Queen has asked you to return
and shake the hand of your deliverer!'

He folds the map, places it by his side,
and rises to offer a hand so limp and pale
you'd mistake it for a lady's kid-leather glove.

'There!' he says. 'There! My goodness, you were less
cautious when you were freshly dead. What rogues
have stripped you of your trust?'
                              There was a time
when I'd have snapped his bait and gulped it down.
And yet it feels like bait, despite that Thorpe
is genuine, I think.
                    'What does the Queen
recall me for?'
              'My dear, what else? A play!
A comedy again – you must forgive.
You are so good at them.'
                        'Where would I stay?'

'In London, sir. With me.'
                                'But can I not
pen the play here, send it the usual way?'

Why now? Have Whitgift's spies got wind of me
and hired this friendly face to tempt me home?

He cocks his head, surveys me as a dog
will stare at a thing he doesn't understand.

'You prefer it here?'
                                'I'm getting used to it.'
'There is a woman?'
                                'No!'
                                'Then why would you—
I thought the exile's only dream was home.'

And he conjures, with that word, the London streets,
their cries and smells, horse hoof on cobbled stone
and a thousand once familiar things I've missed –
yet pushing through this vision's loveliness
someone who thinks he knows me, swift arrest,
and me clapped in a cell, awaiting death.

I rub my neck free of imagined hemp.
'You have my pardon?'
                                'What?'
                                'My pardon, sir.
A paper signed by Her Majesty to show
that Christopher Marlowe is no heretic.'

Thorpe sucks air through his teeth. 'I've no such thing.
Only the Queen's request that you should come

disguised, preparing for Orsino's own
visit to Court some months away. I bring
his invitation also.' Pats his chest,
where the royal seal must be. 'But I should first –
she stressed this most precisely – speak to you.'

He flatters me. I know he flatters me,
a speck in her larger vision. Yet the hope
that I am vital to her plans, that she
should even think of me to call me home,
softens the pardon's absence. And perhaps,
while in her compass, close enough to see
the powder crease on ageing royal cheek,
if I could demonstrate my loyalty—

'I've watched a spider in my room,' I say,
'spinning a web so delicate, a girl
could wear it on her marriage day. And yet
the only nuptials that it renders there
are those of flies, wedding eternity.'

He laughs. 'You are the rarest. Come, sit down,
and save the nonsense for your comedies.
If you were wanted dead, would I be here,
and not some Poley, some more slippery fish?
Have I worn out a pair of boots for this?
Come. Come!'
                    The host who will not take a 'No'
unless you punch him on the nose with it,
and I'm not inclined to violence.

                              'So. Is that
not better? In the shade? The legs at ease?

What was the thought that kept you standing up?'

'That you were sent to kill me,' I reply,
worn out by subterfuge. Thorpe rubs his chin
in laughing disbelief.
                              'You've cooked too long
in the sun, my friend. What must you think of me?
What, murder the man who fathered Juliet,
broke Romeo with that one word, *banishéd*,
and with the woeful error of their deaths,
christened each woman's face and forced each man
to say it was dust that watered in his eyes?'

'Not you, then, but the Queen.'

                              'Indeed. Rare fellow.'
He stares at a foal and mare beneath a tree:
the mare stripping the willow's drooping leaves,
and swatting her flanks with undramatic tail.
'You're worth more than you know. Truly, you think
she'd have you killed? More likely that grey mare
would kick the flop-eared creature in its shade.
She has no wish to hurt you. Though you caused
embarrassment in your more careless days,
she likes your plays the best. Even the ones
that have a dig at her. Titania dear,
indeed. And you're the ass, we must suppose.'

The foal flap-shakes its ears free of the flies.

'Archbishop Whitgift, then.'
                              Thorpe folds his lips
in on themselves. 'Indeed, he is a man

who'd like you soundly dead, I grant you that.
And should you return and shout out in the streets,
"I am Kit Marlowe, whom God did not punish,"
the Queen has made it plain, he'll have his way.
A special cell in Bedlam is reserved
for any maniac who makes that claim
or says Kit Marlowe never died. There's five
immured already. No one you know,' he says
in response to my face's question. 'Just the sort
that found your death's convenience too slick
to swallow, and do not trust official oaths.'

I recall those nights, threaded with Bedlam's moans,
mad cries and laughter, as I tried to write.
Its windows dark, no ounce of soul in them.

'So why must I come to London? Is it safe?'
'I would deceive you if I answered yes.
But safe enough, if you are well disguised,
to cast your eye about those men at Court
who most deserve to be a Sovereign joke.
The Queen grows weary, since Lord Essex has –
been absent. She laughs so little. There's concern . . .'
and here he whispers, though an olive grove,
a mare, a foal, and a high-circling hawk
are all our company, 'The Queen grows old.
Her health has lessened since she banished him
from her company.'

        I quickened, I confess,
at the thought she might be waning. Hand me a lute
and I'll write a song to sing the Queen to death.
Hasten King James, a man to boldly reign

and overturn the past's injustices.
If I could be in London when the news
breaks of her death, his kingship; collar a friend
to make a plea for me while power is fresh
and generous in bestowing its rewards . . .

'But what disguise could keep me safe at Court,
which brims with agents? Or the London streets?'
'The work's half done,' he says. 'Thanks to the sun
you have the very semblance of a Moor.
All we need now is appropriate attire.'

TWELFTH NIGHT

Guests are arriving at the great Noon-Hall,
and snow is falling like small promises
as I cross the courtyard 'wrapped as a corpse should be,
in winding sheets'. (As Thorpe said, when I swam
through my ancient haunts, first time in seven years,
without a flicker I was seen at all.)

A small and foreign man, his skin deep brown
through race or cobbler's dye; they wouldn't care
to look close enough. In the country, people stare,
but London chooses not to notice who
takes shelter in her, bumped as if he's air.

Three months I've ducked through mishap and mischance,
scribbling a play to celebrate misrule,
which tonight, by the grace of the Lord Chamberlain's Men,
will play before Her Majesty.
                              'Percy!'
A young man dressed in finery hails a shadow
lighting a pipe outside. 'You coming in?'
The answer both sweet and tart, like damson jam.
'Not yet. I'm waiting for a visitor.'
Puffs at the pipe, his eyes searching for stars
that the falling snow obscures.
                              'My lord,' I say.
'My lord Northumberland.' He shakes my hand
distractedly, his gaze towards the gate
where others enter. 'Delighted. We will speak
later, perhaps, when we are introduced.'

He takes me for a foreigner, unschooled
in proper etiquette. I hold my ground,

and remember a line that he will recognise.
'Above our life, we love a steadfast friend.'

He stares at me intently.
                              Then,
                                    'My word!
The note – I'd not imagined your disguise.
Your mother would fail to know you.'
                                        'Then all's well.'
He reads my face intently as a page
of mathematics. 'You are keeping safe
in this monstrous lie?'
                        His breath surprises me:
enriched with liquor.
                      'I am glad to be
in England again.' He huffs. 'If England knew
she'd have you quartered. Such does England treat
its poets and thinkers. We're all heretics.
You'd like some tobacco?' Offering the pipe.
'It doesn't suit this Moorish outward show.'
He nods, 'A shame,' and puffs as if for me.
Taps out the glowing heart. 'Shall we? Inside?'

Noon-Hall is lit for Christmas with enough
candles to burn a thousand heretics.
A crush of courtiers and titled guests
mingle, or sit, before the fervent hush
preceding the Queen's arrival.
                              Here she is,
gleaming and pale, her dress a nest of pearls
but in that nest a thin-armed woman, frail
as eggshell after hatching. Power rests
in her hawkish eyes alone: as if shrunk there,
withdrawn from withered limbs until it set

in two blue points of purpose. Yet the dress,
the dress is the outfit of the freshest girl.
And with her Duke Orsino, and with him
Archbishop Whitgift. Like a pair of cruets –
one oil, one vinegar – these opposites
who, singly, threw me out or took me in.

At the back of the hall are Heminges and Condell
in their livery as the Lord Chamberlain's Men:
not acting tonight, but managing the purse,
guarding the props. And here a thought occurs.
'Is Shakespeare here?' I whisper.
       'Never comes,'
Northumberland says. 'Or, rather, he came once.
He rarely comes to London, to avoid
requests for improvised revisions, but
he did come to a court performance, yes.
Hoping to meet the Queen.'
       'And did they meet?'
'Most certainly they did. And never again.
Your stand-in had not reckoned on the depth
of the Queen's own knowledge of this matter. She
humiliated him.'
     'What did she say?'
I confess myself eager to imagine him
deflated by the monarch he admired.

'"Why have you brought this puff-cheeked, small-chinned man
towards me like the pudding course?" she said.
When told he was the author, she replied,
"Of his own conceits and folly. Send him home."'

My heart glowed then with more love for my queen
than a pup feels for its mother. For this night
I dropped all longing for her death, and grinned
so madly, on and off, that servants stared.

These are my notes. Yet I was taken past
the point where words have any use at all.
For how to describe the sharp surprise of tears
as the lute and harp began to pluck my song
before the Queen, and my words echoed there
to the thousand-candled ceiling glittering
on a scene now more than my imagining:
'If music be the food of love, play on.'

An Execution

Essex was exiled only to his house.
Yet how exclusion wounds a righteous man,
bruises his heart. I know the depth of it.
And though he had his country and his name,
his reputation tattered in the wind,
like a standard flag with endless residence.
And though he had wife and child, wine and friends,
the nearness of the thing denied to him –
his queen, the Court – buzzed madness in his brain
as a bee will knock against a window pane
to sense the flower outside, so bright, so close.

The year turned, and he sickened. So unjust
to be condemned for speaking truthfully –
and he more loyal than those whisperers
who fawn and aye and bow extremely low,
unpicking the seams of kingdoms as they go.

Determined to speak to her, and right these wrongs,
he gathered those who loved and honoured him,
would vouch for his loyalty and love for her,
and marched on the Court. Not in rebellion,
yet the boots, in concert, had a martial ring,
and the righteous anger spurring them towards
their queen caused dogs to growl and doors to bolt.
And those who'd cheered him on for Ireland
peeked behind curtains, mimed they were at work.
The wind had shifted unaccountably,
and the streets fell silent, empty bar the march
of Essex and his band. And then a shot,
a challenge, lines of soldiers shuffling up
and aiming nervously at noble heads.

How blind and mindless do old rulers grow,
afraid for their legacies; more fearful still
of their snuffing. Jealously extracting oaths
as insubstantial as a smudge of soot
from those who do not love them, while the pure
untainted soul is viewed suspiciously:
as if some bitter motive lies beneath
his love, as if his constancy's a plot
to inherit the crown and all its fractured woes.

It's said that Essex rose against his queen.
The word that fills the streets is 'uprising',
a word so bloodied by its history
it can't contain its entrails. Thus his love,
his desperation to be seen and heard,
is treachery; and all who followed him
to swear his honour are made traitors too.
Including Hal. The boy is in the tower.

Today I passed the pikes on London Bridge.
There was the head of Essex, scabbed and black,
a March wind ruffling that reddish beard
like the fingers of a mistress. Upturned eyes
rolled back and white as if to know the brain
that read, so grievously wrong, his circumstance.
Three dozen years of bold entitlement
severed and sacrificed to bitter gods.
And knots of people stood awhile and stared
into that face for remnants of the faith
they had in him.
                    Unwound.
                              Went on their way.

WILLIAM PETER

Thorpe's home, in Southwark, rattles in the rain.
Leaks through the beams upstairs, like crying saints.
Makes noise as if at sea, a creaking ship
sailing us down the street towards the Thames.

Thorpe ushers in the youth who lately knocked
so softly we had thought it was the wind
tapping a branch on something.
                                        'He's for you,'
Thorpe says, with a servant's smile, as though the lad
is my dessert. He is eighteen, no more,
wet as a man who's swum in all his clothes,
and nervous, making note of Thorpe's retreat
before he speaks.
                        'Will Hall?'
                                        That makes his task
a governmental one. And I detect
a delicate air.
                        'I might go by that name.
Who asks?'
                        'I'm William Peter,' he declares,
as love's declared, full-hearted, passionate.
'I'm sent to remove you to a safer place.'
'What place?'
                        'Abroad.' Vibrating on his heels.
'There is some urgency? Must we go now?'
'No,' he replies, attempting to be still,
though his eyes are darting to the door.
                                        'A drink?'
I cross the room to where a bottle of sack
sits half exhausted by two pewter mugs.

He nurses his, unsure. I gulp from mine.

'First, I will know about this place, Abroad.
Is it very far? Is its population fair
or dark-skinned? Can you name its capital?'

An earnest reply: 'Abroad is not a place—'

'It is a place, I promise you. I was
in residence there myself some seven years.'

He offers back a doe-eyed blink, confused.

'Abroad. You know, Abroad, that wave-arm place
where awkward squirts are sent. Within its bounds
no man may settle, since there is no house,
no job or friend that will not slip from him
as sand shifts underfoot. Its very streets
become the hairs one brushes from one's pillow
and the cities scabs one must apologise
to lovers for.'

      He's barely understood
a word of my invective. I regret
impaling him so.
            'Go on. Drink up, return
to your master. Tell him William Hall's retired.'

'My master?'
         His eyes are very wide and pale.
His clothes are leaking rain on to the floor
in rivulets.
        'You work for Robert Cecil?

It was his father christened me Will Hall.
I'll not work for the son.'

                    He doesn't leave.
'Go on. Be gone, I say!'
                    And still the boy,
his lips as full and pink as ripened figs,
stands motionless. Then, quite as though the broom
of his spine is stripped from his puppet's back, he falls,
translated to laundry.

                    Gathered in my arms,
and heavy as conscience rests on murderers.
He seems all gone, and yet there is a breath
on my cheek when I bend close enough, as soft
as sudden sleep.

                    Heeding my cry, Thorpe comes
and stares as though he witnessed an assault.
'Bring water,' I say.
                    'The wound?'
                              'There is no wound.
Bring water! The boy has fainted.'
                              And his eyes
come open slowly, beautiful and pale
as two moons rising on a lake.
                              'You fell,'
I say, to explain his body in my arms –
though neither he nor I yet move away.
I feel a pulse that might be mine or his
where he rests against my shoulder.
                              'Now you know.
I have the falling sickness,' he replies.

Thorpe comes with water, and I mop his face,
gesture for sack, and let him sip at it.
'You think me defective.'
                              I wring out the cloth.
'I think you most dramatic. What a ruse
to claim a man's attention.'
                              'It's no ruse,'
he says, with boyish petulance. 'It is
a curse. A curse by which you gain the power
to have me dismissed.'
                              'I will do no such thing.'
'You'll keep a secret?'
                              'Certainly. Can you?'
I tip the cup towards him, motherly.

'You are in danger, and must come away,'
he says, refusing more.
                              'With you?' I ask.
I see the danger clear. His cheek, his neck,
the tempting lips that he is speaking with.

'I'll serve you and protect you,' he replies.

'If my protection rests on sickly boys
I'm doomed indeed.' I help him to a chair

and he recounts the mission: Elsinore.
Two gentlemen I met in Padua
acquainted me with that court, and with their tongue.
Now my smattering of Danish marks me out
to visit the very castle where my ghost
ranges the battlements nightly in my play,
urging my murder be avenged: the boy

can hardly know, and yet he seems to know,
that Denmark will hook my curiosity
more firmly through the lip, and fling me out
of my native waters.
                          'You seem better now.'
'It passes,' he says. 'So will you come with me?'

'What if I don't?'
                    He blanches, very pale.
Paler than when he fell, and for a breath
I wonder if he'll pass out in the chair,
or fake a fit to make me leave with him.

'Tell me the danger.'
                      'Please,' he says. 'Just come.'
'The danger.'
              The boy sighs heavily. His breath
defeated.
          'If you'll not co-operate
I'm told to give this message, word for word.
Your name will be exposed. And every child
you've sired in secret will be put to death.
If you care not for your life, then care for them.'
He cannot know what he's delivering;
only I know the children are my plays.
For, from his face, he must believe them flesh,
and dandled in some mother's lap somewhere.

'You threaten me?'
                   'Not I, not I, sir, no.
I am a messenger.'

A pretty one
to carry such poison in his beak. I go
to the window. Rain is muddying the street
and across the way a candle flickers on
to quell the early dark. A neighbourhood
I've kept myself apart from, like a cyst.

I gather my things, as many times before,
to leave my country. Go to Elsinore.

ELSINORE

Forgive that the boy is in my bed. The cold
in Denmark is persistent. As I write,
he breathes as softly as a passive sea
laps to announce a ship has passed through it.

Upon all hours, they set off ordnance:
a savage shout to the surrounding hills
that power is here, and not to challenge it.
And still I startle, not quite used to it.

My own commission to disarm the Danes
rests on my wit. For I am sent to woo
the brother-in-law of our most wanted James
with the benefits of patience. Should he force

his kin's succession, bolstering the case
with men, and horse, and blunderbuss, the Queen
will melt her promise, fling the crown elsewhere.
Patience, all patience, for the Scottish king.

For my fate hangs as perfectly with his
as if we shared a skin. As if our cloaks
might side by side be hooked, the doors pushed wide
and both together launch our lives, begin.

I Lie with Him

'What would your children think of this?' Will asks,
his sweet cheek on my arm.
                                    'Of this?'
                                                'Of us.
Are any of them as old as me?'
                                    I breathe
and calculate how I might lie to him
whilst being truthful. '*Dido*'s as old as you.'

'Dido!' he says. 'After the Carthage queen!
You know the play? My Oxford tutor said
it was abominably poor. The speech
on Priam's slaughter dragging on and on—'

'Excuse me,' I interrupt. 'The play I know
requires skill to act. I hear it has
been sawn apart by actors, but the text
is delicate. The humour of it missed,
as often as the tragedy is clanged.'

'I don't mean to offend you.' He's concerned
that I've sat up in bed, and strokes my back.
'I'm not offended.'
                        'You seem very sore.'
'*Dido*'s so much derided.'
                                    'Will, the play
reflects not on your daughter.' Strokes, and strokes.
I lie back with my eyes upon the beams.

'You write yourself,' he says, without the curl
of a question mark.

                   'Letters and ciphers, yes.'
Twice, these past weeks, he's entered while my desk
is thick with papers, watched me shuffle them,
fast as a trickster's cards, into my trunk.
My need for privacy's unclear to him,
and must remain so, if he's to be safe.

He's silent awhile. Then slides himself beneath
our blankets.

                   Five nights on, a fearful wail
curls up the staircase. 'Jesus' nails, what's that?'
the boy says, shocked to a students' curse.
                                        'It is –
I fear it is the Queen.' Anne Catherine
is lying-in with Denmark's future king,
just one week old. The wail grows like a wave
carving sheer cliffs of grief, which topple now
to capsize the castle's peace. From Danish shouts
first piercing, and then tangling the air,
I tug this thread: 'The baby boy is dead.'

With I a sort of father, he in my arms,
we drift as the cries, the wailing, dissipate;
perhaps he is more bothered for my sake,
for I must be asleep and he awake
when he murmurs, 'Unimaginable pain
to lose a child.' And, like an open gate
one's cherished horse escapes through, I reply,
'Then let us both stay childless.'

                    His response,
speechless and motionless, breaks through my sleep
as though that flow had met a heavy stone.

'You like to lie with me?' he says at last.
I let time pool. 'You like to lie with me?'
He takes my hand and rests it where the lie
in question is defined.
                    'I do.'
                                'Then truth –
and only truth – should be your currency.'

He sits up, lights the taper. In the glow
he shines, a bronze Adonis, freshly cast.
'You only confirm what I have reasoned out.
When will you trust me? When I bare my chest
and ask you to thrust the sword in? I am yours
in every sense you wish, and I am sworn
to protect you for Her Majesty the Queen.
What does a lie suggest you think of me?'

I sit up, grip his shoulders. 'Not a lie.
Not *one* lie, William Peter, but a cloak
of lies so vast it's hard to breathe beneath.
Why would I want to smother you with that?
Why would I throw this shroud on both our heads?
I'd need to cleave to you till death.'
                                'Then *cleave*,'
he says, intensely locking eyes with me.
'I sense you are extraordinary. That,
whoever you are, a greater spirit beats
inside *this* heart' (his palm upon my chest)
'than I'd be blessed to meet in *any* life.

Cleave to me. Let me be your certainty.
And shed your burden. These most hateful lies.'

May Fate have mercy. Had you seen his eyes
you would have tipped up baskets of your truths
to soak in their redemption. If that youth,
regaled with an understanding of my sins,
had opened the door and called the torturers in
I'd help them break my spine in disbelief.
Let love be dead if he's no love of mine.
Let me: for as you once said, I was honest;
too honest to live submerged within deceit.
And borne alone, the heaviness of lies
had worn me so extremely that I cared
no longer, truly, if I lived or died.

He's pacing then, across the naked floor.
'Your children are books.'
                              'Are plays.'
                                        'Are plays,' he mouths
and slowly comprehends. '*Dido* is yours!
Forgive me—'
              'How could you know?'
                                    His eyes ride up,
racking some mental library of facts,
'Your name,' he murmurs.
                          'Don't be concerned with that.'
'You're Marlowe!' he cries, and sits hard on the bed.

I wait for the weight to sink in him. 'Not dead,'
he murmurs. Then, 'Where's your injury? Your eye
was stabbed.' Inspecting my face.
                                    'No, no, not I.

A substitute.'
                    'Don't tell me any more.
No, tell me everything.' His switch as fast
as a dog sent mad by fleas. 'No, lie no more!
Marlowe was a blasphemer, heretic.
You're no more Marlowe than the rising sun
is a chamber pot.'
                    He pales and smacks his mouth
on invisible cake; the first sign that he's gone,
snuffed out by his brain's crossed purpose.
                                        When he wakes
from this second fit in twice as many days,
I offer this: 'There's not a man alive
whose death won't change him. And what tales are told
posthumously may not reflect the man
in any case. It's true I freely spoke,
shared inklings that, at Cambridge, passed as jokes,
but in London taverns stank of blasphemy;
and through my speaking, lost my liberty.
But I'm not the devil they have painted.'

                                        He
breathes calmly now, and takes me in, like air
from an opened window.
                    'I am glad of that,'
he says. 'Too poor that I should suffer this
and fall in love with a devil.'
                    There, a smile,
the parting of clouds. And I will have my love.

DELIVERANCE

Tonight, I remove the label from the trunk.
The fading ink of some address in Kent
where someone I loved dearly holds his life
close to his bosom: wife and child, estate,
the breeding pigs, the stables by the gate,
the plip of lively fishponds. Friend, you were
all things to me. I let you go with love.
This trunk, these papers, were the things I braced
against the fear that I would leave no trace
and disappear into the muddy roads
of Europe, insubstantial as a cough.
But time has passed. And you have shrugged me off.
What I addressed to you, you cannot want
to know. I suspect they were only for my eyes
in any case. And for posterity,
should such a thing alight upon them. So,
I scratch off the label. Though not easily.
Like scar tissue, it's bonded to the lid.
But I pick, and scratch, and in an hour you're gone.
My 'you' now is larger, wider. Is the world
I wish to know me. And would dream upon.

More Sinned Against
than Sinning

1602. September. Exeter.

I came to live close to him. Close as a coin
in the pocket, or a scar upon the skin:
drunk on the boy's devotion, and the joy
of unloading every feeling into him.

Rewrote, revised, and focused on the thought
of the Queen's impending death. But all the while,
like the scabrous itch that crawls beneath the skin,
the knowledge I was just a ride away
from the man whose name, attached to every play,
was shaking London's hands, retiring quiet
to his manor to count the coins I earned for him.

Anthony Bacon died with us abroad.
The old route for the scripts, once copied clean
by his brother's hired boys, closed up like sand
that a stick is drawn through. And my loyal love
stepped in to scribe, and to deliver them.

'Give my regards to the Turnip.'
                                    Will is shocked,
and breaks from lacing a riding boot to say,
'He shields your life!'
                                    'He is a parasite,
born to suck glory from the quills of men
too wise for the age to stomach them. His name
and his silence are his finest attributes.'

'When the Queen dies—'
                        'When? That woman has the art
of hanging on, finer than any tick.
Pull off her body, still the jaws would clamp
on crown and kingdom.'

                        Uncomfortable with me,
he finishes dressing silently, and slides
the play into a satchel.
                        'You should write
this poison out,' he says. 'Before you find
you're muttering treason in the street. Or worse.'

He packs a travelling bag, resignedly,
and starts to go. 'I'll be six days.'

                        'You're right.'
I catch his arm. 'You're right. I apologise.'

Sighing, he sits beside me. 'That you want
to claim these plays as yours, I understand.
Your soul sings through the lines as though through bars.'
A flash of Southampton, locked still in the tower;
the axe through the neck of Essex, juddering.
I shudder.
            'What thought?'
                        'The head that spoke to me
of restoration, falling in a bowl.'
'Which is the fate we must protect you from.
Write, and say nothing. I will plant this seed
with the Turnip, as you call him, and in time
you'll harvest it. Be cheery while I'm gone.'

'Cheery?'

     'Not melancholy. I will send
my sister to see you. Liz. She'll cook and clean
and listen to you politely.'

                     'Does she know?'
'She knows we're the closest friends. The best of friends.'
He kisses me. 'I'll leave you to your pen.'

Liz

How like him she was. As if he was made twice,
but one time female, softer than the brush
of a flightless wing. A he with breasts, with skin
as velvet as mole's pelt, but as light as light.
She filled his absence with a gentle hum
of kindness, and forgiveness. Left a scent
behind her that I dreamt of, when she'd gone.
Four days, and I had drawn her to my tongue.

I loved her bruisingly, the way that ground
loves a fallen apple. She had all his eyes
and an inches softer bosom: all the love
that a carer for foundling kittens satisfies
herself to give another came to me.
Beyond lust, I admired her as I had
the Virgin Queen, when I was twenty-one
and first her servant. Will was not surprised.
He read the air between us in a blink.

We argued, certainly. I challenged him:
and will you not get married? Yes, he would.
He wanted children. So, I said, do I.
And won't your sister keep us close enough?
Convenient cover for an illegal love,
he swallowed it.
                    The week the old Queen died
Will Peter's sister, Liz, became my wife.

IAGO

Oh, foolish heart, to store your beating hope
in the whim of an unmade king. The wind blows in
from the north, as icy, suddenly, as glass
stuck in the throat.
                              A friend will ask a friend
to ask a friend to ride and put to him
the case for my resurrection.
                              How my heart
thumps strangely in my ears, keeps me awake
beside my wife through hours that only those
haunted or haunting come to know so well.
It knocks like a stranger not at any door.

And every day, no message, though the King
is riding southwards, closer.

                              In the square,
where Exeter's merchants come to chop and chat,
I hear Southampton has been freed. This is
the king to set injustice straight. But still
no end of endless sentence comes to me.

A Never Writer to an Ever Reader. News.

'A letter!'
> Will Peter's panting from the ride.
He drops it in my lap, a baby bird
he prays I might revive, and stares at me –
all fear, all hope, all sharp expectancy.
The seal is still intact.
> 'So you don't know
what's written here?'

> Will Peter shakes his head.
'For God's sake, open it.'

> 'You couldn't tell
from his face?'
> 'His servant brought it. Open it!'

'I can't.'
> 'Then *I* will!' Lunging for it.
> 'No!'
I snatch it flat to my bosom. 'No. Call Liz.'

'I'm here,' she says, appearing from behind
the doorframe.

> Hands that shiver (as she slides
a paring knife beneath the waxen seal)
like new-sprung beech leaves rattled by the wind.

The night before we said our marriage vows
I told her who she married; that she might
one day be Mrs Marlowe. You would laugh
to know how she shuddered at the very thought:
'Then I'll be married to a heretic!'
'No,' I promised, 'I'll not take the name
until it's cleared of every blot and stain
the world has heaped upon it.'
                                        'So a royal
pardon is necessary?'
                        'As the blood
that keeps these sweet lips red.' I kissed her then,
but sensed her fear my past would swamp us both,
King's blessing or no. Thus it was her I chose
to open the letter, knowing what would thrust
a knife in my ribs might be my wife's relief,
so that her joy could temper breaking grief.

And should that letter free me up to live,
to witness her love for me throw over fear.

Her lips are trembling and her eyes have filled.
Just for a moment, grief and joy are one,
impossible to tell apart as twins.
'He –' she says '– you—' and cannot tell me what.
Will Peter is impatient. 'Give it here!'
He snaps it from his sister's floured hands
and, as he reads, grows angry.

                        Now I know,
and a cold seeps from the ground into my feet,
my legs, my waist, my chest, as liquid soaks
up a wick prepared to take it.

                    'He cannot,
apparently, risk restoring you. He feels
such action is impossible, would be
dangerous – for you and also him –
damn him, the coward! "That I must unite
these countries bleeding from religious wounds
is difficult enough without the taint
of a decade-long deceit."'
                           My dearest boy
punches the door shut. Grunts, then slaps his head
as if it were the King's. 'Not least, he says,
that no one will believe your innocence.
Your name is too deeply blackened. Curse the man!'

Liz on her knees before me, takes my palm,
anoints it with tears and kisses.

                      'This is wrong!'
Will Peter storms. A wasp caught in a jar.
'You've been nothing but loyal to England. Saints alive,
all this has come from one man's double-cross;
a personal vendetta. If the King
were any kind of man at all . . .'
                          'William—'
His sister chides him, all her eyes and mind
on me, in case his words unstitch me.
                             'No!
I'll not be stifled. There has been enough
silencing here to stuff ten monasteries
till kingdom come. Only a damned man hangs
the truth and lets the lie perpetuate
for convenience!'

'And yet he's right,' I say,
so quietly Will Peter almost rides
across my words, all driven by his ire –
until the sense breaks through and trips him. 'What?'

'I fear he's right about the name,' I say,
afraid of my own calmness; for the calm
is a dressing over such a gaping wound
I dare not look at it.
                  'What can you mean?'

'You know yourself what Marlowe meant to you.
The name is this age's bogeyman. "Beware!"
say mothers, hearing children fudge their prayers,
"or God will smite you, swearing, in the head
as he did that Marlowe."'

                  'You exaggerate.'

'You think so. Tell me, do those pamphlets sell
that have Marlowe on them? No, they're tucked away
in back rooms for the connoisseurs of shame.
For being Marlowe's, dozens are tossed on fires.'

How we shield ourselves from what we fear to see.
A part of me has known this all along;
steps forward only now, when the part of me
that hoped against hope is struck entirely dumb.

'And all the plays that I've adopted out
beneath a name untainted by my sins –
those plays that are lauded, loved and lifted high –
should we shout, "This is the father! This cur, here,

who is thought in league with Satan"? Every line
reads differently through judgment. "To the fire
with the atheist's plays!"'
                                   'Or with the atheist,'
Liz whispers to my hand. I lift her face.
'Fear nothing, my sweet Liz. A king is wise
who knows his power's limits; that his scope
remains outside the made-up minds of men.
And I will bend with him.'
                                   Her kiss, my skin.
I'm playing courage. Playing some strange part
I wrote not for myself but for a man
better than me. A man I dreamt to be.

Will Peter stares at me as at a prayer
whose text he can't decipher.
                                   Soft, to him:
'Can a king's pardon shift a nation's curse?
Unpick a belief grown hoary with old age?
No. Marlowe is fully dead. No more pretence.
We have to live with this.'

                                   I stand, and he
crumples into the chair that I have left,
Liz watching me as if I'm darkened sky,
holding her breath for where the lightning falls.
I ground myself.
                       'Hand me the letter, Will.'

I read it as a man stands in the rain
whose love has betrayed him, soaking to the bone
until, into his sorrow, he's dissolved.

I let the words run through me like a sword
on the battlefield – I watch my body, slain,
fall separate from me; my spirit still
where all of me was a blink ago, and now
so without substance that my killer walks
across and through me, and I'm undisturbed.

And when those words are wholly understood
I let our fire burn them, and the warmth
brings a desire for liquor, which we drink,
all three of us, talking of trivial things.

And only later, when I'm skin to skin
with the woman who shows such tenderness to me,
and only when I have set desire free
in that mock of death, that sudden, pure release
where hope and love and sorrow close their gap,
do I sob, and sob, and sob, into her lap.

'There is a plan hatched at the Mermaid Club.'
'Whose plan?'
             'Ben Jonson's.'

                              Six months since I wrote,
and in that half a year I've understood
how clever writers are. How good at code;
at understanding what's beneath the line.
How able, some of them, in tracking style
back to its source like water. And how loyal
on discovering one of their number wrongly bound.

The knowledge grew like fungus; underground
but quietly sprouting in the still of night.
I saw hints in the prefaces of books.
Where Shake-speare fell in two, as though it led
these soldier authors to a private fight,
I knew who knew, how far the knowledge spread.

How it spread safely I can only guess.
A voiced suspicion to a friend, a *shush*,
and each initiate sworn in with an oath
and a prick of blood. It seems I have more friends
than the tree outside has pears. The Mermaid Club
is the name they've chosen. William Peter grinned
to tell me of its existence, share the name.

'You are the mermaid. Mythical, never seen.'

'Half girl half fish?'
                'Leander, as you wrote him.
But Leander Club sounds too much linked to you.'

'And what is their purpose?'
                              'Build so great a myth
around the silent author of these works
that the Turnip rattles in the heart of it,
falls out like a weevil with the smallest shake.
To ensure his claim is stumped at every turn.
To keep you safe, and lift your plays so high
no flames can touch them.'

                              He sat on the bed
where I've lain weeks now like a sunken ship
unmoved by tide, unable to expel
the heaviness inside me. 'Honest aims,'
I said. 'What motivates them, do you think?'

'An admiration for your work.' His glance
alighting on all the crossings out upon
the papers at my bedside; on this play
I have so little heart for.
                              As I stacked
their smudgings together, 'How do they propose
to prevent him being William Shakespeare? Given
he is?'
          'But not the author.'
                              'Known to us
and the Mermaid Club. But he has passed for years.
And well enough for Heminges and Condell
to believe his inkless fingers are the source
of their meat and gravy.' Will reached for the hand
withdrawing from him.
                              'Liz!' I called. 'Dear wife!'
She came, as she does. 'We have wine in the house?'

'It's midday. Will you eat?'
                              She asked so timid
I knew she expected 'No.'
                              'Perhaps some bread.
But mostly wine,' I said, and watched her wince.

The bread came quickly. 'Don't forget the wine!'
I called, breaking a little off. 'My boy,
whatever the Mermaid Club cooks up, he has
the name. We rented him like lodgings, left
my precious belongings there. And when he sees
I can't be back to claim them, sure as cats
kill mice, they're his by default. Ah, the wine!'

'Stop sending him plays, then.'
                              'God!' I ruffled his hair
with violence. 'Beautiful boy. Would that I could.
But he is my only means to reach the stage.
You think I should write, but keep my creations close?
Though pus beneath the skin builds to a boil?
I write for all the world, and he's the tap
through whom the writing pours. You know this, Will.'

We drank. Will only to keep me company.
He fudged and flailed, said it was all in hand,
that every mind was devising measures.

                              Today,
he imparts the plan. Master Ben Jonson's plan.

'A lawyer friend of Marston's, Thomas Greene,
will keep him in check.'
                              'How so?'

                              'He'll lodge with him
in Stratford-on-Avon.'
                        'What if he objects?
Or his wife does?'
                        'Then the fake will be revealed
for what he is without revealing you.
In Stratford they know nothing of the claim
he is a playmaker, nor that his wealth
comes so much from the theatre, with all
the immorality the stage implies:
actors who make dishonesty an art,
pet boys, loose trulls, et cetera. He would
be ruined.'
            'And you are quite a ruin yourself,'
I observe, of his dusty face and clothes. He feels
self-conscious then, and crosses to the bowl
of water by the window; washes skin
free of the dirt kicked up on London Road.
'Marston and Greene have drawn up documents
and he has signed them.'
                        'Why would he do that?'
'To protect his honour and his income. Greene
will simply ensure that nothing due to you
is passed to the Great Pretender.' Dries his hands
and pats his cheeks. 'Tell me you're pleased with this.'

'So Greene is his legal shadow?'
                              'Close as fug
to a beggar's armpit.'
                        I rise from the chair
where I've sat all morning, wrestling with a scene
that won't reveal its story.
                        'And yet still

he will be credited,' I say. 'His shares
in the players' company and in the Globe
will see to that. He need not say a word
when blind assumption follows him around.'

The window shows me England, undisturbed
by my lack of recognition. June unfurls,
full of its own perfection, ripe and green.

'Assumption has kept you safe these last ten years,'
Will Peter replies. 'And we rely on it.'

He touches the small of my back as though he means
to push me, fatherly, gently, in to swim.
In a pool of my own reality, perhaps.

I turn to him. 'You must think me stone-headed,
repeating the story I have told to you.'
'And do you not need reminding?'
                                        'Yes, I do.'

'You must believe, you *are* Will Shakespeare now.
People,' he takes my hand, 'they love your plays.
Your new work speaks to humanity with a depth
that must come from your circumstance; the pain,
perhaps, or the perspective granted by
this exile you are forced to. Your new work—'

'Not *this* new work—' But he is undeterred.

'The plays you have finished in these last four years
surpass for greatness all the plays yet written.
If you've lost heart, gain heart. Believe it's true.

The future will right this wrong,' he says. 'It will.
So long as your work survives, and Marlowe's too,
posterity will see how Shakespeare blooms
out of the bud of Kit.'

                    'Posterity?
Some promised future that will never come?'
I turn from him again, and when he speaks,
his voice has softened passion into care.

'You may not live to see it, Kit, it's true.
But come it will. We'll leave too many clues.
Not least the silent Stratford man whose hands
are legally bound. He will not claim the plays,
and no one will ever testify he wrote.
When all who were involved are safely dead –'
'Including me?'
                    A pause.
                                'Including you –
your safety is all our care.'
                                And I have stopped
his speech, it seems. I turn, and see a tear.

'Go on,' I say, more gently. 'When we're dead?'

'It will not be a hundred years, I swear,
before intelligence will sift the truth
and you will be restored your every work;
all credit to your name, and every play
and poem yours again.'
                                'I'll wait that long
if we're eternal.' I reach for the wine
that's never far away.

                    'Then believe we are,
and decades just a blink when we are souls.'

He is so beautiful. 'That is the plan?
This plan's as long as the sort that built cathedrals.'

'And they were built,' he says. 'And are admired.'

'And you believe I'll be admired too?'

'Your friends will see to it.'

                              I touch his face.
A frisson. A shiver. He looks to the door
as if his sister might walk in and see
our tenderness. I say, 'It's market day.'
A kiss as juicy as the purple cherries
my wife is haggling for.
                              'Oh, Kit,' he breathes.
'I'd forgotten who you were.'
                              'Yes. So had I.'

One tale before I go. A tale of drink.
A London tavern where a stranger sits
lining his guts with ale. He shouldn't be
so close to the playhouse. But the play is his,
It's mine, he tells himself; this time out loud
from the look on that wench's face. He's here to feed,
to re-create those nights worn years ago
when he revelled in glory seeded from his pen,
full-grown and showering blossom on his head.
Weathering admiration. Not long now
till the groundlings enter, high on their own applause.

Another beer while he's waiting. Then, sweet joy,
they're spilling through the doors, full of his play,
rattling with the violence of the scene
where the hero dies, the mute face of the Queen
as she poisons herself.
                        And how he breathes it in,
leans back against the wall, closing his eyes
imagining how each word is due to him,
until he hears:
                '''E's odd that 'Amlet, though.
'E shoulda killed the King two hours ago.'
The man has a nose bashed as a cobbler's awl.
The stranger's swallow sticks as the men agree,
and he contradicts them, under his hand. They hear.

He might have drunk up then, and left. But no.
Good Lady Drunkenness has slipped her hand
half up his thigh, encouraging desire
to be a part of almost anything,

so no, he argues. And they argue back.
And the five of them (for there are five of them)
all hold the same opinion: he is wrong,
and they tell him so.
                              'Aha, but *you* are wrong'
(and he may have slurred a little), 'I should know.
I am the author.'

              A decade's secrecy
snuffed in the puff of a pointless argument,
as gossip said his life was.

                    Idiot.

Perhaps you are surprised it took this long.
But a decade built me to the point: this snap,
this wild attempt to resurrect myself
unthought-through, yet imagined many years
through long nights painting my head's scenery
where thought played every possibility.
And now to find what's on the untried page.

'You're Shakespeare?'
                    'No, he's not. I've seen the man.
And he isn't fond of drinking, that I know.
He doesn't mix with the likes of us.'
                              'That arse
is not the author.'
                    Swaying like a tree
caught in a gentle westerly, I cling
to my beer-fuelled boldness. 'This is my play. *My* play.
I'll tell you why Prince Hamlet dithers so.
He isn't of a violent temperament.
Simple as that. Though simpletons like you

will throw a punch rather than hurt the brain
to work out something cleverer, the Prince
(I mark how you restrain him; excellent;
and you, Fist Man, thus name yourself a clod),
the Prince of Denmark, if I may continue,
prefers a quip to murder. As all do
who value the art of thinking. (Hold him well!
I'm really not worth the bruising.) There is much
to think about, surely. Is his father's ghost
a figment of Hell? Did not the Christian God
say, "Vengeance is mine"? Then who is he to slay
another? Yet the urging drives him mad.
And at the same time, into a sanity
more clear than any of you will ever know.'

'Lads! Let me go!' the held-back brawler shouts,
and I see a look pass through them like a breeze
that will furnish the ground with apples.
                                        'No, you don't!'
says the wench who served me. 'No more breakages.
Broken noses is one thing, broken stools
I've had enough of. Out.'
                          'Who – me?'
                                        'It's you,
or the five of them, and you look easier
to get to the exit. Help me, darlin', please,
come willingly. It's best.'
                          I let myself
be coaxed from the tavern like an orphaned calf
is coaxed from its field towards the marketplace.

To steady me, she pulls my arm around,
and draped, *faux*-passionate, around her neck,
'You know I tell the truth,' I say. 'I am

the author of that play.'
                              'You are, you're not,
what does it matter?'
                      Her arm around my waist
as if she's my lover, steadying my sway
towards the door. And I, outraged, begin
my heart's defence.
                      'What does it matter? Why—'
I stop to concentrate upon the words
that will convince her.
                      'Not here, love, outside.'
She tugs at me. 'Now, darlin'.'

                              In the snow.
We're in the snow. She is so practical,
so tiny-nosed.
                      'If they enjoy the play,
what does it matter?'
                      'That I wrote the play?'
'That they know you wrote the play. What does it matter?'

It's falling fast. She's cold. Crosses her arms
across a goosebumped bosom. 'Anyways.
Drink's done you in. You didn't write that play.
You're soft in the head with boozing. Silly man.'
She pats my cheek. 'You're maybe clever enough.
But I've seen him, Shakespeare. Comes in now and then
when he visits London. From a country house,
they say, a big one. Wears a velvet cap.'
I'm outraged, though I've broken sumptuary laws
more often than I've broken wind.
                              'How can
a man of so mean standing—'

                    'Not so mean.
He is a gentleman. Was granted arms.'

'Bought them more like.'
                        She squints me with an eye
expert at filling just below a pint
without attracting notice.
                       'That may be.
But he comes across more gentleman than you.'

'And does he boast about his plays?'

                         'No, no.
'Umble as mumblin'. Not so in his dress,
but in his manner. None of yer spoutin' off.'

My spouting off. The dart's not aimed at me,
but it hits the bull – what landed me right here,
in a filthy street, tipped out like so much turd
from an upper window, wrenched free of my plays,
condemned to stay anonymous Will Hall,
is my spouting off.
                  'You're right,' I say, 'I'm not
called William Shakespeare. That man is a fence.'
She fast objects, 'There's no offence in him!'

'A fence of the sort that keeps intruders out.
A broker of plays behind whom any man
who wishes to stay anonymous can write.
I'll tell you a secret.'
                    She laughs. 'I'm sure you will.
Six pints of my husband's brew would turn a priest
on to his head and rattle him upside down,

for a neighbourhood of secrets. Go on, then.'
'I'm Christopher Marlowe.'
                                    She squawks like a bird.
She folds in half where her apron strings are tied
and hoots out disbelief until she can
stand up half straight.
                         'You fool,' she says. 'He's dead.
And you look nothing like him, anyways.'

'What does he look like?'
                         'Why, a corpse!' She grins.
'All bone and worm food. But I saw him once,
when he was alive. A young bloke. Lots of hair.
Wild in his manner. Loved to pick a fight,
I heard.'
          'So I've lost my hair. And aged ten years.'
She cackles. 'Go on with you! Put on some weight
and shrunk some too.'
                      'Shrunk some?'
                                      'Why certainly!
He was five or six inches taller.'
                                    'And how old
were you, when you saw him?'
                             'Twelve, thirteen,' she says.
'And shorter?'
               'Listen, sir,' her finger wags,
'I'm not the one who's making up this tale.
Now stop your nonsense and be off with you
or I'll call the constables.'

                          She'd more than call,
had she believed me. She'd have shouted, yowled,
summoned the brawlers out to hold me down

until the law came. I'd be bundled off
to prison, and the executioner.
Though often I've wished for that oblivion.

But, friend, this lie we fashioned from our need
has taken sustenance, and grown, and bred.
It nests in the heart of all who gave it ears,
devouring truth, which cannot be recovered
even by shoving fingers down its throat.
The lie has fully digested me, and can't
vomit me out.

               And yet, I tasted there
for the smallest moment, all my pain resolved.
Before their disbelief, before her squawk
of extraordinary laughter, for a breath I was
entirely me, and honest with the world.

How glittering a resurrection feels,
when what was gone for ever is regained,
its value multiplied by loss, reclaimed.

And I shall know it more, shall write it through
in every play until I die; a prayer
that by its repetition may come true.

Again, and again, the posthumous will rise
to claim their crowns, their loves, amaze their friends,
confound their enemies, rewrite their tales.

And I will live that drama yet. I swear.

Author's Note

Not every word that appears in *The Marlowe Papers* was in use in the sixteenth century. In order to avoid cod Elizabethan and strike a balance between authenticity and readability, here and there I have chosen 'barmaid' over 'wench', let Robert Greene refer to Marlowe as 'bent', and given 'Muslim' when 'Musselman' would be more historically accurate. Though in the fifteenth century, 'lunch' was the sound made by a soft body falling, and in the sixteenth, a hunk or chunk of something, I have allowed it to mean a meal on the single occasion where no substitute would do. Some decisions of this sort were made in order to keep within the allowable variations of iambic meter. For the syllable counters among you, it is worth noting that iambic pentameter does not always have ten syllables; it can have as many as twelve (and variations in pronunciation can in places make scansion a somewhat subjective art): so long as it has five metrical feet, and the majority of those iambic, the line should qualify.

Following are notes that are not in any way essential to the understanding or enjoyment of *The Marlowe Papers*, but I hope some readers will find them interesting or useful.

Notes

DEATH'S A GREAT DISGUISER
'the plague pit where Kit Marlowe now belongs' Marlowe is supposed to have been buried in an unmarked grave in the grounds of St Nicholas Church, Deptford.

CAPTAIN SILENCE
'You learnt the tongue from Huguenots?' After the Paris massacre of 1572, Huguenot refugees flooded into southern England. Many settled in Canterbury, where Marlowe was born and spent his boyhood.

TOM WATSON
Tom Watson was a poet and playwright who wrote in Latin. A documented friend of Marlowe, Watson was nine years his senior and a friend of Thomas Walsingham, first cousin once removed of Sir Francis Walsingham, Secretary of State, who set up the first English intelligence network to help Queen Elizabeth gauge and contain the Catholic threat.

Richard Harvey was rector at St Nicholas, Chislehurst, in Thomas Walsingham's parish.

Gabriel Harvey, his brother, was a don at Cambridge while Marlowe was a student. He published numerous references to Marlowe and quarrelled bitterly with his friend Thomas Nashe.

Lord Burghley, as Lord Treasurer one of the most powerful men in England, signed the 1587 Privy Council letter testifying that Marlowe 'had done Her Majesty good service . . . in matters touching the benefit of his country'.

'my only other option was the Church' The scholarship under which Marlowe attended Cambridge for six years, graduating both BA and MA, had been bequeathed by Matthew Parker, the former Archbishop of Canterbury, and under its conditions Marlowe would have been expected to take Holy Orders.

THE LOW COUNTRIES
The Low Countries include the modern countries of Belgium, the Netherlands and Luxembourg. From 1581 parts were under Spanish occupation, while others, such as

the area around Flushing and nearby Middelburg, were held by the English. Protestant England had been under threat from Catholic Spain since the beginning of Elizabeth's reign, as the Spanish king, Philip II, had been made King of England and Ireland through his marriage to the previous queen, Elizabeth's half-sister, Mary.

'the daughter stumbles in/with bleeding stumps for hands' alludes to *Titus Andronicus*. The first recorded performance of this play, on 24 January 1594, suggests it was written in 1593, and though some consider it an earlier work it includes, like *The Rape of Lucrece* published in the same year, the rape and brutal silencing of a heroine.

'the silenced woman turned to nightingale' In *Titus Andronicus*, Lavinia, whose hands and tongue have been removed by the rapists so she cannot identify them, points to Ovid's tale of Philomel to explain what has happened to her. Philomel was raped and had her tongue cut out by her brother-in-law Tereus, but wove a tapestry to tell her story, and was transformed into a nightingale.

Armada Year

In May of 1588, the Spanish Armada would set sail.

'Still hiring the horse, though' Marlowe had hired a grey gelding and tackle when first arriving in London in August 1587, a status item he clearly had problems affording. In April 1588, he borrowed money from fellow Corpus Christi alumnus Edward Elvyn and was sued for non-repayment six months later. In the same law term he was sued by the hackney man for failing to return the horse.

'who now is qualified a gentleman' Marlowe's MA gave him gentleman status, meaning, among other things, he was allowed to carry a sword.

'The execution of the Queen of Scots' Mary Stuart, Queen of Scotland, had been executed the previous February, after the exposure of the Babington Plot. Several people connected to Marlowe – including his patron Thomas Walsingham and the two official witnesses to his 'death' in 1593 (Robert Poley and Nicholas Skeres) – were involved in the government's framing and unmasking of this plot. The messages that led to Mary's execution for treason were passed through double agent Gilbert Gifford, whose name is an intriguing reversal of that of the man arrested with Marlowe in 1592.

'Tom had been writing plays for Ned for months' Though no plays are extant, Tom Watson's employer, William Cornwallis, testified that devising 'twenty fictions and knaveries in a play' was his 'daily practice and his living', and Francis Meres in 1598 lists him as among 'our best for Tragedy'.

MIDDELBURG

Middelburg is adjacent to Flushing (or Vlissingen), their centres being less than five miles apart. It is here that Marlowe's translation of Ovid's *Amores* was apparently printed – a book that the Archbishop of Canterbury and the Bishop of London ordered to be banned (and burnt) in 1599.

Le Doux and his trunk suggest one way in which Marlowe might have led his 'posthumous' existence. Marlovian researcher Peter Farey's discoveries among the Bacon Papers in Lambeth Palace Library include a list of books in a trunk belonging to a Monsieur Le Doux. The Bacon Papers are the papers of Anthony Bacon (brother of lawyer and philosopher Francis), a spy who lived abroad from 1579 and sent intelligence back to his uncle, Lord Burghley, and Sir Francis Walsingham. Returning to England in 1592 he became spymaster for the Earl of Essex, gathering intelligence through an international network of agents. One of these was Le Doux, who Farey and fellow Marlovian A.D. Wraight speculate was an English agent posing as a Frenchman, as other English agents, such as Anthony Standen, had done. The presence on the book list of French and Italian dictionaries, but no English one, supports this theory, as does the fact that the list, though in French, is written in English secretary hand rather than the italic hand a French writer would have used. According to the International Genealogical Index, the only occurrence of the name Le Doux in England in three hundred years (sixteenth to mid-nineteenth centuries) was in the Huguenot population of Marlowe's home town, Canterbury; Louis Le Doux was more or less the same age as Marlowe and therefore a possible boyhood friend (Farey, 2000). The trunk contained numerous books identified by scholars as Shakespeare sources, and a number pertinent to Marlowe's canon. Le Doux was in Exton, Rutland, in late 1595, in London briefly in early 1596 and then abroad (Wraight, 1996), writing to Bacon for the last time from Middelburg on 22 June 1596.

'the outline of a marigold' Two different versions of Marlowe's *Hero and Leander* were published in 1598. On the title page of the quarto published by Paul Linley a woodcut shows two marigolds, one open to the sun, the other closed at night, with the motto *Non Licit Exigius*, which means either 'not permitted to those of mean spirit' or 'not permitted to the uninitiated'. The marigold was a flower with strong Catholic connotations; often linked with the Virgin Mary, it was also explicitly linked with Mary Tudor.

T.T. are the initials under the mysterious 'Mr W.H.' dedication of *Shake-speare's Sonnets* (1609), usually taken to be Thomas Thorpe. Thorpe, it was recently discovered, worked (like Marlowe) as an intelligencer, and was connected to Catholic figures who were considered a threat to the realm. In autumn 1596, he was in Madrid as 'the guest of Father Robert Persons, the outspoken Jesuit opponent of the English government and close adviser to the Spanish' (Martin and Finnis, p.4).

TAMBURLAINE THE SECOND

Robert Greene was a popular writer of romances and plays, described by the *Oxford Dictionary of National Biography* as 'England's first celebrity author'.

'Alphonsus, King of Aragon' is widely acknowledged as one of Greene's several attempts to cash in on Marlowe's success.

Thomas Walsingham was Marlowe's senior by three or four years. He was in Paris with Tom Watson in 1581, working from his older cousin Sir Francis Walsingham's embassy. At one point involved with intelligence operations, he was to become Marlowe's friend and patron.

HOTSPUR'S DESCENDANT

Hotspur's descendant In 1592 Marlowe claimed to be 'very well known' to Henry Percy, 9th Earl of Northumberland, also known as the Wizard Earl, a direct descendant of Henry Hotspur of *Henry IV, Part I* fame. Marlowe's friend Tom Watson dedicated two works to Northumberland. The earl, who amassed a library of over two thousand books at Petworth in Sussex, visited the Low Countries in 1588. His librarian, Walter Warner, was named by Thomas Kyd as an associate of Marlowe's (Nicholl, p.508).

'a history play' The fashion for English history plays began with Marlowe's *Edward II* and the *Henry VI* trilogy, plays attributed to Marlowe by scholars for two hundred years until the late 1920s (Riggs, p. 283).

First Rendezvous

Venus and Adonis, registered anonymously six weeks before Marlowe's 'death', was on the bookstalls two weeks after it. It is the earliest historical record to associate the name 'William Shakespeare' with literature (and there are no theatrical records mentioning that name before this date either). Scholars recognise 'compelling links' between this poem and Marlowe's *Hero and Leander*, which was not to be published for another five years (Duncan-Jones and Woudhuysen, p.21).

Richard Field, printer of *Venus and Adonis* and originally from Stratford-on-Avon, is usually referred to as a 'school friend' of Shakespeare's. He worked frequently for Lord Burghley, whose ward was the Earl of Southampton, to whom *Venus and Adonis* was dedicated.

'Let base conceited wits admire vile things./ Fair Phoebus lead me to the Muses' springs' is Marlowe's translation (from *Amores*) of the two-line Latin epigram on the title page of *Venus and Adonis*. This poem closes, 'Then though death racks my bones in funeral fire,/I'll live, and as he pulls me down, mount higher'.

The First Heir of My Invention

'The first heir of my invention' is the author's description of *Venus and Adonis* in his dedication to the Earl of Southampton.

The Jew of Malta

Thomas Nashe, one of the University Wits, was a writer of satirical and topical pamphlets. He, too, was educated at Cambridge, but by summer 1588 was living in London. Gabriel Harvey referred to Marlowe and Nashe as 'Aretine and the Devil's Orator'; Nashe defended Marlowe as one of his 'friends that used me like a friend'. His name appears with Marlowe's on the 1594 quarto of *Dido, Queen of Carthage*.

'Religion is made by men' 'That the first beginning of Religion was only to keep men in awe'. This and other of Marlowe's views on religion are listed in the famous Baines Note. (See note on 'A SLAVE WHOSE GALL COINS SLANDERS LIKE A MINT'. Three versions of the note exist. The transcripts of these, and other documents relating to Marlowe, can be found in Kuriyama (2002)).

William Bradley In March 1588, William Bradley borrowed £14 from John Alle(y)n, innkeeper, manager of the Admiral's Men at The Theatre, and Edward Alleyn's brother,

promising to pay it back the following August. This defaulted loan caused the subsequent feud between Bradley and those associated with John Allen, including Watson, his brother-in-law Hugh Swift, and Marlowe (Eccles, pp. 57–68).
Hugh Swift is thought to have acted as John Allen's lawyer after Bradley's loan defaulted. In autumn 1589 he was threatened by Bradley's friend George Orrell and took out a surety of the peace. A similar surety was lodged shortly after by Bradley, naming Hugh Swift, John Allen and Tom Watson.

That Men Should Put an Enemy in Their Mouths

'A comedy' It is a common misrepresentation of Marlowe that he couldn't be funny. We know there were comic scenes in *Tamburlaine* which the printer confessed to omitting, thinking them too frivolous for the serious subject matter. *Doctor Faustus* contains a number of comic scenes and *The Jew of Malta* can be played as a farce. There is also a great deal of comedy in *Hero and Leander*. Marlowe was widely referred to as a wit, and one has only to read the accusations in the Baines Note to appreciate Marlowe in full comedic flow.
Padua was the university attended by Danish students named Rosencrantz and Guildenstern in 1596.
Chronicles *Hall's Chronicles,* chief source for the history plays.

The University Men

Poley Robert (Robin) Poley was a key figure in the Elizabethan government's intelligence service. Described by Ben Jonson's tutor William Camden as 'very expert at dissembling', he had been instrumental in trapping the conspirators associated with the Babington Plot, which in turn led to the execution of Mary, Queen of Scots.
Cornwallis William Cornwallis (not to be confused with his cousin the essayist) bought Fisher's Folly in Bishopsgate from the Earl of Oxford in autumn 1588. A suspected Catholic recusant, he was under government surveillance. Watson, appointed as the family tutor not long after his arrival in London, was likely part of this surveillance.
Arbella Stuart was first cousin to James VI of Scotland, and at this time, like him, was considered a strong contender to succeed to the throne. In spring 1589 (when her tutor 'Morley' was appointed) she was fourteen years old.

The Tutor

Perhaps on account of his 'bad boy' reputation, and a belief that Arbella was resident in Derbyshire when Marlowe was in London, scholars have discounted the idea of Marlowe as Arbella Stuart's tutor without thorough investigation. However, the 'Morley' described by Bess of Hardwick, the **Countess of Shrewsbury**, who was the orphaned Arbella's grandmother and guardian, in her September 1592 letter to Lord Burghley, is a better fit for Marlowe than any other proposed candidate. Writers were frequently employed in this capacity and Marlowe's experience as an 'intelligencer' would make him well suited to such a sensitive position. That he had previously been employed by the State in a matter of extreme trust is confirmed by the 1587 Privy Council letter signed by Lord Burghley and other members of the Privy Council. That the 'Morley' in question asked for forty pounds a year, complaining of being 'so much damnified by leaving of the university' and that in the very month that Marlowe was called an atheist in print the countess writes of 'withall of late having some cause to be doubtful' of the tutor's 'forwardness in religion' fits Marlowe perfectly. Marlowe's documented presence in London at points during 1589 to 1592 does not clash with Arbella's known movements. We know that in 1589 Arbella spent much of her time in London with her aunt and uncle (Gristwood, p. 99) and was there with her grandmother from October 1591 to August 1592.

The Hog Lane Affray

The most authoritative source on this incident remains Eccles' *Christopher Marlowe in London*, but details can be discovered in any Marlowe biography.

Limbo

Marlowe was in Newgate prison from 18 September to 3 December 1589. In November, just before Marlowe's release, Thomas Walsingham inherited Scadbury on the death of his brother Edmund. Watson was not released until 12 February 1590. **Sir William Stanley** fought loyally for the Queen in Ireland and at the taking of Deventer in the Low Countries in 1587, but shortly afterwards handed Deventer back to the Spanish and converted to Catholicism, maintaining an 'English Regiment' loyal to the Catholic cause. He favoured his cousin Ferdinando Stanley for the throne, or Arbella Stuart, whom he planned to kidnap (Kendall, p. 170).

John Poole was a Catholic counterfeiter, brother-in-law to Sir William Stanley. The Baines Note tells us that Marlowe was acquainted with Poole, and that he met him while imprisoned in Newgate. For more on Poole, see Nicholl (pp. 286–98).

Ferdinando Stanley The future Earl of Derby was, until his father's death in 1593, known as Lord Strange. Marlowe claimed to be 'very well known' to him in 1592, according to Sir Robert Sidney's letter to Lord Burghley. Nashe (see note on 'The Jew of Malta') was connected to him also, and is thought to have dedicated to him a bawdy poem known as 'Nashe's Dildo'. Strange's Men staged both late Marlowe and early Shakespeare plays.

POOLE THE PRISONER

'we're in a place the State denies exists' Limbo being a Catholic concept. The official State religion had been Protestantism since Queen Elizabeth had succeeded to the throne in 1558.

A TWIN

'never blots a word' In the *First Folio* (1623) Heminges and Condell, Shakespeare's business partners (as shareholders in the Lord Chamberlain's Men), say, 'We have scarce received from him a blot in his papers'. Ben Jonson, in a private notebook published posthumously, says, 'I remember, the Players have often mentioned it as an honour to Shakespeare, that in his writing, (whatsoever he penned) he never blotted out a line. My answer hath been, Would he had blotted a thousand. Which they thought a malevolent speech.'

'shareholder in the players' company' The first mention of William Shakespeare in connection to the theatre is a payment in the accounts of the Treasurer of the Chamber in March 1595 for company performances at Court during Christmas 1594. There is good evidence he was a shareholder in the Lord Chamberlain's Men but no reliable primary source to support the idea he was an actor.

'Nashe is in prison' Thomas Nashe was imprisoned for *Christ's Tears Over Jerusalem* in 1593.

NECESSITY

Thomas Kyd wrote *The Spanish Tragedy* and is considered by some to be the author of an early version of Hamlet, known as the *Ur-Hamlet*, on the basis of a reference by

Nashe in 1589 to 'whole Hamlets, I should say handfuls of tragical speeches' just after an apparent allusion to Kyd. Kyd's first letter to Lord Keeper Puckering after his arrest in 1593 testifies that he and Marlowe were 'writing in one chamber two years since'. A version of *Hamlet* was certainly staged in 1594.

Bedlam The original Bethlehem Hospital (for the insane) was situated in Bishopsgate, directly opposite the Cornwallis house, Fisher's Folly.

'Ann Watson's there' Ann Watson's brother, musician Thomas Swift, was brought up in the Cornwallis household.

THE SCHOOL OF NIGHT

The School of Night refers loosely to the free-thinkers who gravitated to the Raleigh/ Northumberland circle.

Sir Walter Raleigh In an anonymous agent's report on Richard Cholmeley, Marlowe is said to have 'read the Atheist Lecture to Sir Walter Raleigh & others' (Kuriyama, p. 215). The Baines Note quotes Marlowe as saying that 'Moses was but a juggler, & that one Heriot being Sir Walter Raleigh's man can do more than he.'

'I have a mathematician in my pay' Thomas Harriot's connection to Marlowe is mentioned in the Baines Note, and by Kyd in his first letter to Lord Keeper Puckering. Mathematician and astronomer Harriot was employed both by Raleigh and by Henry Percy, 9th Earl of Northumberland.

'Come Live With Me and Be My Love' Raleigh famously wrote a verse response to Marlowe's lyric poem, 'The Passionate Shepherd to His Love', entitled 'The Nymph's Reply to the Shepherd'.

George Carey Second cousin to the Queen, brother-in-law of Lord Strange, and Lord Chamberlain from 1597, when he followed his father as patron of Shakespeare's company of players.

Matthew Roydon Poet, intelligencer, an associate of Marlowe, according to Kyd.

THE BANISHMENT OF KENT

King Leir was performed at the Rose Theatre on 6 and 8 April 1594, and registered for publication that May. Widely agreed as a source of Shakespeare's *King Lear*, this earlier version of the story was published as *The True Chronical History of King Leir and His Three Daughters* in 1605. It does not contain the sub-plot of slander revolving round

Gloucester, Edgar and Edmund, or the banishment of Kent. Some scholars argue the same author wrote both versions.

TOBACCO AND BOOZE

That Marlowe did not originally say 'tobacco and boys' but rather 'tobacco and booze' was first suggested by Stewart Young (2008). The word in the Baines Note is 'boies'. 'Booze', though it sounds modern, is a variant of 'bouse' (*c.* 1300) and *OED* examples of its usage include 'bowsing' ('boozing') in a 1592 pamphlet by Thomas Nashe.

BURYING THE MOOR

'**Moor**' was the Queen's nickname for Sir Francis Walsingham. He died on 6 April 1590 owing the Queen about £42,000, 'largely from expenditure on the Crown's business without obtaining privy seal warrants'. According to the *Oxford Dictionary of National Biography*, his burial at night was to avoid his creditors.

'**the tomb of his son-in-law**' Walsingham's daughter Frances was the widow of Sir Philip Sidney, courtier poet, to whose sister, the Countess of Pembroke, Marlowe was to dedicate Tom Watson's posthumous *Amintae Gaudia*.

'**Phaeton**' Ovid tells how Phaeton, son of the sun god Helios, obtains his father's permission to drive the sun chariot, but fails to control it, with fatal results.

SOUTHAMPTON

'**Why should I marry who that man decrees?**' Henry Wriothesley, 3rd Earl of Southampton, was a ward of Lord Burghley, who wanted him to marry his granddaughter Lady Elizabeth Vere (neglected offspring of the Earl of Oxford). That the first seventeen of '*Shake-speares Sonnets*' are addressed to the Earl of Southampton, who would turn seventeen on 6 October 1590, was first proposed by Nathan Drake (1817) and has been widely supported.

ARBELLA

The Earl of Essex Arbella Stuart had a fondness for the Earl of Essex which she continued to express for many years (Gristwood, pp. 105–6).

'**your cousin Frances had his child tucked in her belly**' The birth of a son in January

1591 indicates that Essex and Lady Sidney conceived their child around the time of her father's funeral.

'the Duke of Parma's son, Farnese' Arbella's possible marriage to Farnese was being brokered in Flushing by Robert Poley's man Michael Moody only weeks before Marlowe's presence there.

POISONING THE WELL

Richard Baines was an English intelligence agent who penetrated the Jesuit seminary at Rheims and was ordained as a priest during the time that Tom Watson and Thomas Walsingham were in Paris. He confided to a friend his plan to murder everyone at the seminary by poisoning the well. The friend betrayed him and he was subsequently tortured, his wrists being tied behind his back before he was suspended by them (the strappado). Boas was the first to recognise him as the model for Barabas in *The Jew of Malta*. Roy Kendall's book on Baines is invaluable in understanding his relationship with Marlowe and espionage (Kendall).

DANGER IS IN WORDS

'I go as Morley' Elizabethan names were flexible. Marlowe was known by many names including Merlin and Marlin (at Cambridge), Morley, and Marley. He is referred to as Morley on a number of official documents: the Privy Council letter of 1587, the Coroner's Inquest document, and Tom Watson and Ingram Frizer's pardons. As Sarah Gristwood observes in relation to his dual lives as intelligencer and writer, he 'managed to split the different sides of his life completely' (Gristwood, p. 459).

FLUSHING

Richard Cholmeley claimed that Marlowe made him an atheist. Cholmeley was 'a companion' of Thomas Drury in 1591, and arrested with him, but it seems he was subsequently released and paid for his role in turning Drury in to the authorities (Nicholl, p. 332).

Drury Thomas Drury describes Richard Baines as one who 'used to resort unto me', and appears to claim that it was he who procured the Baines Note, in a letter to Anthony Bacon dated 1 August 1593 (Kendall, p. 336).

A Resurrection

Gilbert Gifford, known by his alias Jaques Colerdin and his Cipher '4', was a double agent who, like Baines, became a Catholic priest. He spent time at the Catholic seminaries at both Douai (during Tom Watson's time there) and at Rheims (missing Baines on several occasions, and by the smallest margin). After gaining the trust of Mary, Queen of Scots, and being given the key to papal ciphers, he was instrumental in unravelling the Babington Plot. His death in a Paris gaol is supported by the scantiest of evidence: in a letter dated November 1591 from Henry Walpole, Jesuit chaplain to Sir William Stanley's regiment. Two months later 'Gifford Gilbert' appears in Flushing in the company of agents Marlowe and Baines (Kendall, pp. 144–51).

The Fatal Labyrinth of Misbelief

'I've as much right to coin as the Queen of England' Marlowe was quoted as saying this in the Baines Note.

Governor Sidney Sir Robert Sidney, brother of the dead courtier, soldier and poet Sir Philip Sidney, and of Mary Sidney, Countess of Pembroke, was Governor of Flushing in 1592.

Betrayed

'To see the goldsmith's cunning' The reason for the counterfeiting that Marlowe gave to Sir Robert Sidney, as stated in his letter to Lord Burghley dated 26 January 1592, where other details of this conversation appear.

Returned to the Lord Treasurer

'the Strand' Cecil House, Lord Burghley's London home, was an imposing house on the Strand.

Collaboration

'My play' *Henry VI Part I* is widely considered to be co-authored, and somewhat of a mess. F. G. Fleay (1875) argued the authors were Marlowe, Greene, Peele and an unknown writer of limited skill, whom A. D. Wraight identifies as Edward Alleyn (Wraight, 1993, pp 251–76).

'the Crow' Despite a well-established belief that the 'upstart Crow' in Greene's *Groatsworth of Wit* alludes to William Shakespeare, there are good reasons to believe it actually refers to the actor Edward Alleyn (Pinksen). That actors take precedence over writers in the public's mind is at the heart of Greene's complaint. Plays were associated with theatre companies, not their authors, and the line Greene quotes from *Henry VI Part III* would evoke in his readers' minds not the unknown author but the actor who played the part. In the main text of *Groatsworth*, Roberto (whom Greene identifies with himself) meets a 'substantial' Player, who asks Roberto to write for him, promising he will be well paid. In 1592, readers would have recognised this wealthy Player 'thundering on the stage' as Edward Alleyn, chief shareholder and manager of Lord Strange's Men. Greene wrote for Alleyn. In a letter following the main text, Greene reports he is now dying from poverty, and urges fellow playwrights Marlowe, Nashe and George Peele not to trust actors, 'those Puppets . . . that speak from our mouths', and in particular one 'upstart Crow' who believes himself 'as well able to bombast out a blank verse as the best of you': this last phrase aimed specifically at Marlowe. From April to June 1592, Lord Strange's Men were performing *Tambercam*, a probable rip-off of Marlowe's *Tamburlaine*: Phillip Henslowe, buying it from Alleyn in 1602, refers to it uniquely as 'his book'. Thus converging lines of evidence identify Alleyn as Greene's singular target: the Player and upstart Crow who imagined he could write, left his writers to die in poverty after benefiting from their talents, and was 'in his own conceit the only Shake-scene [actor] in a country'.

THE SCHOOL OF ATHEISM

'An anonymous agent' Richard Verstegen is believed to be the author of *An advertisement written to a secretarie of my L. Treasurers of Ingland, by an Inglishe intelligencer as he passed throughe Germanie towardes Italie* (1592), a condensed version of Jesuit Robert Person's *Responsio*. The attack, focused on Lord Burghley, accused Sir Walter Raleigh of running a 'school of atheism'.

'teach scholars "to spell God backward"' This claim, directed at the 'school of atheism' in *An advertisement,* can be read as a reference to *Doctor Faustus*: 'Within this circle is Jehovah's name,/Forward and backward anagrammatiz'd' (Act 1, scene iii). Marlowe was thus implicated in this dangerous public accusation of atheism.

HOLYWELL STREET

Holywell Street Robert Greene died in the house of one Mistress Isham in Dowgate, but he had previously fathered a son with the prostitute Em Ball. He seems to have fallen out with her by the time he was approaching death, but Marlowe's biographer Mark Eccles notes the possibility that 'Greene was staying in Holywell, where his mistress lived, at the same time that Marlowe was bound over to keep the peace toward the constables of Holywell Street in May 1592' (p. 126). Less than five months later, and following Verstegen's tentative allusion to Marlowe's atheism in *An advertisement*, Greene was the first to finger Marlowe as an atheist in a direct and identifiable manner (in *Groatsworth of Wit*).

A GROATSWORTH OF WIT

Greene's *Groatsworth of Wit* – and despite the current scholarly consensus it is almost certainly Greene's rather than Chettle's (Westley) – was registered on 20 September 1592, seventeen days after Greene's death. Gabriel Harvey shows familiarity with the contents as early as 8 September, so it may have been published before this.
'St Paul's' The area around St Paul's churchyard was the centre of the publishing trade, full of stationers and booksellers. Thomas Kyd, Thomas Thorpe, Gabriel Harvey and Sir John Davies all speak of it as one of Marlowe's haunts.
'Thom Nashe was gone to spy on the Church' Nashe, in a secretarial capacity, was staying with Archbishop of Canterbury John Whitgift at his palace in Croydon.

THE COBBLER'S SON

Corkine On Friday, 15 September, just below the Chequers Inn, Canterbury, Marlowe attacked the tailor William Corkine with a stick and dagger. He was bailed by his father, John. In October the case was dropped by mutual consent (Urry, pp. 65–8).

A SLAVE WHOSE GALL COINS SLANDERS LIKE A MINT

'There is a note' The dating of 'A note Containing the opinion of one Christopher Marley Concerning his Damnable Judgment of Religion, and scorn of gods word' is uncertain. The carefully edited final version endorsed 'as sent to her H' says it was 'delivered on Whitsun eve last', but this date (2 June 1593), falling after Marlowe's apparent death, would make the Note (and its two carefully altered versions) pointless.

Drury was sent to 'stay one Mr Baines' as a condition of his release from prison the previous November. He writes of delivering to Lord Keeper Puckering and Lord Buckhurst (Whitgift allies) 'the notablist and vilest articles of atheism that I suppose the like were never known or read of in any age', saying the Note was 'delivered to her Highness and command given by herself to prosecute it to the full' (Kendall, p. 336). Most scholars, assuming error rather than deliberate obfuscation, assign the Note a delivery date of 26 May, a week before the 'Whitsun eve' declared, but it may have been in existence much earlier. Historians of Chislehurst in the nineteenth century stated that the Baines Note was the reason for Marlowe's retreat to Scadbury, and Tucker Brooke arrived independently at the possibility that the Baines Note preceded the arrest warrant of 18 May (Kendall, pp. 308, 281). Gabriel Harvey (a contemporary of Baines who was with him at Christ's College, Cambridge for five years) thanks an unnamed person for 'his invaluable Note, that could teach you to achieve more with the little finger of Policy, than you can possibly compass with the mighty arm of Prowess' and paraphrases the Baines Note's first line, in a letter dated 27 April (Barber).

'To Scotland, where your friend went' Thomas Kyd said of Marlowe 'He would persuade with men of quality to go unto the King of Scots whither I hear Royden is gone and where if he had lived he told me when I saw him last he meant to be.' Roydon had left for Scotland some time after 26 April 1593 (Nicholl, p. 312).

THE PLOT

'the Verge' was defined as an area within twelve miles of the Queen's person. Any killing occurring within the Verge would be handled by the Queen's Coroner.

Ingram Frizer, a loyal servant of the Walsingham family, often acted as their business agent. After apparently killing Christopher Marlowe he received the Queen's pardon with unusual swiftness (in one month). He was doing business for Thomas Walsingham the next day and remained in the family's service until his death. On the accession of King James I in 1603 he was granted numerous leases in reversion on Crown lands (Bakeless, vol.1, p. 165).

Nicholas Skeres was a minor player in the Babington Plot, a business partner of Ingram Frizer (in conning gullible young gentlemen out of their money) and had loaned money to Matthew Roydon.

John Whitgift In 1593 the Archbishop of Canterbury and his supporters on the Privy
Council had growing influence on the Queen, and were in conflict with Lord Burghley
(now ageing and in ill-health) over the prosecution of religious dissenters. Peter Farey
has recently argued that Marlowe's disappearance – which would be unlikely to succeed
without official sanction – was essentially a compromise between those members of the
Privy Council who wished to keep him in the service of the nation (Burghley, Essex)
and those who wished him prosecuted for atheism (Whitgift, Puckering). A faked death
not only allowed him to be silenced and controlled, but to be paraded by the Church as
an example of the punishment God would inflict upon sinners. Puckering's involvement
in the cover-up may be read from the fact that amendments to the Baines Note,
including the alteration of 'sudden and violent death' to the more equivocal 'sudden
and fearful end of his life', are in his hand (Nicholl, p. 323). Whitgift's knowledge of it
may be indicated by the fact that he personally signed the licence for *Venus and Adonis*
when it was 'relatively unusual' for him to do so (Duncan-Jones, p. 743), and from his
subsequent suppression (through the Bishop's Ban of 1599) of works where doubts
about the identity of Shakespeare were aired.

'FLY, FLYE AND NEVER RETURNE'
The title is from a line in the Dutch Church Libel. This poem in iambic pentameter,
posted on the wall of a Dutch churchyard on 5 May 1593, looks like a deliberate
attempt to implicate Marlowe in the recent unrest against foreigners, referencing his
plays *The Massacre at Paris* and *The Jew of Malta*, and being signed 'Tamberlaine'.
'Walter Ráleigh spoke against the Dutchmen' In late March 1593, Raleigh was 'the
lone voice of dissent' in opposing a House of Commons bill to extend trade privileges
to immigrant (largely Dutch) merchants (Nicholl, pp. 358–9). Government policy was to
welcome the immigrants on the grounds they were Protestants. Raleigh and Marlowe
were connected to each other, and to atheism, in government documents.

KYD'S TRAGEDY
'They arrest my former room-mate' With Marlowe being absent from London, the
direct result of the Dutch Church Libel was the arrest (and, probably, torture) of his
former room-mate, Thomas Kyd (Freeman).

'some lines against the Trinity' The papers contained anti-Trinitarian arguments similar to the tenets of Arianism that had been published openly four decades earlier in John Proctor's *The Fall of the Late Arian* (1549).

'from the fact he set inquisitors on me' Kyd's letter and note to Puckering were written when he believed Marlowe was already dead. (He says, in Latin, 'the dead do not bite'). That 'the ignorant suspect me guilty of the former shipwreck' suggests he was being blamed for what had happened to Marlowe.

BY ANY OTHER NAME

'Machevil' The spelling favoured in Marlowe's *Jew of Malta*: 'Make evil'.

'It's Marlowe on the warrant' The Domestic State Papers record it as 'Marlow'. On his appearance before the Privy Council two days later, he is 'Marley'.

DEPTFORD STRAND

'Come from The Hague' Robert Poley was carrying urgent letters from The Hague, yet inexplicably delayed their delivery by ten days. For two of those days, the so-called 'feast' on 30 May, and the inquest on 1 June, he was in Deptford. A payment to Poley covering 8 May to 8 June states explicitly that he was in the Queen's service 'all the aforesaid time'.

John Penry was 'one of the most important martyrs of Congregationalism'. The possibility that John Penry's corpse was substituted for Marlowe's was first suggested by David A. More (More). Sentenced to death on 25 May, Penry was executed at St Thomas-a-Watering, two miles from Deptford, on 29 May. His body is unaccounted for, but would have been within the control of Queen's Coroner William Danby, who conducted Marlowe's inquest (Farey, 2007).

THE GOBLET

If Marlowe's detractor is the same Richard Baines who was hanged at Tyburn in 1594, as Kendall argues persuasively, the parallels between his case and the cup-stealing scene in *Doctor Faustus* between Robin and Dick, smack of something more than coincidence, strongly suggesting the scene is a post-1594 addition. Richard can be shortened to 'Dick' and Robert Poley was often called 'Robin'. In *Doctor Faustus*, Robin gets Dick to hold the cup while he is searched (Kendall, pp. 322–8).

'No benefit of clergy. He was hanged' Ben Jonson, on killing a man, escaped execution through 'benefit of clergy', the abilty to recite from memory Psalm 51 (referred to as 'neck verse'). The Richard Baines hanged at Tyburn was found guilty of robbery (a crime for which one couldn't plead benefit of clergy) rather than burglary (for which one could); the distinction being that the victims were present in the property when the theft took place.

THE HOPE

'the Phoenix' An emblem commonly associated with Queen Elizabeth I, possibly after the Phoenix portrait by Nicholas Hilliard (c. 1575).

SICKENING

'Even to be accused of heresy' Leading legal adviser to Archbishop Whitgift, Richard Cosin, had published *Apology of sundry proceedings by Jurisdiction Ecclesiastical*, a 700-page defence of ex-officio oaths, by April 1593. In it, Cosin explains that against 'a grievous crime' such as heresy or atheism, a judge has the power to proceed even without evidence (Shagan, p. 559).

MONTANUS

Pietro Montanus Peter Farey has explored a number of possible Marlowe aliases in addition to Louis Le Doux. One of these is Montanus. On 9 May 1595, someone calling himself Pietro Montanus arrived in London, ill and without funds. He had entered the country using a forged passport, which alleged he was a French servant of Anthony Bacon. Bacon looked after him while he was ill. On 15 and 23 March, he wrote two letters (in Latin) to an espionage agent of Lord Burghley, Peter Edgcombe, in which he complains he has not been supplied with the provisions, money and safe conduct he was promised. He speaks not only of his illness, but of his 'great calamity'. Farey notes that in *Hamlet*, the original name of the man sent by Polonius to spy on Laertes was not Reynaldo, but Montano (Farey, 2000). Anthony Bacon's documented connection to Marlowe begins with Thomas Drury's letter to Bacon two months after the Deptford incident. Le Doux is associated with Bacon throughout 1595 and 1596, and the Bacon Papers contain several letters from and about Le Doux in this period.

Bishopsgate Street Anthony Bacon rented a house in Bishopsgate Street, almost next door to the Bull Inn, and within easy reach of the theatres of Shoreditch, from April or May 1594 until September 1595 when he moved to a suite of rooms in Essex House (Du Maurier, pp. 131, 154).

MADAME LE DOUX

'The Earl of Derby's death' Ferdinando Stanley died 16 April 1594 after a mysterious illness. It was widely suspected he had been poisoned after informing the government of a Catholic plot intended to place him on the English throne. After his death, key figures from his acting company formed the Lord Chamberlain's Men.

'He comes to London only twice a year' Despite the sustained myth of his deep involvement in the day-to-day business of the Lord Chamberlain's Men, there is little evidence to support William Shakespeare's continuous presence in London (where his lodgings were of a temporary nature) and much that argues against it.

INTERVAL

the Earl of Rutland Friend of the Earl of Southampton and, with him, an avid theatre-goer, Rutland was at Padua University at the same time as two students named Rosencrantz and Guildenstern.

A CHANGE OF ADDRESS

Sir John Harington of Exton, Rutland, was first cousin to Sir Philip Sidney (the soldier poet, first husband of Sir Francis Walsingham's daughter), Sir Robert (governor of Flushing) and their sister Mary Sidney, Countess of Pembroke, to whose sons Shakespeare's *First Folio* Shakespeare was dedicated in 1623. His daughter Lucy married at fourteen to become Countess of Bedford.

Burley on the Hill Le Doux arrived at Burley in October 1595 and remained there until 25 January 1596 when he left with Sir John Harington.

HOW *RICHARD II* FOLLOWED *RICHARD III*

Posthumous is the unusual given name of the hero of *Cymbeline*, a man of low birth but high personal merit, who is banished from the kingdom for exceeding his station.

It was also the name of the first cousin who connected Anthony Bacon to the Haringtons.

NOTHING LIKE THE SUN

Jaques Petit Anthony Bacon's Gascon servant Petit was to arrive at Burley on 10 December 1595. The woman known as Ide du Vault, appointed as governess to Harington's small daughter, had preceded him.

Ide du Vault/Madame Vallereine The woman depicted here as the *Sonnets*' Dark Lady was indeed known by both names. She signs her name 'du Vault' on her letters, but they are endorsed as being from 'Madame Vallereine'. In one of his letters, Jaques Petit refers to her as Ide du Vault, and in another plays on both names by calling her Miss-worth-nothing (Mzel Vaultrein). (Wraight, 1996).

'ruined nun' Petit says du Vault is a defrocked nun. He refers to her as '*la nonain*' but also calls her a whore.

WILL HALL

Unconfirmed evidence of an agent named 'Will Hall' is reported but not referenced in *The Shakespeare Conspiracy* (Phillips and Keatman). Hall's first appearance in the records is allegedly recorded in Canterbury in 1592 in connection with writer and intelligencer Anthony Munday. A payment to 'Hall and Wayte' for carrying messages to the Low Countries was supposedly made on 19 March 1596. (It is a William Wayte who takes out a surety of the peace against one William Shakespeare in November of the same year.) In October 1601 'Willm Halle' returns with intelligence from Denmark. The *Sonnets*' dedication famously begins, 'TO THE ONLIE BEGETTER OF THESE ENSUING SONNETS MR W.H. ALL HAPPINESSE' and Donald Foster has demonstrated that 'begetter' at this time was, with one deliberate exception that plays on the convention, always a reference to the author. Foster's solution is that 'W.H.' is a typo for 'W.SH.' (Foster). A solution suggested by Peter Farey is that the author is at this point going by the name of Will Hall (Farey, 2000).

MY TRUE LOVE SENT TO ME

'Pembroke's Men to come from London with a play' The Earl of Pembroke's Men played *Titus Andronicus* at Burley on the Hill during the Christmas Le Doux was there.

Reporting on the Christmas festivities in January 1596, Petit notes that 'the tragedy of Titus Andronicus' was played, adding 'but the performance was better than the subject matter.'

HAL

Ganymede in Greek myth was abducted by Zeus to be cup-bearer to the gods, and his sexual plaything.

THE AUTHORS OF SHAKESPEARE

'A lawyer playwright' A reference to John Marston who, with Joseph Hall in various publications from 1597 to 1598, discussed an author they nicknamed Labeo, whom Marston implies is the author of *Venus and Adonis*. He identifies Labeo with a heraldic motto used exclusively by Francis and Anthony Bacon, 'Mediocra Firma'. H. N. Gibson, who argued against a range of authorship candidates in his book *The Shakespeare Claimants*, calls this 'the one piece of evidence in the whole Baconian case that demands serious consideration' (Gibson, p. 63). All copies of the books in which Marston and Hall discussed 'Labeo' were subsequently ordered to be burnt by Archbishop Whitgift and the Bishop of London (1599).

'Picks up a play from Bacon' On 25 January 1595 – incidentally the day that Le Doux left Burley – Francis Bacon wrote to his brother Anthony from Twickenham Lodge: 'I have here an idle pen or two, specially one that was cozened, thinking to have gotten some money this term; I pray send me somewhat else for them to write out besides your Irish collection which is almost done' (Cockburn, p. 147). Cockburn says, 'Bacon evidently had several young men at the Lodge doing copying work for him' (p. 148). That Francis Bacon (or his scribes) had possession of several Shakespeare works, including *Richard II* and *Richard III*, is supported by The Northumberland Manuscript (pp. 164–83). On this mixed inventory of works from 1595 to 1597, the name 'William Shakespeare' is scribbled repeatedly as if for practice. No play was published under the name 'William Shakespeare' until *Richard II* and *Richard III* in 1598. The *First Folio* comments of Heminges and Condell regarding blotless manuscripts make it clear that they only received fair copies of the plays, and that this was unusual.

'verse fit only for lighting fires' Oxford's talent in the poetic arts can be determined from examples of his work at www.elizabethanauthors.com/oxfordpoems

Mr Disorder

On 14 December 1595, Petit complains that 'Christmas is the cause of 'much vain expense' for 'des tragedies et jeux de M. Le Desordre': tragedies and plays by Mr Disorder'.

In Disgrace with Fortune and Men's Eyes

'letters for two friends in London' Ide du Vault wrote two letters dated 24 January 1595, one to Jean Castol, minister of the French Church in London and friend of Anthony Bacon, the other to a Madame Vilegre. Le Doux was to be the carrier. Someone copied both letters on to a single sheet of paper and sent these copies to Bacon.

The Earl of Essex

'cousin of the Queen' The maternal great-grandmother of Robert Devereux, 2nd Earl of Essex, was Mary Stafford, née Boleyn, elder sister of the Queen's mother, Anne.

'a memo' Essex issued Le Doux with a passport on 10 February 1596 and another a month later (Wraight, 1996, pp. 55–6). A document headed 'Memoires Instructives' (LPL MS 656 f.186) details what the Earl of Essex expects from his new agent on the continent. He is particularly keen for intelligence from Italy. Intimate first-hand knowledge of certain Italian cities has long been one of the arguments against the man traditionally attributed with the authorship of the Shakespeare plays and poems. The author's detailed knowledge of a fresco in the northern Italian town of Bassano, as revealed by passages in *Othello*, has led one scholar to propose recently that he *must* have visited Italy (Prior). Twenty years' research on this subject has just been published in *The Shakespeare Guide to Italy: Retracing the Bard's Unknown Travels* (Roe).

'a seal' In the Manuscripts section of the British Library, Peter Farey found a seal, identified by the Library as sixteenth century, bearing the name Louis Le Doux. It depicts a man in Elizabethan dress, in all respects normal except his face is covered by a blank mask.

Merry Wives

'some scraps of me' In *The Merry Wives of Windsor* (Act III, scene i) the verse that Sir Hugh Evans sings to cheer himself up is from Marlowe's 'A Passionate Shepherd to His

Love': 'Mercy on me! I have a great dispositions to cry,' he says, and on a second attempt, mixes Marlowe's poem with words based on Psalm 137, 'By the rivers of Babylon', which Farey points out is 'perhaps the best known song of exile ever written.' Sir Hugh also mangles 'fragrant' to 'vagram', perhaps as close to 'vagrant' as the author dares. Further details in Chapter 5 of *A Deception At Deptford* (Farey, 2000).

In the Theatre of God's Judgments
The Theatre of God's Judgments was a bestselling tract by Thomas Beard, detailing the punishments God metes out to heretics, atheists and blasphemers. First published in 1597, it was reprinted several times over the next fifty years.

A Kit May Look at a King
'Burghley is dead' William Cecil died on the 4 August 1598.
'working for the French' A letter dated 28 October 1598 reveals a man named Le Doux is working for Lord Buzenval, French ambassador at The Hague, carrying messages and money between him and the King, Henri IV, in Paris. Le Doux continued travelling between the two for the next eleven months, spending marked periods with the King (Gamble).
'France signed peace with Spain' In a diplomatic move, the Protestant Henri IV had converted to Catholicism in 1593, saying, 'Paris is well worth a mass'. On 2 May 1598, to the dismay of the English, he signed a peace treaty with Spain. The money he was sending to Lord Buzenval, however, appears to have been in support of Dutch resistance against Spanish occupation.
Navarre The King had formerly been the King of Navarre, and Anthony Bacon had formed a strong friendship with him during his twelve years in France (1580–92). The inexplicably detailed references to the court of Navarre contained in *Love's Labours Lost* include the pointed caricature (as Don Armado) of a man both Anthony Bacon and Henri IV knew well, Antonio Perez. Le Doux mentions both Perez and Edmund Walsingham (Thomas Walsingham's brother) in a letter to Bacon dated 20 April 1596. Two and a half years later, a man named Le Doux is in direct contact with the former King of Navarre (Gamble).
Wittenburg The real-life Faustus attended this university, as did Shakespeare's Hamlet.
'he is announced' The Earl of Southampton had arrived at the Paris embassy in April

1598 and remained there until November, bar a short return to England in August to marry Elizabeth Vernon, a cousin of the Earl of Essex whom he had impregnated. Le Doux delivered a letter to the French king in late October 1598.

'She's in the Fleet' Queen Elizabeth, always outraged when one of her maids of honour got married without her permission (and especially when they got pregnant) had imprisoned her.

A ROSE

'some sixteen years ago' The anonymous author of *Ulysses upon Ajax* (1596) speaks of 'witty Tom Watson's jests, I heard them in Paris 14 years ago', putting Watson there in 1582.

'It's said you died blaspheming' This myth began with Beard (1597).

Ned Blount Edward Blount published Marlowe's unfinished *Hero and Leander* (1598) with a dedication to the recently knighted Sir Thomas Walsingham, describing Marlowe as 'the man, that hath been dear unto us'. The other 1598 edition, published by Paul Linley, in which George Chapman had completed the poem and broken it into sestiads, also carried the dedication from Blount to Walsingham, in this version signed only with the initials 'E.B. Thorpe' addresses Blount as Marlowe's friend in a letter accompanying Marlowe's translation of *Lucan's First Book* (1600). Blount was also publisher of the *First Folio* (1623).

George Chapman completed Marlowe's *Hero and Leander* and published it in 1598 with a dedication to Thomas Walsingham's wife Audrey, contributing more lines than Marlowe had written and altering the structure.

CHAPMAN'S CURSE

'fresh from communing with the spirit world'

> 'Was it his spirit, by spirits taught to write
>
> Above a mortal pitch, that struck me dead?' Sonnet 86

It was chiefly these lines that caused a number of scholars, starting with William Minto in 1874, to identify George Chapman as the Rival Poet. Chapman claimed to have been visited by the spirit of Homer while writing his translation of *The Iliad*, published the same year. The chief reason this identification was not ratified was that no connection could be found between George Chapman and William Shakespeare.

Concerning the English

'I'm falling sick' On 24 September 1599 Essex set sail from Ireland against the Queen's express command; his decision to do so would have been taken days earlier. On 25 September 1599, Buzenval writes to King Henri IV, 'I will shortly send you Le Doux who has been here three days, unwell.'

'Cecil' Lord Treasurer Burghley's son, Robert Cecil, now a privy councillor.

Orsino's Castle, Bracciano

Orsino Duke Orsino's seat was a castle at Bracciano, in a mountainous region north of Rome. Inspired by Leslie Hotson's work on *Twelfth Night*, A. D. Wraight speculated that Marlowe may have spent some time there around 1600 (Wraight, 1993, pp. 369–423).

'Oh, you will like it' *As You Like It*, where all the central characters are living in exile, contains a discussion of *Hero and Leander*, of the 'feigning' nature of poets, and an allusion to Marlowe's death (paraphrasing a line from his *Jew of Malta*) that reveals inside knowledge. (That the dispute resulting in Marlowe's apparent death was supposed to have been over 'the reckoning' (the bill) was not in the public domain until 1925. All early commentaries from Beard onwards gave different and conflicting causes.)

'a stupid William' The exchange in Act V, scene i between William, Touchstone and Audrey – characters not present in the source story – is a curious one. The self-confessed unlearned William is recognised by scholars to be a parody of the Stratford-born William Shakespeare, but if it is a self-parody, Touchstone's reaction to him is inexplicably vicious. Touchstone, whose name symbolises a reference point against which other things can be evaluated, tells Audrey that William 'lays claim' to her and tells William 'that drink, being pour'd out of a cup into a glass, by filling the one doth empty the other; for all your writers do consent that *ipse* is he: now, you are not *ipse*, for I am he'. (*Ipse* = 'he himself'.) Touchstone is determined to marry Audrey (whom Wraight suggests stands for the Audience) and threatens to kill William 'a hundred and fifty ways' if he doesn't 'abandon' his claim to her. *As You Like It* was registered in 1600, but its publication was stayed until 1623.

GHOST

'Kyd's fishwife tale' See note on the *Ur-Hamlet* in 'Necessity'.

'the speech from *Dido, Queen of Carthage*' The speech recounting Priam's slaughter of which Hamlet makes so much in front of the Players (and on which Polonius comments, 'This is too long') is in imitation of an even longer speech by Aeneas on the same subject in Marlowe's earliest play.

IN PRAISE OF THE RED HERRING

'red herring' Thomas Nashe's final prose work, *Lenten Stuff* (1599), is also known as *The praise of the red herring*.

'no one's seen Thom Nashe's corpse, or grave' Nashe disappeared around 1601. Two epitaphs appeared that year, but we have no idea when or where he died, or in what circumstance. He was thirty-three.

T.T. & W.H.

'Bedlam is reserved for any maniac who makes that claim' Thanks are due to Peter Farey for this excellent suggestion on how the secret of Marlowe's faked death could be enforced by the State. There is a long history of Shakespeare sceptics being accused of (or even committed for) insanity, and that this might have begun in the late sixteenth century seems entirely possible, given the level of State suppression at the time. Committal to Bedlam in the early 1600s was a threat not to be considered lightly.

TWELFTH NIGHT

Leslie Hotson suggested *Twelfth Night* was written to celebrate the visit of Duke Orsino to London in early 1601. A. D. Wraight developed a Marlovian version of this theory, speculating that the author might have been present, perhaps disguised as a Moor.

'As Thorpe said' In the letter that fronts Marlowe's translation of Lucan, published in 1600, Thorpe addresses Marlowe's publisher thus: 'Blount: I purpose to be blunt with you, and out of my dullness to encounter you with a Dedication in the memory of that pure elemental wit, Chr[istopher] Marlow; whose ghost or Genius is to be seen walk[ing] the Churchyard in (at the least) three or four sheets. Me thinks you should presently look wild now, and grow humorously frantic upon the taste of it.'

'And did they meet?' Orthodox scholars assume Shakespeare was frequently at Court. However, there is no evidence to support the idea that Shakespeare performed at Court or met the Queen. Indeed, Diana Price has demonstrated he was in Stratford on several key occasions when the Lord Chamberlain's Men were performing at Court (Price, pp. 32–5). In payments for court performances, his name is only once recorded among those of other company shareholders.

AN EXECUTION

Following his bursting in on the Queen, unwigged and ungowned, when he returned unbidden from Ireland, the Earl of Essex was ordered to remain in his own house. He remained there from October 1599 to August 1600. Though his freedom was then granted, his basic source of income had been stopped and the Queen would not allow his presence at Court. The earl grew increasingly desperate, and on 8 February 1601, supported by a party of nobles and gentlemen, he marched from Essex House into the City in an attempt to force an audience with the Queen. He was opposed and forced back to his house, where he eventually surrendered. On 19 February 1601, he was tried for treason. On 25 February 1601, he became the last person to be beheaded in the Tower of London.

WILLIAM PETER

Elsinore *Hamlet* was written some time between 1599 and 1602. Between the publication of the first and second quarto, Danish 'flavour' was added, according to John Michell (p. 221). As noted above, William Hall was supposedly paid for returning from Denmark with intelligence on 2 October 1601.

ELSINORE

'brother-in-law of our most wanted James' James VI of Scotland was married to Anne, sister of the Danish king. The Earl of Essex had been a strong supporter of James's succession to the English throne. After Essex's execution, there was concern that James would forcibly depose Queen Elizabeth with the help of his Danish brother-in-law's army.

LIZ

'The week the old Queen died' Queen Elizabeth I died on 24 March 1603. We know nothing of the marriage of Will Peter's sister Liz. But one of the curious anomalies in that privately printed poem *A Funeral Elegy*, which claims to be by one 'W.S.' but is now attributed to John Ford, is its statement that the coyly referenced 'subject of this verse' had been married for nine years when John Ford was well placed to know that the putative subject, William Peter of Whipton near Exeter, had only been married for three. Thus is drawn into a Marlovian framework the possibility daringly suggested by Richard Abrams; that even though *A Funeral Elegy* is not written by Shakespeare, it may be *about* him (Abrams).

IAGO

'A friend will ask a friend' On 28 March 1603 Francis Bacon wrote a letter to lawyer and writer John Davies – apparently the John Davies, later to be knighted, whose epigrams had been published alongside Marlowe's translation of *Amores*. Davies was riding north to meet the new king, James, as he travelled from Scotland to London. Bacon closes with the phrase, 'So desiring you to be good to all concealed poets'. Baconians assume this is a reference to Francis himself but there is no necessity for it to be self-referential, and nothing supports the idea that Francis Bacon possessed any capacity for writing verse (though his brother Anthony did). Bacon's biographer Spedding said, 'the allusion to "concealed poets" I cannot explain' (Cockburn, pp. 14–15).

A NEVER WRITER TO AN EVER READER. NEWS.

The title is copied from an open letter attached to the 1609 quarto of *Troilus and Cressida*, published, like the *Sonnets* in the same year, by George Eld.

THE MERMAID CLUB

'Shake-speare' The frequent hyphenation of Shakespeare's name is not, as is sometimes claimed, due to the requirements of kerning fonts (the need to separate the tails of a long *k* and a long *s*) since the name is often hyphenated in the absence of them and also left unhyphenated at times when they are present. Its frequent hyphenation in early texts is highly unusual when compared with the treatment of other names, and it has never been satisfactorily explained.

Thomas Greene No relation to Robert Greene. A writer and lawyer whom John Marston and his father sponsored to enter the Middle Temple in 1595. Greene was appointed steward of Stratford-on-Avon in August 1603, and is believed to have lived with the Shakespeare family at New Place from 1603 to 1611 (Newdigate). A published poet himself, whose works include a sonnet praising Michael Drayton, he shows no awareness of his host's reputation as a writer, and though he keeps a diary, and the *Sonnets* were published during his stay at New Place, he makes no mention of it. Nor does he comment on William Shakespeare's death in 1616 (though he mentions the deaths of others) (Jiminez). However, he appears to have taken that event as a cue to resign his clerkship, sell the Stratford house he had moved into in 1611, and go to live in Bristol (Fripp).

BIBLIOGRAPHY

Abrams, R. (2002), 'Meet the Peters', *Early Modern Literary Studies*, 8.2, 6:1–39

Bakeless, J. E. (1942), *The Tragicall History of Christopher Marlowe*, Cambridge, Mass., Harvard University Press

Barber, R. (2009), 'Shakespeare Authorship Doubt in 1593', *Critical Survey*, 21:2, 83–100

Boas, F. S. (1949), 'Informer against Marlowe', *Times Literary Supplement*, 16 September

Cockburn, N. B. (1998), *The Bacon Shakespeare Question: The Baconian Theory Made Sane*, Limpsfield Chart, N. B. Cockburn

Du Maurier, D. (2007), *Golden Lads: A Study of Anthony Bacon, Francis and Their Friends*, London, Virago

Duncan-Jones, K. (2009), 'Shakespeare, the Motley Player', *Review of English Studies*, 60, 723–43

Duncan-Jones, K. and Woudhuysen, H. R. (eds.) (2007), *Shakespeare's Poems*, London, Arden Shakespeare

Eccles, M. (1934), *Christopher Marlowe in London*, Cambridge, Mass., Harvard University Press

Farey, P. (2000), 'A Deception in Deptford', www2.prestel.co.uk/rey/title

Farey, P. (2007), 'Hoffman and the Authorship', www2.prestel.co.uk/rey.hoffman

Fleay, F. G. (1875), 'Who Wrote "Henry VI"?', *Macmillan's Magazine*, XXXIII, 50–62

Foster, D. W. (1987), 'Master W. H., R. I. P.', *Publications of the Modern Language Association (PMLA)*, 102, 42–54

Freeman, A. (1973), 'Marlowe, Kyd, and the Dutch Church Libel', *English Literary Renaissance*, 3, 44–52

Fripp, E. I. (1928), *Shakespeare's Stratford*, London, Oxford University Press

Gamble, C. (2009), 'The French Connection: New Leads on "Monsieur Le Doux"', *Marlowe Society Research Journal*, 6, www.marlowe-society.org/pubs/journal/journal06

Gibson, H. N. (1962), *The Shakespeare Claimants*, London, Methuen.

Gristwood, S. (2003), *Arbella: England's Lost Queen*, London, Bantam

Jiminez, R. L. (2008), 'Shakespeare in Stratford and London: Ten Eye-Witnesses Who Saw Nothing', *'Report My Cause Aright': The Shakespeare Oxford Society 50th Anniversary Anthology 1957–2007*, New York, The Shakespeare Oxford Society

Kendall, R. (2003), *Christopher Marlowe and Richard Baines: Journeys through the Elizabethan Underground*, Madison, N.J., Fairleigh Dickinson University Press; London, Associated University Presses

Kuriyama, C. B. (2002), *Christopher Marlowe: A Renaissance Life*, Ithaca, London, Cornell University Press

Martin, P. H. and Finnis, J. (2003), 'Thomas Thorpe, "W.S.", and the Catholic Intelligencers', *English Literary Renaissance*, 33, 3–43

Michell, J. (1996), *Who Wrote Shakespeare?*, London, Thames and Hudson

More, D. A. (1997), 'Over Whose Dead Body – Drunken Sailor or Imprisoned Writer?', *Marlovian Newsletter*, Vol III No 3 www.marlovian.com/essays/penry

Newdigate, B. H. (1941), *Michael Drayton and His Circle*, Oxford, Basil Blackwell

Nicholl, C. (2002), *The Reckoning: The Murder of Christopher Marlowe*, London, Vintage

Matthew, H. C. G. and Harrison, B. (eds), *Oxford Dictionary of National Biography* (online edition), Oxford, Oxford University Press

Phillips, G., and Keatman, M. (1994), *The Shakespeare Conspiracy*, London, Century

Pinksen, D. (2009), 'Was Robert Greene's "Upstart Crow" the Actor Edward Alleyn?', *Marlowe Society Research Journal*, 6, 18, www.marlowe-society.org/pubs/journal/journal06

Price, D. (2001), *Shakespeare's Unorthodox Biography: New Evidence of an Authorship Problem*, Contributions in Drama and Theatre Studies Number 94, Westport, Connecticut and London, Greenwood Press

Prior, R. (2008), 'Shakespeare's Visit to Italy', *Journal of Anglo-Italian Studies*, 9, 1–31

Riggs, D. (2004), *The World of Christopher Marlowe*, London, Faber and Faber

Roe, R. P. (2011), *The Shakespeare Guide to Italy: Retracing the Bard's Unknown Travels*, London, Harper Perennial

Shagan, E. H. (2004), 'The English Inquisition: Constitutional Conflict and Ecclesiastical Law in the 1590s', *Historical Journal*, 47, 541–65

Urry, W. (1988), *Christopher Marlowe and Canterbury*, London and Boston, Faber and Faber

Westley, R. (2006), 'Computing Error: Reassessing Austin's Study of *Groatsworth of Wit*', *Literary and Linguistic Computing*, 21, 363–78

Wraight, A. D. (1993), *Christopher Marlowe and Edward Alleyn*, Chichester, Adam Hart

Wraight, A. D. (1994), *The Story That the Sonnets Tell*, London, Adam Hart

Wraight, A. D. (1996), *Shakespeare: New Evidence*, London, Adam Hart

Young, S. (2008), 'That all they that loue not Tobacco & Boies were fooles', *Marlowe Society Newsletter 30*, 22–5

ACKNOWLEDGEMENTS

This book would not exist were it not for Mike Rubbo, Jonathan Bate, and the Arts and Humanities Research Council (AHRC). Mike Rubbo's documentary *Much Ado About Something* exposed me to the Marlowe theory of Shakespeare authorship for the first time and included interviews with Jonathan Bate, who provided me with my lightbulb moment when he said, of the 'crazy' idea that Marlowe faked his death and escaped into exile, 'I do think there is a really good novel in here'. Without the generous funding of the AHRC, I could not have taken four years out of my life to research and write this book, and I wish to express my sincere thanks to those who selected this project for funding, and the British taxpayers who continue to fund research in the arts and humanities. It is the mark of a civilised country.

The Marlowe Papers was built on a sturdy skeleton of research that was largely the work of others. Numerous contributors to the *Marlowe Society Newsletter*, the *Marlowe Society Research Journal*, and Carlo DiNota's blog The Marlowe-Shakespeare Connection will recognise aspects of their work in mine. My deepest gratitude goes to Peter Farey, author of the Marlovian website to which I most often returned, for arguing with integrity and logic, correcting my misapprehensions, and sharing with me his data, research, microfilms, and theories. My chief (if virtual) company during this adventure has been the founder members of the International Marlowe Shakespeare Society: not only Peter, but Mike Rubbo, Daryl Pinksen, Isabel Gortazar and Carlo DiNota; all have, through discussion, helped me shape my ideas. Alongside Peter Farey, the late Dolly Wraight provided a significant proportion of the foundations on which this narrative is woven; David More furnished it with John Penry, and Tom Chivers (who would probably wish me to point out he is not a Marlovian) must be credited with The Flanders Mare. Anthony Kellett proved excellent at sourcing particular research materials, as did a man at the Open University whom I cannot name.

Thanks must go to Blake Morrison for his support from beginning to end, and for fathering a small family of postgraduate writers at Goldsmiths with whom I could share progress and the occasional free glass of wine (writers' oxygen). Lavinia Greenlaw's early criticism, though hard to swallow, prevented me from travelling any further down a narrative dead-end. Andrew Hadfield gave me an excellent grounding in the Early Modern literary and political scene, kept me on track, and facilitated my research despite the fact that I have a worrying tendency to be heretical. My earliest readers Catherine Smith, Clare Best and James Burt helped me identify places where the text was unclear, and the first wave of anachronisms. Kate Miller alerted me to the Marlovian leanings of Ted Hughes. To all, thank you.

It is likely this novel would be mouldering with others in my bottom drawer were it not for Robyn Young, Rupert Heath and Hilary Mantel. Robyn took the first twenty pages of *The Marlowe Papers* onto a train and so enthused about it to her agent that he swiftly became mine. Rupert's faith in the book allowed him to achieve something others believed impossible. While many established novelists routinely ignore writers seeking their approval, Hilary Mantel said nice things when it mattered. All writers need angels: these were mine.

Especial thanks to Carole Welch at Sceptre for her vision in taking on so unusual a beast, for her keen editor's eye, essential to making a good book better, and for teaching me more about etymology than I ever imagined I would know. Thanks also to Hazel Orme for her painstaking corrections and to Lucy, Nikki, Bea and Jason at Sceptre for everything they have done to help *The Marlowe Papers* on its way.

The largest thanks I have left almost to the last. Stephen Knight was the only person with whom I shared the novel-in-progress. He

accompanied me patiently and unstintingly through the long seques-
tered years of this novel's writing, rekindled my faith in the work
when I had lost it, and managed to be both gentle and incisive,
suggesting cuts with the kindly phrase, 'Well, this part might not
make it into the final draft, but . . .' It is little wonder his students
call him Saint Stephen. Without the guidance of his novelist-poet-
dramatist's eye and his ability to see the wood when I was lost in
the trees, I would probably never have emerged into the light.

Finally, to my husband and children who put up with seeing very
little of me for several years, kept the house ticking over despite my
physical and mental absence, and largely respected the 'No Entry'
sign on my study door. It may be that none of you read this book
for a very long time, but should you ever do so, I hope you feel it
was worth it.

Ros Barber

Ros Barber is the author of three collections of poetry, the latest of which (*Material*, Anvil, 2008) was a Poetry Book Society Recommendation. Her poems have appeared in many publications including *Poetry Review*, *London Magazine*, the *Guardian* and *Independent on Sunday*. They have also featured in anthologies published by Faber (most recently in *Poems of the Decade*, 2011) and by Virago, Anvil and Seren.

Her short fiction, which won prizes in the Asham and *Independent on Sunday* short story competitions, has been published by Bloomsbury and Serpent's Tail.

She was awarded the Hoffman Prize for *The Marlowe Papers* in 2011. The book was written as part of a PhD funded by the Arts and Humanities Research Council.

Ros Barber lives in Brighton and has four children.

www.rosbarber.com